THE SURVIVORS BOOK IV: SPRING

V. L. DREYER

Paperback ISBN (Legrand Cover): 978-0-473-31307-4
Paperback ISBN (Frank Cover): 978-0-473-41358-3
Kindle ISBN: 978-0-473-31309-8
ePub ISBN: 978-0-473-31308-1

Written by V. L. Dreyer
Published by Cheeky Kea Printworks
Cover art by Rebecca Frank Design
Edited by Holly Simmons

The following is a work of fiction. Any resemblance to persons living or dead is purely coincidental, or used in the form of parody.

Second Edition.

To Holly Simmons, the best editor I could ever ask for. This series is almost as much yours as it is mine. And now, after more than two years, hundreds of hours of work, countless arguments, and gallons of blood, sweat, and tears, we've reached the finish line... for now. Mwahahahahahahahaha!

TABLE OF CONTENTS

THE JOURNEY SO FAR…

Ten years ago, I lost my family and all of my friends to the devastating plague that came to be known as Ebola X. I've spent the last decade running for my life, always alone, constantly afraid, with nobody that I could trust.

This summer, everything changed. I met a group of good people. For the first time in my adult life, I've started to feel like I belong again. I've found friendship, a family, and love. Through all the turmoil, I've found a reason to keep going: Tumanako, the city of Hope.

It's been a difficult journey so far and it's not going to get any easier. We've battled bandits, gangs, and the ravenous dead to make it this far, the half-way point in our journey. I won't give up now. We're so close. I will see my dream reach fruition, if I have to fight to my last breath to make it happen.

Humanity needs this. I need this. One way or another, we will see this through.

www.vldreyer.com

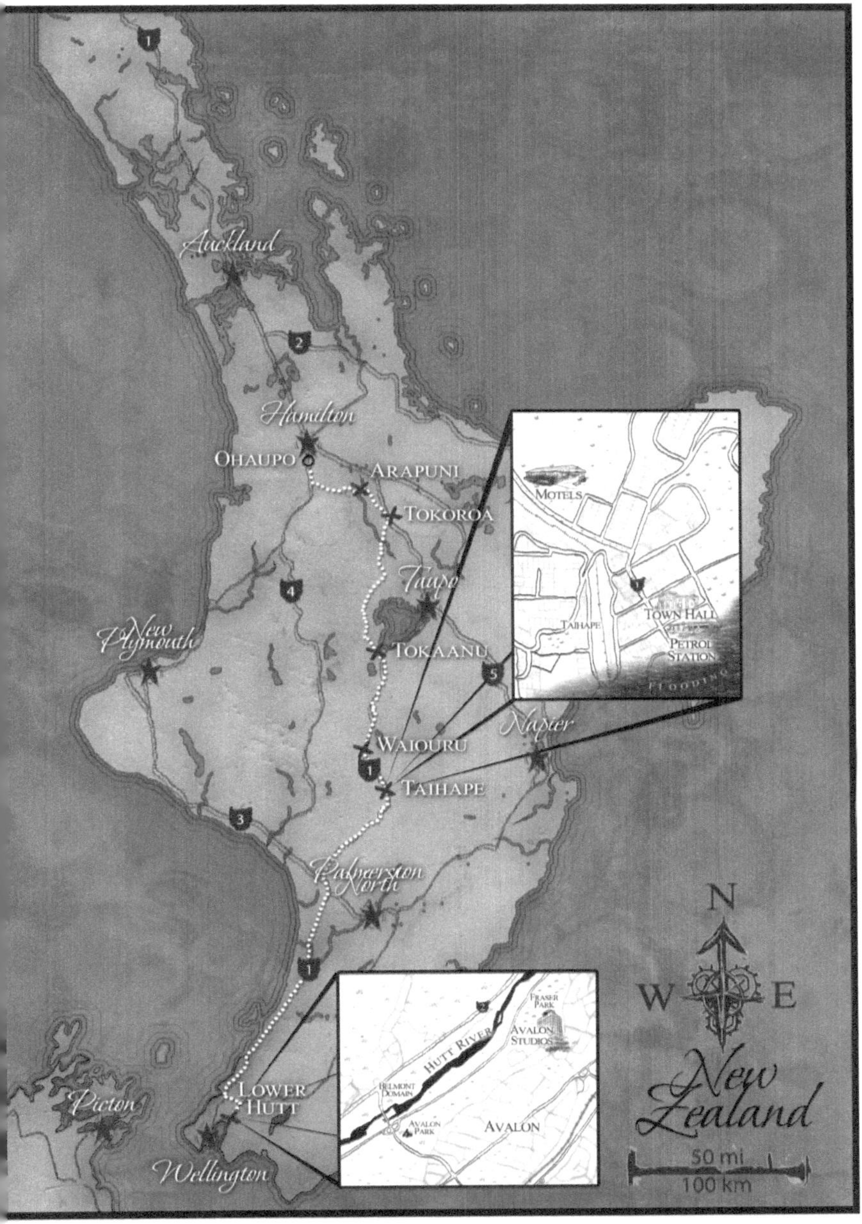

Auckland
Hamilton
OHAUPO
ARAPUNI
TOKOROA
Taupo
TOKAANU
New Plymouth
WAIOURU
TAIHAPE
Napier
Palmerston North
Picton
LOWER HUTT
Wellington
1
2
4
5
3
1
1
MOTELS
TOWN HALL
PETROL STATION
TAIHAPE
FLOODING
FRASER PARK
AVALON STUDIOS
HUTT RIVER
BELMONT DOMAIN
AVALON PARK
AVALON
N
S
W
E
New Zealand
50 mi
100 km

Chapter One

"Whoa!" I cried, yanking the reins as hard as I could. The horse ignored me and took off in the wrong direction.

Sergeant Bryce laughed uproariously and shouted instructions after me, "Keep your heels down, McDermott! Lean back in the saddle, and pull gently on the reins. Gently! Stop sawing her mouth, you'll make her mad."

"Make *her* mad? She's making me mad!" I yelled back, but I followed her instructions anyway. To my surprise, the horse responded: she slowed to a walk, and then stopped.

Bryce nudged her mount forward and trotted up to my side. "That's it. Just try to remember that she's a living thing, same as you. I'm sure you wouldn't like to have someone tugging on your mouth."

"No, I suppose I wouldn't," I agreed grudgingly. I sighed and leaned forward to pat the horse's neck. "Sorry, Buttercup. My bad."

"Boudicca," Sergeant Bryce corrected. "Her name is Boudicca. I name all the horses after historical figures."

"To honour their memory?" I asked. "I like that."

"Exactly," Bryce replied. She ran her hand down her horse's mane affectionately. "This old fellow is Pericles. It seemed appropriate, somehow. He talks a lot."

I laughed, but the levity didn't last long. "Are you sure you won't come with us, Erica?"

"Oh, I'm sure." She smiled at me, her sun-browned face aged far beyond its years by all the time she'd spent outdoors. "We'll follow eventually, once we're sure there are no more stragglers coming this way. Your message is bound to bring more people over the Central Plateau. We'll stay as a rear guard and direct them after you."

"The satellite phone you gave us should help us keep in touch," I replied. "We can contact you when we need to, and you can update the broadcast for us. That'll save time."

"Yes. The road south of here is going to be quite tough on you, even with the horses." Bryce sighed heavily and shook her head. "We've got plenty of trucks to spare, but not nearly enough fuel."

"It's fine," I replied. I gently nudged my horse around and guided her back towards the base, with Bryce close behind me. "The horses are more useful to us right now than trucks, anyway. We've managed to convert a couple of ours to propane, but if we don't find more petrol soon then we're going to have to start abandoning the vehicles."

"Let's hope it doesn't come to that," Bryce replied. "You're going to need all the resources you can get once you reach Avalon. In the mean time, I suggest that you keep following the highway south. It'll take you across the mountains, down onto the plains, and then along the coast. You'll have to swing eastwards at Porirua and double back a bit, but that's better than going the other way. The central route would take you across the Rimutaka Ranges, and with this cold I can guarantee the pass will be blocked by snow before you get there."

"Yeah, that's what we were planning to do," I said. "If we don't find any gas in Taihape, we may have to risk a detour through Palmerston North to search for supplies, though."

"You might get lucky," she said. "Not many people around Taihape, so there's a good chance you'll find what you need. If not... my understanding is that the riots pretty much ripped Palmerston North apart, but I haven't heard of any gang activity in the area. At least that's something."

"You keep tabs on gang activity to the south?" I asked, suddenly very interested.

She shrugged, her expression unreadable. "We do what we can to keep civilization afloat, but there are only three of us. The least we can do is attempt to keep track of danger and warn travellers."

"I'd really like to take a look at your maps before we leave, if you wouldn't mind." I glanced at her and gave her a smile. "Are you sure there isn't anything we can do for you before we go, Erica? You've helped us so much that I feel a little guilty not giving anything back."

"No, we don't need anything," she answered simply. "The base is well-stocked. We may be isolated, but we're all trained to live off the land. As soon as we realised that we were all alone out here, we planted a big garden inside the base and rounded up as many stock animals as we could find. I'm just giving you a small fraction of our surplus." She paused for a second and gave me a long look. "Though, if you really do feel indebted, there is something you can do for us."

"Anything," I replied immediately. "Well, anything within reason, of course."

The Sergeant barked a sharp laugh and gave me a smile. "Well, when I say 'us', I mean it in the broadest sense of the word. It's been, what... three days now? I've gotten a good feel for you and your little pack of misfits. What I see is a lot of people struggling to find a bond with their lost culture. I want you to help them find it."

I stared at her, confused. "You want me to help my mates to find their lost culture? How am I supposed to do that?"

Erica laughed again and shook her head. "I'll explain in a second, I promise."

She fell silent as we approached the small paddock where the rest of the horses waited, along with our friends. With the exception of the people on guard duty elsewhere, everyone was in the field talking to, playing with, and learning to ride the horses. Priya cried out a greeting and waved to me enthusiastically. Michael hurried over to open the gate for us, and then once we were safely inside he helped me dismount.

I smiled and gave him a kiss by way of greeting, ignoring the teasing hoots from all around us. Since our wedding three days earlier, my instinctive need for discretion had all but faded away and I no longer felt the desire to hide our relationship behind closed doors. It felt... good. I felt good. Despite the long journey ahead of us, I felt better than I had in a very long time.

"Hey. I'm not done with you yet, McDermott," Sergeant Bryce joked gruffly. Although it had made me a little uncomfortable at first, I'd gotten used to her rough-and-tumble sense of humour. She reminded me of Jim in many ways, except she was far more willing to open herself up and make friends.

"Sorry, sorry!" I joked right back, holding my hands up in mock self-defence. "We were talking about culture?"

"Yes, we were. Come with me." Sergeant Bryce gave Michael a long-suffering look, and added, "Yes, Mrs McDermott. You can come, too."

Michael laughed, just as he'd done every time she called him that. "You know I'm stuck with that nickname now, right? Thanks, Ricky. Much appreciated."

"You keep calling me Ricky, and I'll keep calling you Mrs McDermott. That's the arrangement," she replied, snapping her fingers playfully at him.

Michael started to chuckle again, then suddenly he froze and gave her an embarrassed look. "Wait — It just occurred to me that you might genuinely not like being called 'Ricky'. It wasn't intended as an insult or anything."

"And it wasn't taken as one." Her broad face relaxed into a smile and she made a dismissive gesture with one hand. "I like Ricky. Erica, Bryce, Ricky, Sergeant — it doesn't really bother me"

"Okay, so long as you're not actually upset," he replied, putting on that whipped puppy expression I knew so well. "I hate to admit it, but... I don't really understand. You, I mean. Not the name thing."

Erica sighed and glanced at me. "I've already had to explain it at least twice a day since you guys arrived. Explain it to your man, will you?"

"Sure," I agreed. I gestured for her to lead on, and took Michael's hand. While we were walking back towards the base that the soldiers called home, I explained the Sergeant's identity as she'd explained it to me. "Sergeant Bryce is bi-gender. That means she identifies as both male and female simultaneously." I glanced at her. "Did I get that right, Sarge?"

"Bang on, McDermott," she replied with a grin. "Good to know that you were listening."

"I'm always listening," I answered dryly. "You're just not always good at making yourself clear."

"I'm still confused," Michael admitted sheepishly. "Can I ask a question?"

"Of course, son," Sergeant Bryce responded, her expression easing back into a friendly smile. Despite the constant teasing, it was obvious that she'd developed a bit of a soft spot for him. That didn't surprise me at all, since they were birds of feather. Both of them had a wicked sense of humour, but at the core they just wanted to protect and serve. The only difference was how they'd chosen to do it.

"I'm sorry, I don't know how to ask this politely," he admitted, looking more and more sheepish by the moment. "Does that... does that mean you... have both guy *and* girl parts?"

Sergeant Bryce and I exchanged a stunned look, then we both cracked up laughing. We laughed so hard that we had to stop walking, and I started seeing stars from lack of oxygen. When my laughter finally faded, I glanced at the Sergeant to check if she was offended, but it was immediately obvious she wasn't.

I took a deep breath and looked back at Michael, struggling to keep myself under control. "No, honey. Biologically, she's a woman. I don't understand it well enough to explain it in great detail, but the simple answer is that she is who she is and we should try to respect that. She'll tell us if there's something we need to know."

"Well, that I can do," Michael agreed, his expression brightening. "Sorry if I've said anything offensive. Please don't hate me."

"I don't hate you, son," she said, her tone turning gentle again. "I don't hate anyone who's willing to learn. Learning is the most important part of life – and that's why I'm dragging you both home with me. Now, if we're done picking apart my gender identity, let's get inside before the rain comes back."

We fell into a comfortable silence as we walked the rest of the way, though once the humour was no longer distracting me I began to worry again. The rain had been nearly incessant for the last few weeks, and every droplet increased the risk of a serious flood. Still, there was some part of me that told me that we had to keep travelling. If we could just get out of the highlands and away from the Waikato, then we'd be safe.

A few minutes later, Erica shoved open a door and led us up a flight of stairs into what had obviously once been crew quarters. There were no crewmen anymore, though – just hundreds and hundreds of books. Maybe thousands. She'd managed to collect at least a dozen bookcases, but it clearly wasn't enough; books, CDs, and DVDs sat in neat piles on the floor and stacked up on the old bunk beds. In one corner, framed artwork rested beneath drop-cloths to protect it from the dust. A few small sculptures and stuffed animals sat on another small table near the door.

"Whoa," I gasped. "Is this what you meant by culture?"

"Yes. You see this? This is just a book, right?" Erica went over to one of the nearest piles and picked a book up off the top of the stack. She turned back to face us with the book in her hand, her expression intense. "Wrong. It's not just a book anymore; it's a piece of our history, our intellectual, spiritual, and cultural legacy. Someone made this, McDermott. Everything in this room was created by another person, and that's important. They're not just books anymore. Not just movies, or paintings, or albums. Not just things. These objects are a record of who we were. One day, these things may be all that's left of us. Isn't that worth protecting?"

"I never thought of it like that," I said softly. Understanding struck me like a solid wave of force, and suddenly I found tears in my eyes. I brushed them away hastily and took a deep breath. "You're right. That is worth protecting. That's the whole point of museums, isn't it? We preserve the past so that future generations can better understand their own roots. What's the point of saving lives if we can't save their identities as well?"

"Then we'll just have to figure out a way to do that, too," Michael said resolutely, all traces of humour gone from his voice and replaced by steely determination. "I have faith in us – all of us. We can do it."

"Yes." I stood up a little straighter and glanced up at him, seeking solace in his eyes. "Once we've established our new city and the weather clears up, then we'll figure out a way to transport all of this to our new city."

"Don't forget that the National Library is in Wellington," Erica said, absently trailing her fingers across the cover of the book. "The National Library is a repository of everything made by Kiwi creators over the years. Assuming that it survived the riots, we should be able to salvage a lot of material."

I nodded and took one last look around the room, then I glanced back at her. "We need to get back on the road. If we leave now, we should be able to get half way to Taihape before we run out of daylight."

Sergeant Bryce just nodded. She put the book back down and led us out of the room, back to face the mission that seemed to be taking on a life all of its own.

Chapter Two

It took longer than anticipated to get the convoy ready to move again. Along with half-a-dozen horses, the satellite phone, and fresh supplies, Sergeant Bryce had given us a spare wagon and tracings to help us in our voyage. She accompanied us for the first few kilometres, while our people learned the art of driving a team. Skylar had insisted on taking the first shift behind the reins, for reasons that I could only guess at.

"It's a good thing you picked patient horses," I called to Sergeant Bryce. Boudicca snorted and flicked her head, not quite sure whether I was talking to her, but she calmed down when I reached out and patted the back of her neck. It had taken a while for us to get a feel for one another, but we were swiftly becoming fast friends.

"Skylar's doing just fine," Sergeant Bryce replied, her voice firm and confident. "It just takes practice."

"See? I'm doing fine!" Skye called, looking about as proud as I'd ever seen her.

I gently leaned back in the saddle and eased my mount into line beside them. "Who said anything about Skylar? I meant all of the horses, not just the team. It can't be easy for them to have to deal with a bunch of newbies like us."

"Oh, yeah." Skye laughed and shook her head. "We'll get there. Like Ricky said, it just takes practice. But hey, at least no one's fallen off yet!"

"Thank heavens for small favours," I answered dryly. I glanced up at the sky to gauge the time, then looked at Sergeant Bryce. "You're going to have to head off soon, if you want to make it back to Waiouru before dusk."

"Yes, I am." She glanced at me and gave me a tight smile. "Keep me updated on your progress southwards. I'll set your new message broadcasting tonight."

"Thank you." I hesitated for a second, then I reached over and gently touched her arm. "Not just the horses or the phone or the supplies, but... for everything. I'm glad to know there are so many people out there who share my vision."

"It's hard not to, when our other option is extinction. Safe travels, McDermott." Sergeant Bryce snapped a salute, then she turned her mount around and headed back to Waiouru.

I watched until she was out of sight, then I glanced at Skye. "Looks like we're on our own now."

"And the rain's coming back," she said, gesturing towards the horizon. A moment later I felt an icy wind strike me, and smelt the tell-tale scent of. I sighed heavily and took my radio out of its pocket.

"Button up, everyone," I advised. "Rain's going to be here any minute."

Before I'd finished speaking, I felt the first droplet land on my cheek. I hastily tucked my radio away, pulled my hood over my head, and buttoned my coat all the way up to my chin.

A moment later, the deluge began.

***

We were all cold, wet, and miserable by the time we decided to stop for the night. We found a large farmhouse right beside the road, but it still took us until after sunset to clear the area, bed the horses down in the barn, and set the night watch. I finished grooming Boudicca by torchlight, then ducked out into the turbulent weather to make my way back to the main house.

Skylar was waiting for me at the door. She waved when she saw me, but as soon as I stepped into range of her nose, she screwed her face up and gave me a dark look. "Gross. You smell like wet horse."

"Thanks, sis. You sure know how to make a girl feel pretty," I replied. She stepped back and let me across the threshold; the moment I was inside I realised that something was amiss. "No power?"

"No power," she said with a nod. "We could set up the generator, but that means using fuel."

"Let's try to avoid that, if we can," I answered. "Do we at least have a fireplace?"

"Yeah." She nodded again, pointing through a nearby doorway. "And there's a shed with plenty of firewood up the back of the house. Plumbing seems to be working, though. That's something."

"Better than nothing," I said with a shrug. "How are we for bedding?"

"There are a few beds upstairs, but I wouldn't recommend it," she replied, wrinkling up her nose. "It's pretty gross up there. Doc's decided he wants to risk it, but I think we're better off sleeping in the living room. Kitchen's over there, if you want to grab some grub."

"Yeah, I probably should," I answered. I caught myself with a hand half-raised to rub my belly, and pretended to scratch my elbow instead. Mercifully, Skye didn't seem to notice my lapse; her expression was distracted, and I could practically see her organizing what needed to be done in her head.

Suddenly, her eyes snapped back into focus, and she looked at me. "Oh, one more thing. Doc wants to talk to you, when you have a second. He's already gone upstairs."

"Why am I not surprised? He never did like getting cosy with us," I said, chuckling. I patted her shoulder, then left her side and headed up the stairs.

I found Doctor Cross inside the first bedroom I came across, in a consultation with Michael. Michael was sitting on the edge of the bed with his foot up in Doc's lap. The room was lit only by a small gas lantern, but it was enough for Doc to see what he was doing.

"This seems to be healing nicely," Doc was saying as I walked up to the doorway, touching the bones in Michael's ankle. "It's definitely just a sprain. That's good news."

"Yeah, it's a little tender, but so long as I'm careful with my footing it's fine," Michael replied. He glanced up, and gave me a smile and a nod. "Hey, Sandy."

"Hey yourself," I returned the greeting, leaning against the doorframe with my arms folded across my chest. "So he's not dying, then? I'm too young to be a widow."

"Well, if you want to get philosophical, everyone is dying," Doc answered dryly. He lowered Michael's foot back to the floor and leaned back in his chair. "You're fine, Constable. How are the painkillers working?"

"Well enough that I've got nothing to complain about," Michael replied with his usual impish grin. He eased himself up to his feet and dusted his hands off on his jeans, then came over to stand in front of me. At first I thought he was going to lean down and kiss me, but he stopped just short, close enough that I could feel his warmth without actually touching me. His closeness sent a shiver right through me, and brought a flush to my cheeks. He always knew just the right buttons to push to make my heart race. "We've got duty tonight. You happy with the first shift?"

"Of course," I replied, reaching up to touch his chest so that my fingers could trace the line of his wedding band hidden beneath the cloth. Even after we'd formalized our marriage, we both still chose to wear our rings on necklaces around our throats rather than on our fingers. It felt like that would keep them safer while we were slogging through mud, rain, and everything else nature had to throw at us.

Michael glanced down at my hand, then looked back at me and gave me one of the subtle half-smiles that he saved just for me. "Good. I need to go organise the rest of the roster. See you downstairs afterwards?"

"Definitely," I agreed. "I'll most likely be in the kitchen."

"Then I'll see you there," he said. His hand touched my shoulder and slid down the length of my arm all the way to my hand, then he lifted it to his lips and pressed a kiss against my knuckles. A second later, he brushed past me and vanished into the hall.

Doctor Cross cleared his throat awkwardly. "Well, that was... interesting. Please close the door, Ms McDermott."

I did as I was told, then I went over to sit on the edge of the bed in the spot Michael had vacated a minute earlier.

"You got the test results, didn't you?" I asked, keeping my voice low enough that it was unlikely we'd be overheard. "Am I pregnant or not?"

Doc shot a glance at the closed door, then picked himself up and came over to sit on the bed beside me. "Yes, you are. There's no doubting it. I tested it three times, and each time was positive." He paused for a moment, and gave me a long, considering look. "You seem unusually calm about this, given that you nearly had a nervous breakdown on me a few days ago."

"I've had time to think," I admitted, absently rubbing my belly. This time, I didn't try to hide the gesture. There was no point, since he already knew. "I'm scared, Doc. I'm really, really scared. But this is also kind of what I wanted, isn't it? I mean, I didn't want to single-handedly repopulate the earth, but I want to see us flourish again. That's why I'm fighting so hard for us to make it to the south. For the kids. For the next generation. This just… makes it more personal."

"And more urgent," the doctor finished for me. I glanced at him and nodded.

"Michael and I haven't exactly had a lot of alone-time since the fire," I said. I closed my eyes for a moment and thought back, running over the figures in my mind. "I can pinpoint nearly to the day when I would have conceived. It would have been around the full moon before last. It's almost new moon again now, so I'd be about six weeks along."

"Then we should have another couple of months before you start to show," Doc said. I opened my eyes and found him studying me with a critical eye. "Possibly less, but it's hard to tell at this early stage. Most first-time mothers don't start to show until around twelve to sixteen weeks in, because it takes some time for your uterus to stretch enough to distend your abdomen. You're also quite tall, and that may help conceal it for longer."

"May, but we can't guarantee anything," I said with a sigh. "We're just going to have to play things by ear, and hope that we're worrying for nothing. I'm also going to have to be careful about what I eat and drink, but there isn't really anything we can do about the risk of the baby being born infected, is there?"

"My understanding is that a child can't be born infected," he said, frowning. "I've heard the rumours about Elira's daughter, but we can't jump to conclusions. Stillbirths happen frequently in nature, particularly when twins are involved. The baby should share your immunity until it's weaned, just like it will share your immunity to everything else that you've acquired antibodies to fight against. After that, I don't know. All we can really do is pray."

I raised a brow and shot him a curious look. "I thought you were a man of science, not religion?"

"I am, but sometimes I wonder." He shrugged sheepishly and glanced away. "I've got a granddaughter who can apparently read minds and see into the future. I think that would be enough to make anyone wonder."

"True." I stood up slowly and stretched my back. "Ugh, this horse-riding thing is hard. My back is killing me. Can you recommend anything to keep me from stiffening up like this?"

"Not really," he admitted. "It'll just take some time for your body to get used to it, I think. I can give you some painkillers, if you like?"

"Nah, it's not that bad," I replied, shaking my head. "I'll just ask Michael to give me a back rub. Thanks, though."

"Quite all right, Ms McDermott," he said. "I'll check my stores tomorrow, and see if I have any pre-natal vitamins that might give you and the baby a fighting chance."

"Thanks, Doc," I replied. I smiled at him, and touched my forehead in a rough approximation of a salute. "Have a good night."

The doctor returned the sentiment and waved me out of his room, then closed the door behind me. I fished my torch out of my pocket, and used its light to guide my way back down the stairs, into the kitchen. There, I found Anahera and Ryan washing the dishes by the light of another lantern, and talking softly to one another. I switched my torch off again to conserve its batteries, and went over to pick up a bowl of lukewarm stew that was sitting on the bench.

Anahera glanced over and gave me a stern look. "Why are you always the last one to come and have dinner? Is my cooking really that bad?"

"Your cooking is great," I hurriedly reassured her. "I just have an endless list of things to do, and never enough hours in the day. You know how it is."

"Indeed." Her frown melted into a smile, and she held a spoon out to me. I took it gratefully and settled on a stool to eat my fill. While I was eating, she turned her attention back to Ryan. "You worry far too much, my friend. Just relax and let the cards fall where they may."

"I know. It's just... it's hard," Ryan admitted, his gaze focused on the dish that he was drying. Once he was satisfied with it, he set it down and took another one out of the tray. "She's already moved on. I don't want to... you know, get in the way."

"Skylar," Anahera said to me by way of explanation, then she resumed speaking to Ryan. "I cannot presume to guess how she feels, but there's no reason for you to give up on her completely. Just try to show her that you've learned from what happened and that you really care about her. She may forgive you."

"No one makes decisions for Skye except Skye," I added, using the very same words as when I'd spoken to Hemi a few weeks earlier. "If you think you still deserve her affections, then show her that. One rule, though."

They both glanced at me, brows raised.

I grinned and waved my spoon at Ryan in mock threat. "No more fighting! Understood?"

"Yes, ma'am," Ryan answered, looking shamefaced.

Anahera just laughed and shook her head. "And on that note, I'm going to get ready for bed. All these affairs of the heart are too much for my poor, elderly psyche."

"You're only, like, ten years older than me," I pointed out.

"More like fifteen," she replied, flicking her sponge into the sink. The dishwater gurgled as it drained away, and then she rinsed her hands under the tap. "Not that it matters, I suppose. What is age but a number?"

"Exactly my point," I said, digging around in my stew for a particularly juicy-looking piece of fish. "You're a MILF and you know it, lady. You're just fishing for compliments."

Ryan froze with a dish half-dried in his hand and turned bright red. Anahera hid a chuckle behind a cough.

"Perhaps I am," she replied, amusement dancing across her tattooed lips. "Everyone likes to feel attractive. Goodnight, dear."

"Goodnight," I said simply. I scooped up the morsel I'd been hunting for and popped it into my mouth, enjoying the burst of flavour that came along with it. By the time I'd swallowed it, Anahera was gone, leaving me alone with a beet-red red-head. I looked at him, and raised a brow. "You all right, Ry?"

"Fine!" he replied, a little too enthusiastically. A second later, his shoulders slumped, and he shot a guilty look at me. "I just… never thought of her like that before. I'm not sure how to feel."

"She's not *your* mum, so you can feel any way you like," I replied with a shrug. "So, what was that I walked in on? You thinking of making another play for Skye's heart?"

"Maybe," he said. He turned away from me on the pretence of packing the dishes away, but I sensed that it was more to hide his face from me than any real desire to work. "I still love her. It's hard to see her with Hemi."

"You know there's no reason she has to pick just one of you, right?" I said, shoving another spoonful into my mouth.

Ryan turned back and looked at me quizzically. "What do you mean?"

I swallowed, and gave him a grin. "This is our world, Ry. Our rules. There are a lot more men than women in this group, and I suspect that's going to be fairly standard across the board. For this generation at least, polygamous relationships may be a good idea."

"Polygamous?" he echoed, his eyes widening. "You mean… Skye could be with both of us? At the same time?"

"Not in bed, obviously," I said dryly, then paused to re-evaluate. "Well, unless you guys swing that way. None of my business. But, yeah, why not? Rebecca's hooking up with Tane and Iorangi, and it seems to be working out well for the three of them."

"I don't know," he admitted, looking uncertain. "I mean, maybe. I'd have to think about it. And talk to them, of course."

"Of course," I replied, shrugging again. "Your rules, kid. At least it's an option, and that way no one has to get hurt. If I remember correctly, you liked Hemi before all this."

"Yeah," he agreed. "I mean, I didn't know him very well, but he seemed like a cool guy."

"And do you really want to fight with a potential friend over a girl?" I said in the driest tone I could muster. That made him smile.

"I don't want to fight with anyone, really," he replied, shaking his head.

"Then don't," I said simply. I rose to my feet and went over to wash my bowl in the sink, then handed it to him to dry.

He took it, stared at it for a second, then smiled again and nodded. "Good advice, as usual. Thanks, Sandy."

"Any time, mate." I patted him on the shoulder, then dismissed myself and went off in search of Skylar.

I found her in the living room, supervising the distribution of spare blankets. We were well into our sixth week of travel, and all of us had acquired a set of blankets that we'd come to think of as our own, but with the weather getting colder and colder it was a constant struggle to stay warm. I watched for a moment, until she noticed me standing there.

"Oh, hey," she said by way of greeting. "Can you do me a favour?"

"Sure," I replied. "How can I help?"

"We're running a bit late tonight," she said, tossing a rolled-up blanket to one of the others. "Can you go round up the girls, please? I sent them upstairs to look for extra bedding, but they haven't come back down."

"I'm on it," I said, saluting her playfully. She was so busy she barely even had a chance to acknowledge me. I left her to it and headed back upstairs, flicking my torch on to guide the way. The light under Doc's door had already gone out, telling me that he'd decided to have an early night. I passed his door and moved deeper into the building.

The sound of whispering voices and muffled laughs drew me to a half-open doorway, lit by the faint glow of an oil lamp. I quietly pushed the door open and peeked inside: Melody, Priya, Maddy, and the twins stood huddled around an ornate vanity, playing with something I couldn't quite see. I took another step closer, straining to get a better look at what they were doing. A loose board creaked under my foot, and suddenly the girls all spun to look at me, wide-eyed, guilty-looking, their faces covered in a rainbow of multi-coloured cosmetics.

"Oh, you guys," I groaned, covering my eyes with one hand. "What have you done?"

"Well, we found this stuff," Melody said, straightening her shoulders and flicking her short, ash-blonde hair back out of her face. "So we decided to have some fun while we were up here."

"That 'stuff' will ruin your skin," I said, moving over to the vanity. I picked up one of the pallets, closed it, and squinted at the faded label. "This is twelve years old, guys. Twelve. And it's used. It's probably full of someone else's eye-gunk, and will give you a nasty infection. Go wash it off before you get sick or something."

A chorus of groans answered me, followed by complaints, whining, and then laughter as they filed out of the room and down the hall, taking the lamp with them. I heard running water, then a squeal, some splashing, and more laughter. The sound of it made me smile; there was a growing sense of camaraderie amongst the group, as people discovered similar interests with one another and friendships began to blossom. Melody had swiftly expanded her little gang to include both Priya and Madeline, while Solomon had drifted out of it and gravitated towards Matt and his younger brothers. He still never said anything, but that didn't seem to impede their budding friendship at all.

I left the girls to their own devices and set about the task that Skylar had originally given them. Gripping my torch between my teeth, I yanked the duvet and blankets off the bed near the vanity, and dragged the bedclothes out into the hallway. A musty scent came up from them and tickled my nose, but I ignored it; I didn't have to sleep in there, or even be in the room long enough to worry about mould in the walls or the bedding. We just needed a little extra warmth to ride out the chilly night.

The house was a large one, with four bedrooms in addition to the one that Doc had claimed. By the time the girls had finished disinfecting their faces, I'd stripped all the mattresses and created a fairly sizeable pile of bedding that needed to be carted downstairs. I assigned the twins to carry stuff downstairs, and put the other girls to work searching the rooms for useful objects. Melody and Priya went one way, while Madeline padded along after me.

Despite her youth, Maddy was a quick study and knew what to look for. While I was yanking open dresser drawers and digging out salvageable clothing, she went over to search the wardrobe. We worked in silence for a couple of minutes, expertly sorting what was useful from what was past its prime.

Suddenly, Madeline called my name. "Miss Sandy?"

Something about her tone of voice set me on edge, and the look on her face didn't help. The little girl wrinkled up her nose and held something out to me; by torchlight, I couldn't make out much of it besides the fact that it was a wooden case.

"We need to give this to Mister Michael," she said softly, in that odd, dreamy tone she sometimes got when her head wasn't entirely in our world.

"What is it?" I asked.

"He'll know," she said. Without asking permission, she took the case and walked out into the hall.

I hurried to catch up with her, leaving my findings to be dealt with at a later time. I'd learned to listen when Madeline got that kind of look on her face, even if she didn't make any sense. The other girls stuck their heads out as we walked past their doors, then fell into step behind us. I heard them whispering to one another, but I said nothing. Madeline's movements were stiff and robotic, like a sleepwalker; something about them had me in what felt almost felt like a trance. I was aware enough that I could have broken it if I'd wanted to, but I didn't want to.

We followed the little girl down the stairs and into the living room. She didn't even pause to look around, just walked right up to where Michael was sitting and put the case in his lap.

Michael stared at it blankly for a second, then suddenly understanding dawned in his eyes. "Is that what I think it is?"

Maddy just smiled and sat down on the ground at his feet without a word. A hushed silence fell over the group, and we all watched as Michael opened the case to reveal a violin nestled upon black velvet. He ran his hands reverently across the polished wood, and then lifted the instrument out of the case.

"I haven't held one of these since high school," he whispered, his voice barely audible. He glanced up at me. I stared back at him, but I couldn't think of anything to say. Something told me to follow Madeline's lead, so I did. I heard movement around me as the others sat down, waiting. A flicker of unreadable emotion passed through Michael's eyes as he ran his fingertips softly along the length of the strings, then picked up the bow and touched it to them.

That first note sent a chill right through me and left me shivering with anticipation. His touch was tentative and uncertain as he tuned the strings, but it didn't matter. I wanted to hear the notes, I wanted it so badly that I couldn't have expressed it in words even if I'd tried. When the music began, it was the most beautiful thing I'd ever heard. It was unsteady, imperfect, even a little hesitant, but that didn't matter. My soul cried out for it, and Michael gave it to us.

I felt tears running down my cheeks and made no attempt to brush them away. Music was something we'd taken for granted before the plague, but afterwards our world had become a silent place. Hearing the notes now took my awareness into another place, a place where only my imagination and the music existed. When the piece finally ended, it left me feeling wrung out and exhausted, but satisfied beyond belief.

A hand touched my cheek, stroking away the tears that had fallen upon them. I opened my eyes and found Michael watching me with the kind of tenderness that he reserved just for me.

"Are you all right?" he asked softly, trailing his thumb across my skin. I just nodded dumbly and smiled at him, though I couldn't find the words to express how I felt.

I didn't need to, though. Michael understood me — and for once, everyone else did as well.

CHAPTER THREE

I awoke the next morning in pre-dawn gloom, hemmed in on all sides by sleeping bodies. Michael stirred but didn't wake as I gently extracted myself from the circle of his arms. Priya didn't even open her eyes, though she did snuggle a bit closer to Alfred for warmth. It was freezing cold despite our best efforts to keep warm overnight, but at least my clothing had managed to dry on the lines we'd strung across the kitchen.

I plucked my clothing off the line and headed into the bathroom to go through my usual morning ablutions. A thorough scrub with a washcloth was the best I was going to have in terms of bathing; it was far too cold for a full shower without the luxury of hot water. Once I was dressed, dried, and groomed, I opened the door – and almost fell over Tigger, who had chosen to ambush me by sitting right on the threshold.

She mewed at me, then hefted her tail and pranced off towards the back door, leaving no mistake about what she wanted. I rolled my eyes and followed her. Gavin was on watch by the door, wrapped in a couple of blankets. He nodded a greeting when he saw me and unlocked the door to let us outside. While Tigger was busy fussing around on the wet, frosty grass, I sat down on the stoop to put my shoes on and admire the sunrise.

"Red sky in the morning," Gavin said quietly. He stepped outside and pulled the door closed behind him. "Looks like we're in for another cracker of a day."

"If by 'cracker' you mean 'terrible', then yes," I replied with some amusement. The cold made the scar on my foot ache, but as soon as I put my shoes and socks on, it felt a bit better.

"Yep," he said, with a long, deep sigh. "It's going to be a harsh winter this year, I think. I can feel it in my bones."

"We had a long, hot summer, so I guess we're about due for it," I replied. "We just have to find ways to stay warm until spring or Avalon, whichever comes first."

Gavin chuckled softly. He leaned against one of the posts supporting the porch roof and gave me a thoughtful look. "Your group seems to be good at that."

"*Our* group, Gav," I scolded gently. "It's been over a month now, mate. You can start thinking of us as friends — or even family, if you like."

"I know," he said, his gaze drifting away to study the horizon. "I'll get there eventually. You know how I am."

"Better than most," I said, reaching up to pat his hand. Then I hesitated for a second, considering my options. I had to be careful who I told about my situation, but Gavin was one of the few people I felt I could trust to help me without giving things away before I was ready. "Gav, I need your help with something, but it has to stay just between us. Can you keep a secret?"

He glanced down at me again, his expression shifting to one of open curiosity. "Of course, Sandy. Anything."

I took a deep breath and a moment to organise my thoughts, then I looked up at him again. "I told you what happened to my sister, right? And her baby?"

He nodded silently, encouraging me to continue. I glanced away and shifted on my seat. Even though I knew it was far too small to actually feel yet, I imagined I could feel the baby inside me with every movement and it distracted me in ways I wasn't used to yet.

While I was still trying to figure out the right thing to say, Gavin chuckled and his voice took on a note of genuine amusement. "Oh, I know that look. My wife used to do that when she was pregnant with our daughter – sit there looking uncomfortable, hugging her belly. How far along are you?"

"About six weeks," I said, relieved that he'd guessed what I was trying to tell him. "I don't want to tell Michael just yet, not after what happened to Skye's baby."

"Your husband is a smart man," Gavin said. "He'll figure it out sooner rather than later – particularly if you keep doing that." He pointed at my hands, which were still wrapped protectively around my middle.

"I know," I said, hugging myself a little tighter. "And I'll tell him once we get to Avalon. I just can't deal with it right now. Michael's very protective, and he desperately wants a family. As soon as he finds out that I'm pregnant, he's going to try and wrap me up in cotton wool and pamper me like a princess."

"I think you're the only person I know who would put this much effort into *not* being treated like royalty," Gavin answered dryly. "Would it really be such a bad thing?"

"Under normal circumstances, it would just cramp my style," I replied. "But right now, I don't have time for it and neither does anyone else. We don't have the luxury of letting me indulging myself. There's just too much that needs to be done. I need to stay strong and put on a determined face, to keep the group together and travelling in the right direction."

"That makes sense, but... I'm not sure I'm comfortable lying to him," he said. "If I were in his position, I'd want to know. Aren't you concerned that he's going to be annoyed when he finds out?"

"A little," I admitted. "I have no intention of lying to him, though. If he asks me outright, I'll tell him the truth. But if he doesn't ask, then I'll just keep it to myself a little while longer. Just until Avalon. Just until everyone is safe and settled."

"All right," he replied, nodding slowly. "Just until Avalon. What do you need from me, then?"

"At this stage?" I glanced around, then shrugged. "Just keep an eye on Michael and let me know if you see any sign that he's on to me. He seems to like you, and we're used to you being weird and secretive. You're Mister Mysterious. That's your whole schtick. I swear, in a past life you were an international super-spy or something."

Gavin laughed at that and offered me a hand to get up. "Right, right, whatever you say, funny lady. Shouldn't you go have breakfast now that you're eating for two?"

I opened my mouth to answer him, only to be interrupted by the demanding mew of a little tabby at my feet. Tigger had one thing on her mind, and it sure as heck wasn't the contents of *my* belly.

***

We made good time along the road towards the next stop on our voyage: the small but pretty town called Taihape, which was famous for nothing but being a waypoint along the route between Auckland and Wellington, and a statue of a giant gumboot. Melody and I rode together in the vanguard. We hadn't seen anything that resembled a threat in quite some time, so we were both starting to let our guards drop just a little, but we knew better than to relax completely. Coming up on a new town could mean anything, or it could mean nothing. Whatever happened, we were ready for it.

Just as we were closing in on the outskirts of town, a human figure jumped into view, waving frantically. Melody shouted an alert and tensed up, but I held up a hand to keep her from taking any rash action.

"Are you carrying your gun?" I asked her. She didn't bother to reply, just shot me a scathing look. Of course, she had her gun. Stupid question. I chuckled softly to myself, and pulled my walkie-talkie out from inside my coat. "Halt the convoy; we've got someone up ahead hailing us. Watch the back and sides, this may be a trap." I put my radio away and glanced at Melody. "Ask questions first, shoot second. Got it?"

She grunted and rolled her eyes. "Fine."

"Good," I said. "If they run when we get close, we'll know it's a trap. Don't follow them, just get back to the convoy as fast as you can." This time she just nodded, her natural hostility fading in the face of potential danger. Whatever else she might think of me, she knew that I'd watch her back in a fight and that I expected her to watch mine. I gave her a quick smile, then I touched my heels to Boudicca's sides and guided the horse up to a trot.

I felt a familiar tension building up inside me as we closed the gap between us and the mysterious figure, one that made me forget all about the discomfort in my back and thighs from hours in the saddle. I found myself sitting up a little straighter, stretching my muscles in anticipation. Erica's maps said that Taihape wasn't gang territory, but it never hurt to be prepared.

I needn't have worried, though. The person made no attempt to attack us. As soon as we started moving towards him he raced out to greet us, then skidded to a halt and stared up at us wide-eyed. He looked back and forth between us, then fixated on Melody.

"Are you Sandrine McDermott?" he asked, as excited as a teenager meeting his celebrity crush. He was about the right age for it, too: maybe fifteen or sixteen at the most, with skin so black that it shone like polished onyx in the rain, and a grin like lightning in contrast.

Melody snorted a laugh and shook her head, pointing at me. The boy's gaze shifted to me and his eyes widened even more. "You? You're Sandrine McDermott? Really?"

"The one and only," I answered, struggling to keep my expression serious.

The youth yelped and jumped back. "You are! You are! I recognise your voice! Wait here, I need to go get my dad." He spun around and started to dash away, only to skid to a halt again and turn back. "I mean, please wait here? Please? I won't be long, I promise."

"Go on, then," I said. I gave up on trying to keep a straight face and just grinned at him, suddenly caught by his infectious humour. The youth grinned back, then let out a whoop and ran off as fast as his legs could carry him.

As soon as he was out of sight, Melody shot me a dubious look. "Are you sure this isn't a trap? That guy was a bit weird."

"Not weird, just excited," I replied with a shrug. "My instincts say he's not a danger to us. What do yours say?"

Melody paused and thought it over for a minute, then she shrugged as well. "My instincts say the same. I think he's been waiting to join us."

I glanced in the direction the youth had gone, only to do a double take in surprise. "I would say you're right."

Melody followed my gaze, and then her jaw dropped. There were people coming out of the buildings nearby, watching us and whispering excitedly amongst themselves. I glanced at Melody and saw her fingering the hilt of her gun, but after a few seconds she relaxed.

"I don't see any weapons," she said quietly. "But there sure are a lot of them."

"There are," I replied, gently squeezing her arm to try and keep her calm. "There must be twenty-five people down there."

Melody gasped and pointed towards the group. "Look! That woman has a baby!"

"Well, that settles it, right?" I said. "She wouldn't bring her baby out here if they meant us any harm, would she?"

"No, she wouldn't," Melody said quietly, her tone suddenly filled with fascination and awe. "She's so tiny. I haven't seen a baby since the twins were little."

"I get the feeling you're going to see one up close very soon," I replied. Before we could discuss it any further, a tall man with ebony skin that matched the youth's pushed his way through the crowd and stepped out into the rain. He was dressed all in leather, much as I was, but his shaved head was uncovered and glistened with raindrops. He closed the distance between us with long, powerful strides, his son hot on his heels.

"Greetings, Sandrine McDermott and friend," he called, raising a hand to wave. "Welcome to Taihape!"

I returned the gesture and called a greeting back. "Hello there! And who might you be, mate?"

"My name is Johan Abrahms, and you've already met my son Dominic," he said as he came to a stop in front of us. "We came from the east when we heard your message, and picked up as many folks along the way as we could."

"By friendly means, I hope?" I asked, determined to get the uncomfortable questions out of the way before I let my guard down all the way.

Johan let out a deep, merry laugh and nodded. "Definitely. We just spread the word about what you were hoping to achieve, and all these people came with us willingly. There are some others who decided to travel on their own, but what you see here is most of the people left alive between here and Hastings."

I looked over the group of people watching us, and saw an odd mixture of expectation, hope, and fear written across every face.

"There are so many of them," I said quietly, frowning to myself. "And yet, so few at the same time. I had hoped more of us survived."

"I know what you mean," Johan said understandingly. He offered his hand to help me down from my horse; after a moment's hesitation, I accepted the help and dismounted. "We did what you told us, and brought as much as we could carry. We've been here for a few days, so we've already found a few sources of fuel that seem to be good."

"That's a relief," I admitted, letting out a long, deep sigh. "We're running low on petrol."

"Well, we're not, so you're not anymore!" Johan grinned at me, the same kind of vibrant grin that I'd seen on his son's face a minute earlier. It seemed to light up the whole world, and drew a smile from me in response. "There is one teensy problem, though."

My smile faded. "What's that?"

"Well, it's the road south," he said, looking back at me with a sheepish half-smile. "It's somewhat... underwater."

"What?" I exclaimed. "Oh no, don't tell me it's washed out?"

"Unfortunately, it is — and the water's still rising," he said. "The news gets worse from there: the water is creeping towards the petrol reservoir we found. We were just trying to work out what to do when you arrived. If it keeps rising at this rate, then we're going to lose that reservoir overnight. I've got a couple of men down there trying to seal it up right now, but they're not having much luck. The seals are just too worn."

I swore softly under my breath and pulled my radio out of my coat. "Then introductions are going to have to wait. We need to get down there and empty that reservoir before it's too late. You rally your troops, I'll rally mine. We need as many water-tight metal barrels as we can find — metal, not plastic."

"I know where we can get some," Johan answered without hesitation. "There was a bunch in a shed near one of the truck stops."

"Good," I said with a nod. "Get as many able-bodied folks as you can down there and bring them to the reservoir." I glanced over at Melody. "Mel, I'm putting you in charge of guarding the injured and children. I presume I can rely on you to take care of that for me?"

Melody nodded sharply, guided her horse around, and then took off at a gallop back towards the convoy. Once she was out of sight, I looked at Johan and Dominic again. "Dominic, can you show me where the reservoir is?"

The youth looked at his father for approval, then beckoned for me to follow him. "Yes ma'am. It's this way."

"Ma'am? What am I, your headmistress?" I said with a laugh. "Call me Sandy."

Dominic grinned broadly and nodded, then he raced off towards the township proper. I followed after him, leading Boudicca behind me. The horse followed obediently as we made our way into the pretty little township – or at least, what was left of it. I'd passed through the town of Taihape many times in my youth; it was a pit stop along the main route south, so we'd either driven through it or stopped in it every time that we'd gone south to visit my grandparents. Like every other town, it had seen better days. The brick storefronts along the main drag of the shopping centre were marred by graffiti, and many of the windows had been broken. Storm damage was very evident, and forced me to step carefully to avoid injuring myself or my horse.

"Are there many infected here?" I asked Dominic when the youth finally paused to get his bearings.

He glanced at me and shrugged. "Some, but we left them alone. They weren't hurting us."

I took a deep breath and nodded my understanding. I usually made a point of putting the infected to rest, but I knew that for many people the task was too messy, strenuous, or just plain upsetting to deal with. "We're going to need to take care of them before we leave. Don't let me forget, okay?"

"Yes ma'am," Dominic agreed good-naturedly. He paused for a second, and glanced at me with a frown. "Something's wrong."

I cocked my head, listening to the sound of the world around me. A second later, I heard what had alerted Dominic: over the whisper of the rain, I could hear voices raised in anger. I touched my finger to my lips to indicate silence, and tied Boudicca's reins to a bike stand beneath the shelter of an overhanging roof. Once my horse was secure, I slipped my shotgun off my back and carefully checked there was a cartridge loaded and ready.

Dominic's eyes went wide, and he took a few rapid steps back away from me. I held up a hand and gave him a friendly smile. "It's just in case. I'm not going to let anyone hurt either of us, okay?"

The youth stared at the gun a second longer, then he looked up at me and nodded silently. I led the way down an alley, following the sound of raised voices. As we drew closer to the source, I started to make out a few words here and there. One of the voices was an adult male, but the other sounded like a young teenager. Every time he shouted, his voice broke and squeaked awkwardly — but that didn't make the threat in his tone any less real.

"I told you to fill up the damn tank! Do it!" the youth shouted, his voice trembling with an odd mixture of anger and fear. "You think I won't do it? I will! I'll kill you both!"

"Okay, okay!" the adult voice cried back. "Look, we're filling the tank. Please, calm down."

I crept to the end of the alley and held up a hand to halt Dominic, then I peeked around the corner. A hundred meters in front of me, a pudgy youth stood with an assault rifle trained on two older men in the forecourt of an abandoned petrol station. The youth had his back to me, his attention fully focused on the men. I slipped back, and beckoned Dominic in close enough that I could whisper in his ear.

"I'm going to sneak up behind him and try to disarm him," I said softly. "Stay here and keep watch. If you see anyone coming, shout and warn me."

"Yes ma'am," Dominic agreed readily. He puffed his chest up and nodded resolutely. "You can count on me."

"Good man." I gave him another smile, and then turned my attention towards defusing the hostage situation. The sound of the rain masked my footsteps as I eased myself out of cover and started creeping forward. The footpath was frequently broken up by what had been large gardens, which worked to my advantage. Every so often the youth would jump and look around, but the bushes and benches gave me enough cover to avoid being spotted.

I was tense as a bow-string and ready to snap by the time I got within a few feet of the youth's back. Just at that moment, he shouted again and very nearly made me jump out of my skin.

"Hurry up!" he yelled, his hands trembling on the assault rifle. I was close enough to see his knuckles turning white, and also close enough to see that he had no idea what he was doing with the gun. Just at that moment, one of the two adult men glanced towards us, and I saw his eyes widen. That tiny gesture was just enough to alert the youth to my presence. He spun to face me – and found himself staring down the barrel of my shotgun.

"Your safety's still on, kid," I told him gruffly, giving him a hard stare. He froze like a deer in the headlights, wide-eyed. Whatever his plan had been, he hadn't counted on any real resistance. Now that I was there and at an obvious advantage, he didn't know what to do. So, I made the decision for him.

Under any other circumstance, it probably would have been stupid to make a grab for the gun, but this time I considered it a calculated risk. I lashed out and grabbed the barrel with one hand, then I shoved as hard as I could. The boy yelped in surprise and fell over backwards, landing hard in a puddle of mud. I shoved my shotgun back over my shoulder, and trained the muzzle of the assault rifle on him instead.

"I think I'd better keep this, don't you?" I said, channelling as much power and command into my tone as I could. The youth just stared at me, his mouth gaping open like a freshly caught fish. I slipped the safety off with a dramatic click, and he jumped.

Just at that moment I heard Dominic shout a warning, followed by a female voice raised in panic. "No! No, please, don't hurt him!"

I took a step backwards and turned slowly to face the sound of running footsteps, keeping both the new arrival and the teenager in my firing line. An older woman who could only have been the youth's mother raced across the clearing towards us, her face a mask of anguish. As soon as she reached us, she threw herself down in the mud and tried to cover the boy with her own body.

"Please, don't kill my son," she begged. "He's all I have left."

"I have no intention of killing anyone," I replied without lowering the weapon. "But you'd best explain to me why your dear little boy here was trying to mug my friends."

"What? Mug?" The woman shoved herself back and stared at the boy in horror. "Bobby! Tell me you didn't?"

"I just did what Dad would have done," the youth whined, nervously scooting back away from the both of us.

The woman gasped and shook her head vigorously. "That man was *not* your father, and you know that you're not to call him that ever again. Nor are you to emulate his behaviour! He's dead, and he deserved it." The woman turned and looked at me, her hands raised in a gesture of placation. "I'm so sorry. His real father died in the plague, and we were... taken in by a group of men, who..." She took a deep breath, and even with the rain I could see the tears gathering in her eyes. It was a look that I knew well, and sympathised with better than most. I lowered the weapon and took a step closer.

"Let me guess," I said softly, understandingly. "You did what you had to do to keep your son safe."

The woman nodded and looked down at the ground. "They were bad men, all of them. They did terrible things. They hurt people. I had no choice; if I hadn't done what they told me to do, then they would have killed us."

"But you escaped?" I prompted, offering a hand to help her up. She accepted it gratefully and hauled herself up.

"No," she said, fruitlessly trying to brush the mud off her clothing. It just made the mess worse, of course. "Someone killed them. All of them. I don't know who. The lookout said there were travellers on the road, and Henry took his men out to attack them. They never came back. Bobby and I left Pukeatua the next day. There were... bodies along the road, but we never saw Henry's..." The woman took a deep breath and straightened her shoulders, obviously doing her best to put on a brave face. "It's for the best. He was a terrible man."

I felt a cold chill run down my spine, like the ghost of actions past creeping up on me. I glanced around at the others, then looked back at the woman, doing my best to keep my face expressionless. "This Henry person, was he about six-five, wore a lot of army surplus, had a tattoo on his neck about here..." I asked, pointing to a spot on my own neck.

Her eyes widened. "Yes! How did you know?"

"Because I killed him," I told her bluntly, making no attempt to sugar-coat the truth. "I was the traveller on the road, with my husband and our foster daughter. My husband is Chinese, and my foster daughter is Indian."

"Oh, no!" The woman gasped and clasped her hands to her chest. "Henry hated anyone that wasn't European, he blamed them for the plague. He... please tell me that he didn't hurt them?"

"No, they're fine." I glanced at Bobby, who was still sitting in the mud staring at me, then I looked back at the woman. "He tried to kill my family. I couldn't let that happen. I won't tell you what happened to him in front of Bobby, though. No one needs to know except me."

The woman started to say something, but Bobby cut her off before she could.

"You... you killed my dad?" he said, his voice carrying that strange mixture of fear and anger again.

"Don't call him that!" the woman cried, spinning to face her son. "Henry was not your father! Your father was a good, kind, gentle man. Your father would never have threatened this lady's child."

"He was my dad!" the stocky youth shouted back, shoving himself up to his feet. "I don't know this other person you're talking about. Henry taught me to fight and shoot and drink – he's the only dad I ever knew."

"I'm sorry, Bobby," I said, with as much sympathy as I could muster; after all, my issue was with Henry, not Bobby or his mother. "He didn't give me any choice. He attacked me, and I had to fight back."

"I don't care! I don't care what you say! You killed my dad!" Bobby screamed at me, his florid face turning red. He took a menacing step towards me, but I was no more intimidated by him than I had been by his stepfather. I raised the assault rifle and trained it on him.

"Stand down, Bobby," I told him, my voice cool and firm. "What's done is done. There's no changing that now."

"Shut up! You're a murderer, and I hate you!" the young man bellowed, then he turned on a heel and ran away from us. After a few steps, he slipped in the mud and went down hard on his knees, then picked himself up and kept running.

His mother looked at me again, her face wet with a combination of tears and rain. "I'm so sorry. Bobby... was too young, he doesn't know any better. Henry was the only man he had to look up to since his father died."

"You don't need to apologise," I said, lowering the gun. "I tell myself that I had no choice, but maybe I did. Maybe I should be held accountable for my actions." I glanced at her, and gave her a weak smile. "Amongst my group, we have a code of laws. If someone has a grievance with someone else, then they can pull the other person in front of a magistrate and a group of their peers, and have that person put to trial. If it would help Bobby to deal with his grief, then I'm willing to submit myself to a trial regarding the death of his step-father."

The woman bit her lip and looked away, watching her son slip in the mud again. She seemed to think about my offer for a second and then she was gone, running after

Bobby and calling his name. Once they were out of sight, I took a deep breath to calm my frazzled nerves and turned to look at Dominic and the two strangers I'd managed to rescue.

"I really need to learn to keep my big mouth shut sometimes," I admitted, the strength draining out of me as the adrenaline started to fade. "I'm sorry you had to witness that. We need to deal with this petrol, before the flood water gets here. Let's get to it, shall we?"

CHAPTER FOUR

By the time the others reached us, I could hear the flood-water lapping against the buildings nearby and see glimpses of it down the alleys between buildings. Bobby and his mother didn't return, but the brief encounter left me feeling wrung out and more than a little guilty. I'd tried so hard to forget what I'd done to Bobby's step-father to protect my own family, but now I had no choice but to remember it. Thankfully, the urgency of our situation helped me to keep going, even if worry still nagged at me.

Suddenly, Dominic shouted an alert. I looked up just in time to see my Hilux rounding a corner and pulling into the forecourt of the old petrol station, followed by a couple of unfamiliar vehicles. I glanced at Dominic and raised a brow. "The first truck is mine, but who are the others?"

"Those are our trucks," Dominic explained. "I see my dad driving! I bet they've got the barrels for us!"

"You have better eyesight than me, mate," I answered dryly. "Go give them an update, will you?"

"Sure!" he agreed, then he dashed off to do just that.

I smiled at the two men helping me to get the tanks ready to be drained. "He's a good kid, that one."

"Aye, seems to be," the shorter one agreed pleasantly. He was a stocky fellow named Aaron, with curly brown hair, a faint Scottish accent, and a smile that seemed to be hard-wired onto his face. The other man was tall, slender fellow named Charu. He was somewhere in his early forties but still youthful and handsome, with dark skin much like Priyanka's. That was where the similarity ended, though. Aaron had introduced him to me, but Charu hadn't said a word. He just nodded, shook his head, or shrugged when I asked him questions, and avoided eye-contact. I couldn't tell whether there was something wrong with him or if he just didn't like me, so I decided it was better to ignore his sullen attitude and just give him time to get used to me.

"I think this should be good to go," I told them, kneeling down to examine the haphazard hand-pump we'd assembled from pieces strewn around the buildings nearby. "Just keep your fingers and toes crossed that it doesn't pop loose at an inopportune moment."

Aaron laughed and nodded, but Charu just shot me a look and went back to tightening the bolts. I eased myself up to my feet again, wiped my hands on my pants, and went over to the trucks. As soon as they came to a halt, the doors of the vehicles popped open and people started piling out. Half of them were the familiar faces from my own group, but the rest I'd only glimpsed in passing at Johan's camp.

"Hey, sis!" Skylar called. "I see you found us some new friends." She ducked out of the rain and into the shelter of the forecourt. Hemi followed her a second later, with Johan and Dominic hot on her heels.

"I certainly hope so," I replied, grinning at them. Johan and Dominic both grinned back, and behind me I heard Aaron laugh again. "Anyway, as far as I can tell this petrol is still good – but it won't be for long. If that water gets anywhere near it, it'll be useless to us. We've jerry-rigged a pump, but I don't know if we're going to have enough time to get all of it. We're going to need to work fast."

"I have an idea to buy us some time," Aaron said. I glanced at him and raised an eyebrow, nodding for him to continue. He cleared his throat and stepped forward, joining the ring of people around me. "I came here as a backpacker right after I finished studying, and ended up living here for a couple of years. The outlying farmland gets flooded on a regular basis. I know they kept a supply of sandbags on hand in case of emergencies."

"Oh!" I gasped. "You're thinking that we could delay or divert the flood water long enough to get the rest of the petrol?"

"Aye," he replied, nodding. Suddenly, he grinned and pointed at a large hall just across the road from the petrol station. "And that right there is the town hall. Probably the best place to start."

"I'll agree with that," I said. "Aaron, you're with me. Johan, Hemi, I want you guys to take care of the pumping operation. Skye, you and Dominic are on watch. Show him how to use this, please." I handed the rifle that I'd confiscated from Bobby to Skye. She gave me an odd look in return.

"This isn't one of ours," she pointed out. "Where did you get this?"

"Long story," I replied. "No time to tell it now. But watch out for a kid of about fourteen who isn't part of either of our groups. He's got a grudge against me and might try to stop us."

"If you say so," she said doubtfully, then she shrugged, took the rifle, and turned her attention to Dominic. I unshouldered my shotgun and ran off towards the town hall, leaving the others to take care of their assigned tasks.

"Any idea where they would have kept these theoretical sandbags?" I called as we ran, ducking across a road marked by paint so faded it was impossible to make out what it might have once said.

"Not a clue, but I can make an educated guess," he called back. "Let's try that side door, since it's the only one at ground level. Makes sense that you wouldn't want to lug sandbags up stairs, right?"

"Right," I agreed, adjusting my course towards the door at the back of the building. When I got there, I tried the handle and found it locked from the inside. I glanced around and spotted a couple of windows a few meters farther along the wall. "Stand back and cover your eyes."

Aaron did as he was told and waited patiently while I used the butt of my shotgun to break the glass. I carefully cleared the shards out of the frame, then called him over. He cottoned on to what I was trying to do immediately, and cupped his hands on his knee to give me a boost. A second later, I was crouched inside the dark building, my shotgun at the ready.

Nothing stirred except the dust-bunnies I'd disturbed by letting in a breeze. The place smelt like a tomb, but so did everything that had been locked up for a decade. I pulled out my torch and used its thin beam of light to guide my way to the door.

Aaron joined me as soon as I unbolted the door, pulling a torch out of his own pocket. Our twin beams pushed back the darkness, illuminating a small office with nothing more than a dusty old computer on a desk against one wall, and a couple of doors leading off into other rooms. I opened one and discovered a vast, empty meeting hall. The other revealed a storage room filled with folding tables and stacked chairs.

"Nothing here," I said, disappointed. Aaron blew out a sharp breath and nodded, then he paused for a moment to think.

"Wait – there were other government buildings outside, I think," he said. He hurried past me out the door, and I followed close behind him. Our feet splashed through deep puddles as we raced down the street and across a gravel parking lot towards a low, squat grey brick building.

"The fire station?" I called after him. "You think they'll be in there?"

"Fire-fighting crews did more than just fighting fires, so it's possible," he replied, ducking into the relative shelter offered by the overhanging ledge of the building.

I joined him and took the lead again, my shotgun at the ready in case of trouble. We found the front door wide open, but this time a steady breeze did nothing to help with the stench. It was a smell that I knew all too well: decomposing flesh.

"I think there's someone in the fire engine," I said. I shouldered my shotgun, and pulled out the rag I still carried out of habit. My lifestyle might have improved, but my chances of running into something malodorous hadn't.

"Can I stay here?" Aaron asked pitifully, gagging and struggling to cover his lower face with the sleeve of his jersey. "Sweet mother Mary, that's a foul stench."

"No, we can't split up. Haven't you ever watched a horror movie?" I said dryly. Without waiting for an answer, I pulled out my taser and my torch and led the way into the reeking gloom.

My first port of call was to check the cab of the fire engine, of course; sure enough, there was a human figure sitting there, staring into space, still clad in his uniform and helmet. Not a mutant, just a regular, helpless, pathetic infected. I sighed heavily and vaulted up to the window, so that I could put the poor person out of his misery.

When I climbed back down, Aaron gave me a curious look. "Why bother? He wasn't causing any trouble."

"Three reasons," I replied as I led the way deeper into the station. "One: respect. That was a zombie fireman, who used to be a real fireman, a person who risked life and limb every day to save people. He would have done the same for any one of us. Two: mercy. God knows what those poor creatures feel, or if there's any way for their spirits to move on while their bodies linger here. I don't know, but I care. The only thing I can do for him now is to put him to rest. He deserves that much. And last but not least, three: the virus mutated. As far as we can tell, it spreads from infected to infected, so culling them is the best way to keep it from spreading."

"Oh." Aaron went quiet for a moment, then he made a noise that was somewhere between a grunt and a chuckle. "I see you've thought this through quite thoroughly."

"I've had a lot of time to think about it, yeah," I admitted. "But if it was your mum, you wouldn't want to just leave her... sitting there, rotting. Would you?"

"Hell no," Aaron agreed, his voice suddenly vehement. He went silent again for a couple of minutes while we explored the offices and storage rooms behind the fire station. There we found a few fully-loaded emergency medical kits that I wasn't about to leave behind, so the two of us set about gathering them up to take back with us. Suddenly, Aaron shot me a concerned frown. "You don't think their souls can move on until they're truly dead?"

"I have no idea," I admitted. I lifted a particularly large kit and lugged it out the door, with Aaron close behind me. "I don't know what comes next. I wish I did. I really, really wish I did. But I look at the infected and I watch them going about their business, and it makes me think. If their brains have melted, then how can they still show some of the same traits that they exhibited in life? It makes me wonder how much of what makes me who I am comes from my brain, and how much of it comes from my soul — if I have one, I don't know. I was taught to treat matters of religion with criticism, but... I just don't know anymore. What if that little bit of who they used to be comes from their soul? That means their souls must be tied to their earthly bodies, until... until they're not anymore."

"Oh Lord, that's a terrible thought," Aaron said, staring at me in horror. "I never even considered that. Do you think they're... aware?"

"I don't know," I said softly. "I don't know anything. That's the hardest part. I can only guess and follow my conscience." I shook my head, and gave him a weak smile. "Come on. We've got to find those sandbags."

Aaron nodded silently, and together we returned to the stinking darkness to search. We came up empty handed, but by the time we'd finished we had managed to find a fair supply of emergency rations as well as the medical kits.

"Well, this is shit," Aaron blurted as we were carrying our findings back to the convoy. "This stuff is nice and all, but we really need those sandbags. They must be around here somewhere!"

"Yeah," I agreed. When we reached the convoy, I yanked open the rear cab of the Hilux and piled my supplies into the back seat. Aaron did the same, then we stood back and stared around, seeking some kind of inspiration.

"If I were a sandbag, where would I be?" Aaron asked himself. The question was obviously rhetorical, but something about it twigged just the right chord to make me think.

"You'd be in a shed," I replied. "You're just a sandbag. You don't need a bathroom or food or even electricity. You just need a roof over your head that'll keep you from getting mouldy."

Aaron froze and stared at me, his mouth hanging open. Suddenly, he let out a whoop and pumped his fist in the air. "That's it! There was a big corrugated iron shed in the parking lot behind Town Hall. They must be in there! Why didn't I think of that sooner?"

"Sometimes it's hard to see something hidden in plain sight," I replied, grabbing his arm. "Come on!"

We took off at a sprint together, racing back across the road and down the gravel path behind the town hall. Sure enough, as I rounded the last corner I spotted an ugly, rusted iron shed the size of a small barn, crammed in between the equally-rusted hulks of a few abandoned minivans. I raced over to the sliding door and tried to open it, but it was held closed by a small, tarnished padlock.

"Damn!" I swore, rattling the door fruitlessly. "I don't suppose you have bolt-cutters on you, do you?"

"Aye, I've got a pair of bolt-cutters wedged down my pants, on the off chance you might happen to need them," Aaron replied sarcastically. He came up beside me and peered at the lock, then gave me a thoughtful look. "Actually, I don't think we need bolt-cutters. This is just about rusted through. Give me your gun a moment?"

"Don't waste my shells," I warned as I handed him my precious weapon.

"I wasn't planning to," he replied with a grin. He double-checked the safety was on, then turned the gun around and brought the butt down hard on the iron hoop that the padlock had been threaded through. With a few good, solid blows, the whole lock popped right off.

"Nice going," I said. He grinned again and handed me back my shotgun, then put his weight against the door. It didn't want to move at first, but he was stronger than he looked. It gave an inch, then another, then suddenly it slid all the way open. The dry, dusty interior was stacked very nearly floor to ceiling with pre-packed sandbags, ready and waiting for the moment when they'd be needed again. In the centre of the shed, half-a-dozen hand-carts waited to be filled.

Aaron looked at the sandbags, then looked at me. He flung a hand up in the air, palm towards me; the unexpected gesture just about made me jump out of my skin. I looked at his hand, then looked at him. He looked at his hand, then looked at me and wiggled his fingers. "Come on! Don't leave a brother hanging here. High five for teamwork!"

"Oh!" I cried, suddenly realising what he was trying to do. Laughing, I returned the high-five and then I led the way into the shed.

"Christ, I think the temperature's dropping," Aaron complained. We manoeuvred two of the hand-carts around into a position where we could easily push them out the door, and then combined our strength to pack them full of as many sandbags as we could.

"I think you're right," I agreed. "It feels like we're going to have hail soon."

"No, not just hail," Aaron said. He paused and stared out the window at the dark sky, then looked at me. "Those are snow clouds."

I swore under my breath and picked up the pace. As soon as the hand-carts were full, we raced them out the door and down the road toward the petrol station. Half way there, we were met by Zain and some of the others.

"Sandy!" he cried. "Only so many of us can fill barrels at the same time, and the water's coming fast! Where are those sandbags?"

"Back there," I replied breathlessly. "In the shed behind the hall."

Zain and his group raced past us, and we hurried on. A few metres past the petrol station, I brought my hand-cart to a stop and looked around. The main road was uncomfortably wide, but I saw an opportunity to make that work to our advantage: nearly a dozen parked cars lined both sides of the road. They were rusted, filthy, and otherwise useless, but they did have one use left.

"We can use these cars to build a barricade," I shouted over the howling of the wind. "If we build it between the petrol station and that building on the other side of the road, it should buy us the time we need."

"Good idea," Aaron shouted back. He grabbed a sandbag and carried it over to the middle of the road. "Start here. We line the cars up behind this point, and then pack the sandbags in front of them."

I couldn't find the breath to reply to him, but I didn't need to. I just raced over to help him and that was answer enough. A few minutes later, Zain and the others joined us, each armed with another hand-cart full of sandbags. As soon as they arrived, I flagged them down and pointed at a couple of the cars nearby.

"Drag them over here," I cried. "Smash the windows if you have to, but get them over here. Build an arc across the road – and hurry!"

Zain shouted a wordless reply and raced off again, and this time I went with him. There was no time for finesse, but we managed to get one of the cars open, the handbrake off, and then the others helped us to man-handle the car across the road. It was long, hard, back-breaking work, but adrenaline kept us going. Twice I was forced to sit down for a second when sparkles began to dance around the edge of my vision, but nobody complained or tried to cajole me. For once in my life, for the baby's sake, I took the time my body needed to recover – but not a second longer. As soon as I could, I was back up, helping to shift cars and lug sandbags.

Every second, the water crept closer and closer. Every second, the sky got darker and darker, the rain fell heavier, and the wind got colder. I paused for a second to adjust my hood, and in that moment I glanced up at the sky – but the droplet that struck my cheek wasn't water. It was ice.

"Incoming!" I cried, ducking my head back down to avoid the downpour. Aaron swore colourfully and grabbed me by the arm, dragging me into the shadow of a nearby building. A second later, the sleet turned to a brief but violent bout of hail. We huddled together until it passed, then hurried back out to check on the others. "Everyone okay? Anyone hurt?"

"Everyone's fine," someone shouted back to me. In the chaos, I couldn't tell who it was.

Once I was sure that everyone was safe, I raced back to the barricade and threw my weight behind the last car that we needed to block the full span of the road.

"We're almost there!" I cried, as much to encourage myself as them. My feet slipped on the hailstones, but the others soon joined me and our combined strength was enough to manoeuvre the car into position.

"More sandbags!" Aaron shouted over the wind. I grunted my agreement, grabbed the nearest hand-cart, and raced back towards the shed as fast as I could without risking my safety on the icy ground. The hail might have passed, but the sleet was determined to keep our world wet and dangerously slippery. I ducked into the shelter of the shed's rusted but solid roof, and paused for a second to brush a few half-formed snowflakes off my shoulders. The others arrived a moment later and took over the heavy lifting, giving me a much-needed moment to recover and catch my breath.

Did I? Of course not. I used the moment to pull out my walkie-talkie and called my husband's name. "Michael? Come in, Michael?"

After a few seconds, the radio crackled and I heard his familiar voice. "Sandy! Please tell me you're on your way back now. Waiting with the wounded is killing me."

"I know, honey, but not quite yet. It's taking longer than we expected," I replied breathlessly, lifting my voice so that I could be heard over the drone of the sleet on the roof. "I need to know, do we have power?"

"No, no power," he replied. "It's getting bloody cold, though; I think we should break out the generator and get some heaters going."

"You read my mind," I replied. "We just had hail, and Aaron reckons we're going to have snow. We're all drenched. By the time we get back, we're going to be popsicles."

"I'll take care of it," he told me, using the deep, firm tone he used to reassure people. "Just make sure you're back before sundown. It's going to be pitch black tonight, without street lamps or stars."

"You don't have to tell me twice," I replied. I quickly said my goodbyes, tucked the radio away, and rejoined the others just as they were lugging the next load out into the weather. When we reached the barricade, I vaulted over the bonnet of one of the cars – and swore when I found my feet splashing through shallow water. "It's here! We don't have much time. Half of you get over here, the other half start throwing sandbags over. Quick!"

Everyone jumped to obey. The sleet made the work even worse, but none of us uttered a word of complaint. We worked feverishly, stacking row upon row of sandbags against the cars, until it we finally had a barricade at least waist high across the entire width of the road.

By that stage, the floodwaters had risen almost to my knees, and I was trembling from cold and exertion. I tried to vault back over to the safe side of the barrier, but my arms went as weak as cooked noodles and slid out from under me. Aaron caught me and helped me back over to where Zain waited, and together they rushed me to the shelter of the petrol station. Skylar was still standing guard, perched on the bonnet of the Hilux; as soon as she saw us coming, she jumped down and hurried over to help me.

"Not this again!" she scolded, guiding me over to sit on the front bumper of the truck. "Sandy, you know you're not supposed to—"

"I didn't," I replied, cutting her off mid-sentence. "I did what I was told, and took breaks when I needed it. I'm just cold. We all are. Let me sit down for a minute, then I'll be fine again." I glanced up at the people who'd been helping with the barricade, all of whom were in just as bad a state as me. "Take a second to recover, guys. Once we're functional again, we need to go see if there's any propane in the station itself."

"Dominic and I can do that," Skylar said, shoving a strand of sodden hair back out of her face. "You guys need to rest. Take over the watch, we'll go scout. "

"Okay," I agreed, relieved by her initiative. They ran off without another word, leaving my group to watch for trouble. We instinctively arranged ourselves so that each of us was watching a different direction. All of us had been living the survivor's life long enough that we knew what to do without being told. Once we were settled, I took a deep breath and just forced myself to relax for a couple of minutes.

Suddenly, Skye and Dominic reappeared in front of us, a whole lot wetter but with triumphant expressions on their faces.

"There are a bunch of tanks in a cage tucked around the far side," she told me excitedly. "I think they might be full, but I can't tell. Can you?"

"No," I admitted. "Zain? Can you?"

"I don't really know how anyone could survive without that knowledge," he answered, his voice carrying the faintest note of humour. Zain wasn't usually one to crack jokes, but in the circumstances it was just what I needed to hear.

"Well, time for all of us to learn," I said with a laugh, levering myself back up to my feet. I waited for a second to make sure that I had my balance, then I headed towards the petrol station.

Skylar hurried into the lead, with Zain and Aaron close behind us. Sure enough, just around the corner nearest to the front door there was a steel cage painted an ugly shade of lime green, which was guarding half-a-dozen tanks. I glanced at Zain curiously.

"That's an exchange station," he explained. "It'll be a mix of full ones for customers to buy, and empties that they've returned. Should be at least one that's full, I imagine – if we can get through that padlock."

"You guys head in and see if you can find a key, or any useful supplies," I instructed. "I'll see if I can pick this lock."

They nodded and hurried off. Before I got started, I stuck my head around the corner and called to the team that were still labouring with the petrol. "Yo, Hemi!"

"Yo, Sandy!" he called back, pausing in his work to wave to me.

"How close are we to being done?" I asked. "We're starting to lose the daylight."

"Almost there, mate," he replied, shouting to make himself heard over nature's racket. "We're nearly at the bottom of the reservoir. We should make it before dark."

"Thanks! You guys are doing a great job, keep it up!" I shot him a double-thumbs-up. He returned the gesture with a grin, then went right back to work. I turned my attention on the padlock, and was just unbuttoning my coat to fish out my lockpicks when Aaron came running back out, grinning like a mad-man.

"Don't you worry, lass; I've got this covered!" he announced gleefully, holding up a pair of huge, bright red bolt cutters.

I laughed and took a step back. "Oh, so you did have those hidden down your pants after all, huh?"

"Nope, but I do now!" he said cheerfully. With a mighty crunch of steel on steel, he cut the little padlock off the cage, then handed the bolt cutters to me so that he could start pulling the tanks out of the cage. "I could be wrong, but these seem to be in fine condition. Not a speck of rust on them."

"Well, it's under shelter on the leeward side of the building, and I guess it's never flooded this high before," I replied. "Zain, we're in!"

Zain reappeared out of the building a few seconds later, clutching a few much-needed flasks of motor oil. Aaron handed me a tank, which I passed on to Zain. He examined it for a moment, then nodded his approval and passed it back to me. "This is full. Should be fine, so long as we can keep it dry."

"On a day like today, 'dry' is going to be an issue," I said, frowning.

"No, it isn't!" Skylar interrupted, sticking her head around the corner. She gave me a huge grin and held up an enormous yellow umbrella. "Ta-da!"

"Well, I guess that'll work nicely," I said, chuckling. I set the bolt cutters down and took the umbrella instead. After a few seconds of awkward fumbling, it popped open in my hand. "Good thinking, Skye. How many are there?"

"Lots," she replied, then she started handing out gaudily-coloured umbrellas to the others.

I just laughed, hugged the tank to my chest, and made a mad dash back across the forecourt to the Hilux. The back was already full of barrels of petrol, so I opened the rear cab and set the tank on the seats instead. Aaron and Zain joined me a few seconds later; between the three of us, we had the tanks Zain had deemed to be full transferred to the trucks in no time at all.

We went back and managed to get in a couple more loads of oil and other useful supplies before the deepening gloom made it too hard to see what we were doing. Just as I was depositing my last armful in a safe place, I heard Hemi shouting. "That's it! We're done! We're done!"

I glanced at our makeshift barricade and saw that the floodwaters had already risen almost to the top, and a few ominous shadows were creeping around the sides as well.

"Then let's get out of here," I shouted back, making a broad gesture to the others. "Into the trucks, quick! The water's coming!"

There wasn't enough space left in the trucks to carry everyone. Those of us who could still function made way for supplies or people in worse condition than we were. We huddled beneath our umbrellas and waited until the trucks had headed off, then we followed on foot back to our base of operations on the far side of town.

Johan, Aaron, and Dominic appeared beside me as I trudged through the driving rain. I glanced at them and gave them a weary smile. "Well, we did it. I'm pretty sure the ground is sloping upwards, so that should help us keep above the water for the night."

"Should do, yes," Johan agreed, sounding just as tired as I felt. "I for one will be glad to find my bed tonight."

"I really hope we *can* find beds tonight," I replied, lifting my umbrella a little so that they could find some shelter beneath it. It was a token gesture at best, but Johan gave me an appreciative smile.

"Even if we can't find you an actual bed, I'm sure we can make you comfortable," he replied, his voice deep, soothing, and somehow familiar. He had the same patient, reassuring tone as Michael, and that put me at ease. "There are several motels at that end of town, and we've scouted them all. I imagine Hannah has already helped your people find the best places to set up camp for the night." He paused and shot a glance at me. "That's my wife. My new wife. We married last year. Dominic's mother died in the plague, sadly."

"Ah. I'm sorry to hear that," I said, nodding my understanding. I glanced at Dominic and gave him a smile. "It must be nice to have a mum again, huh?"

"Yeah!" Dominic agreed, nodding vigorously. "Hannah's really nice. She's a great cook, too!"

We all laughed at that. Once the levity passed, I glanced at the others and tilted my head. "I need to go get Boudicca. Who wants to keep me company?"

Aaron gave me an odd look. "I don't know how to tell you this, but I'm pretty sure Boudicca's dead. Like, a couple of thousand years ago."

"Not that Boudicca," I replied, laughing. "That's my horse's name. Don't look at me, I didn't pick the name."

Everyone chuckled again, but Aaron was the first to volunteer to come with me.

"We better move fast," he said as we peeled away from the rest of the group. "We're going to lose the light completely any minute now."

"And here comes the snow," I added, as a couple of stray snowflakes began to drift down around us. They were small, shapeless things, but they were definitely snow. We exchanged a glance, then picked up the pace.

Boudicca was exactly where I'd left her, tied to the bicycle stand and looking no worse for wear. She nickered a greeting to me and nudged me with her velvet-soft muzzle. I reached up and rubbed her nose affectionately, then I untied her reins and looped them around my wrist.

"My back hurts too much to mount up, but you can ride if you want," I said to Aaron.

He shook his head and gave me a wry smile. "After all that lifting? Nah. I haven't ridden in years, anyway."

"Me either," I said. I handed him the umbrella, so that I could focus on leading Boudicca through the mounting snow. At least the snowfall meant the rain had stopped for the time being, and I was grateful for any small favours that Mother Nature had to offer.

The conversation trailed off during the walk back to the northern end of town, so that we could focus on where we were putting our feet. The wet ground and sudden cold snap meant everything was dangerously slippery, and more than once I found my feet sliding on a patch of black ice. Boudicca seemed to have no such trouble, luckily; she was heavy enough that her hooves just broke through the fresh ice.

It was a long walk back, and by the time we got there we'd lost daylight completely. For the last kilometre or so we only had torchlight to guide us, and the distant glow from the motels where our comrades had set up camp. I found myself growing increasingly anxious the longer we were out after dark, but nothing happened that was any more dangerous than Boudicca accidentally inhaling a fluffy snowflake and then sneezing on me.

Suddenly, one of the lookouts spotted us and shouted a greeting. A minute later, Priya came racing out of the darkness and flung her arms around my waist. "Mama!"

"Priya!" I cried back, squeezing her with affectionate exuberance.

She squealed and squirmed for a second, then ducked under my arm and fell into step beside me. "Mama! Baba found a baby!"

I just about swallowed my tongue in surprise. "He what? He *found* a baby? Whose baby did he find?"

"Hannah's!" Priya replied brightly, miming the way one might hold a baby. "He hugged the baby and went 'goo-goo, gaa-gaa', made many silly noises. Why?"

"That's... something adults do around babies," I replied, forcing myself to take a deep breath to fight down the odd mixture of relief and nausea that suddenly fought to overwhelm me. So, Michael liked babies. That was no great surprise. And apparently he was feeling a bit clucky. Considering my situation, that was most likely a good thing.

My thoughts were interrupted when Priya suddenly noticed Aaron, and froze in her tracks. I just laughed and gave her a look. "Oh, don't tell me you're pretending to be shy again. Come here, munchkin."

I held my arm out to her. She raced into it and cuddled up against me, peering curiously at Aaron from the relative safety of my shadow.

He grinned and gave her a wave. "Hello there, lass. I'm Aaron. What's your name?"

Priya hid her face in my armpit, and I burst out laughing. I just couldn't help it. She always did that to me. "This is my foster daughter, Priya. Don't mind her; she plays this game sometimes when she secretly just wants a hug. Isn't that right, honey?"

Priya peeked out, looked up at me, and gave me a huge, cheesy grin. Then she detached herself from me and we all resumed walking.

"You talks funny," she said suddenly. "Why?"

"Sorry, we're still working on her English," I added. "She's asking about your accent."

"I figured as much," Aaron replied, his expression open and friendly. "I'm from another country, a faraway land called Scotland. I moved here when I was fresh out of university, a couple of years before the plague."

"You remember how we talked about how people's mamas and babas coming from different places?" I said, looking down at her. "Aaron comes from the same place as my baba."

"Oh, aye?" he asked, looking at me quizzically. "Well, I suppose I should have guessed from the 'McDermott' thing, but you don't have an accent."

"I never had the chance to visit, unfortunately," I said. "My father moved here when he was a toddler."

"That's a shame," he said thoughtfully, his eyes turning distant for a moment. "It's pretty country. Much like New Zealand, in many ways. I often wonder what it's like over there nowadays. I suppose I'll never know."

"Maybe one day we'll find out," I replied, reaching out to pat his shoulder. "In the meantime, though — Priya, where are the horses being kept?"

"Over here, Mama!" she replied, scampering off towards a field not far away. She opened a gate and led us through it, then guided us across the field to a ramshackle barn that glowed with the faint light of an oil lamp.

Inside, we found the twins hard at work, rubbing the horses down and making sure that they were fed and bedded for the night. Introductions were made, then the girls took Boudicca and led her in with the other horses.

"Do you need a hand?" I asked hesitantly, hovering near the door with the others.

"No, this is our job tonight," Jasmine replied with her usual determination.

Lily gave us a smile and nodded agreement with her twin. "We're almost done, but thank you for offering."

"Okay," I said. "Call if you need anything."

"We will," Lily replied, waving a goodbye. I waved back, then led my little party back out into the snow.

"Lots of kids with you," Aaron commented. "How did they survive?"

"Lord of the Flies-style," I answered dryly, wrapping my arm around Priya. She gave me a curious look, then snuggled in under my arm for what little warmth and shelter she could get with my coat bundled up tight around me. I briefly explained the origin stories of our various children to him as we walked back towards the glow of the motel, until someone called out and interrupted the conversation.

"Hello!" the woman called, waving frantically. "Come inside and get warm; it's freezing out here."

"Amen to that," I agreed, ushering Priya ahead of me up the short flight of stairs.

"Good evening, Hannah," Aaron greeted with his usual friendly smile. "How are things?"

"All's well, so long as you lot get in here before all the heat gets out!" Hannah replied. She chased us all inside and closed the door, then turned to offer me her hand. "Hi, I'm Hannah. I've heard so much about you!"

"Likewise," I replied, shaking the offered hand.

Hannah gasped at my touch and yanked her hand back. "Good God, you're like ice! Come with me, let's get you all warmed up before you get frostbite."

The woman grabbed my arm and all but dragged me down a long hallway flanked by doorways. Somewhere along the way, Aaron and Priya both vanished, though I didn't notice until they'd already left. Hannah paused for a second to check the doors, then opened one on the right hand side.

"Here, this is your room," she said. "Your husband already brought all your things inside, so you should be able change into something dry."

"Oh man, it's toasty in here," I said, reaching out to rest my hands over the radiator. "I take it the generator's working nicely?"

Hannah laughed and nodded. "I'm a little vague on the details, but I think they managed to use your little generator to jump start the big generator out the back. Thank goodness, because we're going to need it tonight. Now, you get that wet clothing off so I can get it in the dryer for you."

"Yes ma'am," I agreed with a playful salute. I closed the door behind me for a little privacy, then pulled my various essentials out of their pockets and set them out on a dresser nearby. My clothing was a mess: my pants were soaked to the knees, my shoes and socks were sodden, and my coat was practically dripping wet. I stared at it for a second, then just dropped it all in a pile on the floor.

A towel and a stack of clothing sat neatly folded on the end of the bed, obviously waiting for me. I recognised them from our stash of spare clothing, and suddenly I was very glad that we'd brought it with us. I changed quickly, and pulled on a pair of thick socks in lieu of my sodden shoes. When I opened the door, Hannah was waiting.

"Much better," she said approvingly. "We've got a roaring fire going down in the common room, so you go join the others and I'll take care of this. Just follow this corridor to the end, and you'll hear them before you see them."

"Thank you so much," I said, grateful to have the responsibility taken away from me for a change. Every inch of me ached, and I longed for the chance to sit down and eat something hot. I left her to take care of my clothes and padded off down the hall in the direction she'd indicated.

Sure enough, I heard them before I saw them. The buzz of human voices in conversation was a pleasantly familiar sound, and it made me smile. I opened the door, and spent a moment just relishing in the wave of heat that washed out. People were gathered around the big fireplace on the far wall, sitting on chairs or cross-legged on the floor. For once, the scent of so many bodies in close proximity didn't bother me. In fact, I didn't notice it. The moment the joy of the warmth wore off, I only had eyes for Michael.

He was sitting in an armchair, rocking a tiny bundle wrapped in a pink baby blanket. I slipped inside without being noticed and closed the door, then crept up behind him, watching with mute fascination. His big hands were so gentle, and his voice was so soft that it made my gut lurch. There was something about seeing a man being gentle with a baby that made my most primal instincts scream out in need, even if I didn't really know what to do with them.

Melody's voice interrupted my reverie. It was raised a few octaves higher than usual, which made it clear that she was upset and on the verge of genuine distress. "Sandy! I want to hold the baby. Make him give me the baby!"

Michael glanced up and gave me that smile he reserved just for me. "Ah, you're back." He looked at Melody and laughed. "Calm down, would you? She's trying to sleep. You can hold her, but you have to sit down and be still and quiet. You wouldn't like it if someone was running around screaming while you were trying to sleep, would you?"

"Fine, fine, I'll be good, just let me hold the baby!" Melody groaned, plopping down to sit on the floor beside his chair. Once she was settled, Michael leaned over and tenderly placed the sleeping baby in her outstretched arms.

"That's it," he said guiding her arms into the right places to keep the baby comfortable. "Like this. If she starts to wake up, just rock her gently like I was doing."

Melody barely even seemed to hear him; she just stared with rapt fascination at the tiny person in her arms. Michael and I exchanged a smile, then he held his arms out to me. I went into them as happily as any baby, snuggling up in the warmth of his lap. He kissed me, hugged me gently, and suddenly I was the happiest I'd been all day.

"I missed you," he whispered, his voice soft and tender. I could hear the frown in his voice, even if I couldn't see his face. "You're so cold. Are you okay?"

"Fine, just fine," I replied, closing my eyes to enjoy the warmth. "We got it all, and some propane as well. It should be enough to get us to Avalon with lots to spare."

"Sounds like we're going to be stuck here for a while, though," he said, his big fingers stroking a few stray tendrils of my hair away from my cheeks. "From what the others were saying, the flooding seems to be pretty bad."

"It is, but we can wait," I said. "Patience is a virtue, and we've got plenty to do in the meantime."

Michael pushed me back just far enough to see my face, and I gave him a mischievous grin in return. He just laughed and hugged me tighter.

Chapter Five

I pressed my taser to the nape of the infected woman's neck, then leapt back out of the way as she collapsed like a decomposing water-balloon.

"Ugh, this one's over-ripe," I called to the others. "Who's on slops duty?"

"Aw, hell. I'm not sure I'll ever get used to that smell," Aaron said, reaching up as though to cover his face with his gloved hands. At the last second, he remembered that his gloves smelt just as bad and jerked them away from his face with a muttered curse.

"You think it's bad over there? Come closer and take a whiff!" I teased, tucking my taser back into my pocket. "You want some more perfume for your mask?"

"Ugh, no," he protested, waving me away. "That stuff smells even worse."

I opened my mouth to make a joke about the heightened sense of smell that came with pregnancy, but caught myself just in time. Instead, I laughed and went for sympathy. "I know, mate. I know. Seriously, though — who's on slops?"

"Charu, I think," Aaron answered. "You want me to go get him? I don't mind, anything to get out of this stink-hole."

"Nah," I replied, shaking my head. "You volunteered for this, so you don't get to escape that easily. He'll still be busy working on that last place. Looks like the infected around here were in the last stages of the virus. What a mess."

"Yeah, but like you said, better safe than sorry," Aaron said, his voice carrying a mixture of disgust and amusement. "That's the last one we had marked. You want to go do one last check around town and make sure we haven't missed any of them?"

"Sure," I agreed. We stripped off our rubber gloves and tossed them on top of the sloppy remains of the infected, then headed out into the street.

Five days had passed since our arrival in Taihape, and water still blocked the road southwards. We had nothing better to do with our time except explore this side of the flood, and gather up as much as we could carry. Combining our groups and resources had more than doubled the size of our fleet; for the first time, we had enough space to carry everyone and everything we needed, with plenty of room to spare. A few days earlier, there had been a subtle air of uncertainty amongst the group, but now it was gone. Everyone was smiling and feeling hopeful about our chances of making it to Avalon – even me.

It had taken us three days to finish stripping the resources out of that pretty little town. At that time, there had been no sign to indicate that the floodwaters were going to recede, so I'd decided we should use the time to clear away the bodies of the infected. It had taken all of my oratory skills and a wee bit of exaggerating to convince the rest of my group that the gruesome task was worthwhile, but I succeeded in the end. I'd argued that every infected we put to rest now was one that we wouldn't have to worry about catching the mutated virus in the future. Even those of us who had never encountered the mutants had heard the stories. Still, it was a victory that I occasionally regretted, what with my nose being as sensitive as it was.

"It's for the best," I said to myself. Aaron gave me a funny look, and I suddenly realised that I was doing 'that thing' again, as Michael called it. "Sorry, yabbering to myself." I paused for a second, then changed the subject. "So, what's his story anyway? Charu's, I mean?"

"Oh, that's an unpleasant tale," Aaron replied. He sighed heavily and shook his head. "Poor lad had his tongue clipped a few years back. I think it was by that big fellow you were discussing with the woman and her kid the other day, but he hasn't said." He barked a sharp laugh, and just as quickly frowned. "Though I use the term 'said' loosely, here. He can... sort of talk, but usually doesn't. He's self-conscious about it. He used to be some kind of Bollywood icon, back before the plague. A singer or an actor or something."

"That's awful," I said softly, my stomach twisting into sympathetic knots. "If he was a Bollywood star, then his voice would have been his life and a huge part of his identity. No wonder he always looks miserable. I wish I could do something to make him feel more welcome."

"I don't think he feels unwelcome," Aaron replied. "He's not the sort to just sit there and sulk if he doesn't like something. He'll find some way to let you know, even if he has to write it out on a bit of paper, wrap it around a brick, and bash you over the head with it."

I laughed and nodded my understanding. "That's good. I don't want anyone feeling uncomfortable."

We continued in silence for a couple of minutes, each keeping our own council. Just as we were emerging from another building, I realised that something was out of place. I froze in my tracks and held up a hand to stop Aaron. He glanced at me quizzically; I lifted a finger to touch my earlobe, silently indicating that he should stop and listen. The part of town we were travelling through was densely overgrown, but the birds in the trees and bushes in front of us were no longer singing. Someone was hiding just out of our line of sight.

I sighed heavily and put my hands on my hips. "I know you're there, Bobby. Why don't you just come out so we can talk?"

Aaron took a nervous step up to my side, fingering the hilt of the long hunting knife on his belt. I lifted a hand to forestall any hasty actions and just waited. Sure enough, a few seconds later there was a rustling sound, and then the youth appeared out of the bushes. I was almost surprised to see him carrying a large wood axe. Almost, but not really.

I felt Aaron tense up at the sight of the weapon, but I wasn't concerned. While a wood axe could be a lethal weapon in trained hands, my previous encounter with the youth had led me to the understanding that whatever training he'd received from the Pukeatua bandits had been rudimentary at best.

"Were you planning to put that in my back?" I asked, keeping my tone conversational rather than accusative. I took a few steps forward, my arms relaxed at my sides, nowhere near any of my weapons. "You know that's not how justice works, right?"

"My dad said that justice meant an eye for an eye," Bobby replied. "You murdered him, so now I have to kill you."

"I didn't murder anyone," I replied, fighting the urge to react in a way that would exacerbate the situation. He was just a kid, after all. A dumb, stubborn kid. I'd been the same way at his age. Everything was black and white, with no room for shades of grey. "Look, Bobby. I know that you're angry, but would killing me actually solve anything? It won't bring your step-dad back. It won't bring back any of the other innocent people your step-dad killed, either."

"I have to do something," Bobby snapped angrily. He gritted his teeth and wiped his eyes with the back of his hand, as though that would hide his tears from me. "He was my dad!"

"I know, Bobby," I said gently. I heaved another sigh, and watched my breath cloud in the frosty air. "It was a terrible situation. I wish it hadn't come to it. But the only other choice was to let him slaughter my husband and my foster-daughter. She's about your age, you know. She's a beautiful, sweet, kind girl with the soul of an angel and a smile that lights up the room. Your step-father wanted to kill her in cold blood, just because her skin is brown. She hadn't done anything to him. You have to see it wasn't right for him to kill someone just because their skin is brown. Do you think I should have just let him do it?"

Silence was my answer. Bobby shifted uncomfortably from foot to foot on the icy ground, his expression tormented and his grip on the axe increasingly awkward. Suddenly, he sniffed and wiped his eye again. "Shut up."

"We can fight if you really want to," I said gently, taking another step towards him. Rather than threaten him, I just slipped my hands into the pocket of my coat to keep them warm while I waited for him to make his choice. "You know that I'll probably still win, though. I've got ten years of experience on you, and I know how to fight. It doesn't have to be like this, though. I have no quarrel with you or your mother. I don't hurt anyone unless they try to hurt me or my family. That's my rule."

"Shut up!" he said sharply, taking a step back and shifting his axe up into an offensive position. I didn't move, didn't retreat, just looked him straight in the eye and smiled at him.

"I told your mum that I'm willing to go before a tribunal of justice, if you want me to," I explained evenly, my hands still resting comfortably in my pockets. "It was self-defence, Bobby. Everyone's allowed to defend themselves and their families from a threat. I mean, what would you do if someone attacked your mum? You'd want to protect her, right? I feel the same way about my daughter." I took another step towards him and shifted to a tone that was kind and gentle, but not condescending. "Like I said, it doesn't have to be this way. I don't know what your dad taught you, but *my* dad taught me that forgiveness is a strength, not a weakness. We're going south soon. We're going to Lower Hutt, to build a new city where everyone is welcome. I'm willing to forget this ever happened and let you come with us – if you can find the strength to forgive me, too. You deserve a chance to be happy, and so does your mum. Everyone does."

Bobby's grip on the axe faltered in his trembling hands. He lowered it until the head rested on the ground and stared at me with tears flowing down his cheeks unrestrained. Then, suddenly, he dropped the axe and fled down the street away from me as fast as his legs could take him.

I watched until he was out of sight, then turned and looked at Aaron with my brows raised. "I guess that's a no?"

"You handled that so well that if you weren't already married, I'd be down on one knee right now," Aaron said solemnly. It lasted for all of two seconds, then his friendly face cracked into a smile. I smiled back, though my heart wasn't really in it. I'd barely recovered from the last encounter with Bobby, and now I was left reliving the guilt and horror about what had happened in the forest near Pukeatua all over again. No matter how many times I told myself I had no other choice, I couldn't shake the niggling feeling that I should have found another solution, somehow.

Some days, I didn't think I would ever be able to forgive myself and move on. Other days, I thought that I didn't want to, that I had to remember so I never reached the point where I could do that kind of thing without feeling sickened by it. The last thing I wanted was to become the very monster I was fighting against.

I took a deep breath to calm my roiling stomach, then looked at Aaron. "Right, let's get back to work, shall we?"

***

It was late afternoon by the time we finished our final sweep of the town and returned to the spot we'd designated as our rendezvous. It was still raining and snowing intermittently, but we needed a way to burn the remains of the infected. The rendezvous was a large shed near the outskirts of town, which was big enough to house all those bodies but isolated enough that we could burn it down without setting the rest of the township on fire.

The volunteers handling what we'd come to refer to as 'slops duty' were the last to come back. They were wrapped from head to toe in disposable plastic suits that we'd found in a veterinarian clinic, with masks and goggles to protect their faces. For once in my life, I hadn't volunteered; my sense of smell was so sensitive that I probably wouldn't have made it through without losing my lunch. It had taken all of my willpower to hide my relief when other people had put their hands up for the gruesome task.

Charu was the last one to return, carrying two huge buckets filled with a horrible red-brown slime that I refused to believe had once been people. I took a deep breath and looked away; the sight alone was nearly enough to make me retch. Michael appeared out of nowhere and put his hands on my shoulders to reassure me. I leaned against him for a second to recover and absorb a little bit of his strength. When I looked back, Charu was emerging from the shed and stripping off his protective gear. It was too splattered with filth to try and save. Once he'd peeled it off, he tossed it into the shed and then silently walked away. I didn't need to ask to know that he was heading back to base to shower and scrub himself raw. I itched just looking at him.

"Douse the bodies with petrol," I said, pasting my mask of strength back into place. "Good thing we've got some to spare now. We need to make sure it gets hot enough to burn them to ashes. We'll bury the bones and anything left over once it cools down."

Michael gave me one last gentle squeeze, then stepped forward to do just that. He and a few of the others had spent most of the day gathering any spare firewood we weren't taking with us and stuffing it around the edge of the shed to make it burn as hot as possible. My rules were fairly simple: we could burn anything that wasn't of cultural significance. No books, artwork, musical or artistic instruments, or anything that still had value to us. Anything else was fair game.

Michael returned to my side once the work was done, leaving Hemi to do the honours. We retreated to a safe distance, where the rest of our little community had gathered to watch. The sun was setting, and it was hard to see exactly what Hemi was doing; I saw a tiny flicker of flame, then suddenly he was running towards us as fast as he could go.

"Why's he running so fast?" I wondered out loud. Before anyone could answer me, there was a small explosion, followed by a cascade of golden sparkles. My mouth fell open in surprise.

Beside me, Michael made a childlike sound that could only be described as a chortle. "Yes! Yes! It's working!"

"What's workin—" I started to ask, only to be interrupted again by another small explosion that turned into a cascade of blue sparkles. Before I could even catch my breath from the last one, a third and fourth explosion went off. Then the shed ignited with a whoosh of air, amid a dozen cascades of multi-coloured—

"Fireworks?" I gasped, my eyes wide. I wanted to turn and look at Michael, but I couldn't pry my eyes away from the impromptu display. "Where did you find those?"

"Oh, a few people had them in their garages," Michael answered breathlessly. "It was illegal to buy or sell fireworks any time except the week leading up to Guy Fawkes' Day, but lots of people used to buy extras and keep them in storage until New Year's Eve. Since the plague hit in December, they never had a chance to use them."

"No, I guess they didn't," I replied softly. I found myself clinging to him without even realising I was doing it "I didn't realise they lasted this long."

"Oh, yeah. Fireworks last forever, if you keep them clean and dry," he said. "Sophie and I used to do this every so often. We'd find some, have a little fun, get a little pyromaniacal, you know, the usual."

Just at that moment, the fire spreading up the walls of the shed reached the roof, and the first rocket shot up into the early evening sky. It exploded in a vibrant white powder-puff, and I gasped in delight. The fireworks on the ground began to fade away, but by that time we were focused on the sky instead, watching rocket after rocket shoot up above us and explode in sparkles, like the forgotten magic of a bygone era.

Which, in a way, it was.

CHAPTER SIX

As soon as we finished washing away the grime of an unpleasant day spent doing the necessary, we headed to bed for an early night, just as we had every night since we'd arrived in Taihape. Even though we had plenty of fuel for the generators at the moment, we were painfully aware that such resources were finite and we had a long journey ahead of us. We had no intention of wasting any more than we had to.

I awoke in the washed-out grey light of dawn, curled up in the warm alcove between Michael's body and the radiator. I stretched languidly and rolled over on my side, enjoying the warmth while I could. There was nothing that urgently needed to be done until the flood waters receded, so there was no real reason for me to get up. I decided to let myself doze for a while. My eyes drifted closed, and I fell into that pleasant space between the world of dreams and reality.

When I opened them again, the sun had crept a few inches higher. The motel curtains weren't exactly the most solid things in the world, and let in just enough light for me to pinpoint the time as somewhere near mid-morning. I glanced at Michael and saw that he was still sound asleep, so I decided I probably wasn't the only one who'd realised we had a lazy morning ahead of us. My urge to doze had been sated and now I found myself awake and alert, so I decided it was time to get up.

I slipped out of bed without disturbing him, and gently pulled the blankets up to his chin to keep him warm. He sighed softly and snuggled into the space I'd left behind, but didn't wake. The sight of it made me smile and drew my thoughts to the child growing inside me. My little secret, for now.

I'd showered before bed and it was too cold to do so again just yet, so I just grabbed my clothing off the dresser and pulled it on. My basic essentials went into their pockets, but I left my weapons and coat behind for the time being. If I decided to go outside, then I could always come back and get them. For now, I just had to worry about my daily check-up with Doc, and it was easier to do that discreetly when Michael was still asleep.

I left the room and quietly closed the door behind me, then headed down the hallway to Doc's room. His door was slightly ajar; I knocked softly, then entered when he called permission. I found him sitting with Anahera, who was holding a notebook open to a page of tidy, hand-written notes. Maddy was sitting on the floor in the corner, playing with her favourite rag dolls.

"Good morning," I said. "I'm not interrupting, am I?"

"No, we were just working on that little project you gave us," Doc replied. "Come in and close the door."

I did as I was told, and plopped down in an old armchair that Doc had acquired for reasons known only to him; my guess was that he liked having somewhere for patients to sit aside from the beds, which made sense. Anahera leaned over and handed the notebook to me. I quickly glanced over the column of figures, then shot them both a curious look.

"This looks more like a census than a training chart," I said, intrigued.

"That's because it is," Anahera answered, her smile radiant as ever. "We know that you keep a list of everyone so that no one gets left behind, but with all these new faces we decided that it would be logical to expand things a bit. Look at the next page."

I turned the page, and skimmed over the contents. "Wait, is this..."

"Yes," Doc said, looking quite pleased with himself. "That's a list of everyone's names, dates of birth if they remember it, occupations, religious beliefs, approximate ages, and unique or useful skills. We've also plotted family trees as far back as we could, which I plan to keep updating as our little group expands."

"Family trees?" I asked, glancing back at him. "Why?"

"Numerous reasons," he replied. "Genealogy is an important part of human nature, and there is no Department of Births, Deaths, and Marriages to keep track of such things anymore. It will also help us keep track of genetic anomalies, so if there's a risk of anyone developing a hereditary disease then we'll have some advance warning."

"Oh, of course," I said, nodding. "There are quite a few people with relatives that are still alive since the immunity tends to run in families, so the likelihood of hereditary stuff reoccurring is a bit higher than normal."

"Only slightly, but yes," Doc said, nodding. "It probably won't help a great deal for this generation, since so many of our citizens were too young to remember their family histories, but if we start the project now and gather as much information as we can from the people who are old enough to know and remember, then it will help in the future. As for the rest, I know that you like to respect people's choices as much as you can, so I figure that the religious data may come in handy at some stage. The career information is useful so we can keep track of who knows how to do what. "

"It is," I agreed. I skimmed the list quickly, then shot him a curious look. "Aaron's a nurse? That's interesting. He's mentioned that he studied, but he never said what. Not that I'm complaining; two nurses are always better than one."

"Definitely agreed," Doc answered dryly, adjusting his spectacles. "My understanding is that Rebecca stopped practicing a few years before the plague, so her knowledge is a little rusty. I plan to bring her and Aaron in to assist me, and to retrain them both as much as possible. With this many people, I'm going to need as much help as I can get."

"How many women and kids are with the new arrivals?" I asked, glancing back and forth between them.

"Seven women of childbearing age," Anahera answered. "There's also one woman past menopause, and sixteen men over the age of eighteen. There are five kids, aged between three months and fourteen years. Three girls, two boys. They've got a few pets and some livestock with them, too."

I drew a deep breath, and let it out slowly. "Twenty-nine new faces. I don't know how I'm going to remember all of their names."

"We already thought of that," Doc replied. He grabbed another sheet of paper, peeled something off it, and slapped it on my chest. I blinked in surprise and glanced down at it.

"Really? A name tag? This is what we've been reduced to?" I commented, laughing. "That's actually kind of brilliant."

"It is, isn't it?" Anahera grinned at me. She picked her own name tag off the sheet and stuck it to her chest. "Your sister thought of it when she found a roll of these stickers in an old stationery shop in town."

"I like it. It's good," I agreed. "Start handing them out as soon as you can."

"We already have," Doc replied. "We've also started pairing apprentices with their teachers. Hemi is due to start training with me later this morning."

"And I'm officially opening classes for the children, too," Anahera added. "We went down and checked the flooding this morning. It looks like it's going to be at least another couple of days before we can get through there safely. In the meantime, we may as well get these kids learning something."

"Sounds good, I approve," I said, not that they seemed to need my approval for anything. Still, if it helped them get things done, then I was happy to provide it. "Has anyone managed to talk to Melody's gang about what they want to do?"

"That's a bit of a funny story, actually," Anahera replied. "I asked the twins, and they both immediately told me that they wanted to join my school. Those two have a voracious thirst for knowledge, if ever I've seen it. Melody... well, that's where it gets interesting."

"Oh, let me guess," I said. "She bit your head off for even suggesting it, and now refuses to talk to you?"

Anahera laughed and shook her head. "That's what I was expecting, but no. I think all that time she's been spending around the baby has woken up her maternal instincts. She told me she wanted to apprentice to me."

I froze and stared at her in shock. "She... what?"

"I know!" Anahera laughed again and threw her hands up in mock-despair. "The sky clearly must be falling, or that girl has gone mad. She's decided that she wants to be a teacher."

"No, no, this actually makes some sense," I said, tapping a finger against my chin. "Think about it. She practically raised the twins. Not well, but she managed to keep them alive for ten years. She was only eight when she found them, and they would have been about two. She must love kids to do that. I think the problem is that we've only ever seen the protective side of her maternal instincts. She must have nurturing instincts as well, or the twins wouldn't love her so much. Not only that, but they were all literate when Gavin met them, which means she must have educated them."

"Huh." Anahera paused for a moment to think that over, then she nodded slowly. "You're right, that does make sense. I must admit, I haven't spent enough time with her to get much of a feel for her, but your logic makes her sound more promising than I first assumed. Shall I take her on, then?"

"If she wants to teach, help her learn to teach. It'll be good for her to feel like she has a reason to be here," I said. "What about Solomon? Has anyone managed to get him to talk yet?" Anahera and Doc paused, and exchanged a look. I raised a brow. "What is it? You look like you know something I don't."

"Solomon's tongue has been cut," Doc said quietly, his expression unreadable. "I found out when he was in here getting treated for a cold a few days ago. Some bastard cut out part of that poor boy's tongue."

I swore beneath my breath and squeezed my eyes closed. "The neo-nazis at Pukeatua. They did that to Charu, too. They must be the reason behind the disappearance of the Samoan gang in Tokoroa. I knew they wouldn't just let their territory markers fade like that. I'm sorry, Bobby, but the more I hear about your step-father, the more glad I am that I took him down when I had the chance."

They looked at me curiously. I quickly explained Bobby's appearance, and what had happened to us when we'd travelled through Pukeatua months earlier. "I told Bobby that I'm willing to stand trial for Henry's death if he wanted me to, but he didn't seem interested. Still, I'm not proud of what I did."

"As you said, you did what you had to do," Anahera said sympathetically. She patted my hand, smiled at me, and rose to her feet. "I should go start class, if we're going to have time to learn anything before lunch. Are you ready, Madeline?"

"Yup!" she cried happily, leaping up to her feet. Maddy scampered over and grabbed Anahera's hand, then she looked at me. "Bobby's gone away, but you're going to see his mummy again soon. Her name is Isabelle. Don't worry, she's a nice lady. Sad, but nice." Suddenly, Maddy giggled and dragged Anahera off towards the door. "Come on! I want to read a big book today, with lots of words!"

Anahera shot us a look of long-suffering amusement and waved, then she was gone. I glanced back at Doc and shrugged. "Well, I guess I'm going to be seeing Bobby's mummy again or something."

"'Or something', indeed," Doc answered dryly, shaking his head. "Sometimes I just don't know what I'm going to do with that girl."

"Eh, so long as she's using her powers for good rather than evil, let her be," I said with a shrug. "She's not hurting anyone, and usually her prophecies help us in some way. I'm not complaining."

"Speaking of which," Doc rose from his chair and went over to make sure that the door was properly shut, then peered at me over his spectacles. "How are we feeling this morning?"

"We are feeling just fine, thank you," I replied, rubbing my belly pointedly.

Doc smiled and returned to his seat on the edge of the bed. "How's the morning sickness?"

"It comes and goes," I admitted. "It's not that bad, though. You were right on the mark about the sense of smell; it seems to be getting sharper every day."

"That's the one common symptom between every pregnant woman I've ever tended to," he replied, adjusting his glasses. "Did you start the notebook, like I suggested?"

"Yeah." I handed him back the census book, then reached into one of my numerous pockets and pulled out a much smaller notebook that I'd scavenged a couple of days earlier. I flicked the booklet open to the page where I'd begun to keep a running tally of the days since I'd conceived. "Today is the forty-sixth day, according to my count. Should be pretty much accurate within a day either side."

"Excellent, that's very good," Doc said approvingly. "Keep that journal up-to-date, it'll be useful for pinpointing when we can expect you to go into labour. I also want you to write down any time you feel strange, in as much detail as you can."

"Okay," I agreed. I glanced at him, suddenly nervous. "God, I didn't even think about having to go into labour.

That's kind of terrifying. I'd ask if it's going to hurt, but that would pretty much be the dumbest question of all time."

Doc chuckled softly and nodded. "Somewhat, but it's an understandable terror. Just remember that once it's over you'll have a bouncing baby boy or girl to add to your menagerie."

"*My* menagerie? Gosh!" I huffed in mock indignation, then shot a glance over my shoulder at the door. "Actually, it is turning into a bit of a menagerie, isn't it? You mentioned that some of the newbies brought stock animals with them?"

"Primarily chickens, but I believe they also have a pair of cows as well," Doc replied, flipping through the census notebook until he found the right page. "Ah, yes. Five more horses, two milking cows, six chickens, four dogs, and three cats."

"Cats?" I sat up straighter all of a sudden and looked at him. "I was wondering why Tigger's been skulking around looking nervous."

Doc made a thoughtful sound, but his interest clearly wasn't on the cat. A few seconds later, he glanced up and gave me a long look over the rim of his spectacles. "No matter how tempting it may be, resist the urge to drink milk from those cows."

"I wasn't planning on it," I replied, raising a brow. "I'm mildly lactose intolerant."

"Good, good." Doc sighed and took his glasses off, pinching the bridge of his nose between thumb and forefinger. "I've been reading more into the prevention and treatment of listeria poisoning. Unpasteurized milk is a particularly dangerous source of the bacteria. Stay well away from it, and anything made with it."

"Got it," I said with a nod. "You should probably speak with the kitchen crew to make sure they don't give it to anyone else who might be at risk. Maybe we can work out a way to pasteurize it ourselves."

"Maybe," he replied, making a note in his book. "Hannah's baby shouldn't be having any, and neither should the youngest children. I'll investigate the possibility of pasteurizing it, and talk to the kitchen crew in the meantime. I think I'll go do that right now, actually." He glanced up at me. "Is there anything else you wish to discuss today, Ms McDermott?"

"No, I'm fine." I took the hint and rose to my feet, stretching languidly. "I should go find some breakfast, anyway. I'll walk with you."

"Very well," Doc agreed, a faint smile touching his face. He slipped on his shoes, stood up, then together we made our way out of his room and down the hall to the common room.

There, we found Anahera in the midst of gathering the children up and seating them around the fireplace. Skylar was watching them with interest, and both Ryan and Hemi hovered near her with equally anxious expressions on their faces. Skye's back was to me, so I didn't notice the reason for their anxiety until I was almost on them: Skye was holding Hannah and Johan's infant daughter, Evelyn.

Doc didn't seem to care about how concerned Ryan and Hemi looked. He marched right up to Skye and cleared his throat. "Miss McDermott, we must speak for a moment. Will you join me in the kitchen?"

"Of course," Skye answered. "What's up?"

"We just need to discuss food safety, because of the new additions to our group." He glanced at the two young men and lifted his brows. "I believe you both help out with the cooking on a regular basis, correct?"

"Yeah?" Hemi asked, looking at him curiously. "You want us to come, too?"

"Please," he said, then he glanced around at the others. "I've already spoken to Anahera and Sandrine; who else is regularly involved in cooking?"

"Just talk to us," Skye said. "Hannah, Johan, and Elly are in the kitchen right now. One of us is always there for mealtimes, so we can disseminate the information to anyone else that needs to know." Suddenly, she turned to me and held the baby out. "Here, look after Evie for a minute."

I took the baby without thinking. Skye led the others off towards the kitchen, leaving me awkwardly clutching the poor child with no real idea what to do with her. My last experience with a baby had been eighteen years earlier, with Skye. I'd always assumed that instinct would tell me what to do, but it really didn't.

Evie squirmed in my arms and let out a disgruntled squawk; suddenly, I realised I was clutching her too tightly for fear of dropping her, and that she wasn't too happy about it. I took a deep breath and shifted my grip, struggling to find a position that was comfortable for both of us.

There was a soft chuckle behind me, then I felt familiar arms slip around me and gently guide my arms into the right places. "That's it. She's old enough that you don't have to support her head. You can sit down, if you want. There's a chair just behind you."

I felt Evie relax as my grip was adjusted, and I finally let out the breath I hadn't realised I'd been holding until that moment. If anyone knew how to take care of a baby, it was Michael.

"No, no, I think I'm okay," I said. I glanced up and caught Anahera shooting amused glances at us from the far side of the room. Suddenly embarrassed, I turned my full attention to Evie instead. If I was going to have to learn to deal with one of my own, then I needed all the practice I could get. "Hello, Evie. I'm Sandy." To my surprise, the baby gurgled and laughed in response. I blinked and glanced at Michael over my shoulder. "Does that mean she likes me?"

Michael grinned back at me. "Evie likes everyone. She's a very relaxed baby."

"That's good. It seems like I'm the only one that doesn't particularly want to babysit," I answered dryly. I looked back down at Evie and gave her a little jiggle, to which she responded with a big baby smile. I took a deep breath and turned towards Michael to ask him something, but before I could say a word Evie spotted him and let out a squeal of delight. She just about threw herself at him, her pudgy little fists making grabby motions. This time, it was my turn to laugh. "Oh, I think someone has a crush."

"She just likes me because I play with her," Michael answered, his deep voice shifting into the soft tone he used when dealing with kids. He held one finger up and wiggled it at her teasingly. "Isn't that right, Evie?"

She grabbed his finger with her little fists, and promptly pulled it into her mouth. My heart melted; she was a beautiful baby, who looked so much like my vision of what Priyanka must have looked like at that age. Her skin was a little darker than Priya's, but she had the same expressive eyes, and round, sweet face.

"Ow, my ovaries," I muttered jokingly as I watched Michael playing with the baby. It was so natural to him, so instinctive. He just... knew what she wanted and gave it to her. Kind of like how he always seemed to know what I needed. "You're such a people person, honey. How'd you get so good at that when there's no one left around?"

Michael laughed, wrapping his free arm around me. That sandwiched little Evie in between us, but she seemed perfectly happy with the arrangement. "Just empathy, I think. My parents raised me with the belief that I should always treat other people the way I'd like to be treated. I just try to take a second to stop and think about that before I do or say anything."

"That's... really quite smart," I said softly, glancing back down at the squirming baby in my arms. I felt a rush of heat up the back of my neck, and suddenly there were tears blurring my vision. I blinked them away and smiled to myself. "Good thing she doesn't have any teeth yet, she's got a heck of a bite on her."

"Yes, yes it is," Michael crooned to the baby, leaning down to until his face was right in front of hers. "But you aren't teething yet, are you? No, you're not. Not yet. Soon, though. You've got a rough bit on your gum right here in the front, don't you?"

Evie released his finger and made a two-handed grab for his nose with a delighted squeal, which she also tried to pull into her mouth. It didn't work out so well, but it left both of us laughing our heads off.

"What are you two doing to my child?" Hannah demanded from the doorway to the kitchen. I feigned innocence, but Michael just grinned shamelessly and waved at her. A second later, Evie spotted her mother and let out another joyful screech, which turned into a demanding whine.

"Uh-oh, someone's hungry," Michael said. He glanced at me and gave me a wink. "They sure look cute, but they just see us as walking, talking, snuggling food-sources. Well, her mother is. Good luck getting anything out of my nipples, kid!"

Hannah laughed and came over to us, holding her arms out to take the baby from me. I surrendered her with more reluctance than I'd anticipated, and watched as she took Evie over to an armchair to feed her.

"Speaking of feeding," Michael gave me a sideways glance and a squeeze. "Breakfast?"

"Breakfast," I agreed, nodding firmly.

Chapter Seven

It took three more days for the floodwaters to recede enough for our convoy to escape from Taihape. It was early morning on the fourth day when the news finally came, and I'd just finished showing a few of the older kids how to recondition a scavenged car battery. Keeping the batteries functional was a constant problem for us, so the more hands we had to help out, the easier our voyage would be.

"Whatever you do, don't get any of the acid on yourself," I warned one last time. The teenagers nodded their understanding. A few hands came up to ask questions, but just at that moment Hemi came dashing up to us, out of breath and excited.

"Sandy!" he cried. "It's time!"

"It is?" I stared at him, scarcely able to believe my ears. It felt like we'd been trapped in that little town forever, and it took a second for the news to sink in.

"Yes!" Hemi shouted, practically jumping for joy. "We're free! We're free! Onwards, to Avalon and Tumanako!"

That brought that reality crashing home. I let out a whoop of joy and punched my fist in the air. "About time! I can't wait to get away from this snow." I paused and looked at the small group of teenagers gathered around me. "Guys, fan out and spread the news. I want everyone packed up and ready to go by mid-morning. Let's get this show back on that road!"

Everyone let out a spontaneous cheer, then they split up and ran off in different directions. I headed back towards our lodge. Along the way, I pulled my walkie-talkie out of my pocket and informed everyone else who had one about the good news. By the time I made it back to my room, the place was abuzz with excited activity. No one wanted to linger in the cold highlands any longer than we had to. Young and old, original members and new faces alike, everyone was practically chomping at the bit.

I headed to my room, grabbed our luggage from the corner by the door, and started packing everything away. Michael and I had agreed to keep our clothing and personal items separate while we travelled, to make it easier on both of us when we had to find something. I was so used to it that I had both of our bags packed before Michael even arrived on the scene. When he did, he was bright-eyed and breathless from running.

"You're such a slow-poke," I teased.

"Hey, I got roped into figuring out how to move the cows efficiently," he replied. "Do these feel like the hands of a cowboy to you?"

Right on cue, he grabbed my bottom and gave it a squeeze. I squealed in surprise and playfully slapped his hands away. Laughing, he grabbed both of our bags instead, and gestured for me to walk with him while he carried them out.

"I heard that we found a horse trailer or something?" I asked along the way.

"A small stock truck, actually," he replied. "I don't know how Zain managed to get that thing working, but he did. The man's a miracle worker when it comes to anything with an engine."

"He is," I agreed without reservation. "A stock truck, huh? There's only two cows, so that should give us some room to spare, shouldn't it?"

"Yep! Heaps of it," he replied with a grin. "We even managed to fit most of the barrels of petrol in. We are going to need to leave a few behind, though."

"That's fine," I said. "We should leave some for Erica, anyway. She's going to need it when she comes south. I'll give her a call when we stop for the night and let her know where they are. Can you make sure that the spare barrels are put somewhere obvious, but safe and out of the elements?"

"Of course." He paused for a second to deposit our bags in the back of the Hilux, then hurried off to do as I asked. I went the other direction, and headed for the barn where our growing herd of horses had been housed during our stay.

I arrived to find Lily and Jasmine hard at work saddling horses, along with a couple of the new faces from Johan's group. I waved to them, and picked my way between bodies both human and equine to find my mount. Boudicca nickered when she saw me and gave me a gentle nudge.

"Hey there, girl," I said in return, reaching up to rub her velvety nose. "Ready to get back on the road?"

The horse snorted at me and whickered again. I'd swiftly come to realise that she was far more intelligent than I'd initially given her credit for, and while she might not understand my exact words she certainly understood the tone. She stood patiently while I put on her bridle and other gear, and held still as I vaulted up into the saddle. When I was ready, I gently nudged her sides with my heels and guided her out into the brisk winter air.

The rain had finally stopped and the snow had melted a little overnight, leaving just a few inches of slippery ice-crust upon the ground. Boudicca had been born and bred in the Central Plateau highlands, though; she was far more sure-footed and agile on the ice than I could ever hope to be. I checked in with the rest of the group and discovered that they had the packing process under control, so I opted to take on the role of scout instead.

I crossed the township of Taihape at a comfortable trot. Just as I was approaching the southern edge of town, a lone figure huddled up in a ragged cardigan stepped out from between two buildings. She waved hesitantly, her fear obvious even from a distance. I reined in near her and gave her a curious look; even with her hood up, I recognised her as Isabelle, Bobby's mother.

"Hello again," I greeted, glancing around to make sure that the angry teenager wasn't sneaking up on me.

"Hello," she said warily, hugging herself against the cold. "I... I'm sorry, but... have you seen my son?"

I glanced back at her, uncertain how to respond. "Not recently. I last saw him five days ago, around midday. He approached me intent on a fight, but I talked him down. I haven't seen him since then."

"Oh." The woman's face fell, and she lowered her gaze to the frosty sidewalk. "I haven't seen him in days, either. I... I don't know what to do. I thought that he'd get sick of being alone and come back, but he hasn't."

Sympathy swelled in my breast in response to the painful emotion I could see in her eyes, and hear in her voice. I eased myself out of the saddle and went over to stand in front of her.

"Your name is Isabelle, isn't it?" I asked, holding up my hands to show her that I meant her no harm.

"Yes," she confirmed. "Isabelle Wright. I'm sorry, I know you probably don't care, but... I don't know who else to turn to. I've never been alone before. Never."

"It's okay," I said softly, reaching out to touch her shoulder. She flinched when I touched her, but swiftly seemed to realise that I was only trying to offer her a little bit of comfort through physical contact. "I'm not holding you to blame for anything Henry did, or Bobby threatened to do. I know that wasn't your fault – and I know how terrifying it is to suddenly find yourself alone."

Isabelle nodded and looked down at her feet, tears welling up in her eyes. "I'm so scared. Even after the plague, there was always Bobby. I just did what I had to do to keep him safe. I don't know how to be alone."

"I know," I said. "God, I know better than most. I was alone for the better part of ten years. It's awful. No one should have to go through that." I paused to take a deep breath, swallowing the tears that were suddenly threatening me as well. "We're leaving today, Isabelle. In the next couple of hours. You're welcome to come with us, if you want."

Isabelle glanced up at me, her face showing a mixture of warring emotions that I couldn't quite decipher. "You'd take me in? Even knowing what my son wants to do to you?"

"I'm not going to hold you responsible for something you had no control over," I replied. "I know that you were only trying to protect your son. But even if that weren't the case, you'd still be welcome. Your son is welcome, too. We're going south to build a new city, and we're going to need everyone we can get. We've all had to do terrible things to survive over the years, but if you're willing to help then we're happy to forgive." I released her shoulder, and took her hand instead. "It's up to you. Think about it. If you decide you want to come, then pack your things and meet us here in an hour. If not, we're going to Lower Hutt; you can always meet us there later."

Isabelle looked up at me for a few long seconds, then she nodded, wiped her eyes, and turned away from me. I watched until she was out of sight, my stomach twisting itself into knots. Then, suddenly, my radio chirped and I heard Michael calling for me. Thoughts of the lone woman struggling with a difficult decision vanished in the face of the arduous task of getting sixty-something people moving.

***

It took longer than anticipated to get our convoy in motion, with so many new people, vehicles, and animals to plan for. It was nearly midday by the time we were heading south, and poor Isabelle nearly frozen to the bone waiting for us. We packed her and her belongings into one of the trucks that had a working heater, and then we were on the move.

The road directly south of Taihape was in good condition, though it was framed on each side by dense bush that cast the world into perpetual shadows. After a couple of hours, the forest gave way to open plains studded with sheep and the occasional tree, but farther in the distance I caught a glimpse of white.

"What is that?" I asked, standing up in the saddle to try and get a better look. "Over there; the white?"

"That would be cliffs," Gavin said, amusement dancing across his scarred face; he and Michael had opted to ride in the vanguard with me. "Just wait until we get a bit closer, then hold on to your lunch."

"Hold onto my lunch?" I echoed, glancing back at him. Gavin just laughed. Michael shot him a dark look.

"That's not nice," he scolded. "You know she doesn't like heights."

"Oh, she doesn't?" Gavin's mirth vanished as swiftly as it had appeared. "I didn't know that, actually. It never came up."

"Wait, wait," I interrupted, holding up my free hand. "Are you guys saying we're going to have to go near those cliffs?"

"Oh dear," Gavin said, suddenly looking worried. "There's a massive canyon coming up. The road follows it for a while, then crosses a bridge over it. After that, it's all downhill to the plains."

"Ah, cripes." I took a deep breath and let it out slowly. "Think we'll get there by dark?"

Gavin glanced up at the sky, then shook his head. "At the rate we're travelling, it'll probably be tomorrow morning."

"Okay, so I've got a few hours to put my big girl panties on, that's good," I answered dryly. "But after that, nice, long, flat plains, right? Forever?"

"All the way to the sea, yeah," Gavin replied with a chuckle.

"Okay, I can do it," I said firmly, straightening my shoulders and putting on my bravest face. Did I feel it? Of course not. I really, really hated heights. But I wasn't going to let them know that, now was I?

***

Thankfully for my pride, the bridge in question turned out to be far wider and a lot less steep than anticipated. By the time we actually reached it, I'd already constructed a terrifying image of three hundred meter drops onto solid stone in my head. What we actually crossed was barely more than a gully, packed with tall trees that made the drop seem nearly insignificant. Just as they'd promised, after that it was all downhill into broad, rolling plains that stretched as far as the eye could see.

For two weeks, we travelled south-west along the highway towards the coast. We stopped at each major town along the way to scavenge for supplies, and to clear away any of the infected that hadn't already found eternal rest. By the time we were done, the towns of Mangaweka, Hunterville, Marton, Bulls, and Sanson were safe and clear for anyone who followed after us.

Every night, I contacted Erica on the satellite phone and updated her about our progress, and she in turn updated our radio broadcast. As we moved south, we occasionally found small bands of people waiting for us. Sometimes it was a single person, wild-eyed and jumpy. Other times, it was a little family group just glad to see a friendly face.

By the time we reached the town of Levin, our group had swelled to nearly eighty souls. Some of them were shy and reluctant to join in with group activities, while others seemed positively delighted by the opportunity. I have to admit that I was one of the reluctant ones at first; although I did my best to always be there when someone needed me, I was still nervous about being around so many unfamiliar people. Michael seemed to sense my distress, and was always on hand with a reassuring arm and a kind word when I started to feel overwhelmed.

As our group grew, so did its needs. We could no longer spend the night in a single dwelling, so we split everyone into three groups and let them organise their own food and watch rosters. Although our fleet and herd grew steadily with each township, we eventually ended up with too many people and not enough seats. That meant people started having to take turns travelling on foot, which slowed our progress further still.

Despite the regular frosts and occasional sprinkling of rain or snow, we found plenty of wild produce growing along the roadside, more than enough to keep us going as we travelled. At Levin, we stopped for a week to rest, recover, and replenish our supplies by fishing in the lake that ran alongside the town. By the time we left, another ten souls had drifted in from the north-east to join us, and we had to create a fourth subdivision for the night rosters.

On the last night before we were due to leave Levin, I walked into the house my group had claimed and found a bunch of people sitting around watching the television with rapt fascination. Michael waved me over and patted a spot on the floor beside him. To my surprise, I discovered that they were all watching the evening news.

"What's got you all so interested?" I asked.

"We just switched it on and he was talking about us," Michael answered. "I don't know how, but he found out about everything. The mutants, our voyage, Tumanako, even you."

We both fell silent after that, and focused on watching the Anchorman talking about us as if he knew us. For the first time in the ten years that I'd been watching his show, he looked excited. He'd even shaved, and somehow seemed less rumpled and miserable than he usually did. Hope shone in his vivid blue eyes.

Suddenly, I found myself with tears running down my cheeks. I rubbed them away with the back of my hand and took a deep breath to try and steady myself, but it wasn't going to happen. Simon Wentworth, the Anchorman, had been my only human contact for so long. I remembered with such clarity the feeling that he was my only friend, even though he didn't know I existed. Now, I was hearing my own name spoken from his lips. It felt unreal.

"The New Exodus is scheduled to leave Levin in the morning," he said, his voice strong and confident. "All people in the area are encouraged to join the convoy south. Survivors in the South Island are asked to head to Picton as soon as possible. Work is currently underway to refurbish a ferry, to bring you up to the North Island."

"No way!" I gasped, shocked and thrilled at the same time. "How did the South Island find out?"

"That's Simon for you," Anahera said, her eyes gleaming with tears just as much as mine were. "He always was resourceful. I guess he must have heard Erica's broadcast—"

"Shh!" Hemi said suddenly. "He's talking to Sandy!"

"Sandrine McDermott," the Anchorman said, looking straight at the camera. I froze, feeling as though he could see me somehow, even though I knew that he couldn't. "If you happen to see this broadcast, please be advised that you and your people are welcome here. We're waiting for you, and we have some very important news to share with you when you arrive. Good luck."

Then, just like that the broadcast was over. I glanced around at my friends, wide-eyed in surprise and unable to form a coherent word for nearly a minute.

"News?" I said at long last. "He's got news for us? Important news? But he can't share it on his show? What on Earth could it be?"

"There's only one thing it could be," Skylar said softly, her tone low and reverent. "The one thing that makes all of this change."

"No," I said, shaking my head. "I know what you're thinking, but it couldn't be that. That kind of news... well, we'd have heard about it by now, surely."

"Not necessarily," she said, turning to stare at me with enormous eyes. "They wouldn't want to get people's hopes up, would they?"

"What are you two talking about?" Michael asked.

I turned and stared at him, unable to say the words. Skylar felt no such compulsion, and she said them for me.

"A cure," she said, her voice barely above a whisper. "Someone's finally found a cure."

Chapter Eight

Our slow but uneventful southward march continued for several weeks across the rolling, green plains of the Horizons Region, and down into the outskirts of the area that had once been known as Greater Wellington. The winter solstice came and went, and then the days finally started to get longer again. The fourth full moon since our departure from Ohaupo blossomed in the sky, giving us a way to mark the passage of time as our ancestors had in earlier generations.

With every day that passed, the baby within me grew. I marked the 90th day off my list while we were clearing infected out of the city of Paraparaumu. By the 93rd day, we were travelling south again. I was sitting in the passenger seat of the Hilux reading a book when I heard Priyanka frantically calling for me.

"Mama! Mama!"

I glanced up and saw her galloping back towards the convoy, her short hair blowing in the breeze. "God, would you look at her? I can't believe how much she's grown."

Michael made a sound that was somewhere between a laugh and a grunt of annoyance. "I know. I keep catching Dominic and some of the other boys peeking at her when they think we're not watching. At this rate, she's going to turn into a woman before I've figured out how to cope with that. I'm going to need a bigger stick."

"We're just going to have to trust that she's smart enough to take care of herself and know when to ask for help, which I'm pretty sure she is," I replied. By the time I finished speaking, Priya had brought her horse up beside our truck and was frantically pointing to the south-west.

"Mama, we see something!" she told me, practically vibrating with excitement. "Come and look!"

"Okay," I agreed readily. Michael didn't even bother to stop the truck; we were only moving at a snail's pace, and we'd all gotten used to climbing in and out of creeping vehicles during the voyage. Priya slipped her foot out of the stirrup and offered a hand to me. I took advantage of both, and used them to swing myself up to ride double with her.

Once I was seated, she flicked the reins and guided her horse away from the convoy again. She had things well under control, which gave me a chance to study the surrounding landscape. The hills to my left were so steep that it looked like a mountain goat would have struggled to climb them, and were shrouded in low cloud which gave everything a slightly otherworldly feel. I glanced to the right and saw very little: just thick bush at first, which eventually gave way to a few small warehouses, an overgrown parking lot, and a large restaurant advertising specials that hadn't been relevant in a very long time.

Priya rode past them without stopping. Always on the lookout for supplies, I pulled my radio out of my pocket and held down the receiver. "We've got a few buildings coming up, we should probably stop and search them. It's also time for lun—"

Just at that moment, we rounded a corner and the trees suddenly parted. My words died in my throat. I felt my mouth opening and closing like a freshly-caught fish, but no words came out. There were no words. There was only emotion.

"Sandy?" Michael's voice crackled through the radio, laced with concern.

"Oh God," I whispered, my thumb locked on the receiver. "Michael, we… we made it, to the coast. I can see the ocean. I-I forgot how beautiful it was." I muffled a sob behind my hand, unable to keep my emotion in check. "Stop the convoy when you get to the buildings, and bring everyone who wants to down to the beach."

I put the radio away and let Priya help me down from the horse. I barely even noticed the other scouts clustered behind me as we made our way across the gravel and down onto the sand. There was a low, crumbled sea wall not far from the edge of the ocean; I went over to it and sat down, then pulled off my shoes and socks. The feeling of sand between my toes instantly brought me back to my childhood, to all the happy memories shared with my family so long ago. Those summers had been spent on the soft golden sand of the East Coast rather than the coarse black sand of the West, but it didn't matter. The ocean was the ocean, no matter where we were.

I just sat there and watched Priya and her friends examining the shore with great interest, and I was still there when the rest of the convoy joined us. I felt Michael sit down beside me, but we didn't speak. We just watched as more and more people came down to join us. Some of them were confident and playful, but others – like me – had obviously not see the sea in half a lifetime. For many of the children, it was the first time they'd seen the ocean at all.

That didn't seem to bother them, though. Within a matter of minutes, dozens of people were stripping off their clothing and splashing around in the shallows. The water had to be freezing, but no one seemed to care. Everyone was smiling, and that made me happy.

I leaned against Michael for warmth and closed my eyes, enjoying the scent of salt water and distant storms. It was a smell that I wanted to remember forever.

***

We lingered by the seaside for an hour and then we moved on, following the coastline southwards towards the township of Pukerua Bay. We paused there for a few days, both to clear the town and to enjoy spending time playing in the ocean. I'd be lying if I said that the children were the only ones who enjoyed that; the adults loved it just as much, myself included. We'd all forgotten just how different salt water fish tasted. I'd been avoiding fish as much as I could because the smell bothered my nose, but even I was excited to try some. It was exotic and new, and that newness revitalised us.

When we began to move south again, we all did so with renewed energy and vigour. We were so close now that we could barely contain our excitement. The mutants were so far away that we were starting to feel safe again, though not safe enough that any of us would consider loosening our rigid safety precautions. We were still going into unknown territory, and now it felt even more vital that everyone stay safe. Our group had blossomed to over a hundred souls, and I could feel every one of them looking to me for guidance. It was a strange feeling, but wonderful at the same time. My inner council – Michael, Skylar, Anahera and the others who had been with us since the beginning – were always there to help me, and that gave me confidence.

On the second morning after we left Pukerua Bay, we reached another major milestone on our journey: we entered the outskirts of Porirua, the first place that we could rightly call a city instead of a town. At least, it had been. Skylar and I were scouting ahead of the convoy when we arrived. What we saw left our faces grim.

"What happened here?" Skye asked softly, staring at the blackened shells that had once been homes and schools and businesses.

I looked down at the ground and traced my eye towards the edge of the road, where I saw human bones hidden amongst the debris.

"A fire," I said, my voice just as low as hers. Something about the sight made us both want to whisper, even though there was no sign of life. "After the riots, I guess. There was no one left to stop it." I pointed past the ashen husks by the roadside at the hills beyond. "It must have happened years ago. Look, nature's already begun to reclaim this area. One day, this whole city will be forest again."

"Huh." Skylar guided her mount over to the edge of the road to get a better look. "You're right. It looks like there used to be a lot more buildings, but now it's all bush." She glanced at me, and a smile blossomed across her face. "Perhaps we should come back here once we're settled, and see if we can break up those concrete parts that are inhibiting the growth. Give nature a little helping hand."

"Maybe we will," I said, returning her smile. "But for now, we're going to have to try and figure out where our turn-off is in this mess. We're supposed to leave the highway now, and head up into the hills."

"I'll race you!" she shouted suddenly, putting her heels to the horse's sides. They raced off, leaving Boudicca and me in their wake. I guided my horse up to a brisk trot and followed after her, but I did so at a more sedate pace. I was comfortable in the saddle now, but there was no way in hell that I was going to put my baby's life in danger for the sake of a little fun.

***

We found the turn-off without too much difficulty, and then the convoy began its long, slow, painful climb up into the hills that the Wellington region was famous for. For those of us with horses and trucks, it wasn't so bad. For those on foot, it was a miserable and draining trek that seemed to go on forever. We packed as many people as we could into the vehicles and even broke out our quad bikes again, but we still had to stop regularly to switch out the exhausted walkers during the climb. Some parts of the road were so steep that even our four wheel drive trucks struggled with them.

By the time we made it to the top, it was almost sundown and we were all stressed and tired. Thankfully, we discovered that the fire hadn't made it far up into the hills, and we were able to find a few houses intact enough to accommodate us for the night. We turned our animals loose in their overgrown back yards, and slept soundly in our borrowed accommodation.

When morning came, we awoke to a thick sea fog clinging to the hillside around us. It didn't bother us much, though; we were the children of Aotearoa, the Land of the Long White Cloud, and we were used to living in perpetual fog. We reached the peak of the hills in good time, and once we were over the crest it was all downhill. Suburbia gave way to small farms and the occasional lifestyle block perched on the hillside. Rain came again in the afternoon, but it wasn't as cold as it had been before and it didn't hinder our progress.

For nearly a week, we followed the road eastward around the rim of the Porirua harbour, following the old green signs that directed us towards the Hutt Valley. With each passing day, excitement grew in my little group. Not only were we getting closer and closer to our goal, but we could sense the change in the seasons. We'd survived another winter and spring was getting nearer with every passing day. We passed many beds of wild daffodils, and the sight of their bright little faces sent a wave of joy through the entire group.

One day while we were breaking camp and getting ready to move off, Michael came galloping up on his favourite horse. He dismounted dramatically, and bestowed upon me three things: a bow, a goofy smile, and a single white daffodil. Before I could find the words to thank him, he'd leapt back on his horse and galloped off again, leaving me blushing furiously and holding that flower.

My sister took the flower from my hand and slipped it behind my ear. Everyone saw, of course, and a flurry of flower-giving and receiving began soon afterwards. A new tradition bloomed, with men and women of all ages presenting a single flower to the object of their affections to display their love proudly to the world.

By that evening, Skylar had one flower behind each ear. We didn't talk about it, but we didn't have to. I could see her radiant smile as while she went about her work, and I saw the way both Ryan and Hemi were looking at her. The three of them had found a balance that made all of them happy, and that was all that mattered to me.

The next morning, we began our descent into the Hutt Valley. The road was long, straight, and in perfect condition, flanked by rolling hills covered in dense bush on one side, and the sparkling expanse of the Hutt River on the other.

"There should be a bridge coming up in a couple of minutes," I said into my radio, then I put it away and glanced around. My family and several of my dearest friends rode around me: Michael, Priya, and Anahera were on my left, Skylar and Gavin on my right, and Alfred was dancing along happily between us. None of them had wanted to stay back with the convoy, and I wouldn't have tried to make them.

"This is it," Michael said quietly, his voice husky with anticipation. My heart was hammering in my chest at a mile a minute, so I could only imagine they all felt the same tension. I just nodded, swallowed hard, and guided my mount onward. The road ran parallel to the shimmering ribbon of the river, but on the far side there wasn't much to see beyond bush, trees, and the occasional flash of a building.

A few minutes later, we saw a sign guiding us to the bridge which would take us to our promised land. Miraculously, both the bridge and the sign were still intact. We guided our mounts out onto the bridge, heading towards the far side and whatever lay beyond.

"The river is so beautiful," Skylar said in a voice filled with awe. "If it looks like this now, I can only imagine what it's going to look like in summer."

"Even more beautiful, I think," I replied, struggling to keep my emotions in check.

"Look!" Gavin said suddenly, pointing at the side of the bridge. I looked and my eyes widened. There was a fallen signpost, emblazoned with a word that I'd started to think I would never see anywhere but my own imagination.

"Avalon," I said softly, reverently. "One hundred and four days on the road... and we made it. We finally made it."

Michael gave me an odd look. "You were counting?"

"Of course I was counting," I said, quickly making up an excuse to divert him from the truth behind why I'd been counting the days. He'd find out soon enough. "This is going to go down in history one day. Weren't you counting, too?"

"Oh, I didn't think of it like that," he admitted, shrugging sheepishly. "Well, I guess it's good that one of us was countin—"

"Mama, look!" Priya cried, pointing at something her sharp young eyes had managed to spot that we hadn't yet. A second later, Alfred let out a bark, but it wasn't one of warning. It was one of greeting. I looked straight ahead and saw a human figure standing on the bridge, waving frantically at us.

Anahera gasped. "That's Simon! It's been so long I barely recognised him, even after seeing him on television."

"Well, then," I said, glancing around at the group. "We better go and introduce ourselves, don't you think?"

Chapter Nine

A few more people appeared out of the buildings on the far side of the road while we were dismounting and walking our horses the rest of the way across the bridge. They gathered in a little pack as far away from us as possible, watching us with tense, nervous expressions. Anahera obviously felt no such reservations; the moment she was close enough, she tossed her reins to Priya, raced over to Simon, and hugged him fiercely.

"It's so good to see you," she said, her voice earnest and full of emotion. "I should have come south sooner, but I had my own group and the journey was just too far for us."

"No, I understand," Simon replied, shaking his head. "It's been so hard…" He paused for a second and glanced at the rest of us. "Well, you two are obviously the McDermott sisters I've heard so much about, but I'm afraid I don't recognise the rest of you."

"I'm Sandrine, and this is Skylar," I said to clarify which of us was which, then I pointed at each of my companions in turn. "This is my husband, Michael Chan, former police officer and our security chief. That's Gavin over there, our expert in communications, and this is Priyanka, my foster daughter." I looked back at him and grinned. "You know, this is really quite eerie. I've been watching you on the telly for so long that it was starting to feel like you weren't even a real person, just a fictional character or something."

Simon laughed and nodded. "The feeling is mutual. One of the locals picked up on your radio broadcasts a few months back, and we've been following your exploits ever since. It took you so long to get here that it was starting to feel a bit like The War of the Worlds. You remember that?"

"I never heard it but I know the stories," I replied. I caught Skye and Priya looking confused, so I took a moment to explain the story to them. "The War of the Worlds was a classic novel about aliens invading Earth. In the 1930's, a company in the United States adapted it into a radio show, but they did it in a manner that made some people think it was a real news broadcast. It caused mass hysteria."

"Really?" Skye wrinkled her nose, looking doubtful. "People believed aliens were invading Earth?"

"'Mass hysteria' is a bit of an overstatement," Anahera said, her dark eyes twinkling with amusement. "Only a few people genuinely believed it was true. Most people worked out that it was fiction, even back then. They were less worldly than we are now, but they weren't stupid."

"I'm not sure anyone counts as worldly these days," I said. "I mean, when was the last time any of us communicated with a person outside New Zealand? We don't know if the United States exists anymore. It could have sunk into the sea and we'd never know. Hell, we don't even know if there's anyone alive in Australia these days." I sighed and shook my head, then I glanced at Simon. "So I guess you know why we're here, then?"

"I do, and we've already started," he replied. He turned towards the group of people hovering nearby and waved at them. "Come on, you lot! Let's show Sandrine what we've been up to while we were waiting for her."

The people nodded and vanished without a word. I raised a brow. "That was weird. What's up with them?"

"Don't mind them, they're just not much on talking," he replied. "They showed up here a couple of weeks ago, and told me that they wanted to help build the city. From what I've managed to piece together, they're from some type of religious community that lived up in the hills, but beyond that I don't know much. There are a few other folks scattered around between Wellington and Upper Hutt that I see on occasion, but these guys are definitely the weirdest." He glanced in the direction they'd gone and shrugged helplessly. "Still, they're good workers and never complain. They've helped a lot so far."

"Then you'd better show us where we're at," I replied, gesturing for him to lead on.

"Follow me," he said. He turned and led us down the road, looking about the happiest I'd ever seen him. The Anchorman I'd become so familiar with over the years was generally a miserable soul, rumpled and worn with haunted blue eyes that seemed to reflect the sadness of the world all around him. Today, he was smiling, loquacious, well-dressed, and clean-shaven. My grandmother would have been so proud.

"I have no idea how you knew, but Avalon Studios is the perfect location to build our new city," he said. "The river is teeming with trout, so we've got a nearly unlimited source of food right on our doorstep, plus it's right beside the park. If we put fences up, it'll be perfect for grazing livestock. The studio itself is a huge complex that already has fences all the way around, so we can all stay inside the grounds without worrying that we're going to trip over one another. See that big tower over there?"

I looked in the direction he was pointing and nodded. "The office block with the—is that solar panels I see on the top there?"

"Yes!" he replied proudly, his smile widening. "One of the locals helped me hook those up years ago, to keep the news broadcasts going. The national grid is pretty much non-existent down here."

"That's quite brilliant, actually," I replied, studying the lay of the building in the distance. "I wonder if we can hook up enough to keep the whole city going indefinitely."

"We can," he said with absolute confidence. "I know where to find more panels, and I know how to install them now. We'd probably need a car or a wagon to bring back enough panels to light up the city, though."

"We've got trucks, no worries," I replied. I handed Boudicca's reins to Michael, then pulled my notebook out of my pocket and flicked to the back page to start making notes about what needed to be done. "Let's prioritize that high. We don't want to live in the dark more than we absolutely have to, and fuel for the generators is limited. Now, you were saying something about living inside the compound?"

He nodded enthusiastically, and led us off the road into the long grass of what had obviously once been a park. "There are a bunch of really nice houses just outside the fence that we should be able to do up eventually, and also a few inside that used to be used for filming, but in the meantime we've got the tower." Simon glanced back and gave me a wry smile. "We used to call it that as a joke. It's only ten stories. I've seen stacks of pancakes taller than that."

We all laughed at that. Once the levity subsided, he continued. "The inside of the tower is divided up into a mixture of offices, film studios, sound studios, and equipment rooms. There are toilets, showers, changing rooms, and small kitchenettes on every level. Once we get a few more solar panels up, we should have no trouble powering the whole building, including the elevator."

I grinned at him, suddenly understanding. "So what you're saying is that we turn the tower into a bunch of apartments?"

"Bingo!" he said. "There's a full cafeteria on the second floor, and it's set up to feed twice as many people as this. I haven't used it in ages, but it'll be fine once we give it a good dusting and a scrub."

"Excellent." I scribbled another note and nodded to myself. "Do we have a basement? A parking garage or something?"

"No," he replied, "but there are a bunch of big buildings around that we can use for storing vehicles."

"I was thinking about stuff like our food and medical supplies," I said. "We're close enough to the river that I'm slightly concerned about flooding."

"There should be plenty of room on the second floor," Simon said reassuringly. He reached out and clapped me on the shoulder in a friendly fashion, an unexpected gesture that almost made me jump out of my skin. "Don't worry, I've got this all planned out. Didn't Ana tell you that I was studying to be a city planner before I changed my major to journalism?"

I glanced back over my shoulder at her, but she just laughed and shrugged. Who could tell if he was being serious? It didn't really matter, anyway. We'd arrived, and it was time to break ground on our new home.

***

"Well, I don't know about you but I like this one," Michael said, glancing around the little suite on the third floor. It was nothing more than a lobby with an office off to one side, but it was bright, airy, and the afternoon sun poured in through the west-facing windows.

"You're just saying that because this is the lowest floor we're turning into apartments and you know I don't like heights, but I appreciate the sentiment," I teased. I gave him a playful pat on the rump, then went over to stare out the windows at all the people milling about in the parking lot. The convoy had arrived not long after we had, and now everyone was in the process of exploring the building.

"Maybe," he said with a grin, "but it is perfect for just the two of us. Priya told me she wants to bunk down in the girls' dorms, so we don't have to worry about her."

"The girls' dorms?" I asked, shooting a curious look back over my shoulder. "This is the first I'm hearing about it. Since when are we setting up dormitories?"

"It was Ana's idea," he replied, wandering up behind me. He put his arms around my waist and stared down at the parking lot over my shoulder. "It's nothing formal at this stage. She suggested that we give the older kids the chance to live in communal dormitories, so that they can socialise with one another and we know where to find them if there's an emergency. She said it'll also make it easier to organise their classes and apprenticeships."

"Huh, I had no idea," I admitted. "I guess she's taking the whole headmistress thing pretty seriously. Glad someone is. What about the younger kids?"

"They can sleep in the dorm or with their parents, whichever they prefer," he replied. "Like I said, it's nothing formal. The kids don't have to stay there if they don't want to. Ana said that the teens she's spoken to are all excited about the idea, though."

I turned within the circle of his arms and rubbed my face against his chest. "I can't say I blame them. They've been alone for so long, they're just starting to learn how wonderful it is to have friends around them."

Suddenly, a voice spoke up from the doorway. "What's really funny is that Melody just proclaimed herself 'Queen of the Girls' Dorms, and now she's prancing around the place in a plastic tiara."

I pulled away from Michael, laughing. "Oh, hey Skye. Didn't hear you sneak up."

"That's 'cause I'm a ninja," she replied without missing a beat, a giant grin on her face. She wandered into the room and looked around curiously. "So this is you guys, huh?"

"I think so, yeah," I said, glancing up at Michael. "You sure you want this one, honey? Last chance to change your mind."

"I'm not changing my mind," he replied. "Hell, I'm already thinking about how to arrange the furniture."

"What furniture?" I asked, looking around at the barren interior. "The desk, the chair, the tiny couch, the tiny armchairs, or the dead house plant?"

"Hey, it's not great furniture, but it's a start," he replied. "We'll head out into town and start collecting proper furniture once we've got the basics handled."

"Speaking of which," Skye interjected, drawing our attention back to her. "I wanted to talk to you guys about something."

"Oh?" I raised my brows and looked at her. "What's up, little sis?"

Skylar sighed heavily, and went over to sit in one of the armchairs. She immediately grimaced and shifted in her seat. "Wow, these really are tiny."

"I told you," I replied dryly. "I think they're made for kids or something."

"We'll find something better later," she said absently. "Anyway, I wanted to talk to you about my role within the group." Another sigh, and she glanced up at me thoughtfully. "Now that we're here, you don't really need me to keep the provisioning and rationing under control anymore. I just... I dunno, I don't want to go back to being useless. You've got Gavin now to handle any radio communications, so you don't need me for that. Michael handles security, Anahera handles schooling and organises the kids, and Doc's already setting up a medical bay down by the cafeteria. Everyone has their place except for me. I don't want to live my life in your shadow, just being 'the other McDermott sister', you know?"

"Aw, you'll never be that," I said. I disentangled myself from Michael and went over to sit on the couch. "We need you to keep doing what you're doing, now more than ever. We've got so many people looking up to us, and we need to make sure that we've always got enough resources to feed them, clothe them, and keep them warm and clean. Hell, now we've got to think about the acquisition of furniture for everyone, too. We need someone who knows exactly what we have and what we need, and can tell us what we need to make or find before it's too late."

"Oh." Skye paused for a long moment, then she looked at me. "Oh! I can do all of those things! I didn't even think about that. Great. So I can be the... what's the word?"

"The quartermaster?" Michael suggested.

"Yeah!" She nodded enthusiastically, her golden curls bobbing around her face. "I can be the quartermaster! Well, quartermistress, I guess. Quarterperson?"

"You can call yourself whatever you like," I said, reaching over to squeeze her hand. "The job is yours, if you want it. We want to try and avoid people helping themselves to more than we can spare, so it's best if we set you up with an office and keep the supplies under lock and key when you're not there. Can you find something suitable?"

"Just watch me!" she said, leaping up out of the armchair so fast that she almost knocked it over. Halfway out the door, she paused and glanced back at us. "Oh, Simon's looking for you. He asked me to ask you to meet him in his recording studio, which is up on Level Five."

"Will do," I agreed. She waved and ran off, then I glanced over at Michael. "Coming?"

"Absolutely," he replied. "I've got to find out what this big news is before it kills me. Give me a second, though."

I nodded my agreement and waited while he vanished into the room which had been an office, and was going to be our bedroom. A minute later, he came out with a roll of tape and a piece of paper with our names written on it. He taped the sign to the front door, tossed the tape aside, and offered me his hand.

We made our way back to the stairwell and up to Level Five. Along the way, we passed a few familiar faces who waved to us; we waved back, but kept on walking. It took a few minutes for us to find Simon's recording studio. I eventually spotted him through an open door; he was sitting at a desk surrounded by sheets of paper and assorted stationery, intensely focused on writing in a worn exercise book. He was so focused that he nearly jumped out of his skin when I cleared my throat and knocked.

"Oh, Sandrine!" he cried, almost levitating out of his chair. "I've been waiting for you. Come in, please." He glanced at Michael and nodded a greeting. "Hello again... Michael, wasn't it?"

"Yes," Michael confirmed, nodding. "Sorry, we came as soon as we heard you were looking for us."

"Well, I was just looking for her but you're welcome to come along," Simon admitted, with an embarrassed smile. "Come in, have a seat."

We went over to the indicated couch and seated ourselves. A moment later, Simon plunked down in an armchair nearby.

"We caught one of your broadcasts where you mentioned having news for us," I said. "Care to tell us what you were hinting at before we all go crazy?"

Simon laughed and nodded. "I will, don't worry. First of all, though, we must make some plans for tonight's broadcast. I need you up there with me."

"What?" I froze, staring at him. "You want me to be on the news?"

"I believe I said 'need'," he answered dryly. "I definitely need you to appear on the show. We can do a recording if you don't want to go on live, but the people have to see you. They need to see your face, and hear your voice. They need to know that you're a real person, not just a rumour."

"Oh, that makes sense," I said softly, struggling to fight down the wave of nausea that rose inside me. "I'm going to need some time to think about what I'm going to say. Do we have very long?"

"If you're happy being on the live broadcast, then you've got a couple of hours," he said. "If you're too nervous to do it live, then we'll need to get recording as soon as possible."

I took a deep breath and nodded. "We'll do it live. I need as much time as I can to work my speech out. In the meantime, tell us the other news. When you dropped that little titbit on your show, it started a whole slew of rumours that someone's found a cure for Ebola-X."

"They have," Simon said simply.

My jaw fell open in shock. "What? Really?"

A faint smile touched his lips, and his deadpan relaxed. "In a roundabout sort of way."

"Er, what?" I glanced at Michael, then looked back at him. "Explain, please."

"It's probably best if I let him explain it himself," Simon said. He pulled a remote control out of his back pocket and pointed it at a large flat-screen television hanging on the wall opposite us. "While I was out scavenging about two months ago, I found a USB flash drive taped to a door in a plastic bag. It was too weird to ignore, so I decided to open it. I think you'll find it as interesting as I did."

The screen lit up, and a moment later a video began to play. The camera shook for a second, then a scrawny young man in thick glasses and a lab coat sat down in front of the lens.

"If you've found this, I'm probably dead — but you're obviously not, so... hey there!" the young man on the video said, waving to the camera in a way that just made him look even more awkward. "It's February 23rd. We've been down here for forty-three days, trying to find a way to kill the goma ebolavirus before it kills us. We've been making slow but steady progress, but this morning there was a setback: Collins tested positive for the virus during our regular screenings. We've had to put him in the isolation ward and everyone else has come up clean, but we're all a bit shaken."

"Wait," I said, holding up a hand. Simon paused the playback and looked at me quizzically. "Is this what I think it is? I heard rumours about an underground laboratory, but we always assumed it was just that: rumours."

"I thought it was, too – until I found this," Simon answered, his voice losing all traces of humour. "I found a facility, up in the hills. I didn't feel safe exploring it by myself, but this was taped to the front door. We'll need to go back and look for more information, but for now just keep watching." He resumed playback, and we turned our full attention back to the screen.

"Yeah, so um... I'm Clyde. Clyde Russell. Dr Russell – or I would have been at the end of next year." The young man threw his arms wide and grinned at the screen. "Dr Russell, boy genius and geneticist to the stars!" He slumped and heaved a long sigh. "Okay, maybe not. I guess there probably aren't any stars left out there anymore. But we have to keep working, just in case. Maybe there's someone left alive. Maybe someone survived this mess. Well, I guess if you're hearing this then someone has, right?"

"Russell!" someone shouted from out of the view of the camera. "Where are my goddamn cultures?!"

Clyde squeaked in surprise and slapped the camera off. Simon pressed a few buttons on his remote control, then a second video began to play. The screen shook for a few seconds, then Clyde sat down in front of it again. His clothing had changed and he was looking tired and frazzled. "It's day forty-five now, and something's gone wrong. I don't know how. We're deep underground, and we're on filtered air, filtered water, sterilized food. Everything is sealed up tight, nothing's coming in from the outside at all. It should have been enough. It should have! But Dr Scott's caught the virus now, we tested her this morning. I don't know how this is happening. How is this happening? Argh!"

He made a frustrated sound and slammed his fist down on the table, then sighed and looked into the camera again. "We're all going to die. It's inevitable. There's an immunity gene, but none of us are carriers. We've been trying so hard to prevent exposure... it doesn't matter. I'm recording this because I don't want to die without my life meaning something. I think we might be onto something. Maybe. I'll update as soon as I know more."

He leaned over and switched off the camera again. Simon set a third video playing without a word. This time, the young doctor was looking tired and rumpled, his eyes bloodshot with dark circles under them. "Day fifty-three. Collins and Scott are dead. They hung themselves in the isolation rooms. We can't even go in and cut the bodies down; Professor Fa'amoe says it's too dangerous. I don't think it's going to make much of a difference, to be honest. It's too late for us, we'll be joining them soon enough – but at least we've made progress.

"We've determined that a cure is impossible," he said, absently removing his glasses and rubbing the bridge of his nose between finger and thumb. "The virus does too much damage, too quickly. Once the damage is done, it's impossible to reverse. But we think we've worked out a way to engineer a course of vaccines based off blood samples we took from people with the immunity gene before we had to go full dark. I have no idea whether it will do much good for whoever has survived, but I hope it'll help. If not... well, there isn't much else we can do. I'm sorry. We tried."

The screen went dead again, and this time it was permanent. I sat up straight and looked at Simon. "Is that all of it? What happened to him?"

"I don't know yet," he admitted. "There was more data on the flash drive, but the files were corrupted. I didn't want to risk going into that facility alone, so I've been waiting for you to arrive."

"How much good would a vaccine do us, though?" Michael asked, a deep frown on his face. "We're already immune."

"I'm not sure, but if they have it then we should try and find it," Simon said. "It might be the most important discovery of our time."

"It is," I said, hugging myself against a chill that only I could feel. "But it's not for us. It's for our children. We still don't know for certain whether or not the child of two immune parents will always be immune herself. A vaccine would eliminate the chance altogether. If they completed it, it works, and we can figure out a way to make it, then we'll never have to worry about losing a baby to Ebola X. Ever."

Neither of them had anything to say to that.

Chapter Ten

"You ready for your television debut?" Michael asked, squeezing my shoulder in a way that somehow managed to be both teasing and reassuring. We were waiting off to one side of the stage while Simon was running through the last few smaller bits of news at the beginning of his show.

"No, not really," I admitted.

Michael laughed and shook his head. "Well, I think you'd better get ready, because it looks like you're up."

Sure enough, Simon turned and gave me a nod. I swallowed hard, straightened my shoulders, flicked my hair back over my shoulders, and glanced at Michael again. "Do I look all right?"

"...Asks the most beautiful woman on earth," he replied. "Get out there before the Anchorman has a fit."

His comment made me laugh, and gave me the boost of confidence I needed to walk out onto the stage in front of the camera that would broadcast my face to the rest of the country. I already had my entire speech planned out, along with every step, every gesture, and every facial expression. I'd practiced it a dozen times. I knew that I could do it. I came up beside Simon and turned to face the camera with just the faintest smile on my lips.

"Hello, New Zealand," I said, my words practised and even. "By now, I'm sure that you've heard my name. I am Sandrine McDermott, the leader of the group that the media—" I glanced at Simon and smiled wryly. "—or what's left of it, has taken calling the New Exodus."

I put my hands on my hips and looked straight into the camera, forcing myself to project as much strength and kindness as I possibly could. "The New Exodus is over. We've reached our destination. Now, the next step of our journey begins. Today we broke ground on Tumanako, the City of Hope, which we are building out of the ruins of what used to be Lower Hutt.

"One hundred and thirty-four souls call Tumanako home on this, the first day of our new beginning. Men and women, young and old, our citizens cover the spectrum of human society. We have doctors and nurses, veterinarians and engineers, soldiers and teachers – a cross-section of everything you could imagine. Come to us as a friend, and we will welcome you with open arms. Come to us as an enemy, and we will fight you to our last breath.

"You no longer need to live in fear, New Zealand. You no longer need to hide amongst the ruins and run from strangers. I know how that feels, because I have lived that life, and I swear to you that no citizen of Tumanako will ever have to live like that again unless they choose to.

"Come to Lower Hutt, my friends. We're waiting for you to join us. You are welcome here, and you will be safe. Contribute equally, and you will be fed and clothed as one of our own. We'll protect you and your family, and help your children grow up in a world better than the one left to us.

"Together, we will forge a new world, a world like the one we left behind but adapted to fit our ideals and our culture. This is our world now, and we will face the trials it holds together – you, me, and every other Child of Hope. Join us, and we will stand as one to face the future. Thank you."

"No, thank you," Simon said, his voice soft and almost reverent. He smiled at me and nodded his approval. "And there you have it, viewers. The magnificent Sandrine McDermott, in the flesh. Thank you, Sandrine. I can take care of things from here."

I nodded and made my way off the set. Simon's praise was unexpected, and it left my cheeks burning; I'd had a crush on the man for nearly ten years, and some parts of me apparently weren't as dead as I thought they were. The look he'd given me at the end of my speech... it was the kind of look I usually only received from Michael. A special kind of look.

I found Michael waiting for me outside the set. He fell in beside me and matched my step as we walked back towards the stairs. Eventually, I calmed down enough to take a deep breath and let it out as a long sigh. "Well, that was stressful. Let's not do that again."

"I don't think you'll have to," he said, sliding an arm around my waist. I tensed a little, suddenly afraid that he'd noticed my reaction to Simon's praise, but he hadn't. He just smiled at me and gave me a sideways hug. "Simon said something about recording the broadcast, so I assume he can just keep replaying your speech when he needs to."

"Good," I replied. I took another deep breath, but this time I let it out as a playfully grumpy sound that was a hybrid of a growl and a whine. "I am not cut out for television!"

"I beg to differ," he said, squeezing me tenderly. "If I hadn't seen you falling apart before you went on stage, I never would have guessed that you were nervous at all. You did a fantastic job."

"Flatterer," I replied without missing a beat, then I gave him a playful slap on the rump. "Come on. Let's go see what kind of state this kitchen is in. It's almost dinner time, and the natives will start getting restless if we don't feed them."

Right on cue, my stomach rumbled. Michael and I both laughed, and together we headed down the stairs towards Level Two. The majority of that level was taken up by a big cafeteria, with dozens of tables and chairs set up around the middle of the room, and couches and armchairs around the outside. Huge windows gave us a view out across the park to the river, and through them we could see the sun setting on the horizon.

"We're going to need to see about getting curtains up," I said as we walked through the room towards the door at the back that most likely led into the kitchens. "The former tenants may not have cared about all the heat they were letting out those lovely big windows, but we do. No point wasting our precious power, right?"

"Right," he agreed, nodding. "We'll need to get some people in here to clean off these tables. Looks like Simon didn't come in here much."

"Yeah, there's an inch of dust on everything," I replied. I reached the end of the counter and lifted up the little door that was designed to keep the public out, then made my way behind the display cabinets. A few seconds later, I let myself into the kitchen – and almost bowled over poor Elly.

"Oh!" she cried, leaping away from me.

"Ack!" I jumped in surprise and hopped backwards, stumbling into Michael. "Elly! God, you just about gave me a heart attack."

"Likewise," she replied. She swallowed a deep breath, and then gave us a smile. "Sorry, I was just standing here trying to figure out where to begin. They'll be bringing the food up any minute and... well, look for yourself."

I glanced around the big kitchen and cringed. "Wow, I see what you mean. Looks like the folks here left in a hurry."

"Yes, and they left all the food behind to rot," she replied. "We did have one stroke of luck, though. I don't quite know how, but somehow that cooler over there is still working."

"What? Really?" I went over to the big metal door and opened it. The smell of decomposing meat hit me immediately and sent me reeling back, gagging, but the air was still cold. Heavy with the stench of rot, but cold.

Michael reached past me and pushed the door closed, blocking out the worst of the stink. "Let's just leave that closed for now, shall we?"

"Good plan," I replied, struggling to get my gag reflex back under control. I took a couple of deep breaths, then looked at Elly and Michael. "First step is that we need to clean. Let's get as many people in here to help as possible. Many hands make light work. Honey, could you please go round up everyone you can find? We should make this top priority before it gets dark. Oh, and while you're at it, see if you can get the electricians to hook up our generator in here. We're going to need it sooner rather than later."

"I'm on it," Michael replied. He saluted me and hurried out, leaving Elly and me to work out how to handle the mess.

"Okay, you and I are going to get into the cupboards and inventory the cleaning supplies," I said. "You start here, and I'll go check out that room up the back. Sound good?"

"Sure," she agreed readily. While she set to work, I headed across the room to the far side and opened a small door. The room beyond was a storage room, lined with an array of enormous, restaurant-grade tin cans, sacks of flour and rice, and other assorted food items, most of which were way too far gone to be of any use to us. Off to one side, a second door opened into a cleaning closet.

I tried the light switch and found that it was weak and flickering, so I opted to use my torch instead; there was power in the building, but not enough for us to rely on until we had a chance to extend Simon's solar panel array. I sorted through the various bottles and jars of cleaning products, and grabbed the ones that would be most useful to us.

Just as I was bringing out the last load, the door opened and Michael led in a small army of volunteers. I exchanged a glance with Elly, then we started distributing cleaning rags and jobs to everyone.

***

The sun set while we were working, but Jim, Zain, and Gavin appeared right on time with the generator. They managed to hook up lights for us to see what we were doing, and enough electricity to power the cooking facilities as well. As soon as the big, industrial stove had been cleaned, we started it up and got dinner going. With a hundred and thirty-six mouths to feed, we needed every second we could get.

Sure enough, the rest of our settlers drifted in looking for food soon enough. One by one we set them working, cleaning the dining room, scrubbing dishes, or whatever else needed doing. Skylar appeared out of nowhere yet again, her voice effortlessly commanding. Soon we had food ready to be served, and more than a hundred hungry mouths lined up waiting their turn to be fed.

By the time my turn came to be relieved of duty and fed, I was exhausted. I took my bowl of delicious mystery slop out into the dining room and plopped down on a couch beside Michael. Neither of us said anything while we ate. We were too busy shovelling food to communicate with anything more than inarticulate caveman grunts.

When we finished, we went our separate ways. He went off to fetch our belongings from the convoy, make sure that the trucks were safely stowed away, and assign the night watch, while I returned to the kitchen to help with the washing up. There were enough people there that we finished in record time, even without the aid of the automatic dish-sterilizer that sat in the corner of the room. I made a note in my book to get that working again as soon as possible, then mucked in beside the others.

Afterwards, I headed back up to level three and found my way into the ladies room to relieve myself and indulge in a quick cold shower by the light of my torch. A few minutes later, I switched off the shower, dried myself, then wrapped myself in my towel and opened the stall door. My new apartment was just across the way, so I planned to grab my stuff and scamper home to get ready for bed.

It didn't work out quite how I planned it, though. When I stepped out of the stall, I found myself face to face with a group of near-strangers, both male and female, standing in a semi-circle around my shower stall. They didn't say a word, just stared at me, their faces ominously cast in shadow.

"Uh... hello?" I said, taking a step back into the stall. Suddenly, I was afraid for my safety. I was all alone and I didn't like the expressions on their faces. There was someone standing between me and my belongings; the only way to get to my taser would be to somehow get past him.

"We've been waiting for you," one of the men said, stepping forward into my torchlight. I recognised him as a member of the reclusive commune which had come down from the hills, but that didn't really help my confidence. Simon's words had implied that they were fanatics, after all. Nothing good ever came from fanatics.

"Yeah, so Simon said," I replied, trying to keep my voice calm and even. I inched back a little farther and shot a quick glance around, but there was no way for me to get out of the room without passing within arm's length of at least one of them. "So, uh, you guys know this is the ladies room, right? You're not really meant to be in here."

"It was the best way to get you alone," a woman said. I didn't recognise her voice, but I understood the threat in her tone. Suddenly, I caught sight of a glint of steel in her hand. I couldn't tell whether it was a knife or something else, but I leapt back just in time to avoid being struck across the face by whatever it was. It turned out to be a metal crucifix, and pain exploded across my collarbone when its sharp edge bit into my skin. I slammed the door of the shower stall closed and threw the bolt into place; a second later, someone struck the outside of the stall with enough force to make the whole structure shake.

"Blasphemer!" the woman screamed. There was another heavy thud, and I heard the horrible sound of wood cracking and metal shrieking. I threw my weight against the door to keep it closed, but there were a half-dozen of them and only one of me.

"Michael!" I screamed at the top of my lungs, for want of a better option. "Michael! Skye! Someone help me!"

"Silence your tongue, blasphemer!" the woman screamed back at me, and I heard the sound of flesh striking the other side of the door. "New Exodus, indeed? You are not Moses, and you should be punished for your sin of presumption!"

"Wait!" I cried, struggling to keep the shattered door closed. "I wasn't— I didn't choose that name, that's just what Simon started calling us. My only intention was to help people, I swear! All people, regardless of faith, race, or gender. I only want to help our people find a home!"

"Lies! All lies!" the man accused. "We weren't certain of what you were doing until you arrived, but then we heard your people whispering about the prophet in their midst. We know what you're telling them! We know that you are spreading false belief to control them, and we will not let you continue!"

Before I could defend my innocence, there was another blow to the door and it gave in with an almighty crash. I slipped on the wet tiles and fell hard, striking my head on the way down. Stars danced around the edges of my vision and a wave of nausea rose inside me. Before I quite knew what was happening, I felt myself being grabbed by the shoulders and dragged back to my feet, but I couldn't coordinate myself enough to fight back. I was frogmarched towards the door, but then the man holding me stopped suddenly.

"Move, child!" he shouted. "This is none of your concern!"

"Actually, it is," a tiny voice replied, delicate, feminine, and yet supremely in control. I recognised it immediately: Madeline.

"This woman is a false prophet and will be punished as such," one of the women growled. She shoved me so roughly that the man holding me lost his grip, and I slid back to the ground again. When I managed to lift my head, I found Maddy standing over me.

"Miss Sandy isn't the prophet," Maddy told them calmly, her voice carrying a note of derision. "I am. And even if she had tried to claim that title – which she hasn't – violence is not the answer. Now, stop acting like fools and go back to your rooms."

The man took a menacing step towards her, but Maddy didn't even flinch. She looked him straight in the eye, her expression deathly calm. "Your name is Daniel Ferguson. That's your daughter, Mary. You lost your wife, Nicole, to the plague, along with your two little boys. Your youngest son's name was Andrew, and his favourite colour was green. He died holding his favourite toy, a green stuffed dinosaur named Poppet."

I glanced up just in time to see the man turn pale and take a step back. "How do you know that?"

"Because they told me," she hissed, in a voice that sent a shiver all the way down my spine. "They're waiting for you. Now, they're ashamed to see how far you've fallen. Is that what you want, Mister Ferguson?"

"Nicole?" he whispered, his expression changing to one of horror. "They should be in Heaven, waiting for me there. Not here on Earth."

Madeline tilted her head to one side and paused, listening to something that only she could hear. "Not yet. They're still waiting. They'll wait as long as they have to. Time passes differently where they are." Maddy looked at me and smiled. "It's okay, Miss Sandy. They're not going to hurt you anymore. Are you, Mister Ferguson?"

The big man looked down at me and slowly shook his head. He turned and walked towards the door, his movements slow and jerky as though walking in a dream.

The others glanced at one another, then hurried out after him, leaving me alone with Maddy.

She looked at me and smiled. "Don't worry, he'll be here in a second."

"Who?" I asked, dazed and a little confused. Maddy just smiled.

A second later, I heard Michael's voice. "Sandy? Where are you?"

"She's in here," Maddy called before I could answer. "She's a bit dizzy, please come and help her up."

"Dizzy?" Michael stuck his head into the room, and then I saw his eyes widen. "Honey! What happened?"

"I had an encounter with a few people who..." I trailed off and shook my head. "I'm cold and I don't feel good. I just want to go home. Can we go home, please?"

"Of course," he said, his expression softening. He hurried over and scooped me up, as easily as if I were a child. My towel was almost gone, but I managed to pull it around me enough to keep from flashing everyone as he carried me back to our suite. Maddy picked up my belongings from the bench beside the shower stalls and followed after us.

A few people stared as we passed, but Michael didn't stop until we were safely home. He'd apparently managed to drag a thin mattress up to our rooms while I had been in the shower, and now he gently lay me down on the rumpled sheets. He left for a moment and I heard him talking to Maddy, then the door to our suite closed and locked.

A few seconds later, Michael came back and sat down beside me. Without a word, he gathered me in his arms and hugged me close to him, stroking my hair with gentle hands. I closed my eyes and leaned against him, letting his touch comfort me and drive away the feeling of disquiet. The bruises would heal and they hadn't done any real harm, but now I had something new to worry about – and it was something I'd never considered, and didn't know how to handle.

Chapter Eleven

I slept fitfully that night. Every time I started to drift off, something would jerk me awake and leave me tense and nervous. Michael was there to comfort me every time. Whenever he felt me wake up, he stroked my hair and spoke softly to me in the dark until I started to relax again. Eventually, sometime in the middle of the night, I finally fell into a deeper sleep.

The next time I opened my eyes, it was sunrise. There were no curtains in our room yet, just some pathetic blinds that were so dusty we were afraid to touch them. The room was cold as a result, but not cold enough to discourage me from getting up. There was so much that needed to be done, and working would give me a chance to think over the practical ramifications of what had happened the night before. I shuffled out from beneath our blankets and slowly sat up, hyper-alert for any symptoms that would indicate I'd sustained another concussion.

Luckily, this time there were no signs of one. I could feel a bruise through my hair, but my head was steady and my eyes were no more sensitive to daylight than on any other day. Content that I was in my usual rude health, I stood up and pulled on my clothing.

Michael was still fast asleep, and I decided to leave him that way. I leaned down and pulled the blankets up to his chin, then ran one hand affectionately over the back of his head. His hair was perfectly trimmed as it always was, but in the evenings and early mornings there was a shadow of dark stubble on his chin. Those were my favourite times. As much as I loved the fact that he was always so well-groomed, those little moments of imperfection made me feel closer to him.

I sighed softly to myself, adjusted the blanket a tiny bit more, then I left him to sleep. Our bags sat waiting for us in the living room, small and pathetic but somehow enough to give me hope. With time and effort, this place would be our home. Our baby would be born here in a little under six months. I smiled and ran my hand across my belly; there was no sign of her yet, but I knew she was in there somewhere.

Our baby. My baby. Unexpectedly, I found tears in my eyes. To think, I'd been so terrified of the idea not very long ago, and now... I realised with some shock that I was looking forward to meeting my firstborn child. I glanced towards my bedroom and stared at the closed door. I'd have to tell Michael soon, once I worked out the best way to break the news. He was going to be so happy.

A knock on the door interrupted my train of thought and drew me back to the present. I went over to the door, but my hand hesitated on the lock. Was it safe out there? I wasn't so sure anymore.

"Who's there?" I called, my hand resting on the door handle.

"It's Mary. Mary Ferguson," a female voice replied. I immediately tensed up; the last time I'd heard that voice, it had been raised in anger. But now it sounded shy, and just as nervous as I felt. I took a deep breath, unlocked the door, and opened it.

Mary was alone, and her face was a mask of shame. I moved out into the corridor and pulled the door closed behind me. The moment the door was closed, she looked at me and the words tumbled out of her.

"I'm so sorry," she said earnestly. "About what we did last night. We made a terrible mistake – and a stupid mistake, at that." She took a deep breath, then looked down at her feet. "I'm here on behalf of the others. They were all going to come, but we realised that you'd probably be... afraid of us, after what we did. Dad asked me to represent us. Really, we can't apologise enough. I hope we didn't hurt you."

I stared at her while her words sank in, unsure what to make of the apology. It certainly seemed honest and heartfelt, but did that make up for what they'd almost done? If Maddy hadn't shown up when she had, then I might not have survived the night.

"Mary..." I said, a little hesitantly. "Look, I'll be honest with you. You scared the hell out of me. I thought that you and your friends were going to kill me. I'm sorry, but it's going to take time for me to get over that enough to forgive you. I hope you understand."

"I do," she said, awkwardly shuffling her feet. "We weren't... we weren't going to kill you. I don't know what we thought we were going to do. Maybe punish you, scare you enough to see that your path was wrong, but... it doesn't matter now. We see now that we were in the wrong, not you. We should have taken the time to ask, rather than just jumping to conclusions. We can leave, if you want us to—"

"No, you don't have to leave," I said quickly, shaking my head. "Everyone is welcome in Tumanako. You made a mistake, but I'm not going to hold that against you in the long term. It's just going to take some time before I can personally forgive you. But I do appreciate the effort you made in coming here. In future, if you have a problem with anyone, please talk to them first. If it's a serious problem, you can always come to me or one of the other council members and we'll help you work it out."

"I understand," she said, glancing up at me again, her eyes brimming with tears. "Thank you. We'll... we'll find some way to make this up to you, I promise. You were only trying to do the right thing for everyone." She hesitated for a moment, and took a step backwards. "I'll go and leave you be. I hope you have a good morning."

"Likewise," I replied. She curtseyed awkwardly, then turned on her heel and raced off. Behind me, the door opened and Michael stuck his head out.

"What was that about?" he asked.

"She came to apologise for last night," I replied, shaking my head. "I wish they'd thought of that before they attacked me and scared the hell out of me, but I guess the last ten years have been a bit hard on everyone. No one's thinking rationally right now. We're all learning how to be... human all over again."

Michael touched my shoulder and nodded. "We'll get there eventually. All of us. I'm sorry that I wasn't there for you last night."

"It's okay," I said, brushing his apology away with a gesture. "It wasn't your fault. We've all gotten so used to the people with us that we forget some people have conflicting beliefs, or might be offended by the little things we say without thinking. That's an important lesson for all of us to remember: everyone is different. Hopefully, we can learn how to use that to bring us together instead of tearing us apart, because these very different people are the only ones we have left to rely on."

"Very true," he replied. He put his arm around me and gave me a kiss, then smiled. "Shall we go get breakfast on?"

"Yeah," I agreed. "We've got a lot to do today, and it looks like the weather isn't going to be very agreeable. Red sky in the morning..."

Michael just laughed and nodded. Hand in hand, we headed downstairs to get ready to face the day.

***

It was nearly mid-morning before we had everyone fed, clothed, and ready for work or school. I put away the last clean dish and went out into the dining room, where I found just about every citizen of Tumanako sitting around waiting for instructions on where to begin.

That was a big task. I took a deep breath and decided to start with the smallest piece of the puzzle: the kids. Anahera was sitting on one of the couches, surrounded by a mob of adoring youngsters. I smiled to myself, remembering the day I'd first met her. I remembered wondering how anyone could get anything done with someone that beautiful for their teacher, but suddenly it made sense. Anahera wasn't just gorgeous, she was charismatic. The children wanted to pay attention to her, as did most of the men – and not a few of the women, either.

Melody was obviously one of them. She was sitting on another couch nearby with Priya and the rest of her gang, but she only had eyes for Ana.

"Yeah, I see it, too," Skye said softly, right beside me.

I jumped in surprise. "Dammit, Skye! Again with the sneaking!"

"Sorry," she said brightly, clearly not meaning it at all. "But I see it, like I said. Melody's got the hots for Anahera."

I could only laugh. "Everyone's got the hots for Anahera. I've seen you looking at her like that."

"Hey, you have too!" she replied, nudging me with her elbow. "Let's just agree that she's everyone's girl crush and move on."

"Who's got a crush on a girl?" Hemi asked, appearing in the doorway nearby. Skye and I exchanged a look, then laughed and shook our heads.

"I'll let you explain the joke," I told her dryly, then I made my way out from behind the counter and over to Anahera and the kids.

She looked up as I approached, and gave me one of her heart-stopping smiles. "Good morning, Sandrine. You look very well today. You're practically glowing."

"Likewise," I replied with a smile. "I can still hardly believe that we've arrived, and yet here we are! Have you figured out where you're going to hold classes yet?"

"Not yet," she admitted. "I think for the first few days the children and I will set up shop in one of the sound studios on the other side of this level. Once the elevators are working, I'd like to move the children farther upstairs, so they can be closer to the dormitories."

"Sounds good," I said, nodding my approval. "Let me know which room or rooms you want, and we'll make sure to keep them aside." I glanced over at Melody. "I hear you're the new Queen of the Dorms. How was it last night?"

"A little uncomfortable, since we don't have any beds yet," Melody replied. I was surprised to see a smile on her usually sour face, and her eyes were bright and alive in a way that I'd never seen before. "They're up on level seven. It's a bit of a hike, but the view makes it so worth it!"

"Mama, did you see the sky when the sun came up this morning?" Priya asked. "So pretty! So much pink!"

"I did," I said, smiling at her. "I bet it looked much prettier up that high, though. Did you get any sleep at all last night, or did you spend all night awake, whispering with your friends?"

Priya giggled and hid her face behind her hands, which was all the answer I needed. I laughed and shook my head, then I looked back at the others.

"Okay, we need to get started for the day," I told them. "Anahera, Melody, can you take the kids off to one of the other rooms, so I can organise things? I'd like to see class started as soon as possible."

"I have enough books and such put aside that I should be able to find something for them to do," Anahera replied. She rose to her feet and beckoned to the youngsters around her. "Come, children! Time for school. Melody, dear, could you please go fetch the littlest ones from their parents and bring them to us, as well? We can watch them while the adults work."

Melody nodded vigorously. She grabbed Priya and the twins and ran off. Poor Solomon was left behind, looking lost and bewildered. I took pity on him, and addressed him next.

"Hey Sol, you want to work with the adults today?" I asked. He shot a confused look at me for a second, then his eyes brightened and he nodded. "Good man. We're going to need all the help we can get. Come on!"

The youth hurried after me as I went over to a nearby table, pulled out an empty chair, and vaulted up to stand on it. I waved to everyone, but they were too wrapped up in their conversations to notice.

"Hey!" I tried again, but only a few faces turned towards me. I sighed, put aside all attempts at decorum, and cupped my hands around my mouth to shout, "Hey, guys! Shut up for a second!"

The room fell deathly silent for all of three seconds. Then, right on cue, everyone started laughing. I slapped my palm against my forehead. Well, at least I had their attention. The laughter passed swiftly, and when it did they were all looking at me.

"Okay, we've got a lot to do today," I called, projecting as much volume as I could so that everyone could hear me. "I figure eventually we're all going to find our own places and know what needs to be done, but for today I'm going to get everyone started by playing drill sergeant. If any of you can think of something you should be doing that will benefit the group more than what I ask you to do, just sing out. First of all, everyone who has already been assigned guard duty for the day shift, please go stand over there with Michael so I know that you're already occupied. Anyone with technical training or experience with electrical stuff and solar power, come here please. That includes anyone apprenticed to an engineer or electrician at the moment."

A small group of people stood up and came over to me, including Gavin, Zain, and Jim.

"I want you guys to work with Simon to extend the solar grid," I told them. "Requisition whatever you need from the supplies, you have my permission. Simon said something about a stash of extra panels, so talk to him and see what he knows. I also want to get the elevators working again as soon as possible."

"We'll take care of it," Gavin said, saluting me. The rest of the group did the same, then they filtered out of the room and went off about their task.

I waited until they were gone, then looked back at the group. "Okay, plumbers. I think we have a plumber, right?"

"Yeah, me," a voice called from a table on the other side of the room. Someone stood up, and I immediately recognised him as Petera, a member of the Waikato Iwi. He came over to me and gave me a grin. "You want me to make sure all the loos work?"

"How'd you guess?" I replied, grinning back at him. "The loos, showers, sinks. Once you've checked them over, I'd like you to track down whatever makes the water flow and make sure that it's all in working order, right back to the source. You got an apprentice yet?"

"No, not yet," he replied. "I could use some help, though. It's going to be a big job."

I glanced up and looked around at the crowd. "It's not a pretty job, but it's one of the most important. Anyone interested in apprenticing to our plumber?"

Silence was my answer — at least, for the first few seconds. Then, I felt a tug on my sleeve. I glanced down to see Solomon looking at me, his eyes shining with excitement.

"Really?" I asked, a little surprised. "You want to be a plumber?"

The mute boy nodded vigorously.

I raised both brows. "You do know that means dealing with everyone else's poo, right?"

Solomon just nodded harder, then stood up straight and thumped himself on the chest. He tried to say something, but I couldn't quite make out his words.

"I think he's trying to say that he knows how important it is," Petera said, looking at the boy curiously. "And it is. Making sure everyone has clean water is the most important job of all. Right, boy?"

Solomon made a noise of agreement and gave us both a thumbs-up gesture. Petera laughed and clapped the young man on the shoulder, then he looked up at me.

"Well, that answers that question," he said. "Looks like I've got myself an apprentice."

I nodded and grinned at them. "That's great. Thank you for volunteering, Sol. It means a lot to everyone. If you two need anything, go see Skylar. She's handling all our stores."

"Will do," Petera agreed cheerfully. He waved to me, then took Solomon and left as well. I watched until they were out of sight, then looked back at the others.

"We've got plenty of food," I told them. "But I'd like to get some fresh stuff coming in as soon as possible to keep our reserves going until the gardens are reliable. I want ten of you to spend the day down at the river, fishing. Volunteers?"

This time, hands went up all over the room, and everyone laughed. I picked ten people at random, and sent them off about their business.

"Doc, Rebecca, Aaron, and Hemi," I called. The four people I'd named stood up and came over to me. "I want you guys to get the sick bay organised. Consider it a high priority. Every life here is precious, and accidents always happen at the most inconvenient moment. I believe there's a hospital nearby, so I'll arrange a trip out there over the next few days. For now, just make sure we're as prepared as we can be. Make up a list of anything that we're running low on, and I'll send it with the scavengers when they go check out the hospital."

"Of course," Doc replied, adjusting his glasses. He glanced back at his new assistants, then beckoned for them to follow him and headed out the door.

"Johan," I called. "You're a vet, right?"

"I was, yes," he replied, grinning at me.

"Cool. I want you to take care of the horses and livestock," I said. "Find somewhere safe to keep them, and make sure they'll be healthy and comfortable."

"I know just the place," he replied. "I'll need some help getting the fences back up, though. Say, five people?"

"Volunteers?" I said, looking at the others. Sure enough, hands went up all over the room. Johan picked his five people and left. I switched my attention to the next item on my agenda, and looked around for a familiar face. "Richard, where are you? Wait, I see you. I believe you were a gardener, correct?"

"Yes," he replied softly.

I gave him a smile; Richard was a shy soul, but sweet and gentle. Even though he was older than me, my instinct was to protect and nurture him. "I'd like you to be our head gardener, since you know more about plants than any of us. Would you be happy to take on that role?"

Richard gave me a rare smile in return and nodded. "I... would like that, thank you."

"Good," I said, silently pleased that he'd accepted. I'd come to like him a lot in the months that we'd known one another. "What I want you to do today is take ten people out and scout the gardens around here. There will be a lot of plants growing wild. Some of them we can pick now and eat, but there will also be some we can dig up and transplant into our gardens here."

He nodded his understanding and stood up. "We're well past the coldest part of winter now. We should try and get the garden in soon so that it can grow through spring."

"I'll leave that in your capable hands," I replied. "If you need more people, just tell me or Skye."

"Ten should be enough for today," he replied. He cast a nervous glance over his shoulders at the group, then shot me a helpless look. He didn't need to say what he was thinking: he was too shy to ask for volunteers.

"Who wants to help with the garden?" I called. Hands shot up again, and I picked ten people. Richard hurried out, and they followed after him. "Now, the rest of us are on 'unskilled labour' duty," I said jokingly, making air-quotes with my fingers. "That means scavenger duty right now. What we need to do is fan out and search the surrounding area. Bring back everything that's important or useful, so that we can store it safely inside the walls of Tumanako. Eventually, I want that to include things like books, movies, music, and even photographs, but for now let's focus on furniture and supplies, particularly beds. Let's break up into teams of five and six people – unless I'm forgetting something? Or someone has another idea? It kinda freaks me out when you guys are this quiet." The group laughed again, but a hand did pop up at the back of the room. I pointed to the bearer and called his name. "Yes, Nick? What's your idea, mate?"

"A chicken coop," he called back. "I was a tattoo artist before the plague, but that isn't really useful anymore so Ropata's been teaching me his carpentry voodoo. I bet we could build us a real nice coop with a little bit of effort."

"That's a brilliant idea," I replied, pleased by both the concept and the sentiment behind it. "Do you need a few people to help you?"

"Nah, we can handle it," he said. He shot a glance at Ropata and grinned. "Right, Teach?"

Ropata laughed and nodded. The two of them stood without any further prompting from me, and hurried out the door. I looked back at the rest of my people, but no one else had anything to offer.

"Well, then," I said. "Let's get to it before it starts raining, shall we?"

A spontaneous cheer went up from the remaining citizens of Tumanako, and then we divided up and went our separate ways.

***

It was nearly sundown by the time the rain finally started to close in. I'd picked the people no one else wanted for my team: Warren, Quentin, and Kurt, who were the three most standoffish lone wolves of the pack, plus the silent, eternally-sullen Charu, and poor, nervous Isabelle. Even though she'd been with us for over a month now, she was still struggling to settle in and make friends besides me. Whenever she could, she glued herself to my side and followed me like a lost puppy.

At first I'd found it a little confusing, then mildly annoying, but then I'd finally realised that she was just feeling anxious and found my presence comforting. After that, I forced myself to relax and just let her do what she needed to do. She wasn't in the way, and keeping her close meant I could watch for opportunities to help her expand her social circle. The only problem was that her constant anxiety made her a little irritating at times, and not everyone was as patient with her as I tried to be.

I was in the middle of helping the men strip a bed down to the base when she suddenly came rushing into the room, wringing her hands.

"It's raining," she told us, in the kind of voice that usually meant the sky was falling. "Oh goodness, it's getting terribly dark. I think we should go back."

"We will," I said, keeping my tone calm and reassuring. "We're okay, though. We've got lots of time. Why don't you go look in the back bedroom and see if you can find anything useful?"

"O-okay," she stammered, then she hurried off without another word. I glanced back at the others and smiled indulgently. They weren't as tolerant of her antics as I was, but they seemed content to leave it at dark looks and frowns.

"I think we can get this back before dark," I said. They didn't respond, so I shrugged and gave them orders. They'd shown time and again that they weren't interested in debating anything, but they'd follow orders. "Quentin, Warren, take the top mattress. Charu, you and Kurt take the base. Who's got the tarps?"

Quentin raised his hand, then unshouldered his backpack without a word and fished them out. I left them to it and went off in search of Isabelle.

I found her in the back bedroom, looking lost and confused. I cleared my throat, and she jumped.

"Oh, Sandy," she said, letting out a sharp breath as though I'd given her the fright of a lifetime. "Sorry. I'm just not sure where to begin. I'm not very good at this."

"It's fine, really," I reassured her. "Let's walk through this together and I'll teach you. What do you see here?"

"Well, I think it was a baby's room, or maybe a toddler's," she replied, lacing her fingers together in front of her as if to protect herself. "I mean, I guess it must be. There's a crib over there."

"You're right," I said, fighting the urge to laugh. Her obvious desire to please struck me as humorous, even though I immediately felt guilty for feeling that way. I shoved the feeling aside and focused on educating her. "So, we've got the crib, a few baby blankets, some toys, and a chest of drawers. What's in the drawers?"

"Oh, um..." She paused and shot an uncertain look at me. I nodded encouragingly towards the drawers.

"Go on," I instructed gently. "Take a look and see what's in them. They won't bite."

Isabelle nodded nervously and went over to do just that. She opened the top drawer delicately, using just her finger and thumb, then poked the clothing inside. "Just... just baby clothes, I think. Some cloth nappies." Suddenly, she let out a blood-curdling shriek and leapt backwards, almost bowling me right off my feet.

"What? What is it?" I cried, grabbing her shoulders to steady her.

She turned towards me, white as a sheet and trembling all over. "There's a spider in there! A big one!"

Just at that moment, the men appeared in the doorway, weapons in hand and ready for a fight. I heaved a sigh and waved them away.

"Everything's fine," I said. "I'll take care of it."

Charu and the others lowered their weapons and left, but not without shooting scornful looks at Isabelle — and she wasn't oblivious to it, either. By the time they were gone, she had tears in her eyes and was wringing her hands.

"I'm sorry. I just... I don't know how to do this," she admitted. "Henry just sort of took care of everything, even if he was horrible to me. I never had to survive on my own."

I took a deep breath to push down the sense of disdain that kept rising in me. I had no right to feel like that, not after what she'd been through. Ten years at the mercy of a man like Henry would have broken just about anyone's spirit, even mine.

"It's completely okay," I said with as much kindness as I could muster. "Look, I know you're really trying your best, but you've been miserable today. How about tomorrow I assign you house duties instead, something you'll enjoy. What do you like doing?"

"Enjoy?" She stared at me as though I'd just sprouted a second head. "I... have no idea. I'm just, you know, used to doing what I'm told so that he wouldn't hit me. I don't know what I like doing."

"What about before the plague? What did you like doing then?" I asked. She just shrugged. I sighed and nodded. "Okay, here's my idea. Why don't we let you try something different every day, until you learn what you enjoy doing? You can swap it around later, or learn something new – with a population this small, it's not like you're going to be married to whatever career you pick for the rest of your life, you know?"

Isabelle nodded and looked down at her feet. She was silent for a few long seconds, then gave me a shy smile. "Okay. I think I'd like that. Thank you for being so patient with me. I know I'm not like these other people, or... or like you. You're all so strong and independent. I wish I was more like you."

My heart melted more than a little. I reached out and put my hand on her shoulder, giving it a gentle squeeze. "I hope you never have to learn to be like me, Isabelle. You don't need to be. You just need to remember what it's like to be *you* again – and you will, with time. How would you like to help out at the school tomorrow? I know you like kids. Or maybe you could help Skye with the inventory?"

She thought about it for a second, then nodded. "I think I'd like to help Skye. I like Skye. She's very... outspoken."

I laughed and nodded my agreement. "She is definitely that. Come on, let's go home. I'll deal with this stuff another day. We've got all the time in the world."

Together, we headed out of the house and closed up behind us, then hurried to catch up with the rest of our group. Isabelle complained the whole way about the rain and the cold, but I took it with good grace and didn't say a word. We made it back just in time to see Charu and the others manhandling the bed into the stairwell.

"Hey, what are you guys doing?" I called. "You can just leave that down here until the elevators are working, you know. That's why all this other stuff is down here."

They ignored me, with the exception of Charu. He looked at me and tried to say something, but all that came out was garbled gibberish.

"Sorry, I can't understand you," I admitted, hurrying over to help them. As soon as I got close they waved me away.

"He said 'no'," Warren snapped, sounding disgruntled – but he always sounded disgruntled so I couldn't tell if this was a different mood to usual or not. "Leave off. We've got this."

None of them seemed inclined to tell me what they were doing, so I just held my hands up and stood back. "Fine, but I'm just saying that you don't have to do that."

"Yes, we do," Warren replied, but he offered nothing in the way of an explanation.

I decided not to press him. I understood his type better than most: if he wasn't in the mood to talk, then trying to force him to would just annoy him.

"Can I at least get the door for you?" I offered. "I feel bad standing here not doing anything to help."

"Yeah, all right," Warren said. He and Quentin shoved the mattress hard up against the wall, giving me just enough room to squeeze by. I did so, then repeated the process with Charu and Karl's bed base. It was a tight fit, but I made it. Isabelle stayed behind, watching from the bottom of the stairs.

I stayed a few steps ahead of them as the lugged the bed up, waiting silently for the instruction to open the door. They passed the first level without saying a word, and the second as well. Just as we were about to reach the third floor landing, Charu grunted something incomprehensible and jerked his chin towards me. I took the hint and shoved the heavy door open for them.

The four men lugged their burden out into the hallway of level three, and down the passage leading towards the north-western corner of the building. I followed curiously, ready to lend my aid if there was another door that needed opening, but where they stopped took me completely by surprise: they stopped right outside my quarters.

Charu jerked his chin towards my door, and this time I managed to make out what he was saying. "Open."

"But... that's my room," I protested. "Why...?"

"Open!" he repeated, a little more clearly this time. His clipped tongue made it hard to understand what he was saying most of the time, but there was no mistaking his tone. I hurried past them and opened the door.

The men lugged the bed inside without another word, and carried it into the side-room that we'd already decided to use as our bedroom. My jaw fell open as I watched them drag the thin mattress we'd slept on the night before out of the way, then they set the new bed up beneath the windows. Once they were done, they turned and left without another word, all except for Warren.

Warren lingered in the doorway a second longer, watching me with an unreadable expression. I looked at him, fighting the unreasonable urge to cry. "But why me? Any one of you deserves that bed as much as I do."

Warren shrugged and glanced away. "It was Charu's idea. You've been good to us. Better than we deserve. And it ain't right for a lady to sleep on the floor."

Then he was gone, leaving me in shock.

Chapter Twelve

After nearly three months on the road, our new bed felt like sleeping on a cloud. We slept deeply each night, and woke up feeling refreshed and energetic. We and the other new citizens of Tumanako spent the next week getting settled in and working on the various tasks that would eventually turn an office block into a home fit to live in. There was always something to do, never a moment to be bored, and there was certainly no time to miss the freedom of travelling.

Though I'd spent the last decade living the nomad's life, I was not a traveller by nature. Having a place to settle down and call my own was a dream come true. Every day, when Michael and I retired to our beds, we'd have a few little things to add to our apartment. Some days it was something practical, like new sheets for our bed or a pillow. Other days, it was something beautiful and useless, such as a painting to hang on the wall. For the first time, we had the opportunity to really nest together. We'd tried to do it in Ohaupo, but fate had intervened. Tumanako was our second chance, our opportunity to indulge our nesting instincts, and we were both happier for it.

As the days passed, I found myself needing to give commands less and less. People began to find their own niches, and were generally content to trundle off and do their own thing without guidance from anyone. That left me and the other members of the council with more time on our hands, which we all used wisely.

On the fifth morning, I was just leaving for the day when I almost tripped over a colourful gift that someone had left in my doorway: it was a bouquet of artificial flowers, artfully arranged in a porcelain vase. There was no card or tag on the flowers, but the arrangement was beautiful. I accepted the gift for what it was, and set it on our coffee table so that it could bring a little colour to an otherwise bland room.

The next few days passed without incident. Occasionally a new face would drift in or something interesting happen, but mostly I spent my time scavenging. Around mid-morning on the seventh day after our arrival, I was leading my little group of loners back in from another mission with an armload full of small, useful things. I was still working with the same group, minus Isabelle of course, but I hadn't said anything about the bed. It felt strange, but a part of me instinctively knew that they didn't *want* me to thank them. I knew they appreciated just being understood, both by me and by each other. Slowly, my loners were becoming friends – or at least whatever passed for friends amongst people that didn't really speak unless it was vital.

I led the men down the corridor towards the cluster of rooms we'd converted into a storage facility. The door was open, and I could see Skylar talking to a strange woman with a baby in her arms and a toddler clinging to her skirt. Skye spotted me before the newcomer did and waved a greeting.

"Good morning," I said, keeping my tone as light and friendly as I could manage. Despite my best efforts to appear non-threatening, the woman fearfully clutched her children closer and edged away from the door. I sensed that the last thing she needed was more unfamiliar faces, so I stepped back out to address my scavenging party. "Hey guys, can you please just leave the stuff out here and head back out for another load? I'll catch up later."

They nodded, piled their sacks up beside the door, then headed out without a word of protest. This wasn't the first skittish survivor to arrive on our doorstep.

"Hey sis, this is Tala Navarro," Skye said, gesturing towards the petite woman. She hesitated and looked at Tala. "Sorry, what were the names of your daughters?"

"The big one is Nenita," Tala said softly, hugging her baby tightly as if she was afraid I'd try to take the child away. "The baby doesn't have a name yet. She only came a few days ago."

"You delivered her all by yourself?" I asked, suddenly understanding why she was so afraid; that had to have been a special kind of trauma. "You're very brave. I couldn't even imagine going through that on my own. You're welcome here, Tala – you and your girls. My name is Sandy."

"I know who you are," she replied. She drew a deep breath and held it for a second, then I could see her force herself to relax a little bit. "It was... hard, yes. My man vanished not so long ago. I had no choice."

"Oh, I'm so sorry," I said. I put the sack I was carrying down beside the door and took a couple of steps towards them. Tala didn't flinch this time, but Nenita did. She ducked behind her mother's leg and hid from me. I eased myself down into a crouch that put me at eye level with the little girl and waved to her. "Hi Nenita. You're a very brave little girl to travel with your mummy, aren't you? How old are you, sweetheart?"

Nenita just stared at me with huge eyes and didn't say a word.

Tala smiled and looked down at her daughter with obvious affection. "She does not talk much. Losing her father has been hard on her... on both of us. Nenita will be three years old come springtime."

"You're both very brave," I told her, shoving myself back up again. Even though my own child was still so tiny that I often forgot she was there, the hormonal changes in my body left my joints aching from the slightest exercise. I stretched my back for a second, then looked at Skye. "Have you fed them yet?"

"Not yet," she replied. "They just got here. Why don't you go feed them while I sort out a room and bedding?"

"Sure," I agreed. I looked at Tala and gave her a smile. "Would you care for some lunch? You look like you haven't had a proper meal in way too long."

"We've been doing the best we can, but it's hard," she said, her eyes dropping to the baby in her arms. "I can't leave the two little ones alone while I hunt. We were okay before, when Franco was still with us, because there was always one of us to stay with Nenita. When I got too big with the baby, then Franco could go and I'd stay with her. Except one day he didn't come home."

"What happened to him?" I asked, gently reaching out to her, to comfort her and to guide her towards the kitchen.

"I don't know," she replied, her eyes filling with tears. "He just didn't come home. I waited, but then the baby came and... and I didn't know what else to do. I saw you on the television, so I decided to come here." She glanced back at me, studying me with eyes as deep and fathomless as the ocean. "You seemed kind."

"I try to be," I said. I paused for a second as we entered the dining room, then I asked a question as subtly as I could. "Where were you staying before this, Tala?"

"Bodhinyanarama," she replied.

I shot her a bewildered look. "Bodhinwhatawhata?"

"Oh." Tala glanced at me, her expression a little sheepish. "Sorry. Bodhinyanarama was a Buddhist monastery in Stokes Valley. Franco loved it up there..."

I saw the first tear break loose and roll down her cheek. A second later, I had my arm around her shoulders and held her while she silently wept. I led her over to one of the couches and sat down with her. "I know, honey. I know it hurts. But at least you and your babies are safe now. I won't let anything happen to them."

Tala nodded miserably and wiped her eyes. "I know. It's just... so hard."

"You don't have to do it alone anymore," I told her gently, feeling a surge of sympathy towards the woman that I wouldn't have been able to explain in words. "Wait here and rest, I'll go get your food. Is there anything that you or Nenita can't have? Any allergies?"

"No... no." Tala took a deep breath and shook her head. "We appreciate anything that you offer us."

"You're part of our family now," I said, easing myself up to my feet again. "Our food is your food. I'll be back in a minute, okay?"

Tala nodded her understanding, so I left her and her children and went into the kitchen. There, I found Elly and Isabelle puttering around starting preparations for lunch. I waved a greeting to them, but didn't stop and say hello just yet. By the time the door had swung closed behind me, I had my radio out of my pocket.

"Michael?" I said into the receiver.

A few seconds passed, then his voice came on the line. "I'm here. What's up?"

"We may have a wounded man out there in need of our help," I told him. I quickly conveyed Tala's story, and he grunted his understanding.

"You want to send out a search party," he translated without further prompting. "How many people?"

"Six," I said. "You, me, and one of the nurses. Please round up three more people, preferably the best trackers we have, and get the horses ready. I'll meet you down there in a few minutes."

"I'm on it," he replied, then he was gone. Both Elly and Isabelle were watching me, obviously waiting for instructions. They didn't have to wait for long.

"Elly, can you please prepare travel rations for six people?" I asked. "We should be back by dark, but better safe than sorry. Make it a day's worth." Elly just nodded and hurried off without bothering to reply. I looked at Isabelle, and gave her a smile. "Can you please go talk to Skylar for me? I need her to get weapons out of storage for us."

"Okay," she agreed, nervously folding her hands in front of her. She started towards the door, then hesitated and looked back at me. "Anything else...?"

"Yes, if you wouldn't mind," I replied. "Can you please visit the infirmary, and ask one of the nurses to come along? It doesn't matter which one – I'd feel better having someone with medical training on hand."

"Sure," she said, and then she was out the door.

I took a deep breath to calm my racing heart, then turned my attention towards getting Tala's babies fed. I grabbed a couple of plates off a drying rack and went into the cooler to see what was left over from dinner the night before. I found a big bowl of cold stew covered with cling wrap, and some boiled vegetables. It probably wasn't very tasty, but they looked half-starved and food was food when you were hungry. A cold, tasteless meal was better than no meal at all.

Sure enough, when I brought the food out to them, Tala and Nenita set to it without a word of complaint. I sat with them while they ate, until Elly appeared with the rations I'd asked her to prepare. I introduced them, and then I left Tala in Elly's very capable care and excused myself.

Skylar was waiting for me in the hallway, burdened with an armload of guns and bottled water. Once we'd settled in and secured the fence around Tumanako, we'd taken to only carrying weapons when on guard duty or when going outside the fence for long periods of time. I took my favourite shotgun, put it over my shoulder, and stuffed a handful of spare cartridges into my pocket.

"Do you need to go back to your room?" Skye asked. "I can take those rations downstairs with me, if you like."

"Are you sure? You barely have a spare hand," I commented dryly.

Skye just laughed and grabbed the bag out of my hand, then she was off at a rapid clip. I went the opposite direction and climbed the stairs to the third floor to go retrieve my travel gear from my room. Most of it was already on my person, but I'd fallen out of the habit of carrying my GPS unit when I was just visiting the local township.

I quickly found it, checked that it was charged, and tucked it into my pocket, then I wrapped my coat around me and put on my backpack. Michael's backpack sat nearby; I knew him well enough to pack what he needed without a second thought. As soon as I was done, I raced out the door and down the stairs to the lobby.

Michael and Skylar were waiting by the front door, talking softly. Just outside the door, I could see Tane, Iorangi, Warren, and Aaron standing by the horses. I hurried over and gave Michael his backpack, then we divided up the rations, water, and guns between us.

"Be careful," Skye said quietly. "Remember what happened when you decided to play the hero for Anahera's clan. You almost didn't come home."

"What, you still haven't forgiven me for that?" I teased.

She laughed and shook her head. "Nope, and I'm going to keep reminding you about it so that you take better care of yourself in the future. Got it?"

"Got it," I agreed. I yanked her into a hug and planted a kiss on her cheek. "Don't worry, little sis. I have a reason to live these days."

"God, you are so depressing," she answered, giving me a light shove. "Get off me, slobber-puss. You've got work to do."

I released her, then I waved and raced out the door to where Aaron was holding my horse. I put my backpack back on, took Boudicca's reins, and vaulted expertly up into the saddle; if nothing else, the weeks that we'd spent on the road had turned all of us into expert riders. Boudicca pranced and nickered, but I stilled her with a firm hand on the reins and a touch of my heel.

While the others were putting on their gear and mounting up, I pulled my GPS out of my pocket and programmed in the location. Michael drew his horse up beside me and gave me a quizzical look.

"It's a little over eight kilometres away, if we follow the roads," I said, glancing up to study the skyline. "I don't think we'll be able to cut across country. Too many hills."

"The roads are safer," he said. "And eight kilometres isn't far, without a convoy slowing us down. We should be there before midday."

"Agreed," I said, tucking my GPS unit into an easily-accessible pocket. "Everyone ready?"

Everyone called out that they were. I touched Boudicca's sides with my heels and guided her up to a trot, then a canter. If there was even the slightest chance that Franco was still alive, then seconds could prove precious. All our horses were fit and healthy, and seemed to enjoy the chance to stretch their legs.

The gates were open before we even reached them, and the guards shut them behind us before we were out of sight. I led the group down towards the river, then swung northwards and followed the old highway. A surge of excitement rose in my breast as a breeze off the river struck me. It was cold, but there was something exhilarating about it. We rarely had the opportunity to travel at speed unless lives were at stake, and this was the first time that I wasn't worried about wasting precious petrol in the process.

It took all of my willpower to fight down the urge to push Boudicca a little faster, ride her a little harder, but I knew if I did that then she'd end up exhausted before we got there. No, as fun as it was, I had to pace us for the journey ahead. A flock of birds exploded out of the long grass beside the river and up into the sky, leaving me wondering what it felt like to fly. The freedom. The absolute freedom. Riding a horse at speed was probably the closest we'd ever get to feeling like that, and it was glorious in its own way.

The highway was a long, straight road that followed the riverbank for a good four kilometres, until we eventually passed out of the densely-packed suburban jungle into an area that was populated by larger, nicer houses and wide green spaces. Everything was overgrown, but it was still beautiful; green, alive, and refreshing. I lifted a hand and pointed to the right, telling my friends that it was time to make our turn off. Our horses took the turn without breaking stride, onto another road which wound up into the hills.

Much like the area closer to Avalon, the roads here were still in excellent condition and it was an easy ride for both of us. I barely even had to look where I was going, since there was nothing in our way and Boudicca was smart enough to negotiate her own footing. I found myself staring at the hills flanking the valley, watching the dark, ominous clouds gathering above the treeline. We were in for again rain soon.

The first droplet struck my face just as we reached the final leg of the journey, and the road finally began to climb at a gradient that forced us to slow to a trot. We dodged around the rusted hulks of parked cars and one obnoxious purple bus, until we finally reached the crest of the hill. There, several long driveways led off a small cul-de-sac, vanishing into dense forest.

"Which one is it?" Aaron called.

I shielded my eyes from the rain and looked around, then pointed at a small wooden sign nestled amongst flax bushes. "The writing's worn off, but that looks like the kind of thing you'd use to mark a Buddhist monastery, don't you think?"

"If I remember correctly, this place practiced Thai Forest Tradition," Michael said thoughtfully. "It's a branch of Theravada Buddhism." I shot him a curious glance; he returned it with a shrug and a smile. "My mother was very serious about her faith, even the branches that she didn't personally adhere to."

"Makes sense, I suppose," I replied. "Curiosity and all that. Do you know anything about the layout here, or what we can expect?"

"Not specifically, but I have a general idea," he said, turning his attention back towards the shadowy gateway. He pointed to it, then made a broad, all-encompassing gesture towards the hills around us. "These hills will be full of pathways and staircases, leading up to solitary meditation retreats high up the hillside. There should be offices and a public meditation hall closer to where we are, though; the monks in places like this relied on the generosity of their guests to survive, so they needed somewhere convenient for the general public to visit."

"Let's go find out, then," I said. I dismounted and led Boudicca down the driveway. The branches hung so low that I had to push them aside to keep them out of my face, but not for long. A short way in, the bush gave way to a gravel-lined courtyard, surrounded by elegant wooden buildings crafted in a manner that was an odd hybrid of Eastern and Western styles. I paused to admire them while the others caught up with me; even after ten years, they were still solid and quite beautiful in a way that was somewhat alien to my eye.

"This'll be it," Michael said. "The public meditation hall, and probably their office as well."

"What do monks need an office for?" I enquired, genuinely curious to hear the answer.

Michael laughed and shook his head. "No one was immune to the lure of technology. They still had to pay their bills, and probably maintain a website so people knew they existed."

"Oh, good point," I said. I led my horse over to a patch of grass and tied her reins to a low branch. "Let's see if we can figure out where Tala and Franco were living, then maybe we can track Franco from there."

"I'd say in there," Warren said suddenly, speaking up for the first time since we'd left.

I followed his finger towards a smaller building off to one side. "I think you're right. I see signs of recent occupation. Let's go take a look."

Michael and Warren fell in on either side of me with their weapons at the ready, leaving the others to keep an eye on the horses. I climbed the stairs onto the porch and glanced around for a moment, then I tried the door handle. It opened easily, revealing an interior that was dark but smelled relatively clean. I tried the light switch and got no response, so I pulled out my torch instead.

It was immediately clear to all of us that someone had been living there for quite some time. There were beds in one of the rooms, a makeshift couch, and even a television set. We split up to investigate the building as swiftly as possible; I headed down a hall and found myself in a small room with a generator that had either been disabled or run out of gas. I was just about to check which when a shout caught my attention.

"I've got blood!" Warren yelled from the other end of the building. I forgot all about the generator and raced towards the sound of his voice, nearly bumping into

Michael along the way. We found Warren crouched over a large puddle of congealed blood on the floor of a bathroom. He glanced up, nodded once, and stood. It only took me a second to see why he wasn't concerned.

"A placenta," I said, as much to myself as anyone else. "Odds are pretty good that it was Tala's, so this is definitely where they were living. Where would Franco have gone?"

"What did Tala say, exactly?" Michael asked.

"She said he went hunting," I replied, then I paused and glanced around. "There's nothing to hunt in these woods, though. Just possums, I guess?"

"No..." Michael paused for a second to collect his thoughts, then shook his head firmly. "Is English her native language?"

"I don't think so," I replied. "She has a strong accent, and I'd guess by her appearance that she's Filipino."

"Ah, that's it!" he said, snapping his fingers. "I don't know much Filipino, but I learned a bit from one of my friends in the Academy. The word 'hunt' has a bunch of synonyms, just like it does in English. It could also mean that they were seeking something, or scouting, or—"

"Or scavenging?" I finished for him, picking up the idea. Michael nodded and gave me a smile.

"Let's divide up into pairs and go in different directions," he suggested. "We'll have a better chance of finding any sign of him that way."

I nodded and gestured for them to follow me, then led the way back out into the courtyard where Aaron, Tane, and Iorangi were still waiting with the horses. They looked at us expectantly as we gathered in a circle.

"We need to split up to try and find this guy," I said once I'd conveyed what we'd found. "Who has a radio?" Warren and Iorangi both put their hands up. "Okay, good. Michael and I have one each, too. How's your tracking, Aaron?"

"Pretty terrible," Aaron admitted with a shrug. "Never been much of a huntsman."

"That fine," I replied. "You're our medic. Stick with Warren, he can do the tracking for both of you. If Franco's still alive, there's a chance he's conscious. He might be trapped somewhere. It seems safe enough to try calling out to him. Watch yourselves, though: we're pretty close to the bush so there's a chance there might be pigs around, and I see some signs of earthquake damage. Mind your footing."

Warren made an approving grunt and nodded. "Looks like the quake was fairly recent, too."

"How can you tell?" Michael asked curiously.

"I'll show you while we're walking," I said. "We'll leave the horses here and travel on foot. Warren, can you please take Aaron and check around the monastery for any sign he might have gone up into the hills?"

Warren nodded and headed off without waiting for further instructions, leaving Aaron scrambling to keep up with him. I watched until they were out of sight, then took a deep breath and looked back at the others.

"Michael and I will take the left side of the road heading back the way we came," I said. "You two take the right. If you see anything out of the ordinary, check it out – but keep your guns close, just in case."

Tane and Iorangi both nodded and departed, leaving me alone with Michael. I glanced at him and gave him a smile. "I wish I'd thought to bring Alfred along. We could use his nose."

"We'll figure it out," he said in that voice of pure confidence he used when he was trying to reassure me that everything was going to be fine. He reached out and took my hand, then together we walked back down towards the road to begin our search.

The cul-de-sac near the entrance of the monastery was solid tarmac, but the driveways leading to the other properties nearby were all gravel. I knelt to examine the ground, then frowned and shook my head.

"I see a lot of different tracks here," I explained, "but I can't tell how recent any of them are. It's rained a few times, and that's muddled the spoor. Let's head up to that house and see if there's anything fresher that way."

Michael nodded silently and followed my lead. We climbed the steep driveway towards an old wooden homestead set amongst heavy bush. At the top, I glanced back at him and caught him staring at a slender, hairline fracture bisecting the concrete porch.

"That's the earthquake damage," I said by way of explanation. "I'll teach you what I know. Most of it's just logic, really. I mean... look at that planter pot over there and tell me what you see. What's out of place?"

Michael glanced in the direction I was pointing, but he didn't say anything right away. Eventually, he nodded and looked back at me. "I think I get it. The outside of the pot is all green with moss or mildew or whatever that is, and so are the paving stones around it – but not the part underneath where the pot was. The pot was knocked over recently."

"Bingo," I said, pleased but not surprised by his quick uptake. He always had been a quick study. "If we look closer, we can see that there were some spiders or bugs living there and they're all gone now. The moss is also starting to grow over the clear patch under where the pot was. I'd say that it probably fell over a few weeks ago."

"Do you think Tumanako is at risk?" he asked, his voice suddenly filled with concern.

"No more than anywhere else," I replied with a shrug. "We're living on a tectonic fault line. Earthquakes are inevitable no matter where we go."

"True," he said quietly. Suddenly, he grinned. "Hey, at least we're not living in Volcano Land anymore, right?"

I laughed and nodded. "True that. We're living in Flood Plains Land instead."

"Hey, what did I tell you about being negative?" he said. "Anyway, Franco. What now?"

"No sign of him here," I replied. "Let's head down that way towards the back fence. The long grass will help us spot any fresh tracks."

Michael followed obediently as we made our way down to the edge of the yard, and descended into the wet grass. I picked my way carefully, wary of any hidden obstructions or dangers. While we didn't have to worry about snakes like our Australian cousins, my close encounter with a nail six months earlier left me cautious. Plus, now I had the baby to worry about. It was unlikely that me stepping on something would hurt her, but it was better to be safe than sorry.

For half an hour or so, we made our way through the back yards of the houses on our side of the road, looking for any sign of the missing man. While there were plenty of footprints around, some of them as recent as a few weeks old, there was nothing fresh enough to have come from Franco's latest – and possibly last – hunt. Eventually, I stopped and pulled my radio out of my coat to check in with the others.

"Nothing so far on our side," I said into the receiver. "How about you guys?"

"Nothing here," Iorangi replied, sounding as frustrated as I felt.

"Nothing here, either," Warren said. "There's a lot of spoor around, but none of it fresh."

"Yeah, that's what I'm seeing, too," I replied. "Where the hell did this guy go?"

"Hey," Michael said suddenly. "Sandy, what's that? I saw a flash of red through the trees over there."

"Hold on a second, guys," I said into the radio, "we might have something."

I looked where Michael was pointing, shading my eyes against the rain. Sure enough, I saw a brief flash of red, then it was gone. I raised my shotgun and crept towards the treeline. As I drew closer, I saw fresh tracks in the mud and a little strip of red cloth flapping in the breeze. It was firmly attached to the rough bark on the side of a tree.

"Someone came through here in a hurry," I said, easing myself down into a crouch to get a better look at the tracks. After a couple of seconds, I nodded and spoke into the radio again. "We've definitely found something. Head down towards the place with the big pohutukawa tree in the front yard and meet us here."

The others acknowledged my request, while Michael came over to crouch beside me, studying the tracks.

"That looks like **a** boot print," he said thoughtfully, point at a particularly clear mark left in the mud. "A man's, I think."

"Yeah, looks like it," I replied. "There's something else here, though, and it worries me."

"Why?" he asked, glancing up at me.

"Because I think it's pig tracks," I said. I glanced at him and saw all the colour drain out of his face. Even though we'd successfully killed a couple of pigs together, neither of us were eager to take on another – and neither of us wanted to imagine what might have happened to Franco if he'd been chased down by a one of the damn things.

We stood back and waited beneath the shelter of a half-collapsed patio. It didn't do a lot of good since we were already soaked and freezing, but at least I felt a little better for trying. A few minutes later, a familiar voice shouted our names.

"Sandy? Michael?"

"Back here," I called back. Iorangi stuck his head around the edge of the building and waved to us, with the others close behind him.

"Warren," I said, pointing at the tracks. "Reckon that's a pig?"

He went over to examine them more closely, then nodded. "Yep. I reckon that's a pig."

I sighed heavily and swore beneath my breath.

Aaron looked at us curiously. "A pig?"

"Zombie pigs," Michael said sympathetically. "They're a thing. A really *bad* thing. We don't want to tangle with a pig unless we absolutely have to."

"I think we might have to," I said, pointing along the length of the tracks. "It looks like he went through the fence here and I'd say the pig followed him. Let's just hope he was smart enough to go up into the hills rather than try and circle around the base. Pigs can't really climb, from what I hear."

"Zombie pigs," Aaron repeated, as if trying the words on for size.

"Yep. Really a thing," Michael and I said simultaneously, then we glanced at one another and smiled.

"Well, wherever he is, he's probably gotten himself into trouble," I said. "Keep your eyes and ears peeled, guys."

They made noises of agreement and fell in behind me as I led the way towards the rear of the yard. I stepped carefully over a few fallen fence posts and followed the trail into the thigh-high grass on the other side. Mud squelched beneath my shoes but I ignored it, focusing all my attention on the world around us. There was nothing to be heard, except the sound of the falling rain, our footsteps, and our breathing.

The tracks almost made it to the hillside before they turned sharply away and ran parallel to the edge of the forest. I muttered a low curse beneath my breath, but before I could say anything Warren's voice intervened.

"I see blood drops," he said quietly. I frowned and nodded but said nothing. At this stage, blood could have meant anything — it could have even come from the pig.

"Sandy," Michael called suddenly. "What the hell is *that*?"

I looked up and stared into the distance, but this time I didn't have an answer. "I... I don't know. Warren? What the hell is that?"

"I believe that's a crevice," he replied, his voice flat and showing no sign of the shock I felt.

In the distance, a dark shadow yawned like a wound in the skin of the very earth itself, and it looked for all the world like it was sucking in the trees and grass that grew along its edges. It took a second for me to make sense of what I was seeing: a long, slender pit, a fracture in the bedrock. The vegetation wasn't being sucked in, it was sliding in, slowly, courtesy of gravity.

"I think I know what happened to Franco," I said softly. I took a moment to steel myself, then led the way towards the crevice. "Mind your footing, everyone. We don't know how stable the ground is around here."

No one answered, but they didn't need to. We could all see the devastation that the crevice had wrought on the landscape around it. At first glance it looked like the trees around it were going to tumble in at any second, but on closer inspection I realised that many of them had been that way for a while — their trunks were twisted up towards the sun, and their roots were firmly planted in the earth. The crevice had been there for a while. Perhaps Franco had known about it, and decided to use it as a means to escape from the pig.

A dozen meters from the edge, we came to a stop and looked at one another.

"I don't suppose anyone brought rope, did they?" I asked. Everyone shook their heads, except for Aaron.

"Did I mention I used to be a Scout?" he commented dryly. He shrugged off his backpack, pulled out a short length of rope, and handed it to me. "Which one of us goes?"

"I'm the smallest, so it should be me," I said, silently dreading what I volunteering to do.

"No!" Michael protested. "I'll go. You hate heights."

"I know," I answered dryly. "But I'm not strong enough to pull you up if you slip in, and you are."

Michael opened his mouth to say something, then seemed to think better of it. His shoulders slumped, and he nodded. "Just... be careful."

"Oh believe me, I have no intention of falling into a crevice," I replied. I took off my backpack and shotgun and handed them both to Warren, then I wound the rope around my waist. My coat had belt loops on the outside for a terribly fashionable sash that I'd discarded on the first day, but now they finally had a use. I threaded the rope through them, then Michael knotted it at the small of my back.

I took a deep breath to steady myself and began to slowly walk towards the edge of the pit, still following the tracks. With each step, I paused to test the stability of the earth with my shoe before I committed my full weight to it, but it didn't give out or collapse beneath me. When I got within the last couple of meters, I eased myself down onto hands and knees and crawled the rest of the way.

Below me, the crevice vanished into darkness. I reached into my pocket and pulled out my torch, clicked it on, and pointed it downwards.

There was little to see. My tiny light did almost nothing to penetrate the darkness, except show me that the crevice went down deep. I swung the light a little farther to the left, and then I froze: six or seven meters below the lip of the crevice, I saw a flash of crimson cloth.

"Franco?" I called, straining to better make out what I was seeing. "Franco, are you alive down there? Franco!"

The cloth shifted a little, but there was no response.

I called out again. "Franco, mate, please answer me."

Suddenly, there was a bewildered-looking face peering up at me, struggling to block the light of my torch with one hand. "H-hello? Is someone there?"

"He's alive!" I cried. "Guys, head back to the houses. We need more rope, or a chain – anything we can use to get him out of there. We'll need a good ten meters or so to reach him." I looked back down into the crevice and called out to him again. "We're coming, Franco. Just hang in there a little bit longer."

"Tala?" he asked, sounding dazed and confused. Given that he'd been down there for days with no food and only rainwater to drink, I wasn't surprised.

"No, my name is Sandrine," I said to him, switching off the torch and tucking it away. "When you didn't come home, Tala panicked and came looking for us. She thinks you're dead."

"Am I dead?" the man asked, his voice disembodied in the darkness. "I don't know. Everything hurts."

"Don't move," I told him. "I think you're on a ledge. If you move, you might fall again. Just stay right there and keep talking to me. Are you injured?"

"Injured?" he echoed. There was a long moment of silence, then a distant cough. "Yes. My leg. It's broken."

"It's okay, we'll fix it," I said, trying to reassure him as best I could from afar. "What happened to the pig? We saw its tracks."

"It fell in the hole," he said, his words slurred. "I tried to jump, but I slipped. The pig fell into the deep part. I think it's dead, but I don't know."

"He sounds a bit delirious, the poor fellow," a soft voice said beside me. I glanced sideways and saw that Aaron had crept up beside me, lying on his belly. "He'll be in shock, not to mention suffering from hypothermia and probably osteomyelitis." He glanced at me, his brow furrowed in concern. "Blood poisoning."

I nodded my understanding and focused on keeping Franco as alert as I could. The last thing we needed was for him to slip and fall to his death. "We didn't see the pig anywhere, so it probably died when it fell. Don't worry about it. My friends have gone to get some rope to haul you out, so just try and stay with me, okay? Keep talking to me. Um... tell me about Tala."

"Tala?" he repeated her name, a strange wistfulness filling his voice. "Ah, my Tala. I love her. She's a good woman. Have you met her?"

"Yeah, she came to us after you fell," I repeated. "She'll be so happy to see you. The baby's come now, but she hasn't picked a name."

"The baby?" he gasped. "Is it healthy? A girl or a boy?"

"Don't move, Franco," I warned him again. "It's a little girl, and she looked pretty healthy when I saw her this morning. Tala's taking good care of her."

"She's a good mama, my Tala," he said. Even at a distance, I could hear the smile in his voice. "I thought for sure I was never going to see her again..."

"You will," I said, channelling as much confidence as I could into my voice. "Just stay awake. My friends will be here soon. Why don't you tell me about how you met Tala?"

He sighed dreamily and did just that. Aaron and I exchanged worried glances throughout his rambling dialogue, but neither of us interrupted except to prompt him with more questions to keep him talking. Franco wasn't the only one wet and miserable by the time the others returned with more rope, but no one complained.

When I heard Michael call my name to alert me to his return, my relief was so palpable it felt like a weight lifted off my stomach. He tossed one end of the rope to me, and I caught it.

"Franco?" I called, interrupting him. "We've got the rope, mate. I'm going to lower one end down to you, and I want you to tie it around your chest, underneath your arms. Can you do that for me?"

"Anything to get me out of this stupid hole," he replied; the humour in his voice gave me a flash of hope and brought a smile to my face.

"Okay, the rope's coming down," I said. "Tell me when you've got it."

I carefully guided the rope over the edge, while Michael and the others fed it out a little at a time. None of the trees nearby were sturdy enough to tie the rope to, so we were just going to have to do it by hand.

"I've got it," Franco shouted at last. There was a pause of a few seconds, then he spoke again. "Okay, I've tied it around me. This rope is pretty slippery. I hope it'll be strong enough."

"It only has to hold you for a little while," I replied. "Keep hold of it, and I'll be waiting at the top to take you home to Tala. Are you ready?"

"As ready as I'll ever be," he replied.

I glanced up and signalled to the men. They wrapped the rope around their wrists and over their shoulders, and strained with all their might. The rope went taut on the grass beside me, and then slowly it began to creep upwards. After a tense few seconds, I saw a shadow moving beneath me, and then that shadow resolved itself into a slender human figure.

"That's it," I called to everyone. "Keep pulling, just a few more meters."

"Sandrine?" Franco yelled suddenly. "Sandrine, the rope! It's slipping!"

I swore and shoved myself a few inches further forward, peering downwards into shadow. Sure enough, I could see the knot around Franco's chest coming a little bit looser with each tug of the rope. With the rain and the mud, if the knot failed completely there would be no way for him to keep his grip.

"Hang on with both hands," I advised, struggling to fight down the urge to panic. "It's just a little bit more. I can almost reach you." I glanced back again, and shouted, "Keep pulling! We're almost—"

"Sandrine!" Franco's cry was one of pure terror. I glanced back just in time to see the knot slipping the last few millimetres.

"Give me your hand!" I cried, thrusting myself as far forward as I could without falling into the pit myself. Franco screamed something inarticulate and made a grab for it. I felt his hand close around my wrist, nearly tugging my arm out of its socket, and then suddenly I was sliding forward into the gaping abyss.

I felt someone grab the rope around my waist before I had a chance to cry for help, and that saved me from tumbling into darkness: Aaron. A second later, Michael was there with him, then the others. I was briefly buried by a mound of strong male bodies, and when it cleared all seven of us were sitting in the mud. Stunned, but safe.

I looked at Franco, then I looked at the others. I started to say something, but all that came out was a hysterical laugh. They looked at me like I was crazy for all of three seconds, then something in each of them broke and laughed right along with me.

Chapter Thirteen

By the time we'd calmed down enough to be much good for anything, the drizzle had turned into a downpour. All of us were sodden and covered in mud, but that didn't stop us from mucking in to help Franco. Michael and Tane half-helped, half-lifted him to his feet, and carried him back towards the shelter of the monastery – and more importantly, the medical kit we'd left with the horses.

When we finally made it, I was evicted from the room while the men stripped Franco of his soiled garments and Aaron tended to his wounds. I retreated to the small kitchen, stripped off my muddy outer garments, and set about preparing a light meal for Franco to eat once he was ready for it. The others eventually came out to join me, all except for Aaron. I conscripted one of the men to take the food in, then we all sat around just waiting for news. Warren vanished out the door to enjoy his own company, and the rest of us just chatted to pass the time.

Eventually, Aaron finished piecing Franco back together and came out to join us.

"How is he?" I asked, almost afraid to hear the answer.

"Better than he should be, to be honest," Aaron replied. "It's not a bad break, but I'm concerned about the risk of osteomyelitis because it went for so long. We need to get him back to Tumanako as soon as possible. If we don't get him on antibiotics soon, it may end up costing him that leg."

I took a deep breath and nodded. "Can we get him on a horse, or should we send for one of the trucks?"

Aaron went quiet for a moment while he considered the possibilities, then he shrugged. "If wait for a truck, then we'll lose at least an hour and this condition is time-sensitive. If we try and get him to ride double with someone, he may pass out from pain and fall, or make the injury worse. Either way, it's a risk."

"Let's stick with the safest option," I suggested. "I'll call home and get Doc up here in one of the trucks. He should make good time along that road. Can you take care of Franco until he gets here?"

Aaron nodded silently, his face an odd mixture of relief and regret. He vanished out of the room, and I stood to call Warren back inside for a group meeting.

"I need two people to head back the way we came and lead the truck up here," I said. Everyone volunteered. I picked Tane and Iorangi and sent them off, then I pulled out my radio and tuned it to the frequency we'd taken to using around home. "Come in, Tumanako. It's Sandy."

There was a few moments of silence, then the line crackled and a familiar voice came on. "Hey, sis. Any luck?"

"Yes," I replied. "We've found Franco. He's alive, but we need to get him back home for treatment and he's not well enough to ride. He's got a broken leg, and Aaron says he may be suffering from osteo-something – some kind of blood poisoning. I need Doc up here in the Hilux with antibiotics, and I need it now."

"You got it," she answered confidently. "He'll be on the road within 15 minutes, if I have to push him out the door myself. Give me the directions."

I did, then we ended the conversation. I looked at the others and gave them a weak smile. "Nothing to do now except for wait."

"Well, there is one thing," Michael said. "You mentioned Tala arrived with pretty much nothing, just the clothes on her back and her kids. They don't have a lot of stuff here. I bet we could fit it in the back of the Hilux, no problem."

I hesitated for a second, then I smiled and reached out to touch his hand. "Trust you to always know the right thing to do. Good plan. Let's get packing!"

***

It took us virtually no time at all to gather up the pieces of Tala and Franco's life, and pack them into a few bags and boxes. They'd obviously been there since before their eldest was born, but they lived simply and didn't have much. Franco watched silently from the bed while I was in their bedroom, but he said nothing. When I looked at him, he just gave me a weak smile and nodded his approval.

Within an hour, we were ready. Michael and I settled in a chair by the front door, snuggled together watching the rain. I was just beginning to doze off when a strange noise caught my ear. I sat up a little straighter and stared out the window, waiting. Sure enough, a few seconds later Tane sprinted into view, with his brother close behind him. By the time they reached the door, I was on my feet and there to meet them.

"The truck's waiting on the other side of the overgrowth," Tane shouted, pointing back towards the road. I breathed a huge sigh of relief, nodded, and hurried off to convey the news to Aaron. While he was busy getting Franco ready for transport, I pulled my muddy outerwear back on and dove in to help the others carry stuff out to the truck.

I was half way there, lugging a couple of plastic bags of children's clothing, when I spotted Hemi and Rebecca running towards me carrying a makeshift stretcher between them. I didn't bother to ask where they'd gotten the stretcher from, I just dropped one of the bags and pointed back the way I'd come.

"Turn left at the end of the driveway," I called. "You'll see an open door. Whoever's there will point you the rest of the way."

They nodded and ran on without a word. I picked up the bag and resumed my trek down the driveway, picking my footing carefully on the muddy ground. They probably could have driven up closer, but I agreed with their decision; there wasn't much gravel left on the driveway, and the last thing we needed was for the Hilux to get stuck in the mud. When I rounded the last bend, I saw Doctor Cross waiting beside the truck with a slightly sour look on his face.

"Hey, Doc," I greeted. "Thank you for coming out here. I'm sorry you had to come out in the rain, but—"

"But time is of the essence," he replied, finishing my sentence. "Your sister conveyed the message. I presume by 'osteo-something', you meant 'osteomyelitis'?"

"Yeah, that," I replied, nodding. I put my bags down again and went over to open the back canopy of the ute. "I don't know what it is, but Aaron made it sound bad."

"It is bad," Doc said simply. He came around to stand beside me, staring into the back of the ute. "Would there be enough room to lie him flat in here, do you think?"

"I don't see why not," I replied. "He's a pretty small guy. Why not just put him in the back seat, though?"

"You said his leg was broken," he said. "Until we have a chance to set the break, it's best to have him lying flat or sitting with his legs stretched out in a way that won't jostle the break too badly when we gain speed."

"Oh, of course," I said. "We've got some more clothing and bedding coming, we can use it to pad him so that he doesn't bounce around." I heard the sound of footsteps behind me, and turned to see the others hurrying towards us. Michael and Tane had the stretcher, while the others were carrying various boxes, bags, and mounds of blankets.

Doc took command of the situation before I could say a word, and guided the others through the process of creating a comfortable nest in the back of the ute. Once it was secure, they carefully lifted Franco into the remaining space, stretcher and all. I left Doc, Rebecca, and Hemi to deal with the patient himself, and took everyone else back to the monastery to grab our belongings and fetch the horses.

By the time we returned, the Hilux had already left. We mounted up and followed after it as fast as we could safely travel. The rain was coming down in buckets now, but at least it washed away the mud. I tugged my hood down low over my eyes and hunkered over Boudicca's broad back to salvage what little warmth I could from her skin.

It wasn't a pleasant trip back to Tumanako, but we'd spent all winter on the road so we were used to unpleasant trips. Every so often I sat up and glanced back to do a headcount, just to make sure that we didn't lose anyone in the weather. The Hilux managed much better speed than we did, and we soon lost track of it in the gloom. When we finally made it back to Tumanako, we found the outer gates firmly closed and locked, just as they should be.

"Hello?" I shouted, cupping my hands around my mouth to try and make myself heard. A few seconds later, a head popped up in the window of the security shed beside the gate, then one of the people on guard duty jogged out to let us in.

We waved a greeting, but rode past her without stopping to say hello. It was only when we reached the front of the office building and saw the Hilux parked there that I finally relaxed and breathed a sigh of relief. They'd made it.

"We'll take the horses back, if you and Aaron want to go on ahead," Michael volunteered.

"Thank you," I said, appreciating his intuition. "Doc will need Aaron's help, and I should speak to Tala."

"Any time," he replied. "Go, we've got this covered."

I dismounted and handed my reins up to him, then hurried into the shelter of the tower's entrance – and almost bowled Skylar right off her feet.

"Hey, watch it!" she cried, leaping back just in time to avoid being run down.

I yelped in surprise and skidded to a halt so suddenly that I nearly ended up on my ass. "Shoot, sorry! I didn't see you waiting there."

"You never do," she said, laughing and shaking her head. "Took you guys long enough to get here. Doc wants Aaron in the infirmary urgently."

"We figured he'd be needed," I replied. "Aaron was right behind m—"

I didn't hear the door open in time to get out of the way. Aaron barrelled right into me from behind, knocking me into Skye, and all three of us went down in a sodden tangle of limbs.

"Sorry! Sorry! Oh God, sorry!" Aaron cried, leaping back up to his feet with the kind of dexterity that was only born from shock. "The rain was in my eyes and I wasn't looking where I was going. Is everyone all right?"

"I'm fine," I replied. I accepted the offered hand and hauled myself up off the ground, then offered my hand to Skye in turn. She slapped it away. For a second I was worried, until I realised that she was shaking from silent hysterics. They weren't silent for long, though; suddenly, she threw her head back and laughed uproariously.

Aaron and I exchanged an amused look. We waited until she finally got herself back under control, then helped her to her feet and guided her towards the stairs. At the last second, she stopped and looked at us.

"Oh, the elevator's working now," she said. "The electrical crew got it going just after you left."

"That's fantastic," I said, surprised and pleased by the news. "Does that mean that there's enough power coming in from the solar array for the whole building now?"

"Should be, yep!" she replied. She led us over to the elevators and pushed the call button. "I haven't tested every level, but the ones I've been to all have power. Gavin said they're going to keep extending the grid until they run out of space, so there will be enough to cover any extra people who join us, but for now it should be enough for us to have light, heat, and hot water whenever we need it."

"Hallelujah!" I cried, throwing my hands up in the air. "We're civilized again!"

Skye laughed and gave me a light shove. "Civilized? Please, you wouldn't know civility if it up and bit you on the butt."

"It confuses me when you use big words like that," I replied, teasing her back. "Who are you and what did you do with my semi-literate baby sister?"

"Doc made me his pet project," she answered, her expression turning thoughtful. "He's got me up to reading classic novels. I'm reading one right now called *Pride and Prejudice*, by an old-timey author named Jane Austen."

"Oh?" I asked, looking at her in surprise. "That doesn't strike me as your type of book. Are you enjoying it?"

"I..." She hesitated to think over her answer, then she shrugged. "Yeah, actually. I am. A lot of it I don't really understand, but it's fascinating to learn about how people lived back then. And it makes me think Erica's right: we really should try and preserve as many books as possible, so that we don't forget these people. I don't know how to express it, but it feels... important, somehow."

The elevator dinged open. Our conversation halted for a second while we climbed in, then we picked up where we'd left off.

"I agree," I said. "The way Sergeant Bryce phrased it really struck me. She said, 'someone made those books, and that's important.'"

"It's not just that, though," she said, absently hugging herself against a chill that most likely came from within. "Every person is important, even the ones who didn't write a book or make a movie or an album, because those people made *us*. I want to... do something to remember them. I just don't know what yet."

I reached out and touched her shoulder gently. "Whatever you decide to do, you know I'll support you. Just say the word."

The elevator chimed again, and the doors opened to let us out onto the second level. I was just about to step out of the elevator, when I was very nearly bowled right off my feet again. Tala threw her arms around me and hugged me fiercely, then jerked back and planted a succession of kisses on my cheeks. I just froze and took it, not sure how to deal with so much gratitude in one place. Beside me, Aaron and Skylar both burst out laughing, and I could hear a few other people laughing as well.

The elevator doors started to close again, but a hand caught them and held them open. Then Anahera stepped through and grabbed Tala by the shoulders.

"Come here, little mama," she said gently, prying the tiny woman away from me. "Let Sandy breathe."

I gave her a grateful look and a smile over Tala's head. Tala was nearly hysterical and I couldn't make sense of a word she was saying, since most of it was in her native language. We guided her out of the elevator and into the dining room, where we found Melody happily babysitting her two young children. Anahera sat Tala down beside them, then a few seconds later Elly appeared out of the kitchen carrying a steaming hot mug of tea. Anahera took it and placed it in Tala's hands.

"Here we go, dear," she said, her voice soft and maternal. She sat down beside Tala, resting one hand comfortingly on her upper back. "You just sip that, and breathe. Deep breaths. Can you do that?"

Tala nodded and did as she was told. She drew a deep breath and held it for a second, then let it out slowly and took a sip of her tea. It seemed to calm her down enough for her to at least switch to English.

"Sorry," she said sheepishly, looking up at me. "I just...
I thought he was dead. I never expected that you would go
and find him for me." She gulped down another anxious
breath, tears gathering in her eyes. "It seems... it seems
like a miracle. Or a dream."

"Well, it isn't a dream, that much I know for sure," I
said. "But moments like this are the fruition of *my* dream for
Tumanako. This is what we – ordinary people – can achieve
if we work together and share a common goal. This is why
we're all here, every single one of us. Humanity is capable of
creating so many miracles, if we just try hard enough."

"Speaking of which," Anahera said, suddenly fixing
me with an intense look. "You and I need to have a talk."

"Oh?" I replied, raising an eyebrow. "That sounds
somewhat ominous. Should I be afraid?"

"Possibly," she said. She rubbed Tala's back one last
time, then rose to her feet and looked at me. "Best if we do
this now, if you wouldn't mind. Elly can take care of Tala."

"Sure, okay," I agreed, shrugging. "Lead the way."

She nodded and did just that. After a few seconds, I
realised that Skye was following along as well, but neither
of them said anything. They just led me out the door and
down the hall to the storage rooms. Skye unlocked the
door, then locked it again once the three of us were inside.

"Whoa, I'm being cornered," I pointed out dryly,
looking back and forth between the two of them. "What's
going on, ladies?"

Anahera heaved a deep sigh and reached out to lay
her hand on my arm. "You're not going to like what we
have to say, but I think it's important that you hear us out
before you react."

"She's right," Skye said. "There's a chair over here; I think you might want to sit down."

"Just say whatever you're going to say and get on with it," I replied. "I'm a big girl. I can take it."

Anahera and Skye exchanged a look.

"If you insist," Anahera said. "Sandrine, we've noticed a few things that make us think that we might know something that you don't."

"Don't beat around the bush, Ana," Skye scolded. Suddenly, she reached out and poked me right in the tit. "You've gained a good five kilograms, and your boobs are bulging out of your bra. We think you might be pregnant."

Anahera shot her a filthy look. "There's honesty and then there's kindness, Skylar. We discussed this."

"Okay, fine!" Skye threw her hands up in annoyance. "Ana says that you've been 'glowing' and throwing up. Same conclusion: we think that you're pregnant."

I recovered from my shock just in time to muffle an inelegant snort of laughter with my hand. Both their expressions changed to confusion.

"Damn, I was hoping to keep it secret a little while longer," I admitted. "Yeah, I'm pregnant."

Anahera's brows shot up, and Skye's mouth fell open.

"You already knew?" Skye gasped. "And you didn't tell us? You didn't tell *me*?"

"Sorry, sis," I said. "You're not good at keeping secrets, and I didn't want Michael to find out until I was ready to tell him. You know, in case anything happens to the baby. He'd be devastated if anything happened to it."

"Ohh..." she breathed, understanding dawning on her face. "Yeah, that would be pretty rough on him. But—wait, what do you mean I'm not good at keeping secrets?"

I laughed and shook my head. "You're a gossip fiend, Skye. Face it. And the whole point of gossip is sharing juicy secrets. Right now, the only people who know are Doctor Cross, Maddy, and Gavin. Maddy knows because she's the one who told me, Doc knows because, well, I needed his help to make sure I get through this okay, and Gavin knows because I asked him to keep an eye on Michael in case he figures out something's going on." I paused and gave the two of them the hairy eyeball. "I guess I should have asked him to keep an eye on you two, as well."

"I don't think Michael suspects anything at this stage," Anahera said, her expression shifting from surprised to thoughtful. "But you won't be able to hide it from him for much longer. It's still early enough that a stranger wouldn't notice any changes, but we both know you intimately — as does he. His knowledge of female biology is somewhat lacking so he probably assumes the weight gain and missed periods are just because you were so malnourished when you met, but eventually he's going to start to wonder."

"Yeah, especially if you start lactating blood!" Skye said with a salacious gesture.

I shot her a horrified look. "*Blood*? That's not normal!"

"It is fairly normal, actually," Anahera said, a smile dancing across her lips. "Not pleasant, but normal. Don't worry about it too much."

"And this is the other reason I didn't tell you, Skye," I said, fighting a sudden wave of irrational annoyance. "You know how nervous I am about this. The last thing I need is to be told horror stories about bleeding nipples!"

"Hey!" She scowled at me, planting her hands on her hips. "It's not my fault that happened! Don't make me pull the 'pity me, I lost my baby' card again."

"Girls, stop," Anahera said, holding her hands up in a placating gesture. "Skylar, your sister is very anxious about this, and with good reason. Don't forget, she had to *watch* you lose your baby. That's almost as traumatizing as what you had to go through. You both need to calm down and try to see things from one another's perspectives. You're sisters, after all. What do sisters do?"

"They stand together, no matter what," Skye said grudgingly. She heaved a sigh, then looked at me. "Sorry. I didn't think."

I nodded and gave her a weak smile. "I know. My problem is that I think too much, and work myself into anxious knots. After what happened to you, and then hearing about what happened to Elly's baby... I've been trying not to think about it too much."

"What happened to Elly's baby?" Skye asked.

"Javed told me that Ommie originally had a twin sister," I explained, "but she was born infected. Doc says that isn't possible, but... I don't know, I still worry."

"Elly and I have spoken about it," Anahera said, touching my arm reassuringly. "The female twin was definitely not born infected. There was a complication with the birth, and only Ommie survived. The other baby lived for a few minutes, but there was something wrong with her lungs and she couldn't breathe. Neither Elly nor Zain had the tools or knowledge to save her."

"Oh, God," I whispered, an oddly mismatched flood of relief and distress pouring through me. "That's why she didn't cry? It was Javed's comment about her not crying that made me worry most. But if she didn't cry because she couldn't, because of her lungs... that's different. Poor Elly."

"The good doctor and I have discussed the topic at length," Anahera said, her expression turning thoughtful again. "I was worried, too. Tumanako cannot grow if we don't have children, after all. He's reassured me that the child is not at risk while she's being breastfed, only once she starts to wean."

I heaved a deep sigh and nodded. "At least that gives us a bit of leeway, but it makes finding that vaccine even more important. Most of the kids are old enough to be past the danger point, but we still have Evie and Tala's baby to worry about. Evie's got to be pushing six months old now. She's going to start weaning eventually, and after that it's up to us to protect her." I stood up straight and looked each of them in the eye in turn. "Tomorrow morning, we're going to go find the vaccine. One way or another."

Chapter Fourteen

Going after the vaccine felt like a big decision, but I still slept soundly after making it. That might have had something to do with the electric blanket that we'd found two days earlier, though. I'd forgotten the sheer bliss of climbing into a warm bed at the end of a long day, and sliding my legs between sheets that were almost – but not quite – hot enough to burn. It was wonderful, and it put me into such a coma that I slept late again.

Michael eventually woke up and started nibbling on my neck, and there was no way I could sleep through that. Not that I minded in the least; there were far worse ways to be woken up than by a handsome man in a playful mood. I rolled around in the circle of his arms, and swiftly discovered that his mood wasn't exactly *playful*, per se. It was something else entirely – and that something matched my mood exactly.

We made love languidly in the early morning gloom, enjoying the closeness shared only by two. When we were both satisfied, we lay back and stretched, talking quietly about nothing in particular until it was time to get up.

Michael was on the team I planned to take with me, of course. We'd been together for more than half a year now, and in that time he'd become absolutely integral to my world. He wasn't just my husband, but my best friend, my partner, my protector, my confidant, and my soul-mate. I don't know how I knew it, but I just did. Michael was the one that made me understand what the phrase 'The One' meant.

I glanced up in the middle of getting dressed and watched him opening the curtains we'd installed to keep our bedroom warm and private. Despite how I felt about him, I was still lying to him by omission about the one thing that had the potential to bring us closer together: our baby. I may have had a good reason in the beginning, but I was running out of excuses to avoid confronting the inevitable. I took a deep breath and let it out slowly, then looked back down at my gear. There was too much to be done to worry about it today. Once we had the vaccine, then I'd tell him.

"That was a big sigh," he pointed out. I felt his arms creep around my waist from behind, and his breath warm across the side of my neck. "What's the matter, sour-puss?"

"Nothing," I said, turning within the circle of his arms to give him a smile. "Everything's just perfect. That was a happy sigh."

"Really?" he said dryly, raising one eyebrow.

I just laughed and gave him a light shove. "Yes, really. Put your clothes on, nudist; we've got work to do."

"God, you're always complaining when I'm naked," he replied, throwing his hands up in mock despair. "Anyone would think you didn't like it. You don't see me complaining when *you're* naked, do you?"

"You're usually too busy to complain," I replied. I pulled away and gave him a slap on the bum. "Just for the record, I only complain about it when we're going out. Can't have you traumatising the children, now can we?"

"All right, all right, I'm getting dressed," he replied, grinning. He went over to the stack of clean clothing on the floor and fished out his gear, then plopped down on the edge of the bed. "I found a wardrobe in one of the houses that I want to lug up here. It'd be nice to get our stuff up off the floor."

"Sounds good," I said, sitting down beside him to pull on my socks and shoes. "I was thinking that it might be nice to drag a few of those big industrial-grade washing machines and dryers into the tower now that we've got power. I don't know about you, but I'm so sick of everything being damp."

"Oh yeah, it's making me crazy," he replied. "Add it to the to-do list, right?"

"You're starting to sound like me," I said. "Careful, or you'll turn into a sour-puss, too."

"You're not actually a sour-puss," he said, his tone and expression softening. "I was just teasing."

"I know, and I'm teasing back," I replied with a laugh and a nudge. "I thought you would have figured out my deadpan sense of humour by now."

"I don't think I'll ever figure out your deadpan sense of humour, honey," he replied, leaning down to plant a kiss on the top of my head. I grinned and hugged him, then we both turned our attention towards getting ready to leave.

*****

Within the hour, our chosen team was fed, ready, and sitting around a table in the dining room, talking quietly about what we had to do.

"It was up around here," Simon said, touching a point on the map spread out in front of us. "I'm not a hundred percent sure of the exact location on the map, but I can find it again once we're in the area. There's an unmarked building, surrounded by chain-link fences and barbed wire. I can't be sure, but it had the feel of a government facility about it."

"What makes you think that?" I asked.

"It was big," he replied. "Really big. Like, it went all the way back into the hills. But there were no signposts, no branding, no logos. If it had been a corporate facility, they would've had signs posted, right? But like I said, I didn't go inside so I don't know for sure. The flash drive was taped to the door in a plastic bag, with a piece of paper that had a short message written on it. It said 'Don't give up hope.' I picked the bag up and was looking at it when I spotted movement inside. I think it was just an infected, but... I was alone and pretty freaked out by that stage. I shoved the bag in my pocket and ran my ass back home as fast as I could."

"Well, now I'm not creeped out at all," I said dryly. "Thanks, Simon."

"You're so very welcome," he replied, grinning. "In retrospect, I think I made the right choice."

"You did."

The voice came from behind us, and by this stage of our journey I almost expected to hear it. Madeline came up to the table with a very serious look on her face, and climbed into my lap without being invited.

"What do you mean, Maddy?" I asked. I'd learned not to question the accuracy of her instincts, even if she wasn't always clear about her meaning.

"Mister Simon made the right choice by waiting," she replied, snuggling comfortably up against me. "He couldn't open the door. Not without me. That's why I'm here."

"You've lost me, kiddo," I admitted, putting my arms around her and giving her a hug. "Talk us through it from the beginning."

"I'm not sure," she admitted. "Sometimes the things I see don't always make sense. But I know that I have to be there or you won't be able to find the vaccine. You need to take me with you."

I shot a startled look at the others over top of her head. "Uh... have you told your granddaddy that you want to go yet? He's not going to like that."

"He doesn't have a choice," she replied, in a voice that sounded entirely too old to be coming out of such a small child. "We need that vaccine, and you need me to get it." She glanced up, and gave me an endearing smile. "Don't worry, Miss Sandy. I'll be fine. I'd know if something bad was going to happen to me."

"That's true," I agreed grudgingly. "Okay. Go tell your granddad. He's the one you need to convince, not me."

"Okay!" she agreed cheerfully. She gave me a quick hug, then wriggled out of my lap and ran off, leaving the rest of us staring after her with an assortment of different looks on our faces. Aaron was the first one to voice his concerns.

"That wee lass can't be more than six," he said. "Are we really going to take her with us?"

"She's almost eight, she's just a bit small for her age," I corrected him. "And... if she says that she needs to go with us, then we're better off just taking her with us than arguing about it. Maddy has a gift, and she hasn't been wrong yet."

"I've heard the stories, but I don't know what to believe," he admitted, absently rubbing his chin. "I just... I don't know. She's so young."

"When it comes to Madeline Cross, age is just a number," Michael said. "That little girl has saved us numerous times. If she says that she *needs* to come, then we're just wasting our time if we go without her. We'll end up having to come back and get her later on."

"If you say so," Aaron said doubtfully. "Okay, so we've got me in case anyone gets hurt, Simon to guide us, Sandrine for smarts, Michael for muscle, and Gavin because he knows a little bit about everything. Do we need anyone else?"

"You don't need us, but we'd like to come if you'd have us," said a voice from the doorway. I glanced back over my shoulder and saw Mary Ferguson, her father, and several other members of their group standing in the doorway.

I raised a brow and gave her a curious look. "You're not still trying to earn my forgiveness, are you? Because I already forgive you. You guys can stop leaving flowers on my doorstep now."

Mary laughed and shook her head. "Sorry, that was entirely my doing. I do still feel bad, but that wasn't why I left the flowers. I try to do something nice for one person every day, and these rooms are so bland and boring. They need a little colour to bring them to life."

I smiled in spite of what had happened a week earlier. That was a sentiment I understood. "Well, thank you anyway. They certainly have livened up the place. But, why do you guys want to come?"

Daniel stepped forward and rested a hand on his daughter's shoulder. "Word's gotten around about what you're going to look for, and one of these days I'm going to have grandkids to worry about. It's only right that we offer our assistance any way that we can."

Mary shot her father a dark look at the comment about grandkids, then she looked back at me and her expression relaxed again. "We also feel like it's our duty to help protect the Child Prophet. We were listening when she was here, and if she needs to go then we do, too. You've already forgiven us and we appreciate that, but we still feel like we have to earn God's forgiveness as well. Not just for what we almost did to you, but for... everything. Humanity's sins. We believe that the plague was His way of punishing us all for humanity's arrogance, but if there truly is a vaccine then we'll know that we've finally earned His forgiveness." She paused, and gave me a tiny smile. "It's important to us. Please let us come."

"Well, if it means that much to you..." I hesitated and glanced at the others. Michael nodded and smiled to me, while the others seemed fairly ambivalent on the matter. I looked back at Mary and Daniel, and nodded my approval. "Sure. Go get your travel clothes on and grab some rations from the kitchen. We'll be returning here by evening, so pack light. No need to bring overnight gear. If you need some wet weather gear, go see Skylar in the Quartermaster's office and she'll get you kitted out."

They nodded and departed. I turned back to the others, only to find Aaron obviously struggling to keep silent. I smiled at him and made a friendly gesture. "Out with it, then?"

He sighed and rolled his eyes heavenwards. "Look, I consider myself as open-minded as they come... but that bunch weird me out. Do we have to bring them with us?"

"Aren't you Irish Catholic?" I asked, equal parts amused and concerned by his protests.

"Officially, yeah," he said. "But you don't see me ambushing ladies in the women's room, now do you? There's something very peculiar about that lot, and I don't much care for it. I cannot fathom why you let them stay here after what they did."

"Everyone makes mistakes," I replied. "What they did was a genuine misunderstanding. They thought they were doing what was best for everyone by protecting you from a false prophet. There was no real malice or hatred behind it. It wouldn't be right for me to evict them for their beliefs."

Michael lay a hand on my shoulder, picking up the thought where I left off. "Tumanako was always supposed to be a place of acceptance, where everyone is welcome regardless of race or creed. That's what Sandy preached to us in the beginning, and that's what we want to live by now. We know it isn't always easy for different people to live in harmony – there have been enough wars to prove that – but there are so few of us now that we have to try."

"He's right," Gavin said. "You remember what it was like before the plague? All the fear and hatred directed towards anyone who had different bodies or beliefs? Catholics and Protestants, Muslims, Jews, atheists... it didn't matter how innocent you were, there was always someone who hated you. Well, you're Christian, I'm atheist, Michael's a Buddhist, and guess what? We're all good people. The Yousefi family are Muslim, and contrary to what pre-plague society would have believed, they aren't terrorists. Hell, they're some of the best people I know. You heard the story about how they came to join us, right?"

"I haven't," Simon said, looking back and forth between us curiously. "What happened?"

"They gave Skye and Doc concussions and set our house on fire," Michael said, grinning. "We nearly lost everything!"

Aaron's eyes bulged, and Simon's jaw fell open. Before either of them could say anything, I jumped in to finish the story.

"But the point is, we gave them a chance to explain themselves," I said. "It turned out that they were starving, had four kids to feed, and there was a misunderstanding. Everything that happened was an accident."

Gavin nodded and picked up his thought where he'd left off. "If they'd chased the Yousefi family away, not only would there be six more dead people in the world, but we'd have missed out on the opportunity to learn what good friends they can be. My point being, we shouldn't judge people based on what we *think* we know about them without giving them a chance to show us the truth."

I gave Gavin a quizzical look and a grin. "You've been thinking about this a lot."

"I have," he admitted. "I've been spending a lot of time with the engineering crew, including Zain. He told me the story, and how guilty he felt about it in retrospect. It made me realise why you've been trying so hard to be forgiving, even when I know that your first instinct is to push people away to protect yourself from getting hurt. You're trying to lead by example."

I felt a rush of heat in my cheeks and glanced down, suddenly embarrassed. "Everyone deserves a second chance. That's the other thing Tumanako was meant to be: a second chance for all of us. I wish that I could say I lived without regrets, but that would be a lie. I've had to take lives, or have lives taken to protect my own, and I still think about them all the time. I don't want anyone else to have to live with that kind of darkness weighing on their soul."

Michael squeezed my hand, and everyone else fell silent around the table. Everyone except Simon, who looked at me.

"You know, you should write it down," he said.

"Write what down?" I asked, raising a brow. "The darkness weighing on my soul?"

"No, just... your story," he replied, shaking his head. "Everyone should, if they can. One day, people are going to look back on what we're doing here as history. Wouldn't it be better to tell them your story in your own words, rather than have it passed down by goodness knows however many generations of storytellers around the campfire?"

I had to stop and think about that, turning the idea over in my head until I could make sense of it. Suddenly, the pieces clicked into place, and I sat back in my chair.

"You're right," I said. "I mean, what if some kid is looking back on this day in a thousand years, and trying to write a report about us for school? Everyone's voice is a thread in the tapestry that made this happen, and the best way for our voices to be remembered is through our own words. What better way for us to immortalize our families, and those who were lost to the plague? Simon, that's a brilliant idea. Why didn't I think of that?"

"Disseminating information is kind of my business," he answered dryly. "I'll do it if you do it."

"You're on," I agreed, then I looked at Michael and the others. "What about you guys? Michael? Gavin? Aaron?"

"Sure, why not?" Aaron said with a shrug. "If I can find the time, I'll write something."

Michael nodded thoughtfully. "Our stories are pretty closely intertwined since Hamilton, but it's always good to have two different perspectives on the same events."

"I'll... think about it," said Gavin. I glanced at Gavin, but he wouldn't meet my eye. "There are some parts I'd rather not remember."

"I know," I replied, reaching out to touch his scarred hand. "I know better than anyone. Think about it, and take as much time as you need."

Gavin started to reply, but before he could we were interrupted by a commotion in the hall. The door burst open and Skylar dashed inside, her face alight with excitement.

"Sandy!" she cried when she saw me. "Oh thank goodness, you haven't left yet. I was just talking to Mary and she had the *best* idea. You're going to love it!"

"Wait, back up," I replied, holding my hands up to stall her. "The best idea for what?"

"For a memorial to all the people who died in the plague," she replied. She grabbed my hand and pulled me out of my chair, dragging me over to the big, whitewashed wall that ran along one side of the room. "A photo mural, right here. There are photographs everywhere, right? You see them all the time. Magazines, newspapers, even albums in people's houses. So we gather them all up, and we cover this whole wall with them. The whole wall!"

"With pictures of random strangers?" I asked, bewildered. "What good would that do?"

"But they're not just random strangers," she said enthusiastically, struggling to illustrate the idea with broad gestures. "They're *people*. They're our history. Our ancestors. We collect and preserve the photographs, so that we can remember what the world looked like back then. Mary just told me that historians used to look back on Ancient Greece and make guesses about what things looked like based off their art, but if we collect photos then people in the future won't have to make any guesses because they'll just be able to look at the pictures."

"That... actually, that makes a lot of sense," I replied. "Clever. Okay, you're in charge of the project, so organise it as you see fit. We were also just talking about having people write down their personal stories for pretty much the same reason. Can you get hold of a bunch of notebooks and writing instruments?"

"Will do," she said. "There's a big stationery cupboard that we haven't even started to inventory yet, or failing that I'm sure there's a supply store nearby. I'll take care of everything." She paused and glanced around the table, then grinned. "You guys just focus on the vaccine."

"You got it," I replied. I glanced out the window, then looked back at my group. "We better go find Maddy and see what's going on. Looks like the rain's only going to get heavier the longer we wait."

The others nodded and rose. We gathered up our backpacks and left the cafeteria. Michael took the rest of the group downstairs to get our transport ready, while I went off in search of Doc. I found him in his office, a small room off the infirmary, hunched over a book. He didn't notice me at first, which gave me the chance to get close enough to spy on what he was reading.

"Herbal medicine, Doc?" I asked, surprised. "Are our medical supplies running that low?"

He almost jumped out of his skin, then shot a glare over his shoulder at me. "Yes, we are — as your current condition illustrates. I need to work out an alternative, and soon. I can make some things from scratch but not everything. Speaking of which – you need to tell Michael soon. You're beginning to show."

"I'm well aware, don't worry," I replied, glancing back over my shoulder. Tala and Franco were sleeping side by side in the infirmary, but none of the nurses were around. "Skye and Anahera cornered me last night and tried to give me 'the talk', so now they know. I'm planning to tell him tonight, once we get home."

"Not a moment too soon," he replied. "I'm getting tired of tiptoeing around the subject."

"*You're* getting tired of it?" I echoed, laughing. "How do you think I feel? I have to suck my tummy in whenever he's around. At this rate, my baby bump's going to pop out of my back!"

To my surprise, Doc laughed right along with me. "Now, that would be something I don't know how to fix, so you'd best stop sucking it in. However, I do think you made the right choice by not to telling him until you were past the danger zone. I'm surprised you've gotten this far, all things considered."

"What can I say?" I shrugged and grinned at him. "I'm stubborn. Michael's stubborn. Stubbornness is an inherited trait, apparently. I predict tantrums aplenty in this stubborn baby's future. Oh, and speaking of stubborn – did Maddy come and talk to you?"

"Yes, she did," he replied, his smile fading. "I expect you to take care of her, Ms McDermott. She's the only family I've got left."

I lifted my eyebrows, surprised. "You gave her permission to come along?"

"I did," he said quietly. "I don't like it, but... I've come to accept that Madeline's gift is outside my field of expertise. If she needs to go, then she needs to go. I know that I can trust you and Michael to protect her as if she were your own daughter. I sent her off to get her raincoat and boots. She should be back any minute."

Right on cue, the door opened and Maddy scampered in, all wrapped up in her favourite pink raincoat. She skidded to a stop and grinned up at me. "Hi! Granddaddy said I can go, so let's go."

"Did you go and get some lunch?" I asked.

She nodded enthusiastically. "Yup! I'm ready."

"One more thing," Doc said, reaching out to touch my arm. "Once you've told Michael, please bring him by to see me. I'd like to compile as much information on potential problems as possible. Plus, I need to weigh you again to make sure you're gaining enough weight. I'm somewhat concerned that you're still underweight, but we'll find out."

"Will do, Doc," I replied, sketching a salute. Then I offered my hand to Maddy, and led the little girl out into the hall.

"Mister Michael is going to be happy," she whispered as she skipped along beside me. "He wants a baby very much."

"I know," I replied. "Every time I see him cuddling Evelyn and casting furtive glances at me, I want to tell him. I can't hide it much longer."

"It's okay," Maddy said, suddenly turning solemn. "It's almost time to tell him. You'll know when." We rounded a corner into the little alley leading to the elevators, and her seriousness vanished in a flash of youthful exuberance. "Oh! Oh! Can I push the button? Please?"

I couldn't help but laugh at how swiftly she went from stone-faced adult to bouncy child. "Sure. Push the button."

"Yay!" she cheered, and raced over to do just that.

A few minutes later, we headed out the door, and found the rest of the group waiting for us. I bundled Madeline into the back of the Hilux, then I took Boudicca's reins from Michael and vaulted up into the saddle.

"Everyone ready?" I asked, glancing at him.

He nodded and smiled. "We were just waiting on you two, now we're good to go whenever you are."

"Good," I said. I paused to do a quick mental headcount, then I nodded and led the way out into the gloomy streets.

Chapter Fifteen

We travelled east as far as we could go, then turned south and followed the old train tracks through the outer suburbs of Lower Hutt. Even after ten years, even in the middle of a spring rainstorm, it was beautiful country. The houses were run down and overgrown, but they still looked cosy and warm. I found myself looking at them with sadness and longing. Perhaps one day I could have a real home for my family. Maybe we'd be able to raise our baby there.

It was a pointless dream for the moment, though. Until we knew we were safe from the mutated infected, we couldn't leave the safety of Tumanako's walls. But at least now I could hope and dream, and there was a chance that the dream might come true.

A few kilometres before we would have reached the northern shoreline of Wellington Harbour we swung east again, into the industrial zone that lined the inside of the hills. Pretty houses and wild gardens gave way to huge, sprawling factories and the rusted hulks of cars and trucks.

Suddenly, the radio in my pocket crackled to life and I head Simon calling my name. I unbuttoned my coat and pulled the walkie-talkie out. "I'm here. Which way?"

"Left at this roundabout, then keep an eye out to your right," he replied. "You'll see a long driveway going up into the hills."

"Gotcha," I said. I clicked the radio off and tucked it away.

"One of these days, we really need to teach him to ride," Michael commented dryly.

I laughed and nodded. "Sometimes I think he doesn't want to learn, so he doesn't have to get wet."

"Damn!" Michael swore. "Why didn't I think of that?"

"Because you knew I wouldn't let you get away with it," I replied. I was about to make another joke when we rounded a corner, and I spotted our destination. "There! That must be the driveway he was talking about."

"Huh. That's an awfully big fence," Michael said, studying the edge of the property. The fence line was hemmed by a thick layer of bushes and small trees, but beyond it we could see the moss-covered rooflines of a sprawling complex of buildings outlined against the darker green of the hills.

"Hm. No signs, just like he said," I commented. I pulled out my GPS and checked it, then glanced at him. "The maps say it was an industrial research facility, but it's also flagged as permanently closed. Which means it was closed *before* the plague."

"Suspicious and fascinating at the same time," he said.

I nodded my agreement and led the way up the driveway towards those distant buildings. The gate still hung open from Simon's previous visit, but there was no sign of life aside from the birds singing in the trees all around us. I ducked beneath a low-hanging branch and brought my horse to a stop outside the front door.

"This is pretty creepy," I admitted. "No wonder Simon ran off when he was here by himself. I would have, too."

"Says the lady who risked a mutant-infested hospital at midnight because her foot hurt," he said dryly.

I shot him a dark look. "I didn't have a choice. Besides, if I hadn't done that you wouldn't have a wife."

"Touché," he said, and let the topic drop.

We both dismounted and tied our horses to a rusted bike stand in front of the building, then waited while the other riders did likewise and Simon parked the Hilux. Once we were all assembled in front of the building, I took a long look around. "It really does look like a government facility, doesn't it? I don't see a single sign except for that fire exit over there. Weird. Why would they build something way out here?"

"It makes sense, when you think about it," Gavin said. "We're fairly close to Wellington, but it's also far enough away from the capital that it wouldn't be a target if we were attacked by a foreign power. It's within driving distance of the suburbs so the workers could go home at night, but also far enough out of town that you wouldn't have civvies walking past all day."

"He says it's bigger on the inside," Madeline said dreamily. "The facility goes way back into the hills, and deep underground." She paused and glanced at me quizzically. "What's a facility?"

I stumbled over the answer, still struggling to make sense of her words. "It's just a general word for a place or tool that serves a purpose. Who is 'he', Maddy?"

"The big boy," she said, looking at me like I was crazy. "He went inside. He says we'll need his key, so we should follow him."

"The... big boy?" I echoed. I tried to keep my voice casual, but suddenly I found all the hairs on the back of my neck were standing up. "I don't see anything so I'm going to have to trust you on that, kiddo. Can you show us where the big boy went?"

"Of course," she replied. She took my hand and led me into the building. The others fell in behind us, weapons at the ready. The interior of the building was dark, and when I tried a light switch I discovered that the power was off.

"We should have brought a portable generator with us," I said over my shoulder.

"We can always go back and get one," Michael replied. "It's not that far."

"No need," Maddy said in that same dreamy voice. She was very nearly in a trance, I realised suddenly. Her movements were jerky, and her eyes weren't entirely focused. She raised a hand and pointed down a long corridor. "There's a backup generator down there somewhere. He's never been there, but he saw the signs."

"I'll go take a look," Gavin volunteered. "It would help if we could see properly."

"Good," I replied. "Take David, Simon, and Mary with you for backup."

Gavin pulled out a torch, and they vanished into the gloom. The rest of us pulled out our torches and resumed following Madeline. At the first junction, she turned right and led us down another long corridor without even stopping to orientate herself. This one was faintly lit by the odd cracked, filthy skylight, but it wasn't bright enough for me to put my torch away.

Each doorway that we passed was a dark, hollow recess, like a missing tooth in the grim smile of whitewashed concrete walls. I swung my torch into each one as we passed by, and saw offices, laboratories, and even a break room or two. We travelled for nearly five minutes, working our way deeper and deeper into the facility.

Eventually I realised that there were no more skylights above us, and we were probably under the hills.

"In there," Maddy whispered, her voice disembodied in the gloom. I swung my torch towards her and saw her pointing to an office coming up on our right.

I took a deep breath, nodded, and released her hand. "Stay here, honey. I'll go in. Where am I looking?"

"It's around his neck," she whispered. Suddenly, she turned and looked up at me, squinting against the glare of my torch. "Don't kill him, though. If you kill him, he'll will go away. We still need him."

My gorge rose, and I had to force myself to swallow hard to keep my lunch down. "He's infected?"

"Yes, and he's in there," she said, pointing at the doorway again. "We need his key—"

"I know. I'm going," I replied, steeling myself to what I had to do. I shifted my shotgun off my shoulder into a position where I could grab it if I needed it, and walked up to the doorway. A metallic sign glinted in the beam of my torch, which told me that the office had belonged to someone named C. Russell. Someone had taped a bright yellow Post-It note beside the plaque, with a smiley face and the letters 'PhD' written in pencil. I could smell the infected before I opened the door; the stench of decay was one that I was all too familiar with. With one last deep breath of the relatively clean air outside the office, I shoved the door open and stepped inside.

The skinny geneticist's body was familiar even in undeath. He was still wearing the same lab coat that had been a permanent fixture of his videos, though now his glasses were missing. I found them quite by accident, when I heard something crunch under my foot. I glanced down and flinched. "Damn. Sorry, Clyde."

There was no response. Clyde's infected body was just sitting in its chair, randomly poking at the blood-splattered keyboard of a computer that hadn't functioned in years. I cringed when I realised that it had quite literally worked its fingers to the bone, presumably typing away at a dissertation that no longer mattered. It was a heart-wrenching, miserable sight, but Maddy had been clear about what I needed to do. I inched closer and reached out to grab the lanyard around Clyde's neck. On the end of it was a small plastic card, which I assumed had to be the key Maddy had mentioned.

The infected didn't move, didn't look at me, didn't notice me at all. A second later, I was back out in the hallway, clutching my rancid prize and struggling not to throw up. I must have been pale as a ghost, because Michael took one look at me, then he grabbed the lanyard out of my hand, tossed it to Aaron, and pulled me into a hug. I clung to him and buried my face in his chest, drawing long, deep breaths of his scent to get the stink of death out of my nostrils.

After a few seconds, I pulled back and nodded my appreciation. "It's okay. I'm all right. It's just, he's..." I hesitated, uncertain how to express my feelings. In the end, I gave up and shook my head. "We'll be back, to put him to rest once we have what we need."

"It's okay, Miss Sandy," Maddy said, taking my hand again. "He can't feel pain anymore. He says that he's tethered to his body, but it doesn't hurt."

I shuddered and squeezed the little girl's hand. "I always wondered whether the infected could move on, or if they were stuck here. How many... how many people do you see trapped like that, Maddy?"

She glanced around then looked back at me and shrugged. "Only a few in here, but outside there are lots."

"Do they all talk to you?" I asked, fighting a rising wave of horror. What she was describing was my worst fear for the victims of the plague: that they wouldn't be able to rest while their bodies still walked the earth.

"No," she said, shaking her head. "Most of them aren't really there. They're sort of going away on their own, but it's taking a long time. But when you kill them, then they're free. They go away really fast. Not like, whoosh!" She made a gesture to illustrate her noise. "But quieter. They slowly turn see-through. What's the word?"

"Fade?" I suggested.

"Yes!" she exclaimed. "They fade until they're all gone. But they look happier."

"What about Clyde?" I asked. "I mean, I understand why you saw Netty's ghost, she'd only just died. But why is Clyde still here?"

Maddy glanced away, and tilted her head as though listening to a voice that only she could hear. "He says... he says that he's tried to go away, but something stopped him. Every time he started to go, he was pulled back. He says that he had to wait for us to get here. He doesn't know what pulled him back, he just knows that he's not allowed to leave until we're finished."

I took a second to digest what she was telling me, then I nodded. "So what do we do next?"

"We should go find the others," Maddy told me. "We need power to make the elevator work."

"Okay," I agreed, nodding. "Let's go get the power working, then."

We made it halfway back to the junction where we'd gone our separate ways when our radios crackled.

"We've got it," Gavin said. "We found the generator, and it's just powering up. We should start seeing electricity in a few seconds."

The fluorescent bulbs on the ceiling began to flicker to life. I turned to the others and started to say something, but whatever I'd been thinking was forgotten when a bulb a couple of meters in front of us exploded. I yelped and jumped back, pulling Maddy up against me to shield her from the falling glass. Once the socket shorted itself out, I looked at the others. "Everyone okay? Anyone hurt?"

"Aside from a minor heart attack?" Michael asked dryly. "Yeah, just peachy. But hey, at least we can see now."

"What, you weren't enjoying wandering around a pitch black research lab full of zombies?" Aaron quipped. "I'm pretty sure I used to play this game when I was a teenager, but those zombies were a lot more... bitey."

We all laughed, though the laughter was a little strained. We hurried the rest of the way back to the intersection and waited until Gavin's group returned, then took a moment to catch our breath and relay the events of the last few minutes to one another. Once we were done, we all looked at Maddy for further instructions.

"We need to go down," she said matter-of-factly. "Follow me, I know where to go. This way!"

We exchanged glances, but before any of us could say anything Madeline marched off, heading back into the heart of the hills. We all fell in behind and beside her, silently following her through the passageways.

Suddenly, she stopped and pointed. "There, that's it."

"That's a strange-looking elevator," Simon said, frowning. "It almost looks like a freight elevator."

"It was supposed to keep the virus out," Maddy told us solemnly. "But it didn't work."

"Is it safe for us to be going in there?" I asked, suddenly but justifiably nervous. The plague had robbed all of us of our families, so we were entitled to be wary of disease.

"Of course," she said. "We're immune, silly."

"Well, that makes sense," I replied. "Stupid question, I guess."

"It's okay, Miss Sandy." She smiled at me, then she went over to the elevator and pressed the call button. A few seconds later, the doors slid open and she led us inside. Once we were all in, I glanced at the control panel and saw that there was only one choice aside from the floor we were on, but beside it was a security lock and a keypad.

"We have a problem," I said. "Looks like we need a number as well as the key card."

"I know the number," Maddy said. "I'll unlock it, so we can go up and down without the card or the number. He said he'd show me how."

She took the key card, swiped it through the security lock, then punched in a long string of numbers. I glanced at the others, uncertain what to make of Maddy's assertion, but as usual she proved to know far more than she should have. The doors swept shut, and we felt the telltale sensation of descending into the earth.

Aaron made a surprised sound and looked at me. "I'm starting to feel like a fool for doubting her."

I just nodded and said nothing. A few seconds later, the doors swished open with a gust of stale, malodorous air. I shifted my shotgun around into the offensive position, and carefully led the way out into the room beyond. The lights were dim and flickering, and I saw broken glass from other bulbs that hadn't survived the shock of being re-ignited when the generator came back on, but there was enough light that I wasn't forced to rely on my torch.

The lobby we arrived in had obviously been used as a decontamination area, with a heavy door on the other side that probably would have been air-tight if it hadn't been hanging wide open. Biohazard suits hung on hooks on the walls, beside high-pressure showers and coiled hoses that had clearly done no good.

"He was the last one alive," Maddy said softly. "When he got sick, he decided that he wasn't going to die alone in the dark, so he put all his videos onto a... memory thing, and taped it to the door. Then he went outside to enjoy the sun while he could."

I shuddered and swallowed a lungful of stagnant air, trying to ignore the familiar stench of decomposition. "Ugh, it smells rancid in here. From what I saw in the video, they were down here for weeks. Surely there must have been some kind of ventilation system, right?"

"There is one," Gavin said, pointing upwards. I followed his finger and saw a small air vent on the ceiling above our heads. "it's definitely working, I can feel a breeze. It would have gone off when the power died, so it'll probably just take a little while to get going."

"Why is there a vent in the decontamination room?" Simon asked. "They wouldn't have had time to build this just to deal with Ebola X, so it must have been built as a general-purpose facility. Why weren't they thinking about airborne pathogens?"

"They were," Aaron said. "If they went to the effort to build a facility like this for biological research, then there will be at least two separate filtration and recycling systems, probably more. One for out here, a second for inside the facility, and one for each isolated ward. You don't spare any expense on that kind of thing."

"So how did the pathogen get to them?" I asked, glancing back and forth between them. "That door is an airlock, and Clyde said that they were on recycled air and water, and the food was all sterilized. How did they die?"

Without quite meaning to, I looked at Maddy for an answer. She looked back at me, but something about her expression was... wrong. I knew before she spoke that something had changed, and it had all the hairs on the back of my neck standing on end again.

"I never did find out," she said. "Someone must have dropped a culture dish, or not quite sterilized something enough. It's too late to find out now, and I guess it doesn't really matter anymore. Not for us, anyway."

By the time she finished speaking, everyone was staring at her with wide eyes. The voice wasn't Madeline's. Well, it was but it wasn't at the same time. I couldn't explain how I knew, but I just knew. I could feel it in my bones.

"Clyde?" I whispered.

Maddy gave me a lopsided smile and nodded. "She thought it would be easier if we could talk directly. I gotta tell you, it feels pretty weird. I'm not sure how long I'll be able to stay in here."

I glanced at the others, and saw each one of them looking as disturbed as I felt. A couple of the more religiously-orientated members crossed themselves or made other signs to ward off evil. Maddy – Clyde – Madelyde ignored them. She turned and walked away, beckoning for us to follow her.

"I guess my message made it, then?" she asked, pausing in the doorway to make sure that I was following her. I hesitated for a second, then hurried to catch up with her. Behind me, I heard Michael setting a watch near the entrance in case anything happened to us, and I was silently grateful to him for it. The others waited with him to be given instructions, with the exception of Simon; he was way too curious by nature to wait behind when there was an answer to his questions close at hand.

"Sort of," I replied. "We got part of the message, but half of it was too degraded for us to open. The last thing we got was something about him – I mean, you – giving up on finding a cure and focusing on a vaccine made from the blood of the immune."

"Yeah!" she exclaimed. "Pretty awesome, right? I know, I'm just that good. Man, it would have made such a great topic for my dissertation, if not for... well, you know."

"Yeah, we know," I said. "How does it work, then?"

"Well, the main reason that Ebola X was so devastating is because it causes irreparable damage before our bodies have a chance to learn how to fight it," she replied, folding her hands behind her back as she walked. "The only reason that you're immune and I'm not is because your body can produce antibodies straight away. Why? We don't know, it just sort of happened. Evolution, I guess."

"Then why the zombies?" I asked. It was a question that had been bothering me for ten years, and now was the first opportunity I'd had to ask from someone that might actually know the answer.

"Oh, that's a weird one," he replied. "The virus targets the cerebellum – the upper brain, if you like. It's responsible for thought, speech, dreams, the senses, you name it. All the higher brain function. The brainstem is responsible for movement, and the virus pretty much ignores it. I guess it's too... I don't know, chewy or something. Om nom nom, tasty soft higher brain meat, icky brain stem meat."

"Ugh, Clyde, you're in a seven-year-old's body," I protested. "I didn't need that visual."

"Yeah, I know, it's weird being this close to the floor," he replied with entirely too much cheer for a dead person possessing a child's body. "Anyway, you've heard the term 'brain death', I presume. Cerebral death and brain stem death are two totally different things. Under normal circumstances, a person with a dead cerebellum goes into something called a permanent vegetative state. You know, when the lights are on but nobody's home?"

"Yeah, but these people aren't vegetables," Simon pointed out. "They're zombies."

"Well, that's about as far as my research went, so I can't tell you exactly what's going on," she admitted with a shrug. "I went into a persistent zombietative state about sixty days after the outbreak. How long has it been?"

"Uh, ten years," I replied, suddenly fighting the unreasonable urge to laugh. The kid had a sense of humour that I could appreciate, even if it was a little morbid. "Closer to eleven now, I guess."

"Oh wow," she gasped. "And you're only just finding my research now? Damn. That does change things." She paused for a second, and seemed to be listening to a voice that only she could hear. "The power's been off? Okay. My samples of the vaccine are not going to be viable anymore, so you'll need to create your own. I'll give you all my research. If you can find someone that knows anything about pharmacology, they should be able to replicate the vaccine from that."

I breathed a sigh of relief and nodded. "We have a trained pharmacist, I'm glad to say. However, we don't have access to a lot of chemicals."

"That's fine, he or she should be able to get a little creative with the ingredients and it'll still work," she replied. "Like I was saying before we got distracted, the biggest problem with Ebola X is that it does permanent damage before our immune systems can figure out how to produce antibodies to fight it off. So, we do this as a two-step process. The first thing we do is something called immunoglobulin therapy. That's where we take your plasma – that's the clear goop that your red and white blood cells float in – and inject it into the non-immune person. That gives them a boost of your antibodies to protect them while you move on to the second phase. Then while the live antibodies are still circulating, we inject them with a vaccine made from the dead virus. What that does is expose their immune system to the virus without actually infecting them, so their body has a chance to figure the virus out. Their body should learn to produce the antibodies on their own."

"Should?" I repeated, shooting a nervous glance at her. "These are our kids we're talking about. 'Should' isn't really good enough."

"There's no way to be sure until we've had a chance to test it," she replied. "No science is ever a hundred percent guaranteed. Nothing is perfect. But we're only going to use dead viruses, so at least the subject can't get infected from that. The worst that can happen is that their immune system won't kick in, in which case you give them a booster shot of the immunoglobulin and keep trying."

The look on my face must have been pretty intense; I felt Simon touch my arm to comfort me. I took a deep breath and nodded, burying my fear through sheer force of will. Even if there was a small chance that my baby might not be born immune, this still gave us a way to save her. She might have to be on regular injections for the rest of her life, that was still a life. That was more of a chance than so many of us had before.

Madelyde rounded a corner, and entered a small laboratory, one of the many in the sprawling underground labyrinth. She looked around for a second, then went over to a desk and sat down – or tried to, but she wasn't quite tall enough to reach the chair.

"Man, I used to be six-four. Now I feel short," she said, shooting a look at me. "Lift me up?"

I obliged. Once she was settled, she pushed the power button on the computer, and we waited several painful minutes to see if it would boot. While we were waiting, Gavin stuck his head through the doorway.

"It's not going to start," he said. "The CMOS battery will be long dead." He looked at me and raised an eyebrow. "Did I teach you nothing, young padawan?"

I laughed and shrugged. "We never talked about computers, old man. You just taught me important survival stuff, remember?"

"Oh, right." He grinned and winked, though it looked a little odd with his milky eye. "Anyway, I can take care of this. Unplug the machine and we'll take it back with us."

"Sounds good," I agreed, then I looked at Madelyde. "Is there anything else we should take?"

"Um..." she looked around thoughtfully, then pointed at a small stack of notebooks on a bookshelf nearby. "Those. You probably won't need them, but take them anyway. Those are all my hand-written lab notes. And you should probably take the network server, too. It'll have backups of everyone else's research on it."

I nodded and gestured to her. "Okay. I'm feeling a bit light-headed and need to sit down for a minute. Can you please show Gavin where it is?"

"Sure," Madelyde agreed. She jumped out of her chair and scampered off, with Gavin right behind her.

Once they were gone, I took another long, deep breath and sat down in the chair that she'd just vacated. Whether it was the hormones, the excitement, or just the unfamiliar chill of air conditioning, I wasn't feeling my best. Simon put his hand on my shoulder, and looked at me in obvious concern.

"You okay, Sandrine?" he asked gently. "Can I get you some water or something?"

"No, no, I'm fine," I said, shaking my head. "I just need to sit for a second."

He nodded understandingly, then he pulled another chair over and sat down beside me. "Well, I've been wanting a second to talk to you alone, anyway. No time like the present, I guess."

"Oh?" I looked at him and raised a brow. "Is something wrong?"

"No," he said, smiling. He reached over and took my hand, then looked me in the eye. "There's something I've been wanting to say to you since the moment we met, but I wasn't sure if you felt the same way. I think I've finally figured it out."

I just looked at him, bewildered.

"I've been alone for so long," he admitted, running his thumb across the back of my hand. It was a gesture that was tender and intimate, and it immediately set off warning bells in the back of my head – but not soon enough. Before I quite realised what was happening, he leaned in and kissed me.

I froze, shocked by the totally unexpected gesture of affection. Sure, I'd had a crush on him for years, but I'd never, ever imagined that the attraction would be mutual. I was stunned, so stunned that it took a few seconds before the part of me that was totally in love with Michael screeched like a horrified banshee. All of a sudden my body was back under my control, and it was not impressed. I shoved Simon away and leapt to my feet, glaring at him. "What the hell?! I'm a married woman, Simon!"

His eyes flew wide, and a look of absolute horror crossed his face. "But... I thought you were flirting with me! You've been giving me all of the signals! I thought you wanted a threesome relationship, like your sister has. I—"

"No!" I cried, covering my face with my hands. "No, no, no! I wasn't flirting, I was just being nice! I'm nice to everyone!"

"Oh, God, I'm so sorry!" he gasped, slumping forward and burying his face in his hands. "I misunderstood. I thought—"

Suddenly, Aaron raced into the room. "Sandy! What's going on?"

I nearly jumped out of my skin. "What? Nothing! Nothing's going on!"

"Well, something must be going on," he replied, "because Michael went off looking for you a minute ago, then he came tearing back through the lobby looking bloody furious. I've never seen him that angry. He went right up the elevator without a word to any of us. Did you two have a fight or something?"

"Oh, no," I gasped. "He must have seen... Oh no, no, no."

I didn't even try to explain. I just brushed past Aaron and ran off, racing back towards the elevator. There, I found the rest of our party standing around looking bewildered. Mary waved and called out to me, but I couldn't hear her. The only thing on my mind was Michael... and saving my short-lived marriage from a misunderstanding of epic proportions. The elevator pinged open a second later; Maddy had left it unlocked, just as she'd promised. I pushed the button for the ground floor, and then slammed my hand against the button to close the doors and kept pushing it frantically as if that would somehow make it work better. It didn't, but at least it gave me something to do with my hands.

Thirty seconds later, I was back on the ground floor of the research facility, my heart hammering in my chest.

"Michael!" I cried, cupping my hands around my mouth. "Please, it's not what it looked like!"

There was no answer. Tears gathered in my eyes, blurring my vision. I could survive a plague, fight a mutant, and wrestle a goddamn undead pig if I needed to, but the thought of living without Michael was more than I could bear. I took off running, with no idea where I was going or how I'd find him. The logical guess was that he was running away from what he'd seen, which meant that he was probably heading back towards the horses.

My head swam and tears ran down my cheeks, making it harder and harder to see where I was going. I rounded a corner too fast, slipped, and slid into a wall, only to bounce back off again and keep running without falling. By the time I burst out of the front door, I was a mess. I felt it, and I really must have looked it.

All the horses were exactly where we'd left them. I was still staring at them, struggling to make sense of what I was seeing, when a voice spoke from the shadows of the eaves a few meters to my left.

"I trusted you," Michael said softly. I jumped in surprise and looked at him; he was sitting on the ground with his back against the wall, arms wrapped around his legs, his face set in an unreadable mask.

"Michael," I whispered. I hurried to his side and knelt down beside him, but when I tried to take his hand he pulled it away.

"I don't even know how to be mad at you," he said in a tone that wasn't angry so much as bewildered. "I never thought that I'd have to be. Why would you do this?"

"I didn't, honey," I replied, shaking my head. "I swear to you, I'd never betray you. You're the only man I've ever truly loved. I'd never throw that love away."

"I saw you kissing Simon," he replied, his tone harsh and accusative for the span of the sentence, and then it turned soft again. "How is that not what it looks like?"

"Because that was a stupid misunderstanding," I replied, reaching for his hand again. This time, he let me take it. I pressed a kiss to his knuckles, then looked him in the eye. "Simon thought that I'd been flirting with him, and that I wanted to have a three-way relationship with him and you."

A flicker of understanding passed through his dark eyes. "He... what? You've told me again and again that you're afraid of that kind of relationship."

"I am," I replied with a shrug. "But I guess we're not close enough for him to know that. I've never deliberately flirted with him or anyone else, except for you – and you know how bad I am at flirting."

"You're not that bad," he replied, a faint smile tugging the corner of his lips. "Is he going to be sporting a hell of a shiner tomorrow?"

"Nah, I reserve my love-taps for you," I replied, as light-heartedly as I could in the moment. "But... seriously though, he caught me completely by surprise. I just froze. I've gotten out of the habit of automatically punching anyone who tries to touch me, you know? And I do like Simon, just... not like that. I couldn't be like that with anyone but you. You're the only one to earn the privilege."

Michael took a deep breath, and I could see him visibly relaxing. "I should have known better than to assume the worst."

"I can't blame you for doing so," I replied. "I mean, it must have looked pretty bad. But... honey, there's something I need to tell you. I've been putting it off for a while now because I wanted to make sure that it wasn't going to break your heart. I was going to tell you tonight, but I think if I tell you now it'll help you understand how I feel about you."

"Break my heart?" he echoed, confusion crossing his face. "What are you talking about, Sandy?"

"I'm talking about this, you big doofus," I replied, guiding his hand to rest on my stomach. He glanced down at it, and I saw a plethora of emotions cross his face in the span of a few seconds.

"Wait, what?" he asked, looking bewildered. "Are you saying...?"

"I'm saying that we're going to have a baby," I replied. "She's due in about five months. I didn't want to tell you until I made it through the first trimester, in case I lost her. You lost Sophie not even a year ago, and then we both had to watch Skye lose her baby. I knew how much you wanted a child, and I knew it would kill you if I miscarried. Doc said there was a good chance I could lose this one in the first trimester, not just because of the malnutrition thing but because..." I glanced away and swallowed hard. "I've had miscarriages before... after... you know."

"Oh, Sandy," he whispered. I felt his arms close around me, and suddenly I was being hugged. "You should have told me, but I understand why you didn't."

I sniffed and rubbed my eye, brushing away a few tears that were trying to break free. "I know. I just didn't want to make you suffer. You've already lost enough. It's been hard enough watching you grieve for Sophie; I'm not sure I could bear watching you grieve for our baby, too."

"You won't have to," he said, his voice suddenly taking on that tone of total determination I knew so well. "We're going to get through this together, you and me. Nothing is going to happen to the baby on my watch." I heard him laugh, then suddenly his grip around me tightened to the point that I could barely breathe. A few seconds later, he leaned back and looked at me, grinning like a madman. "A baby! I can't believe it! You know I'm going to have to tease you mercilessly for not telling me straight away, right?"

"Oh, I fully expect you to," I answered dryly. "And I deserve it, so it's all good. A few other people already know, but not many. Maddy was the one who told me, and Doc's confirmed the diagnosis. Gavin knows because

I asked him to make sure you were okay, and Skye and Anahera know because they figured it out last night. Apparently I've been gaining weight or something."

"You have," Michael replied, giving me a playful tickle. "I just assumed you were eating more than usual to make yourself extra cuddly for me. I didn't know you were eating for two."

I squeaked and shoved his hand away. "Hey, no tickling! Bladder is weak right now!"

"Sorry, I just can't help i—" he started to say, then suddenly he went stiff in my arms. "Wait... if you've known about the baby for months, is that the only reason you wanted to marry me?"

"Oh, hell no," I replied, with an appropriately sassy gesture. "I married you because I want to claim ownership over you 'til death do us part'. I couldn't care less if our baby was born out of wedlock. I wanted to marry you because you're my Officer Sexy, and I love you." I gave him a cheeky grin, and draped my arms around his neck. "Well, that and the fact I wanted to see you in uniform again."

Michael laughed and I felt him relax again. "Well, if that's what you wanted, all you had to do was ask."

Chapter Sixteen

The building's eaves offered little protection from the elements, so we were both sopping wet by the time we finally finished making peace and returned to the facility, but the look on Michael's face more than made up for the discomfort. His couldn't stop grinning, and I was so relieved to have the burden of secrecy off my chest that I found myself laughing over the most ridiculous things – like the looks on people's faces when the elevator doors opened, and we stepped out. I took one look at the worried faces of my friends, then dissolved into a fit of childlike giggles. Michael grinned even wider and held his hands up to get everyone's attention. "Don't worry, guys! Everything is fine! We had a misunderstanding but it's all sorted now, and we have some really awesome news." He glanced at me and raised an eyebrow. "Do you want to tell them, or shall I?"

"You do it," I said, still struggling to get my laughter back under control.

Gavin looked at me and raised an eyebrow, but he didn't say anything. Michael wrapped an arm around me and pulled me up against his side, then gently rested a hand on my belly. "Everyone, I am thrilled to announce that we are officially pregnant!"

A ripple of surprise passed through the gathered people, then Mary nudged her father in the side and cheered for us. Soon, everyone else joined in – everyone except Simon, who just looked even more embarrassed.

"And about bloody time," Gavin said, breathing a huge sigh of relief. He looked at me again, and gave me a very pointed scowl. "I'm not spying for you again, little miss. That was way too stressful."

"Speaking of which, you and I are going to have words about this later," Michael told him, in a tone of mock anger. "Come on, man! What happened to the bro-code?"

"I'm pretty sure that's not actually a thing," Gavin answered dryly. "And have words with your wife, it was her doing."

Michael laughed and gave me a squeeze. "Oh don't worry, we're going to be having plenty of words. Though now that I think about it, I *was* wondering why you were following me around like a lost puppy."

"I was not!" Gavin scoffed. "I just made excuses every now and then to strike up a conversation. Besides, I think that was secretly her plan all along. She wanted us to spend more time together so that your sense of humour would rub off on me."

"Guilty as charged," I said brightly. Then, I suddenly realised someone was missing and my amusement faded. "Hey, where's Simon? He was here a second ago."

The group glanced around, then exchanged looks and shrugs. I sighed and nodded.

"Honey, I need to go talk to him," I said to Michael. "He's still our friend, after all. He made a dumb mistake, but we can work through it and save our friendship. Can you and the others work with Madelyde to finish gathering up everything we need to take back home?"

"Sure, you just worry about Simon," he started to reply, then paused and looked at me quizzically. "Wait... when did we start calling her Madelyde?"

"Oh, uh, we didn't," I replied, embarrassed. "I've been calling her that inside my head since she got possessed, and it just kinda... came out."

"Ahh." Michael nodded understandingly and gave me a silly grin. "Just your inner monologue showing again. Gotcha. Off you go, talk to Simon. We'll be here when you get back."

He gave me a gentle shove in the direction of the airlock, just enough to get me moving. I caught myself easily and jogged past my friends, who reached out to pat me on the back and offer congratulations as I passed. By the time I was safely around the corner, I could feel myself blushing.

I wasn't sure how to feel about everyone knowing that I was knocked up. In some ways, it was kind of cool. In others, it was embarrassing as hell. I was doing my duty as one of the last women alive by propagating my species, but I still had conflicting feelings about that duty. It was all up to me and the thirty-two other women who had made their home in Tumanako. It was our duty to bear the next generation. It was an honour, but also a burden. In some ways it felt like my right to choose had vanished along with civilization, but in other ways I felt like I would have made the choice — or sacrifice, depending on how I looked at it – willingly in the end.

Without the miracles of modern medicine, carrying a child had become a huge risk again, just as it had been for our ancestors. But I was a Kiwi woman, the latest in a long line of pioneering women. Barely more than a hundred years before the plague, New Zealand had been a wilderness. Now she was a wilderness again, and I was going to help create a whole new type of pioneer.

I laughed and shook my head. Anahera's whole goddess earth mama vibe was starting to rub off on me, just like I'd hoped it would.

A few seconds later, I heard the sound of footsteps. I crept up to the corner and peered around it. Sure enough, there was Simon pacing back and forth, his expression so miserable that I immediately felt sorry for him. I took a deep breath to steel myself, then I stepped into his line of sight and waved. "Uh, hey."

"Oh, hey," he replied. He turned his back to me and hung his head. "I'm sorry. I feel like such an idiot. I guess I've completely lost my knack for reading people."

"It's okay, mate," I said, touching his shoulder. "It was an honest mistake, and an innocent one. Under different circumstances, I might have reciprocated your interest. I had a celebrity crush on you for ages, you know?"

He glanced at me and smiled weakly. "You did?"

"Yeah, totally," I replied, smiling back at him. "If I weren't married, then you'd be my first choice." My smile faded and I glanced away. "Unfortunately, some things happened to me, Simon. Nasty things. Really nasty. I'm not as relaxed around men as my sister is. That's not your fault, either. You're a good person, and you deserve to be happy."

His shoulders sagged and he heaved a deep sigh. "Sometimes I wonder. I did everything I could think of to help, both in the past and now, but maybe it wasn't enough. Maybe I do deserve to be alone for the rest of my life."

I frowned and squeezed his shoulder. "Aw, hey, don't say that. You've given us more over the years than any of us had a right to ask. Keeping the news going gave us some kind of hope that maybe we could find civilization again. You kept me company when no one else did, even though you didn't know I existed. I guarantee that you won't be alone for long."

"You think so?" he asked, shooting a shy, uncertain glance at me.

"I know so." I winked and grinned. "I've caught more than one of the new girls giving you the eye, and I'll bet once the South Islanders get here you'll be fighting the ladies off with a stick. You're a good-looking man, Simon Wentworth – even if you do forget to shave a lot."

Simon smiled and rubbed a hand across his stubbly chin. "Yeah, I'm pretty forgetful. Scatter-brained. I always have been, to be honest. My producer said I was never going to amount to much. I could never remember my lines."

"Well, I guess you proved him wrong," I replied. "Because now you're the only celebrity we've got left."

"I'd disagree with that," he said dryly. "I may be a familiar face from the telly, but the only celebrity these people have – or need, for that matter – is you. You're the rock star here, not me."

"You're sweet," I said, then I gave him a light punch on the arm. "Now stop flirting with me. You keep that sugar for the single girls, you hear me?"

"I wasn't flirting, I was just being nice," he protested, though there was a twinkle of humour in his eyes.

I laughed and threaded my arm through his, then led him back to the rest of the group.

The others were waiting by the time we reached the elevator, in huddle around a stack of old computers, equipment, and filing cabinets. I released Simon's arm and gave him a pat on the shoulder, then went over to admire the stack of information we needed to lug back with us.

"This is going to keep you and Doc busy for days, Gav," I commented.

He glanced at me and heaved a sigh. "More like weeks, maybe even months."

"Take as much time as you need," I replied. "This project takes priority over everything else except food, water, and shelter, and we've got all of those things covered. We need that vaccine ready by the time Evie starts to wean."

He nodded and started gathering up equipment. The others pitched in to help him, all except for me and Madelyde. We had something else to discuss.

I guided Madelyde off to one side so that we weren't in the way, then I knelt and put my hands on her shoulders. "Clyde, we're going to have to go soon. That means we need to figure out what to do about you and Madeline."

"I know," she said matter-of-factly. "Maddy and I have been discussing it at length, and we both think it's best if I stick around until the vaccine is ready – you know, in case you need anything."

I raised an eyebrow and gave her a long look. "And how is that going to work? You can't keep possessing Maddy forever. Aside from the fact that it would be weird and upset her grandfather a lot... well, what would you do when it's time to go to the bathroom?"

Madelyde gave me the kind of look that told me exactly what Clyde thought of that idea. "Don't be disgusting, I'm not going to stay in her body. This was just a temporary arrangement, and she could have booted me out at any time. Maddy says that the key card you took from my body has been close enough to me for long enough that it should be able to act as a focus, so that she can call me to her when you need to ask me questions. There's just one catch, though: it means you can't kill my body yet, and if my body falls apart on its own... well, we don't know exactly what will happen."

I shuddered at the thought, but nodded. "Whatever you two think is best. This is your show. But are you sure you want to linger here for that long? It can't be fun."

"It's not that bad," Madelyde replied with a faint smile. "I mean, it's not like I'm sitting around getting poked by a little devil with a pitchfork or something. There are still a lot of things to see and do. The Patupaiarehe are starting to come back now that most of the people are gone, and they sometimes roam down into these parts when there are no humans around. They don't like people, but they're friendly enough to rogue spirits."

"The Patuparawhats?" I repeated, confused. Madelyde just laughed and shook her head.

"Don't worry, you'll never see them," she said. "Not unless they want you to. Maddy might, but she'll tell you if they're going to be a problem. Anyway, I'd best let Maddy have her body back. As a matter of fact, she needs to go to the loo pretty badly right now. Lavatories are at the top of the elevator, two doors down on the right."

"Oh, well... goodbye, then," I said, shooting a glance at the others nearby.

Maddy blinked a few times, then shook her head as if to wake herself up. "Oh, he's gone. That was weird."

"Maddy?" I asked, touching the girl's cheek. "How do you feel, honey? Are you okay?"

"I'm fine, Miss Sandy," she replied, then she gave me a smile that was very much her own. "But... I really need to pee."

I laughed and nodded, easing myself back up to my feet. "Me too. Come on, let's go home."

***

It didn't take long to find the lavatories, then we loaded the Hilux up and we were back on the road. It was nearly sundown by the time we reached the outskirts of Tumanako. Just as we were nearing the front gate, someone shouted and waved frantically; it took a second before I realised it was Ryan. I glanced at the others, then put my heels to Boudicca's sides and urged her forward at a trot.

"What's wrong?" I demanded as soon as I was close enough to do so without shouting.

"We had an... arrival while you were out," he said, hurrying to open the gate for me. "I've been ordered to take you straight up as soon as you get here."

I raised an eyebrow, then dismounted and handed my reins to Michael without a word. I didn't need to say anything; Ryan's demeanour told us all that something was wrong. Very, very wrong.

Ryan led me in and waited with me for the elevator, but as soon as we were inside he pushed the button to close the doors and held it down so that they wouldn't open again until he was ready.

"Whatever happens in the next few minutes, I want you to know that I'm on your side," he said, his voice almost a whisper.

My heart leapt into my throat. "Ry? What is it?"

"You'll understand soon," he said cryptically. He took his finger off the button, and we rode the elevator up to the second floor in silence.

As soon as the doors slid open, I could hear the commotion coming from the dining room. People were shouting at one another, though I couldn't make out what they were saying. I glanced at Ryan again, suddenly afraid. The voices sounded angry. Were they angry at me?

Ryan took my arm and led me down the hall, into the dining room. As soon as the doors opened, people turned to look at me, their familiar faces so twisted by anger that I barely recognised them. I couldn't tell whether the anger was directed at me or not. I'd never seen so much rage in one place and I didn't know how to react to it, so I just froze.

Skylar appeared out of the crowd, shouting at those around her to calm down. She took one look at my face, then grabbed me and hugged me tight.

I clung to her, bewildered and confused. "What's going on? Why is everyone yelling at me?"

"You remember Bobby Wright, I presume?" she said. "Isabelle's son? Well, he showed up at the gates right after you left this morning, demanding that you be held accountable for the death of his stepfather. I've been trying to tell them that it was self-defence, but they're demanding a trial. It's the only way people will trust you again."

"Well, then," I said, struggling to keep myself rational despite the wave of animal panic that sought to overwhelm me. "Let's give the people what they want."

Chapter Seventeen

As soon as the crowd heard that I'd agreed to a trial it began to calm down, with the exception of a handful of unfamiliar people that seemed to be Bobby's friends. While Skye was busy trying to negotiate with them, I was bundled out of the room and confined to my apartment with guards outside the door.

Still in shock, I sat on the couch and just waited. Michael would be back soon enough, and then I'd have someone to talk to – or a shoulder to cry on, if I needed it. With my current hormone levels, tears were pretty much inevitable.

Sure enough, within a few minutes there was a fuss outside the door. I cringed at the sound of raised voices, but it took a second before I realised that the person shouting wasn't Michael, it was a young female. The door was flung open and Melody stormed in, followed closely by Priyanka and the twins. Priya rushed over and flung her arms around me, her eyes full of tears.

"You'll be all right, Mama," she told me. "We'll stand up for you. All of us. I'll be a—what's the word?"

"A witness," Melody supplied.

"Yes," she agreed, hugging me tight. "I'll be a witness. I saw what happened. You saved my life, and Baba's!"

"I know, honey," I whispered, hugging her back. "We did what we had to do. And now we're doing what we have to do again, for Bobby's sake."

"That stupid brat needs a swift kick in the teeth," Melody snapped, her demeanour tense and angry. "Just give me five minutes alone with him, and I'll show him what's what."

"As satisfying as that would be, we don't want to stoop to that level," I said. "We need to do this, not just for Bobby's sake but for everyone's. People need to know that everyone will be held accountable for their actions, even me. Don't worry, we'll make it through this – and hopefully we'll give Bobby some closure in the process."

The conversation stalled when another ruckus started up outside the door, then Michael stormed in looking about as angry as I'd ever seen him. He took in the people gathered around me at a glance, then planted himself beside me and wrapped his arms around both me and Priya.

"I cannot believe this kid," he said, his voice almost a snarl. "He's down there right now, trying to rile people up. Last I heard was your sister threatening to lock him in a cupboard until he calmed down. It's like he's trying to cause a riot or something."

"I think he is," I said softly, snuggling up against his warm bulk for comfort. "Those people he's with, they're gangers. I'm guessing he found them on his way south and convinced them to come here and 'defend' him. I'll bet if we don't keep a really close eye on them, half our supplies will be gone by morning."

Michael swore under his breath, then shot a plaintive look at the twins. "Girls, can you please run a message for me? I need you to tell Tane and Iorangi to keep a close eye on these new folks, and not to let them anywhere near our supplies." He glanced at me and lowered his voice. "Or the women and children."

Jasmine and Lily nodded in perfect synchronization and dashed off, almost bumping into Anahera as she was making her way inside. She watched the twins go with raised eyebrows, then looked back at me and smiled.

"No wonder your guards are looking frustrated," she commented. "It seems that you've got a steady stream of visitors."

"I think they've given up on even locking the door," I answered dryly. "Not that they really need to. Where would I go? I've invested way too much in Tumanako to just run away."

"You won't have to, anyway," Anahera said with a smile. "This boy, Bobby – he knows he doesn't stand a chance, but he's making trouble because he can. Sometimes people do that. He and his friends have managed to convince a few of the newer members of our community that you are worthy of suspicion, but once they hear what actually happened, they'll understand."

"And if they don't," Melody said, her face set in an angry mask, "then they can leave any time they like!"

I laughed softly and shook my head. "There's your example of people making trouble, in the flesh!"

Everyone laughed right along with me, except for Melody. She just gave me a dark look, then turned away – but not quite fast enough to hide the smile breaking through her stony expression. It was fine, though. We'd gotten to know one another well enough over the last few months that I knew she wasn't offended by my teasing, even if she pretended to be. Still, I didn't want to risk alienating the people I needed most in the coming days, so I looked back at Anahera and changed the subject.

"I told Michael," I admitted. "It didn't quite go how I was planning, but the cat's out of the bag."

"Finally," Anahera said dryly. "At least now I can officially congratulate you both."

"Wait, what'd I miss?" Melody demanded.

"Well, as it so happens, Michael and I are expecting a baby," I told her shyly. "She's due around mid-summer."

"What?" Melody echoed, staring at me blankly. It took a good ten seconds before the news sunk in. Suddenly, her eyes lit up and she leapt on us with a squeal of delight. "Oh my God, you're having a baby?! You're so lucky!"

I yelped in surprise when I suddenly found myself in the middle of a people-sandwich, with Michael on one side, and Priya and Melody on the other.

"Well, it's not really luck," I gasped when I could finally catch a breath, then I paused and looked at her. "Wait — you guys do know where babies come from, right?"

"Of course we do," Melody replied, giving me an annoyed look. "The twins are obsessed with romance novels, remember? We figured it out." She heaved a long sigh, and her expression softened. "I really want to have a baby, but... I don't like boys."

"Well, if you really want to have a baby you could just borrow one for a night," I replied. "It's not like you have to get married."

"No, no, not like that." She shook her head vigorously and gave me a frown. "I don't like boys at all. I mean, I like them fine as people, but I don't want to have sex with them. It's gross. I like girls." Suddenly looking nervous, she shot a glance back and forth between me and Anahera. "Is that weird?"

Anahera smiled and shook her head. "Not at all, dear. There are many different types of people in the world. I like men and women equally. My soul mate just happened to be in a man's body."

The revelation of Anahera's bisexuality didn't faze me in the least. I'd suspected it from the moment I met her. She wasn't the sort to let gender boundaries hold her back. I just gave her a smile, then looked back at Melody. "Yeah, what she said. It's totally normal. Jim and Richard prefer men, and I'm pretty sure Iorangi is bi. You are the way nature made you, no big deal. If you want to have a baby, the doctor can help you."

"He can?" she asked, shooting a look of earnest curiosity at me. "How?"

"Artificial insemination," I replied. "Basically, you pick a guy you like enough to father the child, and if he agrees then the doctor can inject his sperm into you, without you having to have sex with him. You'll still have to have something going up there, of course, but it might be less uncomfortable for you. If you're serious, ask him. It's your choice."

Melody made a thoughtful sound and fell silent. Anahera looked at me again and gave me one of her delightfully radiant smiles. "Speaking of Jim and Richard — did you hear that they're engaged?"

"What?" I gasped. "No! When did that happen?"

"Last night," she replied. "Richard couldn't wait to tell me this morning. I've never seen him looking so happy."

"Oh, that's fantastic," I said, pleased beyond all reason by the news. I elbowed Michael and gave him a grin. "Who's a busybody now, huh?"

"Still you, honey," he replied without missing a beat. "But you mean well, and this time it worked out for the best."

Anahera looked at me with raised eyebrows, and suddenly I found myself muffling a girlish giggle. "I may have sent them on a few missions together, secretly hoping that they'd hit it off."

"You sneaky thing," she replied, a slow smile creeping across her face. "Well, they seem very happy and that's the important thing."

"Then my work here is done," I said brightly, sketching a bow as best I could under the circumstances. "Next project: find Simon a girlfriend."

"Why Simon?" she asked curiously. "He seems perfectly happy as he is."

I cleared my throat and shot a glance at Michael. "That's what I thought, until he tried to kiss me today."

"He did *what*?!" Melody gasped. Priya gaped at me, and even Anahera looked shocked.

"Yep," I agreed. "He thought that I was flirting with him, and that I was interested in a three-way relationship. I set him straight but now I kind of feel bad for him, you know?"

Anahera glanced down at her hands, a thoughtful expression crossing her face. "Perhaps I should go talk to him. We dated for a while, before I met my husband. There was a spark between us once. Maybe it's still there."

This time, it was my turn to look at her in shock. "I thought you weren't going to get involved with anyone after you lost your husband?"

"So I swore, but..." She let out a long, deep sigh and shrugged. "When I made that vow, I still had a young son to fill my life with laughter and love. Now, he's grown up and found a woman of his own, and my home is empty. It is the way of nature for little ones to leave the nest, and build nests of their own, but I still find myself feeling lonely."

"Aw, Ana." I reached for her, and gently touched her hand. "Then talk to him. Your husband would understand. He'd want you to be happy. It's been ten years – that's more than any reasonable person would ask their spouse to mourn for them. Go, talk to him right now. He's going to be feeling really sad tonight, after what happened. I'll be fine."

She nodded thoughtfully and glanced at the door. "I think I will. I'll be there for the trial, though, no matter what."

"Good. It wouldn't be any fun without you," I replied dryly, making a shooing motion at her. "Go on, off with you. The rest of us should head to bed, anyway."

"Have you eaten?" she asked, giving me one of those motherly looks that I'd gotten so used to.

"Not yet, but I've got some rations in my bag," I replied. "That'll do until breakfast. No point poking the hive, you know?"

"If you say so," she said. Melody hopped up and went over to her without being prompted, but Priya lingered beside me. Anahera smiled indulgently and held out a hand to her. "Come, little one. Let Mama and Baba sleep."

"I'm not little!" Priya protested. She still wriggled out of my arms and bounced over to stand in front of Anahera. "I had a growth spurt. See?"

"In more ways than one," Anahera said dryly. "We're going to need to get you a training bra soon, my dear."

I glanced at Michael, just in time to see him turn bright red and suddenly look very interested in a spot on the ceiling. The rest of us just exchanged a glance, then burst out laughing.

***

I woke early the next morning, dragged out of the warm, pleasant haze of sleep by the sound of shouting outside our door. Michael snorted awake and vaulted out of bed before I'd even had a chance to figure out what was going on. He rushed out of our bedroom while I was still struggling to get my clothes on, and I heard his voice join in the shouting. I was just pulling on my shoes and socks when he returned, grim-faced and angry.

"Trouble?" I asked softly, struggling to keep my wits about me and stay strong even though I was terrified.

Michael nodded, glaring over his shoulder at the door. "Bobby. He wants the trial to begin now, and he's angry the guards wouldn't let him drag you out of bed." He looked back at me and his expression softened. "I'm glad I assigned guards who are on your side. This is turning into a witch hunt."

"I knew this was going to get bad the second I met him," I admitted, reaching out to touch Michael's hand. "They may not be related by blood, but that kid is a lot like his stepfather."

"Unfortunately for him," Michael replied, hugging me tenderly. "You're being really patient about all of this. I have to admit, I'm surprised. I half expected you to be out there kicking his ass."

"I need to lead by example now, and I have more to worry about than just myself," I said, resting a hand over my belly. "I can't go rushing off half-cocked anymore. I have to think about her. I should probably stop going on missions outside Tumanako soon – well, assuming I don't get assassinated on the way to my trial today."

"Don't say that," Michael protested, laying his hands over mine. "There are only five of them, and Bobby's the only one actively trying to cause trouble. The majority of the people here consider you their friend and ally, and if it comes to it then we'll fight to protect you."

I smiled and nodded, though I wasn't really as reassured as I pretended to be. "We should go get this over with, but I really need to pee first. This baby thing is hard."

"I'd apologise for that, but I'm not sorry at all," he said dryly, helping me to my feet. He kept his arm around me as he led me to the door, carefully shielding me with his body just in case. I could hear voices speaking outside even before the door opened, but at least they weren't shouting any more. Michael knocked on the door, and waited for the guards to unlock it. When it opened, the first thing I saw was Skylar standing not far from the doorway, speaking calmly and rationally to a mixed group of faces both new and old. On either side of her stood Ryan and Hemi, weapons in their hands and expressions of steely determination on their faces.

"...with us in a second," she said, making a placating gesture. "Just give her time. She made the rules, and if there's one thing I know about my sister it's that she's a stickler for leading by example."

"Skye," I whispered, reaching out to touch her shoulder. She glanced back at me and gave me a reassuring smile.

"See, there she is, just like she promised," she said to the crowd. "Head down to the dining room, everyone. We'll be announcing the adjudicator in a few minutes."

"When did Skylar become such a good bailiff?" I whispered to Michael. She overheard me and shot me a glance, but her expression was unreadable.

"She needs the 'loo before we begin," Michael said, his face revealing no trace of his usual sense of humour.

Skye nodded to the guards, who stepped forward and made a path for us through the wall of bodies. As soon as we were free of the crowd, Michael picked up the pace. By the time we reached the bathroom, we were almost running.

Anahera was waiting there, flanked by every single one of my closest female friends. They took over guard duty from Michael, and protected me while I raced through my early-morning ablutions. Once I was ready, they surrounded me in a wall of protective bodies and led me down to the dining room. The tables had all been pushed back against the walls and the chairs arranged into a makeshift courtroom, with a handful on one side of the room and the rest in rows so that people could observe the proceedings. The seats were already packed, and as I was led inside all eyes turned towards me.

"How are we going to pick the adjudicator?" I asked Anahera nervously.

She squeezed my arm and gave me a reassuring smile. "We drew up a list of eligible candidates last night and held a vote on it. They're just counting up the votes now."

Michael and Priya were both waiting for me up the front. The makeshift courtroom had been set up with a low platform in the middle for the adjudicator and the witness stand, and groups of chairs on each side for the prosecution and the defence. Anahera guided me into a seat between my husband and foster daughter, then stood back to wait.

I glanced at the prosecution and saw Bobby glaring at me from amidst his friends. The boy had grown a couple of inches since I'd last seen him, and gained a rather prominent tattoo on the side of his neck. That set off alarm bells in my head: I recognised the symbol as belonging to one of the gangs that I'd so carefully avoided over the years.

The people with him were male, heavily scarred, covered in tattoos, and practically reeking of danger. I glanced at the crowd, and checked faces against the ever-increasing list of citizens I kept in my head.

As if sensing my concern, Anahera leaned forward and touched my shoulder. "Everyone is safe and accounted for, don't worry. Elly and Rebecca are looking after the younger children downstairs and the people on guard duty are all loyal to you. They have walkie-talkies on them, so if anything happens we'll know about it."

I nodded and took a deep breath, willing myself to relax. It wasn't going to happen, though. As positive as I was that I'd only done what I needed to do to protect my family, Henry's death had always bothered me. I felt guilty about it, and that feeling coloured my thoughts.

The kitchen door opened and Skylar emerged, again flanked by Ryan and Hemi. A step behind her was a tall, dark-haired man I didn't recognise. Although he had the same tattoo on his neck as the other gangers Bobby had brought with him, he carried himself differently, with authority and a confidence that reeked of intelligence rather than violence.

Skye stood in front of the gathered crowd and addressed them without further ado. "We've counted your votes, and Johan has been selected to act as the adjudicator. Johan, please come forward."

All eyes turned to the veterinarian. He came to the front, his expression unreadable. While he was settling into the adjudicator's chair, Skylar addressed the crowd again.

"I will be acting as Sandy's defence," she said, then she gestured to the tall man following her. "This is Owen Gordon. He'll be speaking on behalf of the prosecution. Whenever you're ready, Owen."

"Thank you, Miss McDermott," Owen replied. His voice was smooth and practiced, and something about it sent a shiver down my spine. It didn't take a rocket scientist to guess that he'd probably been a lawyer before the plague. "My client accuses the defendant of murder, for taking the life of Henry Barrett in cold blood four months ago. Sandrine McDermott, the prosecution calls you to bear witness."

I took another deep breath and stood up, making my way up onto the makeshift stage to sit in the witness chair. Suddenly I felt very alone and exposed, looking out across the sea of faces. I swallowed hard and looked at Owen.

"Ms McDermott," he said, "please tell us in your own words what happened that day."

I started in surprise and looked at Skye. "Just like that? Aren't you supposed to swear me in or something?"

"What, you want me to make you swear on a Bible?" she said dryly. "Last time I checked, you were an atheist obsessed with telling the truth anyway. Just tell us what happened."

"Okay, okay." I backed down and closed my eyes, focusing on the story I had to tell. It was a story I'd replayed a thousand times in my head but it still seemed somehow unreal, as if it had happened to someone else or occurred in a dream I only half remembered. "It started when we were living in Ohaupo — 'we' being Michael, Skylar, Doctor Cross, Madeline, and myself. We'd received a plea for help by radio, from Jim and Rebecca at the Arapuni Power Station. We agreed to help them. Michael and I originally set off in our car, but it broke down near Te Awamutu and forced us to travel the rest of the way on foot. Along the way, we met Priyanka and decided to bring her with us.

"While we were passing through the township of Pukeatua, Henry Barrett ambushed us. He came up behind us and grabbed Priyanka by the throat before I knew he was there. He said that I could leave if I wanted, but he was going to kill Michael and Priyanka..." I paused for a second, glancing towards the prosecution, "...because he said he believed anyone who wasn't fair-skinned and of European descent was responsible for the plague."

A stir passed through the crowd at that. While many of us matched that description, myself included, more than half of the people in the room did not.

Owen glanced at the crowd, then looked back at me. "I bet that made you angry, didn't it?"

"I married a Chinese man and adopted an Indian girl as my daughter," I answered dryly. "You better believe that it made me mad."

"Did you try to talk to him?" Owen asked. "Or did you just decide that was enough to warrant his death?"

I shot him a scathing look and a deep frown. "Of course I tried to talk him down. We both did. He wouldn't let us reason with him, and he had a machete against Priyanka's throat. As soon as I saw an opportunity, I took it."

"So, you admit that you attacked him first?" Owen asked, raising his eyebrows.

"No, he'd already attacked us," I argued. "He'd grabbed Priya and was holding a bloody great machete against her throat. He'd left bruises on her and told us twice that he was going to kill her and Michael."

"But you said that he was willing to let you go," Owen said. "Why didn't you just leave?"

"He said he was willing to let *me* go, as in just me," I repeated. "He wasn't going to let Michael or Priya go."

"Doesn't that make it their problem, then?" Owen said cryptically. "Your argument is that it was self-defence, but *you* were in no direct danger."

"But the people I love were!" I argued back, stunned and furious by the implication of his words. "Would you leave your wife and child to die? Of course not! It was my duty to defend them."

"But you weren't married at the time, and you didn't have a formal adoption," Owen said, his expression one of practiced intensity. "So you're telling us that you killed someone because he said threatening things to the man you were sleeping with and a girl you'd just met?"

"I didn't kill him," I snapped, anger clouding my mind. I knew that every word I said was being measured and judged, but for a second I was just too furious to care. "I haven't finished telling everyone what happened yet! Would you just shut up and let me tell the story?"

Someone in the crowd laughed at my outburst, and a few others whooped and whistled. Owen glared at them until they fell silent, then finally nodded to me.

I nodded curtly in return and resumed my narrative. "Henry had Priya pinned, with one hand around her throat, and in the other hand he was holding this massive machete. He got himself so angry while he was ranting and raving that his guard dropped for a second. I could tell by that stage the only way I was going to save Priya was to go on the offensive, so I did. I hit him in the face with the butt of my shotgun to distract him, then I yanked Priya out of his grip."

"So, your foster daughter was safe?" Owen extrapolated. "But you continued the fight?"

"No, I did not," I replied, giving him another scathing look to shut him up. "I stayed on the defensive. He attacked me. I had a shotgun, but I did not at any point shoot him with it. I was trying really hard not to kill him or even do any permanent harm. I can't say he felt the same way." To illustrate my point, I lifted the hem of my shirt up to reveal a deep scar across my ribs from where the machete had cut me. "This is what he did to me. Can you imagine what he would have done to Priya?"

Another ripple passed through the crowd. I glanced over and caught them exchanging looks and whispers, and I could see uncertainty on more than one face. I lowered my shirt and looked back at Owen.

"It's important to note that Henry was a very big man," I said, raising my voice a little more, so that there could be no doubt that everyone could hear me. "He must have been six-five, built like a bodybuilder, outfitted in full battledress and carrying a sidearm in a holster. I mean, Michael's big and even I'm on the tall side, but this guy could have torn Priya in half if he wanted. She was terrified — hell, I was terrified. Any sane person would be when there's a wall of muscle coming at you swinging a machete. I managed to flatten him with a well-placed kick to the groin, but not for long. We grabbed Priya and ran for our lives."

"You ran?" Owen echoed. For the first time, he looked a little uncertain of himself.

"Yes, we ran," I replied. "He had other men with him, all of them armed. I managed to knock one over before he could shoot us, then we all ran into the bush. While we were running, we heard him shouting orders to the other men. He ordered them to kill us. We were travelling on foot and we were heavily outnumbered. I had to do something... something I didn't want to do."

"What did you do?" Owen asked, and this time there was no guile in his voice, just honest curiosity.

I sat up a little straighter and steeled myself. "Priya, honey, I want you to cover your ears."

"Yes, Mama," she replied obediently. I didn't have to look to know that she'd done as instructed. She was still a good girl like that, even with Melody's rebellious influence.

"While we were running, I heard the sound of pigs in the bush nearby," I said, forcing myself to lift my voice high enough to be heard even though I dreaded saying the words. "There were two of them, a boar and a sow. Both infected, of course. I sent Michael and Priya off towards Arapuni, and then I shot the pigs to goad them into chasing me. That was the only time I fired my weapon. Then I turned and ran back towards Henry and his men with the pigs hot on my tail."

There were gasps all around the room, and the whispering increased in volume. I swallowed hard and looked Owen right in the eye. "At the time, I didn't think it was going to work. It felt suicidal. I've fought pigs off before, but never by myself. I made the choice, even if it cost me my life, because it might just buy my loved ones the time to escape. I could still hear Henry shouting for his men to kill us, so I ran towards the sound of his voice. He grabbed me and we scuffled for a second, but I managed to get away and hide just in time. He didn't see the pigs coming. They knocked him to the ground, and they... they killed him."

Tears welled up in my eyes, and I suddenly found myself unable to maintain eye-contact any longer. "I didn't mean for any of it to happen. We were trying to do the right thing, to help the people at Arapuni keep the power going. We didn't know anyone lived in Pukeatua, and there were no warning signs. We had no way to know about Bobby and Isabelle, and by the time we'd fought off the rest of Henry's men we were too exhausted to even think about the possibility that they might have had captives. I've regretted what happened for every moment since, and I don't think I'll ever stop regretting it, but even now I can't think of anything else I could have done."

I finally worked up the courage to look up and found Owen watching me thoughtfully. After a few long seconds, he looked at Johan. "I have no more questions."

Johan nodded and looked at Skylar. "Do you have any questions for her?"

"Nope," Skye said dryly. "As usual, my sister has managed to express herself quite eloquently. I would, however, like to call a few new witnesses to the stand. Some new information has come to light in relation to the nature of the deceased."

"Oh?" Johan raised his eyebrows and looked at her curiously. "That's fine, but who did you have in mind?"

"Solomon and Charu," she said, her expression one of stern resolution. She turned to face the crowd, and beckoned to the young man in question. "Solo, are you still happy to come up here and tell us what Henry Barrett did to your family?"

Solomon leapt to his feet, nodding vigorously. He said something that none of us could understand thanks to his missing tongue – none of us, except for Melody.

"He says that he will, for Sandy's sake," Melody translated. "He says that it's a painful memory for him, but Sandy's always been kind to him so he'll do it for her."

"All right, come on up here," Johan said. He gave me a smile. "You can go back to your seat, Sandrine."

I relinquished the witness chair and rushed back to my place with Michael and Priya. They both hugged me, and then we all turned our attention to Solomon. Melody came up to the stand with him, to act as an interpreter. Solomon looked at me for a second, then looked back at Skylar and began to speak. It was the first time I'd heard more than two words out of his mouth, and listening to him struggle over his syllables hurt more than I'd ever imagined it could. He was so determined to get his story across, though. I'd never seen that kind of look on his face, and it made me proud.

"Solomon's grandfather was the leader of the Samoan gang in Tokoroa," Melody translated as the young man spoke. "They were happy there, and hurt no one. Occasionally people came to trade with them. That's how Henry Barrett got inside their compound. He said that he was there to trade, but once his men were inside the walls they started shooting..."

Chapter Eighteen

By the time Solomon finished telling the gruesome tale of his torture and mutilation, there were tears running down my cheeks and I had my hands clamped firmly over Priya's ears. She had been through enough; I didn't want her to have to think about that kind of pain. It made me sick to my stomach, and if I'd eaten breakfast then I might have lost it. Even Owen looked a little green around the gills.

Skye didn't stop there, though. She called Charu to the stand next, and he came willingly for the same reason as Solomon. Part of me was grateful that they were so willing to help me, but a bigger part was just horrified by what they'd gone through. The emotional onslaught didn't stop with Charu, though. Once he was done, Skye called Isabelle to the stand.

Like the others, Isabelle came willingly, but she was obviously feeling miserable. The only person she'd look at was me, as if looking at me and thinking about how she was helping me kept her focused on what she wanted to do. Hearing her story was too much for me, it struck too close to the bone. I pleaded for a momentary respite to collect myself, and Johan permitted it. Anahera took me by the shoulders and led me out, just as Skye was calling Michael to the stand.

We managed to make it to the ladies room before I broke down and wept as if my heart was breaking. Anahera just hugged me and held me silently, letting me vent my grief on her shoulder like the mother I'd lost ten years ago. That was all I could ask from anyone, even when I didn't have the words to express how much I needed it.

Eventually, my tears ran dry. Anahera helped me over to the sink so that I could wash my face, then she led me back to the dining room where the trial had continued without us. Michael's testimony was over and he'd been released back to his seat. Skylar called Priya's name. She promptly panicked and looked around for me. It wasn't until she saw that I was on my way back that she relaxed again. I gave her a quick, reassuring hug and sent her up to give her testimony.

I barely heard a word she said. I was feeling so drained, both physically and emotionally, that I planted my face in the side of Michael's neck and stayed there. Owen barely had any questions for her, and now when he asked them he was subdued. No more doublespeak, no more trying to catch us in lies or twist our words to make us sound guilty. The time for that was long past; now, he looked as exhausted as I felt. The only person who seemed to have any energy left was Bobby, who was still glaring at me in spite of everything.

Once Priya had been sent back to her seat, Johan looked at Owen and Skylar. "It seems like we're just about done here, unless any of you have any other witnesses you'd like to call?"

"Nope, I think we've made our case," Skye said. Everyone looked at Owen, but he just shook his head.

"All right, well I think the verdict is fairly obvious," Johan said. He glanced around for a second and shrugged sheepishly. "I feel like I should bang a gavel or something, but I don't have one. It's obvious to me that Sandrine was just doing what she had to do to protect the people she cares about, and that she made every reasonable attempt to salvage the situation. I find her not guilty of the charge of murder. If anyone believes I have made the wrong decision, please raise your hand."

We all looked at the gathered crowd expectantly. Not a single hand rose. I let out a deep breath I hadn't even realised I'd been holding until that moment, and managed a weak smile.

Before I could say anything, Bobby rocketed out of his chair, red-faced and shouting. "What?! That's it? She killed him, and you're just going to let her get away with it? That's bullshit! You bitch! I'll kill you, you stupid bitch!"

Gasps of shock and horror echoed through the crowd as Bobby vaulted right over the table and rushed at me, slipping through the fingers of his gang-mates when they tried to hold him back. Ryan grabbed me and pulled me away, while Michael and the guards on duty rushed in to try and subdue him.

He was strong, though. That growth spurt had packed muscle on him, and I could see the other men struggling to hold him back. Ryan tugged my arm and pulled me towards the door, but I resisted him. Too many people I loved were in that room for me to just run away. I wanted to help. I wanted to fight! There were so many bodies everywhere that I could barely make out what was happening – but I definitely heard the scream.

"Look out! He's got a gun! *He's got a gun!*"

The world seemed to slow in that instant, and everything came into perfect focus. I saw Michael lose his balance and fall to the ground, giving Bobby the moment of opportunity he needed to lift that gun and point it straight at me.

A body flew into me just at the moment the gunshot rang out, bowling me right off my feet. I hit the ground so hard that it left me momentarily stunned. By the time I'd regained my wits enough to shove myself up, Bobby had vanished beneath a mound of angry bodies.

Unfortunately, his single shot was enough to turn my world upside-down.

"Ryan!" Skylar gasped, rushing past me. "No, no, no, oh God, hold on!"

She dropped to her knees beside him, frantically trying to staunch the blood pumping from his chest. Doctor Cross flung himself down beside her a second later and joined in the efforts, but the wound was too deep. I could see the blood around the wound frothing and bubbling as air escaped from his lungs with every breath.

"Skye?" he whispered, groping for her hand. His skin was already turning pale from shock, paler than I'd ever seen it before.

"I'm here, Ryan," she said, grabbing his hand in both of hers and holding it to her chest. "Just stay with me. Doc will take care of you."

He tried to answer, but all that came out was a sick gurgling. Skye leaned in close to listen, but I couldn't make out what he was saying from afar. I could see her nodding as she listened to him struggling to speak. People gathered around me, whispering and staring, and I shared the sense of disbelief running through the mob.

"This wasn't supposed to happen," Owen said. I hadn't noticed him come up beside me, and part of me was too deeply in shock to understand what he was saying. I glanced at him and saw the same kind of utter stupefaction on his face. "No one was supposed to get hurt. We just wanted to see what was going on here, and get Bobby justice. This... this wasn't supposed to happen."

"Well, it did," I replied, my words coming out much harsher than I intended. The sound of my own hoarse voice stirred me out of my daze. There was nothing I could do for Ryan now, and he was in the most capable hands we had. In the meantime, there was a situation that needed to be addressed. "Where's Bobby?"

"Unconscious, I think," Owen replied. I looked around, but all I could see was a crowd of concerned faces. At the back of the crowd, I spotted Rebecca and Aaron trying to get through; Bobby was forgotten for the moment, in favour of getting Ryan the medical care that he needed.

"Make way!" I shouted, putting as much force behind my words as I could. "Let them through! Make a hole, people!"

Whether it was my tone of voice or the expression on my face, people moved enough for the two nurses to get through. By the time they reached him, Ryan had lapsed into unconsciousness. Skylar knelt on the floor, just staring into space while the doctor and nurses picked Ryan up and raced him off to the infirmary.

I went to my sister's side and put my arms around her. It was the only thing I could do for her now. Skye hugged me and buried her face in the side of my neck, silent and shivering. Everyone around us fell silent, and when I glanced up I could see them exchanging uncertain looks.

Suddenly, someone shoved through from the back of the crowd, and I heard a familiar deep, husky voice ordering people out of the way. A few seconds later, Michael burst through, his expression frantic. He rushed over to us and wrapped both of us up in a hug. Skye barely seemed to notice, but I was grateful for it.

"What happened to Bobby?" I asked him over my sister's head. "Owen said he was unconscious?"

"He got knocked out in the scramble," Michael replied. "I had my boys move him to one of the spare rooms and lock him up. We can deal with him later. Ryan...?"

"They took him to the infirmary," I said quietly. "We don't know yet, but..."

"It's an unsurvivable wound," Skye said, her voice laced with a mixture of bitterness and regret. "If he's not dead yet, then he will be soon." She laughed, but there was no humour in it. "He knew it. He was trying to say goodbye, but he couldn't speak properly."

I sighed heavily and tightened my grip on her. "I'm so sorry, Skye. After everything you two have been through together... it just isn't fair."

"Life isn't fair," she replied. This time, her voice lost its bitter edge and just sounded exhausted, far more exhausted than any eighteen-year-old had a right to be. "He made a choice, and he chose to save you."

"He didn't just save me, though," I said. "He saved my baby, too. He saved my family. He must have known the risk, but he made that choice anyway." I glanced up and made eye contact with Michael. "At least now we know what to name the baby."

"Actually, I might have to fight you for that," Skylar said. "I think I'm pregnant again. I'm late. Just a few days, but... if I am, it might be his, or it might be Hemi's. I guess I won't know until after it's born."

I felt tears gather in my eyes, and this time I made no attempt to hide them. "Dammit, little sis. When I said that we needed to repopulate the earth, I didn't mean that we had to do it personally."

Skye managed another humourless laugh and wriggled out of our three-way embrace. "I want to... I want to go wait with him. Even if he's not awake. I need to say goodbye."

"Do you want me to come with you?" I asked.

She shook her head. "No. I just need some space, please. I know where you are if I need you."

Part of me screamed in protest about leaving her alone at a time like this, but she'd proven time and again that she was mature enough to cope with far more than I knew how to give her credit for. I was learning, though. I was learning not just how to be there for her when she needed me, but how to take a step back and not pressure her when she needed space. That was a hard lesson for me when all of my instincts told me to wrap her up in cotton wool and protect her from the world.

"Can we at least walk you to the infirmary?" I asked, reaching out to touch her hand. Skye just nodded and threaded her fingers through mine, letting me offer her what comfort I could from physical contact.

The crowd parted in front of us as we walked out of the dining hall, with Michael a step behind us. The infirmary was so close that it was a symbolic gesture more than anything else, but Skye seemed to appreciate it. When we got there, we found Hemi waiting outside the door. He took Skylar's elbow and guided her inside, leaving the rest of us out in the hall.

I looked at Michael, but he had no advice or guidance for me today. None of us had known Ryan for more than a year except for Skye, but he'd touched so many of our lives. I took Michael's hand and sat down on the floor. The least we could do was sit out the death watch in his honour.

Chapter Nineteen

People came and went over the course of the next few hours, but Michael and I stayed. Maddy came to join us, carrying Tigger in her arms. The kitten – now a young-adult – pranced back and forth across our laps, then curled up and went to sleep on my thigh. I stroked her for a while, but there were no words to make my churning gut feel any better today.

Slowly but surely, other people came to join the watch. Priya brought Alfred up, though the old sheepdog had no idea what was going on. He lay down beside Michael and went straight back to sleep, while Priya sat down in front of us and stared into space. Elly, Zain, and their older boys sat on the floor not far away, and Richard and Jim sat across from them. Anahera and the rest of the Waikato Iwi arrived one by one, and then other citizens started to join us as well. Eventually, the hall was packed with people.

I couldn't look at them. Seeing so many people gathered around just made it all seem more real, and I couldn't bring myself to accept the reality of his impending death just yet. I knew that the doctor would do everything in his power to save Ryan's life, but we weren't equipped to treat gunshot wounds, let alone collapsed lungs. My gut told me his death was inevitable, and that was so tragic that it made my mind scream and thrash in rebellion. Too many young people had died. Far too many. Sophie, Dog, Kylie, and now Ryan – they'd barely had a chance to live. It wasn't fair for them to have to die. Netty had broken my heart, but at least she'd lived a full life and gone to her grave on her own terms.

Another friend, gone forever in the blink of an eye.

"This is the last one," I said softly, as much to myself as anyone else. "We can't lose anyone else before their time. We just can't. It's wrong. He's the last one. For his sake, this cannot happen again."

Michael touched my shoulder, a simple gesture that told me he understood, then he rose to his feet. "I'll be back in a minute. I'm going to go get something."

I nodded dumbly, my head a million miles away and busy replaying the collection of moments that Ryan and I had shared together. Our joy over their baby, then despair. The moments when we'd sighed together over Skye's stubborn nature and swapped loving jokes at her expense. In a few minutes, those memories were going to be the only thing I had left of my friend.

I was still brooding when Michael returned and sat beside me, carrying his violin in its case.

"My parents taught me that the dying can still hear, and sometimes music can ease their passing," he explained as he set the case on the ground at his feet.

I just nodded again, closed my eyes, and leaned back against the wall to listen. While I might not share his beliefs, I accepted them for what they were and was happy to let him do what he wanted to do. If there was even the slightest chance that it would help, then it was worth it. More people joined us as Michael played, squeezing into whatever gap they could find in that narrow hallway. It was hard to judge the passage of time without watches or windows, but it didn't really matter anyway. We would wait as long as it took, for the sake of our friend.

Just as I was thinking that, Madeline reached out and touched my hand, then Michael's. The violin fell silent.

"We need to go in now," she said. "It's time."

"Time for what?" I whispered.

"Time to say goodbye," she replied simply. The little girl rose and beckoned for us to follow her, then led the way into the infirmary. Nobody seemed surprised by our arrival, not anymore. Madeline's gift had seen to that. Skye was sitting beside Ryan's bed, her face drawn and red, but no tears shone in her eyes. Doctor Cross and the nurses were covered in his blood from their efforts to save him, but now they'd given up and just stood in a huddle nearby, their expressions utterly devoid of hope.

I went straight to Skylar's side and put my arms around her without being asked. She looked up at me, her face unreadable.

"I can't cry," she told me. "I should, but... I feel like I've already said goodbye to him. I don't know how to do it again. Ever since he told me that he tried to kill himself, I knew we were living on borrowed time. I knew it wouldn't be long until we were saying goodbye for the last time. The man who came back after Kylie's death was never *my* Ryan, the happy-go-lucky kid with the ready laugh and the shy eyes. I buried my Ryan when I buried our daughter. I still love him, and I'll always love him, but... now all I feel is relief. Every minute of our lives is pain and struggle. He's played his part, and now he doesn't have to suffer any longer. He's finally free of the misery, the fear, and the dread, and who knows? Maybe he's gone to be with Kylie and our parents. He's at peace. It's the rest of us I'm worried about."

I looked at Ryan, struggling to process her words but I couldn't. I just stared and stared, and all I could think was that I'd never seen his freckles stand out so much. The rosy glow of life was already fading away, leaving his skin pale and translucent. It was a miserable thing to see. He was far, far too young to die. I felt a small hand touch my back, and then I heard Madeline's voice.

"He wants me to tell you not to worry about him, Miss Sandy," she said, her voice soft and serious. "He always knew he'd give his life to save a McDermott someday, and you've been a good friend to him. He says to make the most of it, and to remember every day as his last gift."

A shiver ran down my spine, much as it did every time she spoke for the dead and dying. I closed my eyes and nodded. "Thank you. Please tell him that I appreciate it. My baby appreciates it. We'll never forget him."

"He says that he already knows that," she replied, then she looked at Michael. "He wants you to know that he's not angry at you. He knows why you treated him the way you did, and he gets it. He says that he's always respected you, and he wishes fate had given him the time to earn your friendship back. He wants you to promise to take care of his girls for him."

Michael drew a deep breath and nodded sharply. "I promise, and... thank you. Please tell him that I forgive him. I made a mistake by treating him the way I did, because I didn't understand his choices until it was too late. But when it came time to make the most important choice of all, he made exactly the same one that I hope I would have been strong enough to make. I'll remember him as a brother and a friend."

"That made him happy," Maddy said with a smile and a nod, then she turned to Skylar at last. "Miss Skye... he wants me to tell you that you made his life worth living, and that you were his first and only love. You were his hopes and dreams, and he'll be waiting for you when it's your time – which he hopes will not be for a long time."

I looked up just in time to see a smile cross Skylar's face. Finally, tears welled up in her eyes. She reached out and took Ryan's pale hand, pressing it to her cheek.

"You silly boy," she whispered. "I'll miss you so much. I'm so glad you came back and I'll always be grateful for the time we had together. You better be waiting for me when I get there. If you aren't, I'll hunt you down."

I hugged her tighter, and felt Michael's arms closing around both of us again. A few seconds later, I heard Maddy sigh. "He's gone."

"May he rest in peace," I said softly. Around me, I heard the stir of people in distress, followed by a wave of grief and confusion. Though few had been as close to him as we were, everyone had known him in some way. Now, for the first time, Tumanako had to grieve as a community.

***

We buried Ryan just before sunset, in the park overlooking the river. Like the graves in Hamilton, we picked a beautiful green place with old trees and wildflowers scattered amidst the long grass. It rained again, just like it always seemed to, but that didn't deter anyone from attending the funeral. Even Owen and his comrades joined us; they stood off to one side with their heads bowed respectfully while I read a short eulogy and shared a few stories from our time together. By the time I was done, everyone was dripping wet, shivering, and red-faced from crying.

One by one, the others drifted away to find dry clothes and warm up, until only a few of my most trusted friends and family remained. I looked around at the ring of faces and heaved a long sigh. "We need to figure out what to do about Bobby."

"If he were a few years older, then the answer would be obvious," Doc said, his expression troubled. "But he's just a child. We cannot execute a child, and exiling him would inevitably come back to haunt us. Imprisoning him seems like the logical option, but we aren't equipped for a long-term prisoner."

"No, we aren't," I agreed. "We don't need to hold a trial to determine whether he's guilty or not this time. We all saw him do it. But… Skye, you're the next of kin. What do you want us to do?"

"He's just a kid," she said, her face sad but thoughtful. "Ryan wouldn't want him to die, and if we exile him then you know Isabelle would go with him and she doesn't deserve to be punished. There must be another option."

"Give him to me," Gavin said. All eyes turned to him.

"What do you mean?" I asked.

"I mean, let me take custody of him for the duration of his punishment," he replied, absently flexing his hands. "You're right that execution is out of the picture, exile is a bad idea, and imprisonment is impractical. That just leaves rehabilitation. Taming rotten youngsters is kind of my field of expertise, isn't it? With enough time, patience, and a firm, guiding hand, I bet I can turn that boy into a productive member of our community."

I looked at Skylar and raised my eyebrows. "If anyone can, it's Gavin. What do you think?"

"I…" Skye hesitated, uncertainty flickering across her face. "If you think you can do that, then I agree. It's what Ryan would want. He was really listening to what you've been saying these last few months, Sandy. About lives being precious, and that we can't be too quick to kill or we risk becoming the very monsters we're fighting against. We talked about it a lot, and I'm starting to believe it, too."

I nodded and reached out to touch her arm, then I looked at Gavin. "You know it's not going to be easy. He's going to fight you every step of the way."

"Of course he is," Gavin replied, a faint smile crossing his scarred face. "Nothing in life is easy. It's not meant to be. It wouldn't feel like an achievement if it were. Still, I'm willing to do it if you're willing to let me."

"Then I'm officially putting you in charge of his rehabilitation," I replied. "Just ask for any resources or assistance you need, and I want a progress report every few days. I'll leave it in your hands."

"You make the public announcement, and I'll take care of Isabelle?" he suggested.

"I better tell her," I said. "As much as I'd love to not have to deal with that conversation, Isabelle trusts me. If it's going to come from anyone, it should come from me. Take Michael and Skye with you, and tell the others what's happening."

We started to head back towards Tumanako, but before we'd made it more than a few hundred meters we spotted a handful of figures standing in the gloom beneath a nearby tree. I held up a hand to halt the others, and went forward to meet Owen on my own.

Less than a year ago, I wouldn't have dreamed of confronting a gang on my own, but so much had changed since then. I was a different person now: stronger, more self-assured, and backed by a group of people that I trusted with my life. I came to a stop a few meters away from them and gave Owen a curious look.

"I thought you lot had gone home," I said, carefully modulating my tone so it was neither mocking nor accusative, but merely interested.

"We're about to leave, but we wanted to talk to you first," Owen replied. He hesitated for a second, then stepped out of the tree's shadow and came over to me. "We wanted to apologise for everything that happened. We knew the kid was a bit unbalanced, but we didn't know how imbalanced. He found us about a month ago, all full of fire and brimstone, shouting something about justice for his dad. If my father had still been in charge he'd probably have sent the kid packing, but I made the mistake of believing him. Dad just died a few months ago, and something about his situation struck a chord with me. I should have known better."

"Okay, fair enough," I said. "I don't blame you for what Bobby did. He's the only one responsible for his own actions. You're free to go any time you want."

"Actually, that's just it," he said, absently scratching his neck. "The lads and I... we don't particularly want to go. We've got nothing to go back to. There are people here — real people, normal people, good people. Underneath the leather and tattoos, we're just like everyone else. We crave normality. We dream about having a home again. We're not bad people, either. I know some of the gangs think nothing of using violence to get what they want, but Dad never let us turn into that. He was a biker, but he was a good man. If you're willing to have us, then we'd like to help you build a home for all of us right here."

In spite of the day's tragedy, a smile crept across my face. "Well, all right. But no stealing from us, okay?"

"If we stole from you, then we'd be stealing from ourselves," he answered. "We never wanted to steal to begin with. Hell, I was a prosecutor for the crown. My job was making sure murderers and child-molesters saw justice. Necessity makes criminals of us all."

"That is very true, unfortunately," I replied. "Okay, let's go see which rooms are available."

"Can I do that?" Skylar asked, coming up behind me. "I'd rather keep myself busy with work than have to listen to Gavin explaining the Bobby deal again."

I sighed and nodded my understanding. "If it'll make you feel better, then go ahead. Assign them rooms and bedding, and then bring them down to Doctor Cross for a physical examination and a workup of their personal histories."

"I know what to do," she answered dryly, then she gestured to Owen and his friends. "This way, guys. Let's get inside before it gets dark."

I watched her gather up the newest members of our community and lead them away, then I looked back over my shoulder to see who was left. Everyone had vanished, except for the last three remaining members of our original group: Michael, Doctor Cross, and Madeline. Michael took my hand and I fell into step beside him.

"We're probably not going to have much time to talk over the next few days, Doc," I said. "Maybe you should ask whatever it was you wanted to ask us now."

Doc sighed and hiked his glasses back up the bridge of his nose. "It wasn't much, really. I just wanted to ask you both a few questions regarding the medical histories of your families so that I can work out what we should be able to expect when your due date comes."

Michael laughed suddenly. "You know, in all this excitement I nearly forgot about the baby."

"You're such a bad liar, honey," I told him, squeezing his hand. "It's okay to show your excitement, it's not going to freak me out. Hell, knowing how much this baby would mean to you was what got me through the first few months."

He glanced at me and gave me one of his silly, sheepish grins, then he grabbed me and hugged me tight. "Am I that transparent?"

"Like glass," I replied, laughing. Almost as suddenly as it had started, my laughter faded away. "Damn, it feels so wrong to be smiling right after a funeral."

"I think that your sister is right in more ways than she realises," Doc said, absently adjusting his glasses again. With a sudden grunt of annoyance, he took them off and started wiping the raindrops off the lenses. "Ryan would want us to carry on. We were never what you would call close, but I knew that much about him."

"You're right, of course," I replied. "Like she said, he's at peace now. After everything we've been through, death is almost a blessing." I shook my head and snuggled in against Michael's warmth. "Not that I plan to embrace it any time soon. Anyway, what did you want to ask?"

"Ah, yes," Doc said. "I want you both to think as far back as you can when you answer, and also consider any extended family you know of. I need to know if there's any history of congenital defects, genetic conditions, or even a history of multiple births in either of your families."

"Multiple births?!" I exclaimed. "Oh, hell no. That is *not* what I signed up for!"

Doctor Cross gave me a dark look. "I'm just asking, Ms McDermott."

"Right... just asking," I echoed, glowering right back at him. "Nothing on my side, as far as I'm aware. I don't really know my extended family, though. Mum used to tell me that both Skylar and I were born a little early, but we were both healthy regardless."

"Sometimes a baby is just more anxious than most to get out into the world," Doc replied, a faint smile crossing his lips. "We'll keep that in mind towards the end. And what about you, Constable? Anything we should know about?"

"Not as far as I'm aware of," he replied with a shrug. "No twins or triplets, heart defects or anything like that."

"Good, good," Doc said, nodding thoughtfully. "Of course, that doesn't rule out difficulties, but it does mean less to worry about."

I grunted and shook my head. "I think the plague is enough to worry about."

"Very true," he agreed. "On a more positive note, I believe we've managed to save Franco's leg. It will be a while until he's up and about unassisted, but he should heal cleanly. It's a very good thing you found him when you did — another hour and he might have lost that leg, or even died from exposure."

"Thank goodness," I said, letting out a long sigh of relief. "You're right, that's a good thing. Do whatever you need to take care of him. You know you have my permission to draw on any of the resources you need."

"I do, and I shall," he said. The conversation halted as we stepped across the threshold, and spotted a small figured huddled up in the shadows waiting for us. As soon as she saw us, she jumped up and rushed towards us.

"You guys go on without me," I said softly. "Isabelle and I have to have a talk..."

Chapter Twenty

Isabelle took the news of her son's rehabilitation about as well as I thought she would, which is to say that she was so grateful, it took me weeks to make her understand that she didn't owe me anything. Eventually, I managed to convince her that it was all Gavin's idea, and then her gratitude transferred to him. Every so often, I'd spot her running after him with some gift that she'd made clutched to her breast, which always left him looking flustered.

As the days passed, Tumanako settled into a comfortable routine. New faces emerged from the wilds to join our community on a daily basis, and every morning the sun shone a little bit brighter. Winter was over and most of us had survived. Most, but not all.

Ryan's death hit Skylar hard, and I'd be lying if I said it hadn't affected me almost as much. I often found myself retiring to the dark places where grief lingered, thinking about another friend lost before his time. Just as I'd been there for him in the wake of Sophie's death, Michael was there for me. He always seemed to know when I needed the space, but never let me mope for long.

We spent as much time together as we could justify, and even when we couldn't be together he found ways to make me feel loved. Some days I'd come home to a bouquet of freshly-picked wildflowers in a vase, or a piece of furniture for our apartment, a new book, or even something for the baby. Somehow, he managed to dote on me without making me feel put-upon. It was a remarkable feat of ingenuity, really. I was secretly impressed – but I didn't tell him, of course. I didn't have to. It was Michael. He just knew.

Still, there were some days when I was in a dark place and the only person I wanted to talk to was Skye. This time, she let me in. Neither of us had to grieve alone. We'd grown close enough over the course of our journey south that she really was my sister again, not just in name but in every way. If we wanted to sit together in silence and cry, we could. No judgement, no awkwardness, just understanding. Something about that was comforting. Together, we both began to slowly recover.

One morning about six weeks after the shooting, I trudged inside after a few hours of pulling weeds in the garden and found Skylar sitting in the dining hall with a petite, dark-haired woman whose name I didn't know. Both of them were hunched over a table, talking quietly.

"Whatcha doing, little sis?" I asked curiously, walking up behind her.

Skylar jumped and shot me a dark look. "Damn it, don't sneak up on me!"

"Honey, I'm a three hundred kilogram placenta-filled water-balloon right now," I said dryly. "'Waddling' and 'sneaking' are two different things. If I scared you, that's your fault."

"Oh my god, you're so over dramatic," Skye replied, rolling her eyes. "You're barely even showing yet. If you think this is waddling, just give it another three months."

"Don't remind me. I'm already getting stretch marks," I said. I invited myself to sit down at the table opposite them, and leaned over to look at the sketchpad sitting open on the table in front of the new arrival. "Hey, what's this?"

"It's going to be Ryan," Skye said, suddenly looking very pleased with herself. She picked the sketchpad up and turned it around so that I could get a better look at the picture. "Isn't it wonderful? Aicel was an illustrator before the plague. I convinced her to draw Ryan for the memory wall."

Aicel smiled shyly and tucked a strand of hair back behind her ear. "You're too kind. It's just a doodle at this stage. Once I complete the painting, it will look much better."

"Oh, you're going to paint it?" I asked, surprised and pleased. "That would be a wonderful tribute to him. Once it's done, would you consider doing some others?"

"We're already planning to," Skye replied, looking happy for the first time in weeks. "This is just the start. Aicel's going to help me with the photographs, and we're going to try to paint everyone we can remember into a huge mural – not just down here, but anywhere there's space. I think we should do Kylie, Sophie, Dog, and Netty first, then move on to our families. It's going to take us years, but once we're done we're going to have a memorial to every person we loved and lost. It's going to be magnificent."

"Wow," I breathed, impressed by both the scope of the idea and the emotion behind it. "Do we... do we have the resources to make that happen?"

"We'll find the resources," Skylar said, her voice firm and resolute. "Aicel says that artist's paints last just about forever, and I know a few stores in town that we can raid. If that isn't enough, then I'm sure there are plenty down in Wellington."

"Another brilliant idea," I said, nodding my approval. "Add it to the list. It seems like every time we start a project, we have another dozen good ideas to distract us."

Skye laughed and nodded. "Yeah, we've got way too many ideas and not enough time, but we'll get there. Speaking of which, I forgot to tell you – I got the notebooks and stuff you wanted. I'll start handing them out over dinner tonight."

"Thank you," I said. I rose to my feet and stretched my aching back. "I have to go do some stuff. Let me know if you need me, okay?"

"You're going to need to start taking it easy soon, missy," Skye said, wagging a finger at me. "Don't make me give you the same lecture you gave me last summer."

"Oh, I won't," I said dryly, running a hand across my growing belly. "I have no intention of doing anything that might put the baby at risk, even accidentally. It's going to be hard when those tomatoes start ripening, but I'm even going to resist eating anything fresh out of the ground until it's been thoroughly washed."

"Good," she said. "I guess we'll see you later, then."

"Absolutely," I agreed. "Nice to meet you, Aicel."

The woman waved a shy farewell. I waved back, and then trudged out of the room and down the hall towards the elevator. A few minutes later, I was making my way towards the suite of rooms we'd put aside for our communications equipment and research facilities when a door opened and Gavin stepped out. He froze in his tracks, blinking in surprise, then he grinned.

"Well, I suppose that saves me coming to look for you," he said. "We just had a call from Sergeant Bryce."

I raised an eyebrow. "Oh? Is everything all right?"

"Yeah, everything's fine," he said, beckoning for me to follow him. I did, and he led me into the room he'd just come from. Through a doorway, I could see Doctor Cross hunkered over his latest set of experiments. Bobby was sitting at a small table in a corner, intensely focused on a book that lay open on the table in front of him. He didn't even glance up when I came in.

Gavin and I hadn't really talked about the details of his rehabilitation regime, but whatever he was doing seemed to be working. I hadn't seen Bobby much, just at meals and occasionally in the garden, but whenever I did he just nodded politely and kept walking. There had been no further attempts on my life, and no sign that he was planning anything untoward. It was entirely possible that he'd just learned his lesson, but I thought it more likely that Gavin was just enough like his former stepfather for Bobby to respect him and be willing to follow his lead. Fortunately, Gavin was a much more responsible father-figure than Henry had been.

Gavin led me through another doorway, into a small room where he kept the various bits of radio and long-range communications equipment he'd scavenged from the area. I settled in a random chair without being prompted, happy to be off my feet even for a moment.

"Sergeant Bryce wanted me to tell you that no one's come through Waiouru in more than two weeks," he said, sitting down in the chair opposite me. "No sign of the mutants, either. She's decided it's time for her to come south, and she's bringing the library."

"Does she need us to send her any aid?" I asked.

"No," he said, shaking his head. "She said that she and her men already have things well in order. She's going to follow the same route we did, and estimates she should be here in under a month."

"That's good," I replied, then I sighed and admitted the truth to him. "I am concerned, though. New Zealand isn't that big. The mutants are going to keep spreading in the north, and eventually they're going to start roaming south. What if we haven't gone far enough?"

"Michael and I have been working on a plan for that," he said. "We've worked out that the mutants aren't a short-term problem anymore. They're a long-term problem. We need to stop thinking about what we can do about them today and tomorrow, and start working on how we can deal with them over the next decade."

I gave him a curious look and said nothing. He smiled sheepishly, but took that as his cue to keep talking.

"Right now, there just aren't enough of us to deal with them in an efficient manner," he explained. "So what we're going to do instead is create a firebreak between us and them. You know what a firebreak is, right?"

I nodded. "It's a strip of land where all the trees and brush have been cleared out, to prevent forest fires from spreading by restricting their potential fuel."

"Exactly," he said with a smile. "So the plan is that we treat the mutated infected like a natural disaster, and build a break around us. The regular infected don't move around much, so we're going to start taking teams out and clearing them from the area surrounding Lower Hutt and Wellington. Once this region is totally clear, we'll start moving north. Obviously we can't take anyone vital to the day-to-day running of Tumanako, so it's going to take a long time for us to even finish the Wellington region."

"But we'll get there eventually," I finished for him. "Just by taking it one day at a time. That's as good a plan as any I've heard."

"Obviously, the mutated infected themselves can cross the break," he added, "but at least this will prevent those plague-bearer things from having any effect on us. Can't spread a plague where there's nothing to receive it, right? Eventually, once we have enough people, we can move up the North Island and clear out the old cities—"

Just at that moment, our conversation was interrupted when the door burst open and Priya raced inside. She glanced around frantically, then as soon as she saw me she scampered over and grabbed my hand.

"Mama!" she cried. "Mama, come quick, must see!"

"Whoa, what is it honey?" I asked, rising to my feet. She just squealed something inarticulate and dragged me out of the room. Gavin leapt up, shouted something to Doc, and hurried after us. The four of us raced down the corridor towards the north-west corner of the building. We completely forgot about Bobby in all the excitement, but he soon caught up with us of his own free will. Priya threw open the door to the corner suite and pulled me over to the window overlooking the front gates.

Outside the gate was a massive crowd of people.

"Good Lord, there must be two hundred people down there," Doc cried. "Where did they all come from?"

I glanced at Gavin, but he had no answer for me.

"I don't know," I started to say, but suddenly realisation struck me. "Wait! Yes, I do. We all do. It's the South Islanders!

Remember, they were camped out in Picton, trying to get the ferry working again? They must have done it, and now they're here! The South Islanders are here! Come on!"

This time, it was me dragging Priya along, with Doc, Gavin, and Bobby hot on our heels. The elevator was too busy to be of any use to us, so we took the stairs instead. By the time we reached ground level, the entire population of Tumanako was gathered outside. The chatter of excited voices and the bright-eyed looks on every face sent a thrill of excitement right through me.

I lost my grip on Priya's hand as I was trying to wriggle my way to the front of the crowd, but it didn't matter. We were surrounded by friends and family, no one would hurt her. Someone shouted my name, and then suddenly I found the way open before me and helpful hands guiding me through. On the far side, Michael and Skye were waiting for me, along with Anahera, Simon, and a few of the other more prominent members of the council.

"Sandy!" Michael cried as soon as he spotted me. "You're not going to believe this."

"Oh, yes I would," I replied.

I grabbed my advisors and led them towards the gates. The gates were still closed, but the people on the other side looked just as excited as my people. There wasn't the slightest hint of a threat in either their voices or on their faces. Someone I didn't know spotted me and shouted my name, then a spontaneous cheer went up from the crowd. By the time we reached them, they were chanting my name like a mantra. I came to a stop on the far side of the gates and held up my hands, but it still took a minute for the chant to die down.

Once it was finally quiet enough for me to be heard, I addressed them all. "I think I can already guess, but where are you guys from?"

"Nelson!" a woman at the front of the crowd shouted.

"Dunedin!" someone else cried.

"Picton!" called a third voice, then the noise level rose to impossible again as everyone announced their home cities. By the time they were done, there was a tear in every eye. Everyone fell silent, looking at me expectantly.

"To be honest with you all, I wasn't sure that you were going to make it," I admitted. "But, you have no idea how glad I am that you did. Welcome, everyone! Welcome to Tumanako! Your new home!"

A cheer exploded from the crowd, both inside the gate and out. I beckoned to the guards to unlock the gate and let the people in, and they did. A few moments later, we were caught up in a flood of happy, crying, excited people, strangers exchanging handshakes and hugs as if they were old friends.

For the first time in my life, I wasn't scared of being surrounded by strangers. I was excited. Truly, unbearably, ridiculously excited. These strangers were not a scary mob of potential danger, they were the living embodiment of the one thing that humanity needed more than anything else in the world: hope.

Chapter Twenty-One

The arrival of our Southern brethren more than doubled the population of Tumanako overnight. Even more critical to the survival of the human species, we discovered that there was a much higher percentage of adult women amongst the South Island survivors than the North. I could only guess that the thinner population in the South Island had given the women a better chance of making it through the years after the plague. Half of them were already married, but the other half... well, let's just say that there was a lot of friendly competition amongst the men of Tumanako to try and win the hands of the new arrivals.

It took us weeks to record everyone's biographical information, but as we worked our way through them we were delighted to discover that we'd gained a number of useful professionals. Once we'd finally completed the monumental project, Doctor Cross called a meeting of the council to update us on what our newest citizens were capable of.

"I am thrilled to advise that I am no longer the only doctor here," he told us as soon as we'd all seated ourselves. We all laughed at his obvious relief, and he glared at us. "Oh yes, laugh your little heads off. You weren't the one faced with the prospect of having to tend the needs of four hundred and seven people!"

"Sorry, Doc," I replied. "We were just laughing at the look on your face. We're thrilled there's someone else to help out. Tell us about the new doctor."

"Oh, yes." He relaxed a little and adjusted his glasses. "Her name is Ngaire Madurrit, and she was a professor of obstetrics at Otago University before the plague. She managed to keep a small group of students from the school together, including a couple who were involved in the medical sciences." Doc paused and gave me a significant look. "One was studying immunology. I've already commandeered her services."

I grinned at him and nodded my approval. "She's all yours. And, is obstetrics what I think it is?"

"Yes, yes it is," he replied dryly. "I've set her up with an office in the other spare room off the infirmary, and I expect you both to check in with her as soon as possible. You'll be spending a lot of time together."

Skylar shot me a quizzical look. "Does he mean us?"

"Yes," I said, laughing. "She specialises in pregnancy and childbirth. Thank goodness she survived — we're going to need her services a lot in the years to come."

Michael perked up and gave me a half-excited, half-terrified look. "We are?"

"That was a general statement about the community, honey," I replied, patting his knee comfortingly. "Don't worry, we've got to get through this pregnancy before we think about having any more kids. We're probably going to get divorced about ten minutes after I go into labour."

Everyone laughed again. Once the levity faded, Doc picked up his list and checked it. "We've also got a handful of builders and engineers who were in Christchurch helping with the rebuild, another plumber, a psychologist, a potter, a tailor, two teachers, three artists, and a bunch of farmers. Oh, and we've got four soldiers from Burnham Military Camp, and two officers from the Air Force base in Blenheim."

I sat up straight and looked at him with interest. "Are they pilots?"

Doc consulted his list for a moment, then nodded. "One is an engineer, but the other was a helicopter pilot."

I glanced around the circle of faces and raised an eyebrow. "You guys thinking what I'm thinking?"

"Fuel is limited, but a helicopter could be useful in a pinch," Michael said thoughtfully. "We need to head down to Wellington to raid the National Library anyway, so we could check out the airport while we're there."

"Maybe," I said, holding up a hand. "Long-term plans. Right now, I want everyone focusing on getting Tumanako self-sufficient. We'll head down to check out the library once Erica gets here; she'll never forgive me if we go without her. How far away is she, Gav?"

"She checked in this morning, said she's three days out," Gavin replied. "She should be here by new moon."

"Hang on a sec, what do you mean 'we'," Skye interjected, giving me a dark look. "You are not thinking about going down to Wellington in your condition."

"Just to watch," I replied. "It should only be a day trip, and I plan to take care of myself. I won't help with the lifting or anything, I just want to be part of the mission. Promise."

Skye crossed her arms and glared at me. "You better not. If I hear about you fainting again, I'll kick your butt."

"I don't doubt it," I answered dryly, then I turned my attention back to the rest of the group. "We need to send a scouting party down to check if there are any books worth saving. No point going if the place is a smouldering ruin."

"I'll take care of it," Michael said, rising to his feet.

"And I'll go organise their supplies," Skye chipped in.

"Wow, I don't need to do anything these days," I said with a laugh. "Thanks, guys."

"You just go see that obstetrician lady and check on our baby," Michael replied, his tone light and playful. "Don't make me nag you, woman."

"All right, all right," I said, easing myself up to my feet. Michael hurried over to help me, but I didn't really need the assistance. I might not have been used to lugging around the extra weight, but I was still an athletic person by nature and pregnancy had done nothing to change that.

Still, he liked to help me and I was happy to let him do it if it made him feel better. We headed down to the second level together, then he kissed me goodbye and hurried off to organise the scouting party. I let myself into the infirmary, where I found Franco and Tala talking to Rebecca. Tala's face lit up with a smile as soon as she saw me, and she waved shyly.

I waved back and returned the smile. "Hey, guys. How's the leg, Franco?"

"Good," he replied. "The doctor says I'll probably have a limp forever, but I'm just grateful to be alive and walking. Things could have turned out much, much worse for me."

"I'm glad to hear you're recovering nicely," I told him. "I'm always impressed when I see you whizzing around on your crutches. You've really got that motion down to an art. I never could get the hang of it."

Franco laughed and nodded. "Practice makes perfect, eh? Life is good here. I'm glad we came." He put his arm around Tala's slender shoulders and kissed her cheek. "I just wish we'd come a little sooner."

"You can't change the past, and regrets won't fix what happened to you," I replied. "The important thing is that you're all okay, and you've been given a second chance at life. Anyway, I shouldn't interrupt your consultation. Is the Professor around?"

"She's in her office, reviewing our patient files," Rebecca replied, pointing me towards one of the doors at the back of the room.

"Thank you," I said, then I went over and knocked on the door.

A few seconds later, the door swung open and I found myself face to face with a tall, slender woman with dark skin, intelligent eyes, and short brown hair frosted with grey. She took one look at me, then smiled and beckoned me inside.

"Sandrine," she said by way of greeting. "I was wondering when you were going to avail yourself of my services."

"Doctor Cross only just got around to telling me what your speciality is," I replied. "I've seen you around, but I had no idea that you were an obstetrician until five minutes ago. I can't tell you how glad we are to have you here. And by 'we', I mean every woman of childbearing age in Tumanako."

Professor Madurrit laughed and reached out to touch my elbow, gently guiding me into a chair by her desk. "I can imagine. Stewart just about had kittens when I told him, and I can understand why. Obstetrics is an intimidating field, where even the slightest miscalculation can cost more than one life. Now, hold still a moment while I give you a check-up. Where did I put your file...?"

I waited patiently while she dug through the mound of paperwork on her desk, then she came back over and ran me through a series of quick tests. Though most of them were the same as what Doctor Cross did, there was something reassuring about being examined by a professional who knew what was best for both me and my baby. When she was done, she sat down at her desk again and made some notes in my file, then turned back to me with a smile.

"I'm pleased to advise that both of you seem to be in excellent health," she said. "I would like you to come back for an ultrasound once the scavengers manage to find a machine in working order, but I doubt there's anything to worry about at this stage. Have you made plans for the birthing yet?"

"Plans for the birthing?" I echoed, giving her a confused look. "What do you mean? It's just point and shoot, isn't it? Oh, and scream. Scream a lot."

She laughed again and shook her head. "Don't worry, most first-time mothers think that's how it is. No, there are an assortment of different options for you to choose from in terms of where and how your delivery takes place. I've got a few books here that we can look over, and then we can start making plans together..."

***

By the time I finally left the infirmary, my head was spinning from all the new information. I'd made my choices, though, and I felt better for having a clearer understanding of what my body was going through. Yeah, I was still fairly terrified by the whole process, but the professor had a way of making it all seem normal.

Which it is, I reminded myself. *Women have been having babies for thousands of years. They got through it, so I can get through it, too.*

I took a deep breath, nodded firmly to reassure myself, then I headed for the kitchen to make myself a nice cup of tea. On my way through the dining room, I spotted Skylar talking to Aicel and a couple of other people I only knew in passing. She waved a greeting, finished up her conversation, and raced over to catch up with me.

"Hey! How did the obstinate lady go?" she asked.

"You mean the obstetrician?" I replied dryly. "Good. She gave me a list of exercises to do to keep my girly-parts in peak baby-pushing condition, and yet another lecture on nutrition."

Skylar laughed and nodded. "Gotta keep them girly-parts working nicely if you want to repopulate the earth, sis."

"I keep telling you, we're not doing that single-handedly," I teased her, which just made her laugh even more. It was a pleasant sound to hear, and one that I decided I was going to squeeze out of her more often because it meant that she was finally recovering from Ryan's death. Once she stopped laughing, I gave her a nudge. "Hey, weren't you supposed to be getting supplies ready for the scouts?"

"I was on my way there when I got distracted," she admitted. "Did you see how well the mural is coming along? I requisitioned all the artists from the South Island group, and some other folks who are willing to learn. You wouldn't think it to look at her, but Melody is really good with a brush."

"I'd believe it," I said, glancing at the mural. With every passing day, it was spreading across the blank stone wall, filling it with colour and faces both familiar and new. Suddenly, I realised that there was something out of place and shot a quizzical glance at my sister. "I thought there were three new artists? I only see two over there."

"The third one is a sculptor," she explained. "I've got him working on another project. It's going to take a while, but I think you'll like it when it's done."

"Oh?" I asked, genuinely curious. Skye wasn't usually the sort to keep secrets.

This time, she just shook her head and smiled mysteriously. "Come on, we've got a lot to do before Erica gets here."

***

The next couple of days flew by. Word spread about the impending arrival of Erica and her books, and I found myself with no shortage of volunteers eager to help me transform a large chunk of one of the spare levels into a vast library. Of course, the rain may have also had something to do with it; the weather closed in on the day we sent the scouts south, and it was still drizzling when Sergeant Bryce finally arrived.

I was hard at work in the kitchen getting get lunch ready when the radio I still carried out of habit crackled to life. "Sandy, you there?"

"I'm here," I replied. I wandered over to the big windows that looked down on the courtyard, and immediately spotted the reason the guards were calling me: there was a slow-moving but determined convoy heading towards our front gates. "Oh, I see it. That's Sergeant Bryce. Let her in, and I'll be down in a second."

By the time I'd washed my hands and fought my way through the crowds to the ground level, Erica had already dismounted and was deep in conversation with Johan. I got there just in time to catch the tail end of a conversation about horse husbandry that went way over my head.

"Don't worry, we've got plenty of space here for the rest of the herd," Johan reassured her, then he spotted me and grinned. "Ah, there she is. I was just telling your friend that the mares are going to start coming into heat any day now, so we should start thinking about expanding our herd. No reason not to, since we've got the space and the numbers to warrant it."

"Sounds good to me," I agreed. I glanced at the herd milling around the courtyard and grinned. "Wow, it looks like you managed to bring the whole lot of them with you, Sergeant. How did you manage to pull that off?"

"It's easier than it looks," Erica replied. "Horses are herd beasts by nature, and tend to follow a single dominant mare. I just rode the dominant mare, and the others were happy to follow. I'll admit, I've never done it over such a long distance, but I'm very happy to say that I didn't lose any of them along the way. Quite a feat, really!"

"Well, I'm glad you managed to pull it off," I replied. "So, those trucks are the books?"

"Yes ma'am," she said, glancing back at the pair of trucks just coming to a stop behind the herd. "We had to leave a few things behind, but we've got the important stuff. Now that we know the way is open and fairly easy, I'm betting we could make the trip back in half the time if we need to."

"I doubt we'll need to," I told her. "We have enough resources here in the south not to worry about it. I think you'll be very pleased once you've had a chance to look around and meet people. It's actually starting to get a little cramped up there, if you can believe it. We're going to need to start moving people out of the main tower and into the houses inside the fence soon."

"There are houses inside the perimeter?" Erica asked, looking both surprised and pleased. "Well, this really was an ideal spot to build your new town, isn't it?"

"It is," I agreed. "This used to be a film studio. We've checked the fence for holes and patched up any weak points, so it's all secure. There's enough space to graze the animals, grow crops, and even expand our living space, all without leaving the security of the complex. We've even been working on a plan to turn that big warehouse over there into a giant greenhouse to keep us in fresh fruit and vegetables come winter. It was being used for sound stages, so the walls are removable and it's got built-in heating to keep it warm all year round."

"Sounds brilliant," Erica said, then she grinned. "I, for one, will just be glad to sleep in a proper bed tonight. I hope you can arrange that for us?"

I laughed and nodded. "Yep, and hot showers for everyone. Let the volunteers take care of the horses and unload the trucks. I've got a lot to show you."

Chapter Twenty-Two

I awoke the next morning to the sound of activity out in the hall. Michael was up and halfway through getting dressed, which meant we were already late. I muttered a low curse and rolled out of bed – or I tried to, but I overshot the edge and ended up in a heap on the floor with sheets and duvets all around me.

Michael took one look at me, then cracked up and raced over to help me up. "Dammit, Sandy. Do I need to keep reminding you that you're not as agile as you used to be?"

"Apparently," I answered dryly. "Well, nothing injured but my pride. How late are we?"

"Not late enough to matter," he replied. He gave me an affectionate smile, then leaned down to press a kiss to my lips. "We're back in that happy no-man's land where time doesn't really matter all that much, honey. Relax. We have a lovely home, we're going to have a family together, and we're safe." I opened my mouth to protest, but he just grinned and pressed a finger to my lips. "Hush. No one's going to leave us behind. Now, go do your stretches before the professor scolds you like a naughty school girl."

Whatever I'd been planning to say vanished in laughter at the mental image he conjured up. I just nodded obediently and headed out into the living room to do the exercises Professor Madurrit had assigned me, while Michael packed a day bag for us to share.

"Think we should toss in a change of clothes, just in case?" he called from the other room.

"Better safe than sorry," I replied. "The scouts reported the building's in pretty bad shape, so it might take us a bit longer than we planned to clear everything out. Ugh, man, when did it get so hard to do squats?"

Michael stuck his head out the door and watched with a cheeky grin on his face. "I'll take the blame for that. You need a hand?"

"Only if I get stuck," I replied.

He laughed and ducked back into our bedroom. "I'll pack a change, just in case. I mean, it's the National Library. It's gotta be pretty big, right?"

"Yeah," I agreed. I paused between reps to catch my breath and stretch my back. "This place is supposed to be a repository of all the literature ever written in or about New Zealand. Assuming it's not burned out, that should be a fairly large amount of information."

Michael came out of the bedroom with my backpack over his shoulder, and wandered over to kiss my cheek. "After all this preparation, it better not be burned out. I'm going to grab some breakfast. Want me to get your usual?"

"Since when do I have a usual?" I asked, surprised.

He laughed and gently prodded my swollen belly. "Since her. I do listen, you know. It's always fried tomatoes this, fried tomatoes that. With parsley. Always with parsley."

I blinked owlishly and felt myself turning red. "Wow, I didn't realise I was that predictable."

"You're not," he replied, his tone softening. "I just know you better than anyone else, remember? So, omelette and fried tomatoes, my love?"

I couldn't help but laugh and nod. "Okay, okay. But don't forget the parsley!"

"I wouldn't dream of it," he replied, then he gave me another quick kiss and left the room.

I spent a few minutes finishing my prescribed stretches, then I headed off to indulge in a long, hot shower. By the time I was done, I was surprised to find myself feeling much better. Whatever else she had going for her, the professor definitely knew what my body needed.

When I finished bathing, I changed into my travel gear – or at least the pieces that still fitted – and made my way down to the dining room. Before I even made it through the doorway, I heard the sound of whoops and laughter, but there were too many bodies gathered around for me to see what was going on.

"Lower!" a voice demanded. It took me a second to recognise it as Professor Madurrit. A few seconds passed, then she grunted in what sounded like mock annoyance. "I said lower, young man! You know what 'lower' means, or she wouldn't have ended up in this condition to begin with."

The people around them hooted and jeered so loudly that I could barely hear the deep, male voice apologise to her. "Sorry, Professor."

"Michael?" I called, struggling not to laugh. "Is that you in there? What's she doing to you?"

"Mama!" Priya's voice greeted me. A few seconds later, she wriggled her way out of the crowd and threw her arms around me. "You're missing the funnies."

"Oh, am I just?" I glanced up, just as the crowd peeled back to reveal the last thing I'd expected to see: Hemi was sitting backwards in a chair with his chin on the top rung while Michael massaged his back, with Anahera and Professor Madurrit watching like a pair of hawks. Michael shot a guilty look over his shoulder. I raised my eyebrows questioningly. "Well? What's this, then? And where are my fried tomatoes with parsley?"

"Skye's making them," he replied apologetically. "As soon as I got down here, the ladies jumped me and insisted I learn the basics of haputanga massage before we leave."

I looked at the ladies in question. "Oh? What is haputanga massage, and should I be afraid?"

"Afraid? No, dear heart." Anahera laughed and came over to me. She put her arm around my shoulders and guided me to the centre of the circle. "Haputanga is an important part of my culture, and one that I think we could all benefit from sharing. While I am not qualified to teach it, Ngaire is. 'Haputanga' is the Maori phrase for pregnancy and pre-natal care. We believe that it is important for both mother and baby to be relaxed, and that the father's help is instrumental in making sure that happens."

"And why is he practicing on Hemi?" I asked dryly. "Last time I checked, he wasn't a pregnant woman."

Everyone laughed at that, including Hemi himself. Anahera shook her head and grinned at me. "Well, if I am to be a grandmother, either by blood or adoption, it seems logical to teach them both at the same time. They're not the only ones, either. Many of our citizens will become parents in the days to come, so we'll be teaching the art of haputanga to anyone who wants to learn."

"Well, if it'll keep my back from playing up, then I'm all for it," I announced, then I marched over to the chair, shoved Hemi out of it, and plopped down in his place.

Again, the people around us whooped with laughter and cheered, and for once I wasn't embarrassed at all.

***

A few hours later, we were fed, dressed, and on the road with all the trucks that were still in working order. Between a hefty dose of fried tomatoes and a good massage, I was feeling sleepy and relaxed. I napped most of the way to Wellington, and woke just as Michael was guiding the Hilux along the last stretch of motorway leading into our country's former capital.

Michael grabbed the walkie-talkie off the dashboard and spoke into it. "I'm seeing a lot of rubble up ahead. Are you sure it's safe to take the trucks this way?"

There was a momentary silence, then one of the scouts replied. "Yeah, the Molesworth Street overpass is down. You should see an off-ramp on your left just before it. Take that, it's still good."

"There," I said, pointing to an overgrown concrete ramp not far from in front of us. Michael nodded and handed the radio to me, then focused on driving.

We crept up the off-ramp carefully, with a few people walking on either side to make sure that the concrete wasn't going to crumble beneath us, but it supported our weight just fine. At the top, we spotted a group of people on horses waving to us; from there, the way was easier. The streets were narrow, winding, and choked with the rusted hulks of old cars, but the scouts had made the most of the last few days and cleared a path for us. A few of the buildings had been reduced to rubble, but I was pleasantly surprised to see just how many were still intact.

"Wellington was always prone to earthquakes, so most of the buildings here were built to a high standard," Michael commented thoughtfully. "Looks like they did a good job of it, huh?"

"Looks like," I agreed. "Shame there are still so many bones, though."

"We're going to bury them," he told me. "As part of the project to put to rest the infected, we're going to bury the bones as well."

I shot him a startled look. "What? You're going to bury the remains of four million people? There's barely even four hundred of us!"

"I didn't say it was going to be easy," he replied, "and I didn't say it was going to be quick – but it is the right thing to do. Hell, it may come down to our kids and grandkids to finish what we start, but you taught me that we need to think about the future. I don't want my daughter tripping over the bones of the dead while she's learning to walk. Do you?"

"No," I admitted. "I'm just having trouble wrapping my head around the scope of what you and Gavin want to do. I never said that I disapprove, it's just... massive."

"It is, but it's the right thing to do," he said firmly. "Not just for the sake of hygiene, but also for respect. Like you always remind us, those bones were people once, people just like us. They deserve to rest in peace. If it were my bones lying on the pavement over there, I would hope that someone would take the time to bury them one day. If I have to work every day of the rest of my life to make this world a better place for the next generation and to let the last generation rest in peace, then I will."

The determination in his voice made me smile. I let the conversation drop and focused on the road instead.

After a few minutes of negotiating the clogged streets, I spotted a sign etched into the side of a building.

"There!" I cried. "That weird-looking one, with the angled front. That's it!"

The scouts guided our trucks up into the tiled arcade that ran alongside the library. I glanced at Michael and started to say something, only to stop when I saw the look on his face. "Whoa... honey, what's wrong?"

"It just..." He hesitated for a second, shaking his head. "It looks so much like the place where Sophie died. It was always the books with her. She loved going to the library."

"I'm so sorry," I said, reaching out to touch his hand.

He wrapped his fingers around mine and drew them up to his lips, then smiled sadly at me. "It's hard to believe it's been nearly ten months since I saw her smiling face. Sometimes, it feels like just yesterday..."

"Do you want to go home?" I asked. "We can leave the guys to take care of this, if you want. We don't really have to be here, they're perfectly capable of doing it."

"No," he said, shaking his head. "I can handle it. It just gave me a shock, is all. I'll be okay."

I frowned and nodded. "If you're sure..."

"I'm sure," he replied. He put the truck in park, then climbed out and hurried around to help me out. Though it usually bugged me when people pampered me because of my condition, this time I just let it go without saying a word. If it gave him something to think about besides Sophie's grisly death, then that was fine by me.

Within a few minutes, all of us had disembarked and gathered in front of the building, standing in a ring around the scouts. Warren stepped forward to address the group on their behalf, his face tense and alert.

"We haven't been able to breach the interior of the building yet," he explained. "The doors are all locked, and we haven't been able to unlock them by conventional means. We decided to wait until you got here before we tried anything more drastic. You bought sledgehammers, right?"

"We've got them, just like you asked," I replied. "You want us to try and break the glass?"

"We can try that, I doubt it'll work," he said, shaking his head. "If the rioters weren't able to break in, then I doubt we can do much unless we resort to explosives. No, we found a weak point in the wall around the back. I'm pretty sure that we can bust through it without too much effort."

"Assuming it's not a load-bearing wall," I said dryly. "Show us anyway. We brought one of the engineers along, he should be able to tell us whether it's safe or not. Eugene?"

A tall, painfully thin man with short, black hair and thick glasses stepped forward and nodded to us. "Show me the weak point, please."

Warren grunted inarticulately and gestured for us to follow him. We picked our way across the crumbling flagstones, down a short flight of steps, and into an alley that ran behind the library. Warren stopped beside a fire door and pointed at the wall just beside it.

"Here," he said, running his finger over the concrete. "If you look closely, there are some fine, hairline cracks running all the way through it. What do you think?"

"Mmm." Eugene leaned in close to get a better look at the cracks — but his inspection was interrupted by a metallic shriek as the fire door swung open unexpectedly.

I barely leapt out of the way in time to avoid being struck. Before I could even think of reaching for a weapon, I found myself staring down the barrel of a pair of rifles.

"Get away from there and go back to wherever you came from," the woman behind one of the guns demanded, her tone cool and professional. She was a few years older than me, with the same intense, wild-eyed look that I'd seen in the mirror every morning up until recently. The man beside her was the complete opposite — small, nervous, and mousy — but while his hands did tremble on the hilt of the gun, there was determination in his eyes that made me think twice about crossing him.

"Whoa, we mean no harm," I said, holding my hands up as if that might placate them. "We were coming to rescue the books, that's all. We didn't know there was anyone here."

The woman raised an eyebrow and took a step towards me, though she didn't lower her weapon. "Rescue the books from what, exactly? And where were you planning to take them?"

"From..." I hesitated, then shrugged and told her the truth. "I don't know, anything. We've founded a new city just north of here, in the Hutt Valley, and we're trying to collect anything we can find to remember and preserve the old world. Since we live so close to Wellington, it seemed logical to come here and try to save whatever we could before it was lost to fire, or the ocean, or just time."

She hesitated for a second, then slowly lowered her gun. "You're not going to try and destroy anything?"

I blinked in surprise and shock. "What? Why would we want to destroy our cultural history?"

"People do strange things," she answered dryly. "We've been locked down in here for four days while your men were nosing around outside, so you'll forgive me for being a little suspicious. We've protected this library for ten years and we have no intention of giving it up without a fight."

"You're... protecting it?" I echoed, then I looked at Erica and smiled. "All this worrying for nothing."

Sergeant Bryce grunted inarticulately and nodded. "We should have known we weren't the only ones around who gave a damn about the books."

Michael laughed and reached out to rub my shoulder reassuringly, then he glanced past me at the woman. "You know, I can't help but feel like I know you from somewhere."

"I was just thinking the same thing, actually," she replied. "Did we go to school together? Or to Police College? I graduated about a year before the plague."

"Oh, that's it!" he said, snapping his fingers. "I knew your face was familiar. I don't think we ever spoke, but I remember seeing your face in my classes. I'm Michael, and this is my wife, Sandrine."

"Valerie, but you can call me Val," she replied. "This is Xander. Don't mind him, he's not much of a people person. He just really loves his books."

Xander shot her a filthy look, then vanished into the building. Val rolled her eyes and gave us a long-suffering look. "Story of my life. He practically lived here before the plague, and nothing much changed when everyone died. He just lets me and the kids stay here because I'm bigger than him and because it means he doesn't have to find his own food."

"The kids?" I echoed. "You have children?"

"I have one," she replied, her expression suddenly turning dark. "My son, Dennis. He's four. Don't ask about his father. The others are foundlings. I couldn't very well leave them to starve after their parents died, so I adopted them."

I grimaced at the implications of the situation regarding her son's paternity, because it was one all too familiar to me. I just nodded my understanding.

"Yeah, we've got quite a few foundlings with us, too," I said, deliberately changing the subject to safer territory. "Like you said, it wouldn't be right to leave them to starve. We founded Tumanako – our little city – in hopes that no child would ever have to grow up alone. You're welcome to come and visit, if you want."

A flicker passed through Valerie's eyes, then she glanced away. "Are there many people there?"

"More than four hundred now," I said softly, gently. "All people like you and me. People who have been alone for way too long, and just want to be surrounded by friendly faces again. Men, women, children – we even have some pets running around. It's not exactly like the old days, but we're doing our best to build something worthwhile."

Valerie sighed and nodded. "I guess it can't hurt to look. Maybe we could think about transferring some of the books there. Are you sure it's secure? Doesn't Lower Hutt flood?"

"Sometimes," I replied. "But we've got a multi-level building, and we've dedicated the top floor to the preservation of cultural artefacts. The plan was that if we fill up the top floor, we'll gradually move the people out of the apartments on the next floor down and make room for books there. We're not sure how many people are left alive around here, but if it's more than a thousand I'll be surprised. Still, we've got plenty of good buildings near our main base, and builders to help us make more as we need them. We just need to find a way to contact the people who didn't see our television broadcast or hear our radio transmission, like you."

"I never was one for TV," she admitted with a shrug. "Well, come on then. I suppose I better introduce you to the others, then you can show me what you've got."

***

I sent the majority of my group off to check out the airport, while Michael, Erica, and I stayed behind to talk to Val and Xander. Once they'd relaxed and gotten used to us, they started opening up to us. Xander and Erica were drawn to one another almost immediately by their mutual intense love of books, and soon vanished out of sight. Val stuck with me and Michael. After the initial wariness wore off, she was perfectly happy to chatter away about whatever was on her mind, which mostly seemed to revolve around two things: the books, and her son.

No matter how he'd come to be, she obviously loved Dennis with an intensity that almost hurt to see. Every so often, I'd catch her looking at me and Michael with longing, but just as regularly she'd shut up shop and shy away from us as if suddenly remembering something painful. I understood, and made no attempt to pressure her into opening up before she was ready.

Unsurprisingly, Dennis and the younger kids gravitated towards Michael, and he to them. Val and I watched on from the relative safety of a couple of plush armchairs while Michael and the kids dashed frantically up and down the long aisles between bookshelves. Their laughter and shrieks of glee filled the library, driving back any shadows of doubt that either of us might have had about meeting one another.

"You know, I've lost track of who's chasing whom," I admitted as they tore past us again.

"Yeah, no idea," she replied. "I'm tired just watching them." She glanced back over her shoulder, then gave me a wink and a secretive smile. "You know, Xander's taken quite a shine to your army friend. I don't think I've ever seen him open up that fast to someone. When I first met him, it took me a week to convince him to even tell me his name."

"Well, they have a common obsession," I said. "I'm not sure what's going on with them, but I'm happy to see it. Erica's a brave woman, and she deserves a friend. She volunteered to stay behind while we came south to establish the city, and I was worried she was going to have difficulty getting used to being surrounded by people again. I know I did."

"She's a soldier," Val replied simply. "Adapt and survive. That's what soldiers are trained to do. Police officers, too. I'm not surprised that she thrived all these years, and I'm not surprised Michael did either. We have the training to help us. I am, however, surprised that you did. You can't have been more than, what... sixteen when the plague hit?"

"Eighteen," I corrected her. "But yeah, you're right. I'm not entirely sure how I survived, either. A lot of it was just trial and error, a lot of it was luck, some of it was reading, and the rest I put down to a few good teachers over the years. My mum and dad taught me a lot of valuable lessons before the plague, and then afterwards I met an ex-soldier named Gavin who's a lot like you, minus the love of books. Smart, quick to learn and slow to forget, and knows a lot about keeping himself alive."

Val laughed and nodded. "No, I get it. There was a lot of luck involved. A lot of luck. I was twenty-two, but I had my training to fall back on. I was assigned to Wellington after Police College, and this was one of the first places that got badly hit by the riots. They wanted us to protect parliament, but we soon figured out that the prime minister and the rest of cabinet had already fled. Why risk our lives to protect something that didn't matter anymore? So we just went home."

"I guess it's safe to say that your parents didn't make it?" I asked as gently as I could, watching her face for any sign that I was crossing a line.

She just shrugged and glanced away. "My dad died of a stroke when I was a teenager, and my mum just sort of... wasted away after that. She died a week after I was accepted into Police College. I think she was just waiting to see me on the road to a good career before she went to join Dad, you know?"

"Yeah, I know." I reached over to touch the back of her hand. She didn't pull away. "Some people are just meant to be together, in life and in death. My parents were like that. It's a long, not-nice story, but they died during the plague. So, is that why you came to protect the books?"

"Pretty much," she said with a shrug. "I went back to the flat I was living in at the time, but it was on fire and there was no sign of the fire service coming to deal with it. I figured out pretty quickly that the whole city was going to go that way if we didn't do something to stop it, so I grabbed the riot gear out of my car and came back into town, looking for some way to stop what was happening.

"I made it to the downtown area, then I was cornered by a group of rioters. They pulled me out of my car, and I thought for sure that my number was up — until someone laid into them from behind and managed to chase them off."

In spite of the fact that she'd obviously survived the encounter, I found myself sitting forward in my seat, anxious to hear the rest. "Who was it?"

"It was my partner," she replied softly. "Him, and a few of the other officers that he'd managed to round up. I found out afterwards that they'd barricaded themselves inside the library because it was the safest place they could find in a pinch, but when they saw me get pulled from my car they'd rallied out to save me. I was bruised up pretty badly, but they carried me back inside the library and took care of me."

"They didn't go home, either?" I asked.

She shook her head and looked down at the floor. "They'd tried. I don't know about the others, but my partner's wife was dead. He couldn't say the words, but I could see it in his eyes. He never told me what happened. It's probably for the best." She closed her eyes and took a deep breath to steady her shaking voice. "Most of the others died over the course of the next few weeks from the plague, until it was just me, Xander, and Dennis."

I blinked in surprise. "Wait, but Dennis is only four..."

Val cringed, then she sighed heavily. "Dennis senior was my partner. He was immune, like us. There was an accident, a few years ago... I don't want to talk about it."

"Then don't talk about it," I said, grabbing her hand in both of mine to offer her some kind of support. "It's okay, you don't have to say anything at all. I'm sorry. I didn't mean to bring up bad memories."

"It's not your fault," she replied, staring down at my hands as if they were some kind of alien life-form that had latched onto her. She swallowed hard, then put her free hand over top of mine and gave it a gentle squeeze. "Every day is hard. Every day, I wonder how I'm going to get through it all alone. I mean, I have Xander and the kids but they're always looking up to me, whether it's for food or protection or even just to play with. I'm not sure how much longer I can put up with this."

"Then come home with me, Val," I said gently. "You can leave the kids here if you want. Xander can watch them for one night. Come and see Tumanako. It's not just a city, it's an idea. The name means 'hope'. People like you are exactly why we founded it. You need something to hope for as much as anyone – and you deserve it."

"Sometimes I don't feel like I deserve it," she admitted, her voice husky. "Sometimes I wonder if those of us who survived did something horrible in a past life to deserve this fate. Like maybe we're suffering because we were mass murderers or something."

"I used to feel that way, too," I admitted. "When I was all alone, with no one to help me, I used to cry myself to sleep every night, wondering what I'd done to deserve my fate. But, you know what? We haven't done anything to deserve this. We all deserve better. The problem is that the people who used to make things better for us are all gone now, so we have to make things better for ourselves. Come with us, Val. Just for one night. No contracts, no obligations. If you don't want to stay, then you don't have to. If you don't want to see us again, you don't have to. But if you do, then you'll be welcome to stay. You won't have to live in a library anymore. You won't have to do everything. Dennis can go to school with the other kids and make new friends. You can make new friends, too. I bet you don't remember what it's like to have friends anymore, do you?"

"Well, I guess Xander counts as a friend, but only because there's no one else," she said hesitantly, then she bit her lip and fell silent. I just waited, watching her, letting her think through the decision without pushing her any more.

Sure enough, less than a minute later, she looked up at me and nodded.

Chapter Twenty-Three

Once we took Val home, we couldn't have convinced her to leave even if we'd wanted to. She lasted about ten minutes before she burst into tears, and had to sit down for a while to recover. Maddy appeared out of nowhere, just as she had that first day I'd awoken in the Hamilton bunker, and her tiny, unthreatening presence helped Val through the shock.

By midday, she'd seen everything we had to see and was thoroughly convinced that she wanted to be part of it. She insisted that we go fetch her son and bring him to Tumanako, and it took all of my wiles to convince her that she'd need to go with us or Xander was unlikely to let him go. She saw sense in the end, but heavy emotion left her a little irrational. She demanded that I come with her, and cried on my shoulder most of the way back to Wellington. Once she got there, the sight of her son's face seemed to steady her. She packed up their belongings, chased Xander and her foundlings into the trucks, and took them all back to Tumanako that very evening.

Val and the kids settled in quickly, but Xander was another story. If not for Valerie and Erica, then he might well have slipped off in the night and never come back. But with their help, he eventually decided to give us an honest chance – and although he wasn't as vocal about it as Val, it swiftly became clear that he liked what he saw.

Val metamorphosed into 'one of us' in no time flat. Within a couple of days, she became the perfect representation of my vision for the people of Tumanako: a lonely, frightened flower that bloomed within the greenhouse of safety and social acceptance into a happy, healthy, smiling rose. Every time I saw her, she was laughing and joking around with her new friends, and something about her unabashed joy was infectious. Even my little group of loners smiled when she was around. I saw her teasing stoic Warren on more than one occasion, and I could have sworn that he actually liked it.

The new kids went through a similar transformation over the course of the first week. At first, they were shy and standoffish, until they met Melody. With that special kind of magic only she was capable of, she took the new kids under her wing and taught them how to be children again. Soon, they were all part of her little pack of wild, fun-loving raggamuffins. There wasn't a morning that went by in silence with her there to lead them. They filled the corridors with happy noise, until it was time for class.

On one such morning not quite two weeks after their arrival, I was sitting in the dining room staring out the window and fiddling with a pen when I heard someone pull out the chair across from me. I glanced over, and was surprised to discover Johan sitting down with a bundle of purring tabby fluff in his arms.

"Wow, I can't believe Tigger's letting you carry her around," I commented, amused.

Johan laughed and nodded. "I have secret vet voodoo, didn't you hear? It's the first thing they teach you when you start studying."

I chuckled, setting put my pen down. "I can't believe how big she's getting. She must be almost a year old by now, but she's still all fluff."

"You're not all fluff anymore, are you?" he asked the cat, stroking her fur. She didn't answer, of course. She just purred and wound herself around his hands, rubbing herself against him. He smiled and glanced up at me. "Did you know she's pregnant, too?"

"What?" I gasped. "Who impregnated my kitten? I'll kill him!"

Johan just laughed again, not fazed by my horror. "It's a natural thing, Sandrine. Life comes, life goes. She seems to be quite happy with her condition, so it's nothing to get upset about. I just wanted to check if you'd like me to spay her after she's had the kittens. She's due in the next few weeks."

"Natural... right." I took a deep breath and closed my eyes for a second to calm myself down, then I shook my head. "Not just yet. There aren't a lot of domestic cats left around here, and we could use them to keep the pests out of the crops. Plus, they kind of help keep people sane. She certainly did that for me."

"Why don't you write about that, then?" he suggested, gesturing towards the blank page in front of me. "You seem to be at a loss for where to start."

"I am," I admitted, absently tracing my fingers over the smooth paper. "There's just so much to tell, you know? Ten years. More, if you count before the plague. Where do I even begin?"

"Start with how you met Tigger," he replied. He placed the kitten – now a cat – on the table beside me and rose to his feet. "See her back home when you're done with her?"

"Of course." I watched until he left the room, then I looked down at the fluffy tabby face staring up at me. I reached out to her and ran my hand across her back, marvelling at her softness.

As I did so, a memory surfaced of a time not so long ago, a time when I'd needed that softness to keep me sane. Ohaupo. It felt like a lifetime ago, even though it wasn't quite a year yet. How much things had changed — and so much for the better. One year earlier, I'd been a shaken, traumatised loner without a friend in the world except for this little feline. Now, I had a home, a husband, a baby on the way, friends and family all around me. I had a life. I had hope. It was a beautiful thing.

Tears welled up in my eyes as I picked up the pen, and began to transcribe the tale to paper for the very first time.

***

Knowing the library was water-tight and secure took the pressure off us and relieved the urgency we felt. We could take our time moving the contents back to Tumanako, and lock the place up when we weren't there. It was a slow, laborious process, but now we could pick and choose the days we went down there. Whenever the weather was fine, we'd send a group down with the best trucks and horse-drawn wagons we had and they'd come back full to the brim with cultural treasures.

As our library expanded, so did my waistline, until it got to the point I could barely waddle from bed to the toilet and back again without significant effort. One of our teams brought back an ultrasound machine, and I was its first victim. After a few minutes of cursing and scowling, and a fair amount of uncomfortable prodding, Professor Madurrit finally smiled and told us that our baby was very healthy.

I was a different story. As the weeks progressed, I started to feel less and less healthy. I could sense the change in the seasons, but summer's impending arrival did nothing to improve my mood. Eventually, I gave up on toughing it out in silence and went to see the doctor and the professor. Again, I was poked and prodded, examined from all angles, had tests run on me, blood drawn, and then they left the room to consult with one another in private.

A few minutes later, they came back in and both of them were smiling.

"You're a little bit vitamin D deficient, but not enough to be worried about," Professor Madurrit told me. "The baby's fine. You just haven't been getting as much sun as you're used to recently, and that's why you're feeling off-colour. Try sitting in the sun for fifteen minutes every day, and you'll feel right as rain in no time."

"No pun intended," Doctor Cross added, giving her a dark look. "And while we have you here, we should mention that we're almost ready to begin trials of the vaccine. Evie isn't showing any signs of wanting to wean yet, so we should be ready with plenty of time to spare."

"Good," I said, nodding my approval. I hauled myself up to my feet and stretched my back with a deep groan. "Are you sure it isn't twins? It feels like twins."

"It's definitely not twins," Professor Madurrit said with a laugh, slipping her arm around me to help. "Nor is it triplets, quadruplets, or an elephant calf. Come, dear. Let's go see if there's any trout left in the kitchen. It's not as good as salmon for vitamin D content, but it'll help."

"Oh, I've been avoiding the fish," I admitted, suddenly feeling guilty. "It made my morning sickness really bad in the first trimester, so I started staying away from it."

"And there's the culprit," Professor Madurrit said, her voice a mixture of teasing and gentle understanding. "It was probably the smell bothering you. I'm sure you noticed that your nose was particularly sensitive in the early days, too."

"It's still pretty sensitive," I replied. "Not as bad, though."

"Good," she said. "Between the fish and a bit of sunbathing, you'll feel better in no time."

She was right. I was back to my normal chirpy, sarcastic self within a couple of days. I made peace with my fishy friends and spent a little time sitting in the sun every day. My skin broke out in a rash of freckles, but I didn't care anymore. I remembered being horribly embarrassed by them when I was younger, but I'd outgrown that phase of my life. I was just happy to have friendly faces all around me, and many of those faces were just as freckled as mine.

As my due date grew closer and closer, I finally managed to convince myself that it was okay for me to sit around and gestate quietly. There were more than enough capable hands to help with the construction now, and people knew what needed to be done well enough that my leadership was only really needed in a spiritual sense. So, I forced myself to just relax, and divided my time between napping, working on my memoir, and organizing our ever-growing library.

Jim and Richard decided to officially get married and I was asked to officiate, which I did with great pleasure. When it came time to exchange the rings, they hit us all with a surprise: instead of physical rings, they announced that they wanted to have matching designs tattooed on their ring fingers.

"Nikora?" Richard asked, his face alive with new-found confidence. "My old friend, I know you studied *ta moko* in the old days, and I've seen you practicing it from time to time. Will you do the honours for us?"

"I'd be honoured to," Nick replied, grinning broadly.

After the reception, I stole a moment to approach the happy couple.

"Hey, guys," I said. "When you get those tattoos done, could I maybe watch?"

They both looked surprised for a second, then they laughed and nodded.

"Of course," Jim said. "Thinking of having it done too?"

"Maybe," I admitted. "It's a good idea, and I think Michael will like it."

"You can't do it until after the baby's born," a voice behind me said. I turned around, and found Nikora and Michael walking towards us. I raised my eyebrows at my husband, but he just shrugged and grinned at me. "I always wanted to get a tattoo, so I figured it couldn't hurt to ask. Nick says we can't get yours done until after the baby, but if you want to, I'm game."

This time, it was my turn to laugh. He really did know me too well. By the end of the evening, plans had been made for the two of us to get inked after the baby was born, and we both felt a strange sense of relief. As much as we loved the idea of our rings, the reality was something that we'd both struggled with. The tattoos gave as an alternative, one that I suspected would spread in popularity just as the flowers had.

One afternoon a few days later, Tigger vanished. When we eventually found her secret hidey-hole, there were four tiny kittens suckling on her belly. She'd never looked happier. The human citizens of Tumanako immediately started fighting over who was going to get to adopt the kittens when they were old enough, until Madeline put her foot down and scolded us all like naughty children.

Priya stuck to me like glue all the way through the last weeks of my pregnancy, and since she was Melody's favourite that meant that I was usually surrounded by a friendly mob of teens and pre-teens. Once I got used to it, it was pretty useful. Michael always looked like he was afraid to coddle me for fear of annoying me, but having the kids around meant that I had someone to help me at all times. That freed him up to be useful in other ways – ways that he was strangely closed-lipped about. I knew there was a surprise coming long before anyone said anything directly, from the stealthy glances and whispered conversations whenever I was around. I didn't know exactly what they were planning, but I knew it was going to be interesting.

Two weeks before my official due date, I was sitting in the library working on my memoirs again when Priya and Melody suddenly came rushing up out of nowhere, with the rest of the gang hot on their heels. I'd gotten used to their sudden appearances and disappearances by now, so I just looked up at them and raised an eyebrow.

Priya looked at Melody, then she giggled and shoved a bundle of cloth into my hand. "Put this on, Mama. We have a surprise for you!"

"That's not how it works," Melody said, her voice halfway between amusement and annoyance. She took the cloth back and held it up to show me that it was a makeshift blindfold. "No peeking, okay? You don't want to ruin the surprise!"

I just laughed and nodded. "Okay, okay. No peeking."

Once she'd tied the blindfold securely, the girls helped me to my feet and led me down the hallway to the elevator. I lost track of exactly where we were after that. I felt the ground change in texture beneath my feet from carpet to concrete, then I felt a breeze on my face. I could make an educated guess that I was outside, but that was about it.

Just as I was starting to wonder what was going on, I heard Michael's familiar voice. "Over here."

The girls led me a few steps closer, then Michael's big hands took over the process of guiding me. He turned me around and removed the blindfold.

I blinked a few times as my eyes adjusted to the bright sunlight – then I gasped in surprise.

"Michael? What is this?" I demanded, fixing my husband with the hairy eyeball.

"Well, I figured our apartment was a bit small to have kids running around in," he replied, giving me an embarrassed look that was so obviously faked I had to laugh.

"Did you deliberately add a white picket fence? I'm pretty sure this place didn't have one before." I paused and gave the little cottage a long, considering look. "Though, I guess it is quite pretty. It must have taken forever to tame the gardens."

"The fence isn't for you," he answered, putting on a haughty, defensive look. "The fence is for *me*. There's something else for you."

"Oh, is there just?" I replied, still laughing. "Should I be afraid?"

"No, you should just open the damn door, woman!" he instructed, folding his arms across his chest.

"Okay, fine. I will then." I stuck my tongue out at him, then I walked up to the door and opened it. It took a second for my eyes to adjust again, but when they did my heart just about melted. "Oh, Michael, it's beautiful. Look at this furniture."

"I thought you'd like that," he replied. I felt his arms slide around me from behind and his lips brushed my cheek. "Everyone helped me to salvage the best antique furniture we could find, and we picked a house outside the floodplain so you never have to worry about losing it. This is for you, honey. You, me, Priya, and our baby. Oh, and Alfred, too."

The dog's ears pricked up at the sound of his name, then he let out a happy yelp. Behind us, the girls giggled.

"There's something else, too," Priya said.

"Yup!" Melody agreed, nodding. "There used to be a tradition back in the old days, and we thought it was a good one to continue. It's called a..."

"Surprise party!" Several dozen voices yelled the words all at once. Right on cue, people sprang out from behind furniture and poured in from other rooms. I almost jumped out of my skin, but Michael was right there to keep me from falling over and hurting myself. He hugged me protectively while the others all cheered and threw flower petals over us. Bouquets of fresh-cut flowers appeared like magic, along with platters of food and bottles of homemade wine and juice. Before I could recover, Michael and the girls swept me into the crowd, and I found myself the recipient of more hugs than I'd ever had in my life.

Eventually, I was guided into a big, plush armchair, and people brought out gifts wrapped in shining paper. The sight of it brought tears to my eyes.

"Oh my God, you guys," I gasped, struggling not to cry. "You didn't have to do this..."

"No, we didn't have to," Anahera said gently, pressing a soft package wrapped in sparkly silver paper into my hands. "We wanted to. There's a difference."

"You've given us so much, Sandy," Gavin said, resting a hand on my shoulder. "And you've given it completely selflessly. You deserve every ounce of happiness that we can bring into your life, because you've brought so much joy into ours."

I sniffed and wiped my eyes, unable to think of any way to reply that would adequately express how I felt. Michael knelt down on the floor in front of me and took my hands in his, then together we carefully peeled the tape off the paper and opened the gift. Inside was a set of tiny baby clothes, little rompers that would stretch as our baby grew.

I picked them up and ran my figures over the fabric, marvelling at its softness. Finally, I looked up at Anahera and the others and gave them a tear-filled smile. "Thank you. Thank you all so much."

"Oh, we're only just beginning," Skye said. She threw her head back and let out the evilest cackle I'd ever heard in my life. We all froze and stared at her, then burst out laughing.

***

We spent the next few hours doing nothing but eating, drinking, laughing, and unwrapping presents, but it felt like food for the soul. Still, despite the relaxed atmosphere there was some part of us that was still conscious of our situation. Nothing went to waste, except for the tape on the presents. Even the paper was carefully salvaged, folded up, and put away to be reused. It used to be that survival turned us into the ultimate recyclers; now, planning for the future had the same result. Once the presents had been opened and everyone had come through to congratulate us and eat their fill, Skylar twined her arm around mine and gave me a wicked little smile.

"We're still not done yet," she told me. "This was all just a distraction while we finished off the last piece of your present."

"There's more?" I asked. "What more could there possibly be?"

"Come and see," she replied mysteriously. She helped me to my feet and led me back out into the sunshine. My new home was close to the Tumanako tower, but far enough away to ensure our privacy. The walk back took a couple of minutes, and I spent the entire time wondering just what she had in store for me. By the time we were approaching the corner that would bring us back to the front of the tower, I'd turned every possibility over in my head, but what I actually saw still took me completely by surprise.

"A statue?" I asked, confused. It took a second before I grasped exactly what I was seeing. "Wait, is that *me*? But... how?"

"Remember the sculptor who came up with the South Island guys?" Skye replied. "He's been working on this in secret for months. We moved it out here while you were at the baby shower. The base isn't quite finished, but he wanted to polish that off when it was in its final location."

"I can't believe this," I whispered. I moved closer and ran my fingertips over the smooth stone. My long hair was unmistakable, and even without me acting as a model the sculptor had managed to carve a striking resemblance of my face. I was carved much larger than life, kneeling on the ground with my head bowed. Opposite me, a smaller female figure was posed in the same way. It took me a second to realise that it was Maddy. We both had our hands cupped around something tiny and fragile. I looked closer, and saw that it was a stylized representation of New Zealand, sculpted to look like a delicate seedling.

"We call it 'The Prophet and the Hero'," Skye explained. "Once the base is finished, we're going to add a plaque with your names on it, so that future generations will remember the spirit that founded Tumanako."

"Everyone was important to the founding of Tumanako," I protested, suddenly upset. "Not just me and Maddy. Every single soul here deserves to be recognised for their contribution."

"And they are," she replied. "This statue has your face on it, but it represents all of us, the founding family of the new New Zealand. You represent our strength, our creativity, our drive, and our stubborn determination, while Maddy's image represents our heart, our soul, our spirituality, and our hope for the future."

"Well, I like it," Maddy said. I hadn't heard her arrive, so her sudden appearance made me jump. She just smiled and reached up to take my hand. "Are you ready, Miss Sandy?"

"Ready for what?" I asked, suddenly perplexed.

Maddy just smiled a little wider. A second later, a terrible pain shot through me, and sent me reeling.

"Ow! Jesus! What was that?" I demanded, clutching my swollen belly. "Ow! Ow, ow, ow!"

"Sandy!" Skye cried, rushing over to grab me and help keep me upright. "What's wrong? What is it?"

"It... it hurts..." I gasped, struggling to articulate my pain.

Maddy let out a girlish giggle and did a little pirouette beside us. "Don't worry, Granddaddy's already on his way. The baby's coming!"

Chapter Twenty-Four

"What?" I cried, horrified. "But it's too early! The baby isn't due for another two weeks!"

Suddenly, Michael was beside me, and both Professor Madurrit and Doctor Cross were shoving their way to the front of the crowd.

"Doc!" I called. "It's too soon! Isn't it too soon?"

"Calm down, Ms McDermott," Doc instructed calmly. "Some babies are just in a hurry to be born. Let's get you upstairs and take a look. And remember – breathe."

"That's easy for you to say!" I complained. "It's taken me a while to accept that I'm going to be a mum, but by God I will kill someone if this baby is not okay."

Michael snatched me off my feet and carried me up to the infirmary without another word, with just about the entire population of Tumanako following along behind us. Once we reached the infirmary, Doc kicked them all out except for the Professor, the nurses, Michael, Skye, and Anahera, who was to act as my labour coach – but even with just them the room felt crowded.

Rebecca and Professor Madurrit stripped me and dressed me in a light robe, then they lifted me up onto one of the infirmary beds. After a few minutes of tests and examinations, Doc smiled reassuringly and patted my shoulder. "Everything's fine, Ms McDermott."

"Thank goodness," I gasped, leaning back against the pillows. Then realisation struck, and I shot him a horrified look. "Wait – does this mean I'm actually in labour? Now? But I'm not ready yet!"

"Ready or not, it looks like your baby is in quite a hurry," Professor Madurrit told me. "I just had a look, and you're already at four centimetres. Nothing's actually going to happen for a while yet, so just lie back and try to relax. We'll tell you when it's time for you to get into the birthing position. You still want to squat, right?"

I tried to answer, but my voice didn't want to respond to me so I just nodded vigorously. If gravity would help the pain be over quicker, then so be it. I'd cursed my way through all those exercises for a reason, now it was time to use the muscles I'd toned up preparing for this day.

Professor Madurrit beckoned Anahera over, and she fell into place beside me. She held my hand gently and guided me through the breathing exercises just like we'd practised. I heard other voices around me as the medical staff organised things, but I just ignored them and, focused on Anahera. There was no chance of an epidural, and even if there had been I would have refused it. Once the initial shock wore off, my natural stubbornness surfaced. If I had to become a mother then I was determined to do it as naturally as possible, unless there was a good reason not to. The health and well-being of my baby was my first concern, even above my own.

"Don't worry, dear," Anahera whispered, brushing my hair back away from my forehead with a gentle, maternal hand. "You can do this. I know you can. Just think, once this is over you'll have a beautiful bouncing baby of your very own."

"I'm not sure I'm ready," I admitted, my voice a harsh whisper. Another contraction clenched my midsection and made me growl like a wild animal, but I pushed past the pain to focus on Anahera. "I've been trying to tell myself I'm ready, but I'm not sure."

"You're never ready to be a mother," she replied. "Everyone is terrified, confused, and anxious the first time, but experience will teach you everything you need to know. Don't forget, you're going to be surrounded by many mothers the whole way through, both new mums like yourself and experienced ones like me. We'll take care of you and help you take care of your baby."

I nodded and tried to answer, but the pain stole my breath away again. Anahera helped me into a sitting position and put her arms around me.

"You'll do fine," she whispered reassuringly. "We've got some time before your baby is ready to actually come out. Sometimes moving helps relieve the pain. Would you like to walk around? Or perhaps take a warm shower?"

The contraction faded again, and I finally found the breath to reply. "Yeah... I think a shower would be nice." I finally looked up and saw Michael hovering nearby looking anxious, while Skye was busy helping the nurses with whatever they were doing.

"Do you want me to help you?" Michael asked nervously. "You're not going to punch me again, are you?"

"I might, but not yet," I replied dryly. To answer his question about whether or not I wanted his help, I just held a hand out to him and gave him a tiny smile. He returned the smile with obvious relief, and hurried over to put his arm around me. He and Anahera did the robe up around my middle to preserve what little dignity I had left, then they marched me off to the bathrooms.

I was surprised to discover that the hallway outside was packed with people, just like after Ryan had been shot, but the atmosphere was completely different now. Everyone was smiling. They looked excited, anxious, and even a little bit nervous, but all of them looked happy.

"They're on birth watch," Michael said suddenly, looking almost as surprised as I felt. "Like the death watch, except the other way around. This is the first baby to officially be born in Tumanako, and they already love her as much as they love you."

The thought made me smile, despite the pain of another contraction. Everyone had a kind word for me as we walked past them, and helping hands were everywhere if I needed them. Michael and Anahera helped me through a quick, hot shower, and then we spent the next few hours just keeping me busy while nature took its course.

Eventually, the contractions started to come closer and closer together. I was ushered back onto the table so the doctors could check on our progress, but by that stage the pain was so intense that I couldn't keep track of what was going on. I heard Professor Madurrit tell me that it was time, then I was ushered over to squat on a birthing stool that they'd salvaged a few weeks earlier. Anahera knelt in front of me, her hands on my shoulders to brace me and help me keep my balance.

"It's time, darling," she told me firmly. "Time to meet your baby. Breathe deep, and push!"

I did as I was told. The pain was intense, worse than anything else I'd ever been through in my life, but Anahera's words rang in my mind and gave me the strength I needed to make it through. I heard myself yelling until my throat was raw, swearing up a storm, and even threatening poor Michael, but all of that stopped mattering when I heard one thing: the sound of a baby's cry. I burst into tears and barely heard Anahera say, "It's a girl!"

I lost track of the baby while Michael and Anahera helped me back into bed, but only for a few seconds. Skye came over as soon as I was settled and placed the squirming newborn in my arms.

"Oh my god," I gasped, staring down at her little face. "I... I made this. I made a people! A tiny people!"

"No, *we* made a tiny people," Michael replied, laughing. "I helped, too!"

"Oh sure," I answered, unable to keep the smile off my face despite the pain and exhaustion. "I just lugged her around inside my body for the last eight and a half months, then tore myself in half squeezing her out, but by all means, take all the credit."

Michael just laughed even harder. He wrapped his arms around me and planted a kiss on my cheek. "I don't want all the credit. Just some. And lots of hugs. You know, daddy privileges."

"Oh, well I guess you can have that," I replied. I gave him a quick kiss, then looked back down at our baby again. She was red, wrinkled, and wriggling like an eel, but to my eyes she was the most beautiful thing in the world. She wasn't just my firstborn child, she was something more. A symbol. A step towards the future. She represented the end of one chapter of my life, and the beginning of something new and wonderful.

I couldn't wait to get started.

***

With Skylar's blessing, we named the baby Ryana. In the days and weeks following her birth, I often found myself struggling to cope with balancing my newfound responsibilities as a mother with my duties as the leader of Tumanako, but everyone was patient with me. To no one's great surprise, Michael look on far more than his fair share of the tasks required to keep our baby content and healthy. I'd never seen him happier than when he was changing her nappy or rocking her to sleep.

Occasionally I found myself struggling to produce enough milk to feed her, but when that happened the rest of the community came to my rescue. Hannah or Tala or any of the other new mothers were always there to help, either by acting as a wet nurse or by bottling their spare milk for us. Their willingness to help left me feeling warm inside, because it was exactly the kind of community spirit that I'd hoped to create when we founded Tumanako. Just as Anahera had promised, the community was there to help us learn to care for our baby, and to teach us how to be the best parents we could possibly be.

It took weeks for my body to recover from the traumatic act of giving birth, but it did. Thanks to the excellent medical care I received from my friends and the exercises that Professor Madurrit had insisted I do every day, I bounced back in good time. By the middle of summer, I was fit enough that I could work in the garden, or even help with the construction projects around the village. Michael and I had our tattoos done, and took our rings off permanently. They meant too much for us to throw away, of course, so we mounted them on the wall above our bed, strung together on a single chain to symbolize our unity.

Our community grew right along with our new baby. Every day, stragglers drifted in from the countryside and new faces joined our community. By the end of summer, Tumanako was home to nearly six hundred souls. Just as we'd hoped, we outgrew the tower and began to spread out into the grounds around Tumanako. Couples began to settle down and start families.

Skylar came to term and gave birth to a healthy baby boy with a shock of red hair. Though it was obvious who the biological father was, Hemi adopted the baby as his without question, and it was a delight to see them both so happy.

Shortly after Skylar gave birth, Bobby approached us both and did the unthinkable: he apologised to us, honestly and sincerely, with tears in his eyes. We were stunned, but once the shock wore off we both accepted his apology without reservation. Matt Yousefi took a liking to him, and the two of them struck up a tentative friendship. With Matt's help, Bobby finally began to integrate into our society. Watching him learn to smile again was one of the most rewarding things I'd ever seen.

Isabelle began to outgrow her nervousness and come into her own, thanks to the friendship she developed with Gavin. I gave in to curiosity one day and asked if there was anything between them, only to be told that Isabelle had finally discovered what she liked best was her own freedom. Whenever I saw her, she was learning something new. One day I saw her working on the mural with our resident artists, and the next she was training with one of the self-defence classes. The combat classes gave her a confidence I'd never seen before, and watching her squeal and jump for joy whenever she won a sparring match brought me great pleasure.

The community became so focused on what was happening inside it that we almost forgot there was a world outside the walls. We kept reminding one another to be aware and watchful, but no one could have predicted the momentous event that would force us to start thinking of ourselves as part of a wider world again.

That event came in early autumn, as the leaves were just starting to think about changing colour. I'd led a short scavenging trip to Wellington to look for anything we could use; winter was coming again, and although we felt secure in our new home we wanted to be prepared. We were half way through loading the truck with salvaged blankets and duvets when one of the scouts came running up to me, frantically flailing his arms.

"There's a boat!" he cried breathlessly. "There's a boat in the harbour!"

I shot him a curious look. "There are always boats in the harbour. They don't go anywhere."

"No!" he gasped, shaking his head. "No, there's a new boat — a frigate! It's just arrived!"

"What?" I froze, staring at him. "Are you serious?"

"Yes, I'm serious," the scout replied. He grabbed my arm and half-led, half-dragged me through the winding streets towards the waterfront. The rest of our party dropped whatever they were doing and raced after us.

By the time we reached the waterfront, the frigate had dropped anchor in the harbour.

"Binoculars!" I demanded.

Someone put a pair into my hand. I lifted them up and stared through them, trying to make out the details of what we were seeing.

"There are people moving about on the deck," I told the people around me. "I can't tell how many. I think they're preparing a boat to come ashore. Wait – there's a flag! It's... it's the New Zealand flag? No– no it's not, there are too many stars. Oh my God! It's the Australian flag! The Australians are here!" Gasps of shock rang out all around me. I lowered the binoculars and looked around, just as stunned as the others sounded. "What are they doing here? *How* are they here?"

"If they're coming ashore, then I guess we're going to find out in a couple of minutes," Gavin said, his expression painfully neutral but I could see the concern in his eye. If this was an invasion, then we were sitting ducks. A ship like that would need almost a third of Tumanako's entire population to man it, which meant that we were seriously outnumbered – not to mention outgunned.

Gavin put his hand on my shoulder and gave it a squeeze, a gesture of silent solidarity that spoke far more than words. We all waited together as the frigate lowered a smaller craft into the water. The inflatable swung around and crept towards shore at what felt like a snail's pace, even though we could see from its wake that it was travelling at a good speed. By the time it was close enough that we could see the faces of the people on board, I was feeling sick with anxiety and anticipation, but there was nothing we could do except wait.

Finally, the boat came to a rest against the edge of the dock not even a few meters away from us, and a single, uniformed man stood up. He gave us a long look, and for a second we all held our breath – then, suddenly, he saluted us.

"Permission to come ashore?" he called, in a voice that carried an accent I hadn't heard in a very long time.

Tears sprang unbidden into my eyes. I pulled away from the group and walked over to offer him a hand up onto the dock. "Permission granted."

Once he was on dry ground, he straightened his uniform and looked at the little group of faces huddled behind me.

"You have no idea how glad I am to see someone alive down here," he said, his voice thick with emotion. "I'm sorry it took us so long to get here, but it took a lot of doing to assemble and train a crew."

"You came to check on us?" I asked, struggling to blink back the tears that very much wanted to roll down my cheeks. "It's been a decade."

"I know," he said. "We never forgot about you. There aren't many of us left, but there are some. We had to find a way to check on our little sister nation somehow. It wasn't easy, but I guess you know that better than most."

"Yes, I do," I replied, suddenly fighting the urge to laugh. "We were so afraid... we thought we might have been the only humans left on Earth, and everyone else was gone forever. I can't believe you're standing here."

"We thought the same thing for a while," the sailor replied, "but we've managed to make contact with little pockets of survivors all over the world. The Royal Family may be dead for all we know, but the spirit of the Commonwealth lives on in us."

Something about that sentence struck just the right chord with me. I burst into tears and threw my arms around the stranger's neck in a hug. We embraced for nearly a minute, then I shoved him back and gave him a watery smile.

"Bring your crew ashore," I suggested. "Let us show you the city we've built for ourselves. It isn't perfect, but it doesn't have to be. It's home."

Epilogue

"...And they lived happily ever after. The end!" The little girl slammed the book closed, and looked expectantly at her teacher. "Can we go now?"

"Sophie!" Kylie exclaimed, struggling to hide her amusement behind a mask of horror. "That isn't even close to the end of their story. Don't you want to know what happens next?"

"We already know what happens next, Mum," Sophie complained, rolling her eyes and crossing her arms. "We read this last year. We don't want to read it again!"

The rest of the class laughed. Kylie hid a chuckle behind a cough, then shook her head. "Come on, kids. This is your great-grandparents we're talking about. Without them, we wouldn't have a home, we wouldn't have the vaccine — most of us wouldn't even be alive. Just one more chapter?"

"No!" Sophie cried, covering her face with her hands. "It's Founder's Day! We want to go to the feasting before the grown-ups eat everything. Please, Mum? Please?"

"Please, miss?" another child asked, and then they all joined in. "Please? Pleeeeease?"

Kylie finally gave in and laughed. "Oh, fine. It's Founder's Day. I suppose the best way you can honour their memory is by enjoying it. Go on, then — but I want you back here bright and early tomorrow morning! Don't forget you've got a maths test."

A chorus of cheers and groans went up from around the class, but it was swiftly drowned out by the screech of chairs and the pounding of footsteps as the entire class raced out of the room. Kylie heaved a sigh, then she stood up and walked around the room collecting the copies of the collected memoirs of Tumanako's founders from the desks. Just as she was returning the last copy to its place on the shelves, there was a light tap on the door. She glanced back over her shoulder, and found a familiar face loitering in the doorway.

"Hello, Mr Cross," she greeted with mock formality. The young man laughed and came over to kiss her cheek.

"Hello, Ms McDermott," he replied. "Did you let your class out early, too?"

"Yeah," she said, absently touching the locket around her throat, passed down to her by her foster aunt, Priyanka; her cousins were all boys, and her aunt had wanted the keepsake to stay on the female side of the family. It could have gone to her mother, Ryana, but they'd decided to pass it straight down to her. Kylie sighed in memory, then shook her head and smiled at her husband. "You know how the kids get on Founder's Day. They don't want to sit around reading books when they could be running around, playing, and stuffing food down their gullets."

"I know," he said, putting his arm around her shoulders. "Just remember, to them these people may as well be characters from a novel. They're not as real to the kids as they are to you and me. They were our grandparents, our aunts and uncles. We knew them. Sophie was only a baby when we buried them. Speaking of which – Nana will want us at the memorial, and you know how much your mum hates it when we're late. We should probably get a move on."

Kylie nodded and went to fetch her coat. Founder's Day fell in early spring, and that meant that the weather was fickle at best. It could go from brilliant sunshine to pouring with rain in a heartbeat. Tumanako was her home, though, and she knew the weather better than her own moods.

Tama linked his arm through hers, and together they left the school building and went out into the city streets. People were everywhere, a swarming mass of smiling humanity out enjoying the holiday regardless of the weather. Kylie smiled and waved to her friends, but she didn't stop to chat. There would be time for that later. Now was the time for remembrance.

The walk to the family crypt was long but ultimately pleasant. She still remembered the day they'd decided to build it. The entire community had gotten together both to collectively mourn the loss of their heroes, and to thank them for a lifetime of service. Beautiful flowers grew in well-tended beds on either side of the path, and the sweeping boughs of trees protected them from sun and rain alike.

Where once the grave of Ryan Knowles had stood alone, they'd built a crypt to honour the memory of every person who had dedicated their life in the name of an idealistic dream all those years ago. A plaque adorned the entrance, carved with dozens of names that were so familiar to her – and in front of the plaque stood a wizened old woman with long hair that had once been raven black, and was now steel-grey with age.

"Nana?" Tama called. It was unnecessary, of course. No one could ever sneak up on his grandmother. Even as a child, he'd never been able to get away with anything when she was around. Somehow, she always knew.

The woman turned and smiled at them both. "Hello, dear. Hello, Kylie — ah, I see you've been reading the stories again. Trying to remember?"

"Every year," Kylie said softly. She walked up beside the old woman and reached out to touch the names of her grandparents, carved at the very top of the list of founders. "I miss them sometimes. I wish that Sophie could have gotten to know them better."

A smile crinkled the old woman's lips. "At least your Sophie will have the chance to grow up safe and healthy. That's the most important thing."

"I know." Kylie sighed and closed her eyes, running her fingers across the cold metal as if that could help the twisting of grief in her gut. "The children don't understand, though. I try to teach them, try to keep the memory alive, but the founders are just stories to them."

"Not stories, my dear," Madeline Cross said, turning to face her fully. "Legends. The founders have passed from our world into the world of legends. That means they'll *never* be forgotten."

"Let me guess," Kylie said, a shy smile dancing across her face. "You know because you've foreseen it?"

Madeline laughed and shook her head. "I don't need to foresee it to know it'll happen, dear. It already has."

THE END

Afterword

When I started this project in December 2012, I honestly didn't believe that I was going to see the end of it. I never could have guessed just how popular *The Survivors* would become. Now, just over two years later, I've written the final book in the series and you've just finished reading it.

Is this the end for *The Survivors*? Doubtful. This is the end of the first arc, yes, but I've already got a few ideas for future novels. There are still so many adventures to be had, and so many concepts to explore. I don't know when it'll happen, but I have no doubt that it will.

While you're waiting for that day to come, why not check out one of my other books? I'm always working on something, so just take a peek at my website to see what's available now. I also have a few more light-hearted (and slightly raunchy) books under my pen name, Abigail Hawk.

If you enjoyed this book as much as I enjoyed bringing it to you, please consider leaving a review. Reviews are the life-blood of all independent authors, and are vital to our success. Plus, I love hearing that people enjoyed my story! Reviews may drive my sales, but it's you — the reader — that keeps *me* going through all the ups and downs.

Please feel free to contact me via any of the following with
your questions, comments, or feedback:

Email: info@vldreyer.com
Amazon: http://amazon.com/author/vldreyer
Facebook: http://www.facebook.com/VictoriaLDreyer
Twitter: @VL_Dreyer
Patreon: http://www.patreon.com/vldreyer

It has been my pleasure and my honour to write this series
for all of you, and I thank each and every one of you for
joining me on this journey.

Where will the future take us? I don't know yet, but like
Sandy said, I can't wait to find out!

V. L. Dreyer

The Cast

THE NARRATOR
Sandrine "Sandy" McDermott

THE OHAUPO GROUP
Michael Chan
Doctor Stewart Cross
Madeline "Maddy" Cross
Ryan Knowles
Skylar "Skye" McDermott
Priyanka
Tigger the Kitten
Alfred the Sheepdog

THE WAIKATO IWI
Anahera Parata
Hemi Parata
Ropata Parata
Iorangi Parata
Tane Parata
Richard Parata
Petera "Peter" Parata
Wiremu "Will" Parata
Nikora "Nick" Parata

THE ARAPUNI GROUP:
Jim Merrit
Rebecca Merrit

THE YOUSEFI FAMILY:
Zain Yousefi
Elira "Elly" Yousefi
Mathias "Matt" Yousefi
Javed Yousefi
Baraz "Barry" Yousefi
Omid "Ommie" Yousefi

THE TOKOROA GROUP:
Gavin Church
Lily & Jasmine
Melody
Solomon

MISCELLANEOUS:
Erica Bryce
Simon Wentworth

DECEASED:
Sophie Chan, niece of Michael.
Henry Barrett, the Pukeatua bandit.
Everyone else in the whole world.
May they rest in peace.

Kiwiana Language Guide

Aotearoa	Maori, New Zealand. Literally "The Land Of The Long White Cloud".
Arapuni	Location; a town in the central Waikato, home to the Arapuni Power Station.
Bush	Specifically, "native bush". Refers to an area of native forest, which is characterised by a particularly thick shrub layer dominated by indigenous ferns and bushes. Native bush is often very thick and dark, and can be very difficult to travel through as a result.
Central Plateau	Colloquial, the Tongariro National Park. It is an area of major cultural significance to the various peoples of New Zealand, and contains numerous Maori sacred sites. Above ground, it is a massive rock desert that covers approximately 795.98 kilometres and is home to the volcanic cones Tongariro, Ruapehu, and Ngauruhoe. Below ground, it is the centre of a massive geothermal field that spreads across most of the North Island. It is one of the few North Island areas that regularly sees snowfall.
G'day	Colloquial version of "Good day".
Hamilton	Location; A medium-sized city in the Waikato

Horizons Region	The Horizons Region is an agricultural region in the lower half of the North Island. The official name of the area is the Manawatu-Wanganui region.
Hutt Valley	An area in the Greater Wellington Region that contains the cities of Upper and Lower Hutt, and the fertile Hutt River.
Kia Ora	Maori, "Hello".
Maori	Relating to the original peoples of New Zealand. May be used to refer to their cultural traits (*e.g. "she tried to live by the traditional Maori ways."*), language (*e.g. "he spoke Maori."*) or ethnicity (*e.g. "my grandmother was Maori"*). The Maori culture evolved from Polynesian migrants that arrived in New Zealand around 1,000 years ago.
Mate	Colloquial, a contextually sensitive word that is usually used in place of the word "friend". Can be used sarcastically or in threat just as readily as being used in a friendly fashion, *e.g. "You're going to regret that, mate."*
Ngauruhoe	Geography; the central volcano in Tongariro National Park. Ngauruhoe is an active stratovolcano.
Ohaupo	Location; a small town in the Waikato region, 17 kilometres south of Hamilton.
Porirua	A coastal city in the Wellington Region.
Ruapehu	Geography; the southernmost volcano in Tongariro National Park. Ruapehu is one of the most active stratovolcanoes in the world.

Taihape	A small town in the central North Island.
Tā Moko	Maori Culture; traditional Maori face and body tattoos.
Te Awamutu	Location; a medium-sized township in the central Waikato. In the *Survivors* world, this town was razed by a large earthquake several years after the plague.
Tokaanu	Location; a small township on the southern shore of Lake Taupo.
Tokoroa	Location; a medium-sized town located in the central Waikato, half way between Hamilton and Taupo.
Tumanako	Maori, "Hope".
Waikato	A large agricultural region in the central North Island.
Waiouru	Location; a small town in the Manawatu-Wanganui region, located approximately 25 kilometres south of Mount Ruapehu. It is home to the Waiouru Army Camp and Airfield.
Wellington	Location; capital of New Zealand, and southernmost city in the North Island.

About The Author

V. L. Dreyer is an international best-selling author from the wild back country of New Zealand. She is best known for her post-apocalyptic series, *The Survivors*, as well as the *Immortelle* series under her pen name, Abigail Hawk. Her earlier works include an assortment of graphic novels, short stories, blogs, and works of art, and her preferred genres are science fiction, post-apocalyptic survival, and romance – and sometimes all three at once.

Ms. Dreyer is the unlikely miracle offspring of a science fiction geek who dreamed of teaching, and a biker computer technician. She penned her first novel at the age of 14, and started her first business at the age of twenty. From 2003 to 2011, she ran the publishing house Blue Scar Productions, then went on to produce numerous literary and artistic works under her personal brand, Cheeky Kea Creations. In October 2017, Ms. Dreyer expanded the publishing division of her brand, Cheeky Kea Printworks, into a full hybrid publishing house, to help others see their ideas take flight.

Ms Dreyer suffers from an advanced form of Meniere's Disease, which has left her with a hearing impairment. In her free time, she is an avid gamer, reader, and enjoys learning new and sometimes completely random things.

www.vldreyer.com

About The Publisher

Cheeky Kea Printworks began as the personal publishing house of author V. L. Dreyer, and later became the brand under which she freelanced as a publishing assistant for other authors. In 2017, CK Printworks took the final step to becoming a publishing house in its own right, by securing the contracts to translate and publish several Polish manuscripts into English.

CK Printworks specializes in science fiction, fantasy, urban fantasy, romance/erotica, and anything else that helps the imagination take flight.

To learn more about CK Printworks and the authors represents, please visit:

www.ckprintworks.com

To receive an alert when new books are released, subscribe to the CK Printworks Mailing List:

www.ckprintworks.com/subscribe